Seeking Samuel Goldberg

Lyn Behan

BehanPublishing

For Shirley, who was the inspiration for this story

Chapter One

February 1965, Rockwood Cemetery, Sydney, NSW

L iesel screwed up her face to stop the threatening tears as the pallbearers lowered her grandfather's coffin into the ground.

'Stop that snivelling,' hissed her mother, giving Liesel a nudge with her elbow. 'Don't waste your tears on that miserable old German. Trust him to have his funeral during a hail storm!' She jerked her umbrella, sending a shower of wet hail over Liesel, and turned to her husband. 'Let's go back to the car, Charles. We don't want to hang around with these people.'

An old man walked up to Liesel. 'He your grandfather?' he said in a German accent.

'Yes.'

'Very good man. Kept our spirits up in Tatura.'

Liesel sniffed loudly and blew her nose. She had no idea what he was talking about, but she said, 'Thank you,' and then followed her father back to the car.

She'd loved her grandfather and could never understand why her mother had always disliked him. Although he'd only lived in the next suburb, just twenty minutes' walk away, Liesel could only remember a few occasions when he'd visited their house. He'd never been welcome there.

'No point in going back to his house; miserable old sod would have nothing worth leaving,' her mother said, shaking her umbrella before they clambered back into the old car, which was all they could afford. 'Lee, there's a lot of ironing to be done,' she continued.

'I have to go back to my father's house, Madge, to clean it up,' her father said. 'I need Liesel to scrub the floors.'

Liesel gave her father a quick look, but he stared straight ahead and started up the car.

Her mother sniffed. 'Well, Charles, she still has to do the ironing when she gets back. Just because she's at college doesn't mean she's too high and mighty to do menial jobs.'

Liesel grimaced as she got in the back of the car with her brother, Archie, who smirked at her. Doing the ironing would mean she'd have to stay up late finishing her assignment.

When they reached their house, her mother and brother got out, leaving Liesel and her father in the car. He remained silent—but then, he usually was.

They drove to her grandfather's house, where after opening the front door, her father turned to her and said, 'Your grandfather wanted you to have something.' Then he led the way through the small fibro house to a bedroom at the back.

Although scrupulously clean, the house was dark and dingy; it hadn't been repainted in years. Liesel looked around. 'It all looks spotless to me, Dad. Do the floors really need scrubbing?'

Charles sighed. 'No, that was just an excuse so I could get you here on your own. Your mother wouldn't have let you come if I'd said Grandad had left you something. She'd have been here like a shot and wanted Archie to have it.'

Liesel followed him into the sparsely furnished bedroom.

'He never liked her; your mother, I mean,' her father said.

She looked at him in amazement. He'd never spoken like this to her before.

Charles Martin opened the wardrobe door, pushed aside the few clothes hanging on the rail and took out a box. Plain, but beautifully crafted in what looked like mahogany. He brought it out, walked to the kitchen and set it on the table. 'He told me years ago that I was to give you this box after he died. He told me that he'd been unable to fulfil a request, and he thought you were the only one now who could ... don't know what he was on about. Open it.'

Her heart thumping, Liesel lifted the lid of the box.

'I think he made it himself,' her father said, sitting down at the table.

Disappointment filled Liesel when she peered inside—just bits of paper, a notebook, old letters and what looked like certificates or something. She lifted them out, then caught her breath. Underneath was something wrapped in velvet. Carefully she took it out and unfolded the material, revealing a miniature violin.'It's beautiful,' she breathed, stroking the glossy varnish with her fingers.

Her father's eyes filled with tears. 'Oh! I remember that! He showed it to me once when I was about ten. He told me he made it himself for his guild master's examination,' he paused, 'after he'd been on his *Wanderjahre.*'

'His what?' Liesel frowned and looked at her father.

'He told me it was something they did years ago in Germany. After finishing their apprenticeships, tradesmen would go from town to town getting work with different masters. It was to increase their experience.'

Liesel barely listened, her attention focused on the violin. 'Look! Inside, behind the strings; it looks like something's written.' She peered closer. 'I'll need a magnifying glass to read it.'

'I think your grandfather had one,' her father said. 'He couldn't see much the last few years and needed it to read.' He stood and looked around the neat kitchen until he found the magnifying glass. 'Here it is.' He handed it to Liesel, and she held it over the opening in the violin.

'Liesel Goldberg,' she read.

'That was my mother's name.' Her father sighed. 'She died when I was about six. I scarcely remember her. But your grandfather adored her. He always said you looked like her. I think that's why he loved you so much. When I told him that your mother was expecting a baby, he asked if it was a girl, would I call her Liesel, after my mother.' He sighed again. 'But Madge wanted you to be called Sheila. I just went and registered you as Liesel before she had a chance. That's why she calls you Lee and not Liesel.'

That explains a lot. Liesel frowned and looked at her father. 'What happened to your mother's violin? The one Grandad gave me that Archie broke? I thought you were going to ask Grandad to mend it.'

'I did, I think it's here somewhere. Your grandfather was devastated when Archie broke it. He was going to try and repair it. It's probably in the back shed. I'll look next time.'

Liesel nodded, then turned back to the papers. 'Most of these are in German,' she said. 'Can you speak German, Dad? Can you translate these papers?'

He shook his head. 'No. I was only four when we left Germany, and I had to speak Spanish until we came here from Argentina.'

'Argentina! Why haven't you told me this before? I never knew you'd been in Argentina.'

Her father shrugged. 'Nothing to talk about; it's all in the past.'

'And look at this!' Liesel held up a small notebook. 'It's full of drawings of furniture.' She turned the pages slowly. 'They're quite beautiful. Was Grandpop an artist?'

'Don't know,' her father replied, looking over her shoulder.

'The last one is of a staircase, and the hand rail and newel post are in detail.'

'Hmm.' Her father took the notebook from her and carefully examined it.

Liesel picked up another of the papers and one word caught her eye. *Jüdische*. 'I know this means Jew!' she exclaimed.

'Yes.'

'Was he Jewish?'

'Yes,' her father replied, slowly. 'Well, we all are. But no-one ever spoke of it. I think he was too afraid. Apparently, there were pogroms in Argentina. Judaism was never spoken of.'

'Afraid?'

'Yes. No one liked Jews, and Australia said at that time that they didn't have a racial problem and didn't want to import one. So they made it difficult for Jews to come here. I think my father must have put some other religion on the visa application.'

Liesel looked up. 'Well, I suppose I'm not Jewish. Doesn't being a Jew have to pass down through the mother?'

'Yes.' Charles frowned. 'However, your mother's Jewish, too.'

'What! She's never mentioned it! How did you meet her if there were no Jews allowed into Australia?'

Charles shrugged. 'There were Jewish families living in Australia since the first settlers. Some came as convicts.'

'So that makes me a Jewess!'

'Yes.'

Liesel's hand flew to her nose. She jumped up and ran to the kitchen sink where a small mirror hung in the window. 'My nose! Is it Jewish?' Her voice squeaked with alarm.

'It's a beautiful nose.' Charles smiled at his daughter, then said, 'Liesel, we'd better go now. Put everything back in the box. I'll come tomorrow after work and get the box and hide it in my shed. Archie and your mother must never know about it.'

Liesel nodded. She understood. 'Just a minute, Dad. What's this screwed up bit of paper?' She smoothed it out. 'It looks like a family tree.'

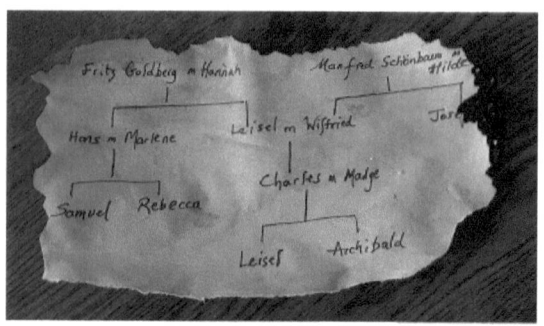

Her father peered at it. 'Manfred Schönbaum married Hilde,' he read, 'that would be my grandparents. They had two children, Wilfried and Josef. Wilfried was my dad, your grandfather. I don't know anything about Josef.' He scratched his head. 'Wilfried married Liesel. Looks like she had a brother, Hans who married Marlene. I don't know anything about them.' He looked at Liesel. 'My father must have done this, as he's got you and Archie on it. We'd better go, love. Put all this back in the box.'

'Just a minute, Dad. Hans and Marlene had two children, Samuel and Rebecca. They would be your cousins. I wonder where they are now?'

Charles sighed. 'They probably died in Hitler's concentration camps.'

'Oh, no!' Liesel's mouth fell open in horror. 'Dad, did you ever try and find them?'

Her father frowned. 'No,' he murmured, then looked up. 'Perhaps you could, Liesel.' He looked at his watch. 'We'd better go, your mother will be jumping up and down.' He stood and walked towards the front door. 'Whoever rents the house next might like the few bits of furniture here. Unless you'd like some pieces? He made it all himself.'

'I'd love to,' Liesel said as she followed him out, 'but where will I put it until I get my own place? That might be years away.'

Her father nodded and locked the front door behind them.

As they walked down the path to the car, Liesel thought about her father's cousins. She wished she'd asked her grandfather more about his past. But perhaps she could find out what happened to these cousins ...

Chapter Two

1903, Frankfurt Am Main, Germany

As soon as he was old enough to totter after his mother, Wilfried Schönbaum helped her polish the furniture in their big lounge. She often smiled at his serious little face and careful actions.

When he was about seven years old, his father took him to his furniture shop in Frankfurt. Wilfried walked around the big store in awe, going to each of the pieces of furniture, stroking the polished surfaces and sometimes sniffing them.

His father came up behind him as he ran his hand gently over a dresser. 'What are you doing, Wilfried?'

'Oh, father! This is so beautiful, and what's this glowing stuff?'

'That's called mother of pearl. It's inlaid into the wood.'

'It smells like the polish Mother uses.'

'Lavender polish.' His father laughed. 'I can see you'll be a great asset in the shop in a few years' time.'

Wilfried took a deep breath. 'When I'm big, I'm going to make furniture like this, Father.'

His father only smiled, but Wilfried knew this was what he would do with his life.

His younger brother, Josef, teased him when Wilfried took the tin of lavender beeswax and polished the sideboards.

'You're like a girl!' he taunted Wilfried. 'Why don't you wear a skirt? And plait your hair?'

Wilfried looked at him. 'If you were not my baby brother, I'd thump you.' He smiled and threw a mock punch at Josef.

Wilfried spent his spare time sketching furniture designs. His father was delighted, he could see that Wilfried would be able to help his customers decide on special-order furniture his suppliers could make.

***

One Friday afternoon, a few weeks before his fifteenth birthday, Wilfried came running down the stairs, a clumsily wrapped parcel in his hands. The smell of baking teased his nostrils, and his stomach rumbled. The light was fading in the warm kitchen as he went in and sat at the table. He watched his mother taking the *challah* from the oven, her face flushed as she hurried to finish preparing the meal for the Sabbath, which would commence at sundown.

'Have you finished all your homework?' she asked without looking up.

'Yes, of course.'

'Where's Josef?'

'He's still finishing his.'

At last she sat down at the big kitchen table with a sigh, folded her hands in her lap and looked at Wilfried, who smiled.

'Mother, I have something for you.' He passed her the parcel.

She looked at him. 'What is it?'

'Open it!' He wriggled with anticipation on the wooden chair.

She unwrapped a pair of carved wooden serving spoons. 'Oh!' Her eyes lit up.

'I made them for you.' Wilfried's face reddened, pleased that she seemed to like them.

'Oh, my clever son!' She got up, went around the table and gave him a kiss.

'Mama, I want to finish school and learn to be a carpenter. I want to make beautiful furniture, like the Roentgens or Chippendale.'

'But Adam Roentgen became a Reformed Christian. A Moravian!'

Wilfried frowned and shrugged. 'Religion isn't important. It didn't affect his craftsmanship.'

His mother blinked and said nothing while she held up the serving spoons and looked at them closely. Then she nodded. 'Yes, I know you've always been sawing and chiselling at pieces of wood since you were old enough to hold a hammer.' She sighed. 'But I don't know what your father will think. You know he's keen for you to follow him into the business, and you've been well educated. You can speak Spanish and French,' her voice rose. 'You would be able to travel and order furniture from anywhere in Europe.'

'But Josef can do that; he's only two years younger than I am, and he's interested in the shop.'

'You're the eldest son; it's expected of you.'

'But we're Reformed Jews; those traditions are changing. I really, really must do this, Mama.'

She stood up. 'I'll speak to your father. Now, it's nearly sundown, get ready for the Shabbat.' She smiled as she shooed him from the table.

***

Wilfried felt on edge for several days after he'd given his mother the serving spoons; he kept wondering if she'd spoken to his father. Now, as they all sat down to dinner, Manfred Schönbaum picked up the spoons and studied them.

Wilfried's heart seemed to stand still.

Manfred turned to his eldest son. 'Wilfried, your mother tells me you want to be a cabinet maker.'

Everyone looked up.

'Yes, Father,' Wilfried said, leaning forward eagerly.

'Well, it's a disappointment to me.' Manfred Schönbaum helped himself to salad and put the spoons back in the salad bowl. He put a forkful of food into his mouth and slowly chewed it.

Wilfried gripped his knife and fork and waited.

'I was sure you would want to come into the business with me; you'd be able to travel for me and find nice pieces of furniture all over Europe.' His father sighed. 'However, as you seem so determined about this, I went to the Carpenter's Guild in Frankfurt, and they suggested a master cabinet maker who might take you on. As it happens, he supplies me with a lot of furniture to sell in the shop, so I went to see him, and he's willing to take you on as an apprentice on your fifteenth birthday.'

A grin spread across Wilfried's face, and he jumped up from his chair. 'Oh, Father! Thank you so much.' He made a move to embrace his father, thought better of it and sat down again. 'I'll be fifteen next month.'

'You'll have to live in the master's house and do all the work he asks you, even menial tasks, like sweeping the floors. And he's agreed to let you come home on Fridays at sunset for the Sabbath.' Manfred didn't mention that he'd had to use monetary persuasion to achieve this.

'Yes, yes, Father. I understand.' Wilfried could barely contain his excitement. He looked at his hands. He loved the feel of wood; the smell of fresh timber; the sense of achievement from turning a piece of timber into something of beauty that would last for centuries.

His brother, Josef, looked at him. 'Can't understand you, Wilfried. Much easier working in the shop with Father, and travelling.'

Wilfried glanced at Josef. He loved him—he was his baby brother—but he knew Josef was lazy. He was also clever. So clever that he never needed to study like he, Wilfried, had to. He wondered if Josef would be happy working for their father. He smiled at him. 'Perhaps,' was all he said.

Their father looked at Josef. 'You'll learn, my son.'

Chapter Three

1909, Frankfurt Am Main, Germany.

W ilfried, now twenty, had finished his apprenticeship and was back living at home, but still working for his master. One evening he came into the kitchen where his parents were sitting; his mother sewing and his father reading the paper. He twirled a walking stick.

His mother looked up from her sewing. 'I don't think we need a walking stick just yet, thank you, Wilfried,' she said with a smile, then broke some thread with her teeth.

'Do you like it?' Wilfried held out the stick with its twisted carving for his parents to examine.

His father took it, looked at it and frowned. 'This looks like a *stenz.*'

'Yes, it is, Father; I've just finished making it. I'm getting ready to go on my *Wanderjahre.*'

His mother looked up. 'What! No, please, no. I can't bear the idea of you going off for three years, working for your board and lodging.' Tears came to her eyes.

'Don't be silly, Hilde,' exclaimed her husband. 'He has to do this as a step to becoming a master cabinet maker, and then he must make something beautiful for the guild to pass him.'

Wilfried looked gratefully at his father. 'Yes, exactly! You see, Mother, my father understands.'

'You may have to sleep rough and not get proper meals.' Her face puckered with distress.

Josef came into the kitchen. 'What? Wilfried sleeping rough? What's happening?'

'I'm sure that won't happen,' Wilfried took their mother's hand and glared at his brother.

'And then'—she tried to suppress her tears—'then, when you come back, you will have to do your national service in the army. We won't see you for years.'

'Come, Hilde,' his father said. 'It will make a man of him! All good German men have to do their national service.'

Hilde Schönbaum sniffed. 'And Josef will be next. At least he is safe at home and working in the shop.'

'What's going on? What's Wilfried up to now?' Josef looked at his mother.

'Wilfried is going on a *Wanderjahre*.' she wailed.

Josef burst out laughing. 'Oh, Wilfried, you make your life so hard.' He sat down at the kitchen table, took Wilfried's *stenz* and twirled it, pretending to drop it and then catch it.

'Hilde, my dear, soon Wilfried will be making beautiful furniture for us to sell in the shop.' Manfred smiled at his elder son. 'Now, don't you have to get special clothes for the *Wanderjahre*? And a gold earring?'

'Earring!' Hilde's hand flew to her mouth. 'My son wearing an earring like a common gypsy? What next?'

Wilfried laughed. 'Mother, you must have seen craftsmen on their *Wanderjahre* with their special hats and waistcoats and flared trousers?'

She nodded. 'Yes, but ...'

'Well,' continued Wilfried, 'The gold earring is in case I run up debts or get sick and die, the earring will be used to pay my debts or bury me.'

'Bury you!' Hilde's eyes grew wide with fear.

Manfred put an arm around his wife's shoulders. 'Come, my dear. That won't happen to Wilfried. He will return to us, strong and healthy.'

Josef gave Wilfried back his *stenz*. 'You're crazy, brother!'

***

Wilfried carefully folded a clean, spare shirt and underwear and placed it into his kit bag. Finally, he was ready to set out on his journeyman years. His father had given him the money for his outfit. He held up the white collarless shirt, looked at it with a smile and put it on. Then the black trousers with flared bottoms and the velvet waistcoat with eight buttons to signify the eight-hour working day. He stood up tall, squared his shoulders and put on the black jacket. Taking his new black boots and the wide-brimmed black hat, he went downstairs to the front door.

He was tying his boot laces when his mother came out from the kitchen. 'Oh, my son! You look so handsome; where are you going?'

'To the town hall to get my official *Wanderbuch*, Mother.'

'Oh!' She bit her lower lip, and without another word went back into the kitchen, closing the door quietly behind her.

At the town hall, Wilfried knocked on the mayor's door.

'Come!'

Shelves of books covered the walls of the musty smelling room. The local mayor sat behind a large, cluttered desk. He looked up at Wilfried, then nodded when Wilfried said he wanted a *Wanderbuch*.

'You understand the terms of the *Wanderjahre*, young man?'

'Yes, yes.' Wilfried nodded, impatient to get the visit over.

'Well, I'll explain it to you anyway, as it is my duty so to do.' The mayor, a well-rounded middle-aged man, took a deep breath, coughed and said in a ponderous tone: 'You must be under thirty years of age. You must be unmarried.' He paused and looked at Wilfried over his half-moon spectacles, as if suspecting him of having entered into a clandestine union.

Wilfried nodded.

The mayor continued. 'You must be clean and disease free. You must be chaste and stay chaste.' Another stern look. 'You must confess your faith in God.'

Wilfried nodded. He twisted his gold earring in his newly pierced ear.

'You must work at least fifty kilometres away from your home, and have no contact with your family, except in cases of death or emergency. Your current master will verse you in the secret signs and codes of your trade so that other masters will know you are a genuine craftsman. You will act honourably at all times so that you do not bring your trade into disrepute and make it difficult for other men on their *Wanderjahre* who come after you.'

Wilfried shuffled from one foot to the other. He wished the mayor would hurry up.

'When you enter a new town, you must go straight to the town hall and present this book,' the mayor continued. 'It will enable the officials to register you. Then, when you go to your trade guild, they will send you to a master craftsman who has work. He will look at what the previous master has written, and only accept you if the report was good. He will keep the book until you leave, at which time he will write his report in this book, sign it, stamp it and give it back to you.' He took off his glasses and glared at Wilfried.

'Yes, Herr Mayor. I understand all that, and I will be bound by those rules.'

The mayor nodded, huffed on the lenses of his glasses, polished them and put them back on his nose, carefully tucking the wire sides behind his ears.

Wilfried tried to contain his impatience.

'Good, good,' the mayor muttered. Slowly he opened one of the drawers in his desk and shuffled some papers. Then took out a blank *Wanderbuch*. 'Name?'

'Wilfried Schönbaum.'

'Date of birth?' Wilfried told him.

The mayor dipped his pen in the inkpot and slowly wrote in the book. He stood up, and beckoned to Wilfried. 'Stand here.' He positioned Wilfried against a wall marking heights, put a ruler on Wilfried's head, then went back to his desk and wrote in the book. Then he studied Wilfried and again wrote in the book. 'Open your mouth.'

Wilfried blinked, but did as the mayor requested.

At last the mayor stamped the book with the official stamp. Then he signed it, blotted it and looked up at Wilfried. 'Sign here.' He handed Wilfried the pen. 'Good, now, go to your master and ask him to sign it and write a reference. God go with you, Herr Schönbaum.' He stood, smiled, handed Wilfried the precious book and held out his hand.

'Thank you, Herr Mayor.' Wilfried smiled back, shook the mayor's hand and walked out with a spring in his step.

***

Wilfried returned home with his official record book eager to show it to his parents.

His mother looked at it and burst into tears when she saw what was written on it:

Description of the Person of the Bearer:

Wilfried Schönbaum

Age: Born 2nd December, 1889

Height: 180 cm

Stature: Average

Face: Long

Hair: Dark brown

Forehead: Ordinary

Eye brows: Brown

Eyes: Hazel

Nose: Slightly hooked

Cheeks: Full

Mouth: Full

Teeth: Good

Chin: Square

Legs: Straight

Distinguishing marks: Skin clean

Above is certified true: [The town stamp and mayor's signature]

Signature of the traveller: [Wilfried's signature] September 12th 1909

'Oh, Wilfried,' his Mother wailed. 'It doesn't say that you are such a handsome young man; that description could be anyone!'

'Hush, mama. It's just to prove it's who I say I am. Look there is my signature if anyone doubts it's me.'

'Well done, son. We're proud of you.' His father patted Wilfried's shoulder, the closest the undemonstrative Manfred had ever come to showing he cared. Then he gave him a piece of paper. 'These are the names and addresses of good Reform Jews. Go to them if you need to. They will look after you.'

Wilfried put the slip of paper in his small leather wallet. 'Thank you, Father.'

He had the requisite amount of money in Marks, and his tools. He would be gone for three years and one day, getting work, food and accommodation wherever he could.

The next morning, he said his farewells to his parents and his brother, his mother striving not to cry, his brother just smiling, wondering how long his brother would last.

'See you soon!' Josef called as he waved goodbye.

Wilfried raised his eyebrows and smiled, then threw the bag containing his tools and the minimum to survive over his shoulder, twirled his *stenz*, put his trademark hat on his head and set off on his journey.

Though fired up with a sense of adventure and keen to go, a little part of Wilfried wanted to stay home and sleep in his own comfortable bed and eat his mother's good food. Apart from his apprentice years with his master, it was his first time away from home.

Under the journeyman terms he was only allowed to either walk or accept an offer of transport from a passer-by, and he was very relieved when, at around midday, a farmer with a hay cart passed him and then stopped along the road in front of him. 'You want a ride, young man?' the driver shouted. 'I'm going to Egelsbach; where are you heading for?

'Well, I was hoping to get to Darmstadt before dark, where there's a guild for carpenters,' Wilfried said, jumping onto the hay cart.

'Hmm,' the carter grunted. 'Well, I'll save you an hour's walk, anyway.'

'Thank you,' Wilfried said. He opened the package of black bread and cheese his mother had prepared for his lunch. 'Would you like to share my lunch?'

The carter shook his head. 'Thank you, but no. My wife will be waiting with my lunch. You'll need all the food you can get!'

Wilfried was grateful. He was starving after walking for four hours, and he probably had another three hours to go. He had the name of the Darmstadt guild, but first he'd have to find the local town hall, register and get his *Wanderbuch* stamped.

As he approached Darmstadt, Wilfried saw a black-clad figure trudging along in front of him. The flared trousers and wide-brimmed hat indicated another journeyman. Wilfried hastened to catch up with him. 'Hello!' he called, 'Are you on your *Wanderjahre?*'

The man stopped, turned around and looked at Wilfried. 'Yes. I'm on my way to the rope-makers' guild in Darmstadt. And you?'

'I'm making for Darmstadt too. The carpenters' guild.' He held out his hand. 'Wilfried Schönbaum.'

'Wolfgang Swartz.' The man studied Wilfried. 'You look very new and fresh. Been on the road long?'

'No; this is my first day.'

Wolfgang smiled. 'This is my second year. Welcome. I'll show you the ropes.' Then he burst out laughing. 'Not my ropes! I mean the way it all works.'

Wilfried felt delighted at this turn of events. The two youths walked along the road, laughing and chatting together.

'The road seems easier with company,' Wilfried remarked as they reached the outskirts of Darmstadt.

'Yes, indeed. Now, first, we must go to the town hall and register. But then I think it will be too late to find our guilds. What I usually do when this happens is go to a local tavern. Generally, the inn keeper will give you a meal and somewhere to sleep for the night. And he might find some kind of work to do to repay him. Is that all right with you?' Wolfgang raised his eyebrows at Wilfried.

'Yes, of course. I'd be happy to do that.'

'Good. Well, here's the town hall; we're just in time to find the mayor and get him to sign our books and tell us where to find our guilds in the morning.'

***

The tavern owner gave them a fine meal and told them they could sleep in the stables for the night. He nodded at Wilfried's insignia and smiled. 'I see you're a carpenter. If you two can repair a door that got broken in the stables, I'll give you both a hearty breakfast.'

They did so, and the next morning Wilfried felt sad to say goodbye to Wolfgang. 'I hope we meet up on the road again,' he said as they went their separate ways. 'And thank you for your help and your company.'

'A pleasure,' replied Wolfgang. 'We have to help each other on the *Walz sein.*'

The two youths shook hands. Wilfried found his guild and presented his *Wanderbuch.*

The guild master nodded. 'Yes, I believe a master craftsman in the town needs someone to help with a new staircase for the belfry tower in the church. This is his address.' He wrote the address in Wilfried's *Wanderbuch* and gave Wilfried directions.

The master was pleased to see Wilfred. 'You've come at the right time,' he said, looking closely at Wilfried's journal.

Four weeks later, the staircase was finished and Wilfried was on his way. The master gave him a good reference.

His experiences were mixed. Most masters were kind and generous; one who had no work for him gave him board for the night and only two others were hard task masters where he worked long hours for a scant meal and rough accommodation.

Sometimes Wilfried felt like giving it all up and going home to his mother's cooking and his own bedroom, but he was resolute, determined to be a master craftsman and make beautiful furniture. As he tramped along the roads, he visualised the furniture he would make: writing desks inlaid with mother of pearl; roll-top desks with secret drawers; sideboards with scroll edged mirrors ...

***

Wilfried approached Mannheim late one afternoon four months after he'd left home. Winter had set in, and he'd left Worms early that Friday morning in pouring rain, gradually becoming soaked through. Tired and hungry, he increased his pace towards the town. He stopped at the town hall and registered, then realised it was too late to find the carpenters' guild. Taking out his father's list of Reform Jews, he asked for directions to an address on the outskirts of Mannheim and then trudged on, his feet slipping on the smooth wet cobblestones of the town. He paused when he reached the address: 9 Pfeffer Strasse. It looked like a house but with a big window of round bullseye panes of glass. He peered through the glass and saw a range of boots and shoes. This must be a shoemaker, he thought. Unsure whether he should just open the door and walk in or knock, he did both. A bell rang inside, and after a few minutes, a young boy appeared. Wilfried nodded to him.

'Hello, my name is Wilfried Schönbaum; my father gave me this address.'

The boy just looked at him.

'Who is it, Hans?' came a voice from inside.

'He said his father sent him.'

'Well, bring him in!'

Wilfried looked at his sodden boots and hesitated, noticing the spotless entry and shop. 'I'm very wet,' he called out.

A middle-aged man appeared from what Wilfried thought must be his workshop. He took one look at Wilfried and shook his head. 'Take off your boots and coat here.' He turned to his son. 'Hans! Ask your mother for a clean shirt, pants and socks of mine,' then he continued to Wilfried, 'Come into my workshop; Hans will bring dry clothes and you can change there.'

An old iron stove warmed the workshop, and the welcome heat hit Wilfried. A smell of leather and wax filled the air. A good smell, Wilfried thought as he closed his eyes and crouched towards the stove, luxuriating in the warmth. Steam rose from his wet clothes.

From his leather wallet, somewhat sodden from the rain, Wilfried took out the piece of paper his father had given him. 'I'm doing my *Wanderjahre*, my *Walz sein*. I'm a cabinet maker. My father, Manfred Schönbaum, of Frankfurt, said to call on you if I needed somewhere to stay. He said you were a friend of his. I'm Wilfried.'

'Yes, I know Manfred Schönbaum, and you are welcome to our home. I'm Fritz Goldberg.' He held out his hand.

Wilfried shook it and smiled. 'Thank you.'

Hans returned with the dry clothes.

'Thank you so much!' Wilfried said as he took them.

'Now change,' Herr Goldberg said, 'and come into the kitchen and join us for the Shabbat. Hans, take those wet clothes to the drying room.'

'Yes, Father.' Hans took the dripping clothes reluctantly, holding them at arm's length.

A woman, her face flushed from the heat of the oven, looked up and smiled as they came into the kitchen. She was busy making *challah* for the Sabbath. Wilfried smiled back. With her hair plaited and coiled around her head, she reminded him of his mother. He looked around the large room, one so like his mother's kitchen at home, except for the upright piano in one corner.

'Now, sit and tell us about your travels.' Fritz indicated a chair at the kitchen table. 'This is my wife. Hannah, my dear, this is Manfred Schönbaum's son, Wilfried.'

Hannah smiled. 'Welcome, Herr Schönbaum.'

'Thank you, Frau Goldberg. I'm a cabinet maker, and I'm on my *Wanderjahre.*'

Hannah Goldberg smiled, then looked at her husband, who kept glancing at the cuckoo clock on the wall.

Fritz looked at Wilfried and nodded. 'I have lots of little carpentry jobs around the place that I can give you to do.'

'I must register with the carpenters' guild on Monday morning,' Wilfried said, 'but I'm happy to do any jobs to repay you. Although I'm a cabinet maker, I can do any kind of carpentry.'

'Good, good.' Fritz Goldberg frowned, and looked at the clock again.

Wilfried followed his gaze. *What was fascinating about it? Was the cuckoo about to come out?*

'What's keeping her?' Fritz muttered to himself.

'Liesel has gone for milk.' His wife smiled at her husband's anxiety.

'She should be back by now; it's getting dark, and she'll be drenched.' Fritz mumbled, then raised his voice. 'Hans had better go and look for her.'

Hans glowered. Clearly, he didn't want to go out in the rain to find his sister.

'I expect she's talking to Helmut,' Hannah said. 'She won't be long.'

Fritz's frown deepened just as the kitchen door burst open, and a young girl came in, shaking her plaits. A shower of rain drops burst over the room. 'Ouf! It's so wet!' she exclaimed, and then saw the visitor. She flushed, and her hand went to her mouth as she put the big jug of milk on the table. Her green eyes sparkled. 'Oh! I didn't know we had a visitor!'

Wilfried stared, entranced.

'My daughter, Liesel,' Fritz announced with a proud smile.

'Liesel, this is Wilfried Schönbaum. He's on his *Wanderjahre* and will be staying with us for a few days.'

Liesel stared at Wilfried as her father continued, 'We must prepare a bed for our guest before sunset. Hans will make a mattress in his room for you, Wilfried.'

His wife looked up from taking the *challah* from the oven. 'Liesel, find bedding please and help Hans.' Wilfried moved to get up and help, but Frau Goldberg held up her hand. 'No, Herr Schönbaum, you stay here and get warm. Drink this.' She poured him a mug of fresh milk from the jug.

'Come, it's getting dark; we must hasten for the Sabbath,' Fritz said. 'Quickly, Hans, prepare the bed for Herr Schönbaum.'

The familiar Sabbath rituals soothed Wilfried, but his gaze followed Liesel. She kept her eyes cast down, but he saw her taking sideways glances at him.

The meal over, Fritz looked up at his daughter. 'Liesel! Bring your violin and play for us!'

She left the room and returned with her violin. She smiled at them, spent several moments tuning it and then started to play.

First, a piece from a violin concerto, then old German songs which caused Fritz and his wife to tap their feet in time to the music.

Wilfried just kept looking at this beautiful young girl, mesmerised by her fingers on the strings of the violin and her rapt expression as she played, until he became aware of the boy, Hans, watching him. 'How old are you, Hans?' he whispered.

'I'm thirteen years old,' came the reply.

'And how old is your sister?'

'She is sixteen, I think.'

Sixteen! And I am twenty. 'Do you play an instrument, Hans?'

Hans screwed up his face. 'I'm supposed to be learning to play the piano, but I have no interest in it, not like Liesel.'

Wilfried nodded. He didn't have much inclination to play an instrument, either. But now, as he looked at Liesel again, he thought the violin a most attractive instrument.

All too soon, Fritz said, 'It's time for bed. On Sunday we will look at work you can do, Wilfried.'

***

On Monday morning, Wilfried took his leave of the Goldbergs.

'Come back on Friday night and spend the Sabbath with us,' Fritz said, shaking Wilfried's hand.

Wilfred was delighted, and even more pleased when he found out that the master carpenter he went to in Mannheim would have at least three weeks work for him. Under the terms of the *Wanderjahre*, he was not allowed to spend more than three months with any one master at a time, but usually they only had a few days' work.

Wilfried was more than happy to spend his Saturdays with the Goldbergs. He couldn't stop looking at Liesel.

On his last day of work, the master gave Wilfried a glowing reference, signed his *Wanderbuch* and Wilfried was on his way to his next place of work. But first he had to say farewell and thank the Goldbergs.

Fritz was happy to see him. 'Please call in the next time you're passing,' he said. 'We'll have found a few more jobs for you by then.' His eyes twinkled.

Wilfried smiled and nodded. 'Thank you, sir.' He glanced over Fritz's shoulders to where Liesel stood in the doorway, and they exchanged a look that made Wilfried's heart beat faster.

'Goodbye, Herr Schönbaum,' Liesel said breathlessly as she stepped forward and offered him her hand.

He took it and bowed his head for a moment. 'Goodbye, Fraülein.' Emboldened by her touch, he gave her hand a gentle squeeze, causing her cheeks to glow.

Fritz looked from Wilfried to his daughter. 'Come, my dear, we had better let Herr Schönbaum continue his journey.' He took Liesel's hand from Wilfried.

'*Auf wiedersehen*, Herr Schönbaum.'

Chapter Four

Germany

Wilfried continued on his journey, becoming more skilled at his work and more adept at surviving in the hard conditions of the *Walz sein*. But his thoughts kept returning to Liesel Goldberg.

A year and a half later found him back in Mannheim, and after registering with the guild, he went to visit the master craftsman where he'd worked previously.

'The Benz Company has nearly completed their new factory in Mannheim-Waldhof,' the master said. 'I'm struggling to finish the interior on time. You're just the man to help. Come in! Come in! Start first thing in the morning.'

'Very good.' Wilfried's eyes shone at the warm welcome. 'But first, may I go and pay my respects to a friend of my father's, and then I will come straight back here.'

'Of course, of course.' The master carpenter, pleased to have such a good and willing worker joining him, clapped Wilfried on the back.

Half an hour later, Wilfried knocked on the door of the Goldberg's shop. He wondered if he'd exaggerated Liesel's beauty in his mind during the long nights alone. The bell jangled as he opened the door.

Liesel answered it. 'Oh!' She exclaimed with pleasure when she saw who it was. 'Herr Schönbaum, oh, please do come in.' She held the door wide open.

Fritz came out of his workshop, his round gold-framed spectacles on the end of his nose. 'Herr Schönbaum, how good to see you again.' He held out his hand.

'Good day, Herr Goldberg, but please would you call me Wilfried?'

'Come into the kitchen,' he said and then called out, 'Hannah, Wilfried Schönbaum is here!'

Wilfried looked at Liesel, who he thought was even more beautiful than he remembered. 'I can't stay,' he said as he walked into the kitchen. He looked around the familiar room—the dresser shelves with old china beer mugs and pretty crockery, just like his mother's kitchen. He missed his family.'I've just been to see the master where I was registered before. He was very pleased to have me back. He's got a lot of work to finish on the new Benz factory and wants me to start work tomorrow. I think I might be in Mannheim for a few weeks.' Wilfried looked at Liesel as he said this and saw her start to smile.

Hannah Goldberg smiled as she watched Liesel's blushes and Wilfried's rapt attention.

'Yes, there is a lot of talk about the Benz motors and the new factory,' Fritz remarked and then frowned. 'But tomorrow is the Sabbath ...'

All the Goldbergs looked at Wilfried, who gestured with his hands. 'I know, but, dear Herr Goldberg, I am afraid this has happened a lot while I've been on my journey, and as a Reform Jew, I think it's acceptable that I respect my master's wishes.'

There was a sudden silence.

'Herr Goldberg, it's been difficult to get work with Jewish master craftsmen. There aren't many ...' Wilfried's tone was almost pleading.

Fritz looked at his wife, who looked perplexed, then at his daughter, who had paled. It seemed she was waiting and hoping for an acceptable response from him. He took off his spectacles and polished them.

The others all watched him expectantly.

'I suppose that is true,' he said thoughtfully. Then he smiled. 'Well, we are Reform Jews, too, but now we must celebrate Wilfried's return!'

The atmosphere immediately lightened. Liesel let out a sigh. Wilfried smiled at her, and realised that it'd been a pivotal moment. If Fritz had been antagonistic to the idea of him working on the Sabbath, and for non-Jewish masters, he would've been torn between giving up his career or giving up Liesel. He felt relieved that he didn't have to make that choice.

'Perhaps you'd help Liesel get the milk and butter from the farm,' Hannah Goldberg said.

Wilfried was delighted to accompany Liesel. As they approached the farm, a young man came out; it appeared he'd been looking out for Liesel.

'Oh, Helmut,' Liesel said, 'this is Herr Schönbaum. He's on his *Wanderjahre* and working in Mannheim at the moment.' She smiled at both men. 'Herr Schönbaum this is Helmut Winkl. His father has the farm here.'

Wilfried looked at Helmut. '*Guten Tag.*'

Helmut frowned and self-consciously mumbled a reply. In his farm clothes, which although clean, smelt of the farm yard, he didn't cut as romantic a figure as Wilfried with his fancy *Wanderjahre* dress.

'I'll get the milk for you, *Liesel.*' Helmut took her hand, lifted it up and pointedly took the milk jug with a proprietorial air. In the dairy he filled the jug and handed it to Liesel.

Wilfried stepped forward and smiled. 'Perhaps I can carry that for you, Fraulein?'

Helmut scowled. 'I have butter and eggs for you, *Liesel.*' He emphasised her name again to indicate that he was on first name terms with her, and as they left, he bid them a surly goodbye.

Wilfried didn't know quite what to say to Liesel, but when she asked him about his work and the travelling, he found it easy to reply and then ask her about her music.

'I'd like to study music and the violin.' She looked up at him with those eyes, which were sometimes green and sometimes amber. 'There's a good music school in Mannheim, but I think I would prefer to go to Frankfurt or Berlin. I don't think my parents could afford that, though.' She sighed.

Wilfried wanted to say, 'If you went to Frankfurt, you could stay with my parents! My room is empty, you could stay there!' The thought of Liesel in his room, sleeping in his bed, made his heart race. Instead he asked, 'So ... Helmut is a close friend of yours?'

Liesel looked up at him from under her eyelashes. 'He's just a neighbour.'

Wilfried felt that Helmut wanted to be much more than 'just a neighbour'.

When they got back to the Goldberg's, Wilfried made to leave. 'My Master is expecting me back tonight,' he said. 'But perhaps I can come and visit on Sunday? I don't think we'll be working then.'

Fritz Goldberg nodded. 'Of course, of course!'

Wilfried worked for six weeks on the new Benz factory, spending any time he had off with the Goldbergs. Eventually the Benz factory was ready for the production of luxury cars, and his master gave him an excellent reference. Reluctantly Wilfried set off for Ladenburg. From there he would go to Heidelberg where he was sure he'd find plenty of work.

***

The following year found Wilfried back on the Goldberg's doorstep.

Fritz clapped him on the shoulder. 'Welcome, dear boy! I think you've grown! I hope the pair of boots I've made for you will still fit!'

Wilfried was touched. 'That is so kind of you Herr Goldberg.'

The years on the road had turned Wilfried from a boy into a man. Tall and handsome and with a newly grown moustache, he looked older and more mature than the previous year.

'I've finished my *Walz sein*,' Wilfried replied. 'I came to thank you for your hospitality and to see if you had any other jobs you need doing before I return to Frankfurt.'

Liesel, hearing the voices, came running to the door. Her face flushed when she saw Wilfried, who just looked at her for a long moment.

He swallowed. 'Hello, Fraulein.'

She smiled. 'Herr Schönbaum.'

A knock sounded on the door as they went into the kitchen. It opened and Helmut appeared. 'I've brought the milk.' He smiled at Liesel; then he saw Wilfried and his smile faded.

Hannah turned to Helmut. 'Thank you, Helmut, will you come in and meet Herr Schönbaum?'

'Thank you.' Helmut walked over to stand beside Liesel. 'We have already met,' he said in an abrupt tone as he nodded at Wilfried, who greeted him.

The two men stared at each other.

Hannah opened her mouth as if to ask something, then saw Wilfried's face, and closed it again without saying a word.

Hans came between them. 'Hello, Herr Schönbaum; I'm now sixteen.'

'Yes, I can see you've grown a lot.' Wilfried smiled at the young boy.

'I need more eggs, Helmut,' Hannah said, breaking the tension, 'would your father have any to spare?'

Helmut nodded.

'Hans, perhaps you would go back with Helmut and get them.'

Hans grimaced, apparently unwilling. He looked at Liesel, then back at his mother. When he saw his mother's glare, he set off without a word with a reluctant and scowling Helmut following behind.

Wilfried smiled; it seemed he had an ally in Frau Goldberg.

After the evening meal, Wilfried managed to get Liesel to himself for a moment. 'Fraulein Liesel, I'm twenty-two now; I should have started my national service when I was twenty, but I was excused until after my *Wanderjahre*. Now I have to do two years of active service in the army before I can return to Frankfurt. I'll be stationed with the Fifth Army Inspectorate in Karlsruhe. If I write to you, will you write back to me?'

Liesel looked up at him. 'Yes, Herr Schönbaum,' she whispered.

'Wilfried,' he said, 'Please call me Wilfried.'

She nodded. 'Please call me Liesel.'

Wilfried smiled. 'There's a train from Karlsruhe to Mannheim. I might be able to visit you. Would your parents allow that?'

Liesel nodded. 'I think so. I'll ask them.'

***

Wilfried only managed to visit the Goldbergs twice during his active service. No battles were fought in those two years, so the

Army Inspectorate didn't travel away from its headquarters in Karlsruhe, but he had to visit his parents as well as the Goldbergs when on leave. When his two years had passed, he was assigned to the Army Reserve, which meant just a two-week refresher training period a year for the following four years.

He returned to Frankfurt and registered with his guild, then went to see his old master where he'd served his apprenticeship. The master was impressed with the references Wilfried had in his *Wanderbuch*.

'I hope you haven't forgotten how to be a cabinet maker after two years of being a soldier,' he joked, 'but now you have to make something special, a masterpiece.'

Wilfried nodded. 'Yes. I'm not sure yet what to make. I've been thinking about it all the time I was in the army. I love the thought of something inlaid with mother of pearl.'

***

Wilfried pondered over various ideas, but thoughts of Liesel kept intruding. He pictured her playing her violin as she had when he'd first seen her. Then he had an idea: a miniature violin! It would be a tribute to Liesel.

Dear Liesel,

I trust you and your family are well.

I have been thinking of what to make for my masterpiece, and now I have decided.

I am still working in Frankfurt with my old master.

If I can pass this test, I will be able to open my own business. Perhaps in Mannheim.

Wilfried Schönbaum

Each evening after his work with his master, he worked on his masterpiece. At last he completed a test violin for himself, and before putting on the tiny strings, he carefully etched his name inside the back of it. It looked good. He decided to make another and put Liesel's name inside. This one was slightly better finished, he thought. He'd keep that one for his masterpiece.

He took them home and showed his parents.

Josef came into the kitchen as Wilfried was unwrapping them from the velvet covering. 'So this is your Masterpiece?'

Wilfried nodded. 'Yes.'

His mother exclaimed, '*Oh! Mein Gott*! So beautiful.'

His father smiled. 'Can I pick one up?'

'Of course.' Wilfried handed one to each of his parents.

His father peered behind the strings. 'Is there something written there?'

'Yes.' Colour flooded Wilfried's cheeks.

Josef peered over his father's shoulder and laughed. 'It says, Liesel Goldberg. Ah ha! So you have a sweetheart you're trying to impress!' He clapped Wilfried on the shoulder.

Wilfried grinned. 'I hope so!'

'They are beautiful, Wilfried,' said his father, 'but why have you made two?'

'The first one was a practice one; I'm going to give it to Herr Goldberg's daughter. They were so kind to me on my *Wander-jahre*.'

Manfred nodded, a twinkle in his eyes. 'Hmm,' was all he said.

*****

The following Sunday, Wilfried got the train to Mannheim and called on the Goldbergs.

Liesel opened the door.

'Who is it?' called her mother.

Liesel stepped back. 'It's Wilfried,' she exclaimed.

'Well, bring him in!'

The Goldbergs all seemed pleased to see Wilfried. Hans was no longer little but a sturdy teenager who rather hero worshipped Wilfried.

'I've brought something to show you,' Wilfried said as they led him into the kitchen. When they were all sitting at the table, Wilfried brought out two packages. 'This one is for my masterpiece,' he said, unwrapping one.

The Goldbergs gave a collective gasp when they saw the flawless little violin lying on the velvet cloth.

'Oh, it's perfect!' exclaimed Liesel. 'And there is mother of pearl on the body!'

Wilfried turned to her and shyly offered her the other parcel. 'For you.'

Carefully Liesel unwrapped it and gasped when she saw the replica miniature violin. 'Oh! Oh, it's so beautiful! For me?'

'Yes. If you look inside very carefully you can see I've put my name. The wood is so thin that it is a bit indistinct. It's so you won't forget me.'

'Oh, Wilfried, how could I forget you?'

Wilfried picked up the first little violin. 'If you look carefully inside this one, you can see your name.' He held it out to her. 'You might need a magnifying glass to read it.'

Fritz looked up. 'I have a magnifying glass in my workshop. Hans will you fetch it, please? I need one these days when I'm doing fine work. My eyes are not so good,' he said ruefully.

Hans came back with the magnifying glass and handed it to Liesel.

She peered into the middle of the violin. 'I can see it,' she breathed.

'Play it, Liesel,' her brother commanded.

She looked up at Wilfried. 'Is there a bow?'

'Oh!' he replied, feeling embarrassed. 'Should I make one? I didn't think of that! I'll make one for my test.'

Liesel shook her head. 'Perhaps you don't need to. I think this will pass your guild examiners.' She carefully wrapped her miniature in the velvet cloth. 'It's beautiful, Wilfried. Thank you so much.'

'We must celebrate!' Fritz jumped up. 'I think we have some of Hannah's cherry wine. Yes, Hannah?'

Hannah smiled. 'Of course. I'll fetch glasses.'

Wilfried and Liesel exchanged looks.

Wilfried looked at Liesel's father. 'My parents have invited Liesel and Hans to visit us in Frankfurt. Perhaps they could come on the train one Sunday?'

'Oh, yes!' Hans said enthusiastically. A visit to Frankfurt was a rarity.

Fritz smiled. He understood that Wilfried's parents would want to repay the hospitality that the Goldbergs had shown to Wilfried while he was on his *Wanderjahre*. And it would be good for Hans to see something of Frankfurt.

A few weeks later, Wilfried met Hans and Liesel at Frankfurt railway station and took them home. The visit was a success. The Schönbaums thought Liesel quite delightful and that Hans was a very well-mannered boy.

After Wilfried had seen them off at the station to get the train back to Mannheim, Josef slapped Wilfried on the back. 'How did you find such a beauty, Wilf? And whatever does she see in you?'

Wilfried smiled. 'I don't know, Josef, but now that I've finished my national service, and as soon as I can save some money, I plan to ask her to marry me before she realises just how dull and ordinary I am.'

Josef grinned. 'I don't want to make you even more conceited, Wilf, but I reckon you're pretty special. For a brother, that is, don't know about husband material.' He dodged away, laughing, before Wilfried had time to aim a punch at him.

About once a month Wilfried managed to visit Liesel, and she and Hans came a few times to Frankfurt.

'Liesel is such a lovely girl,' Hilde Schönbaum said after one visit. 'I would've liked a daughter like her. And Hans and Josef get on very well. The Goldbergs seem a very nice family.' She looked at Wilfried, who smiled and nodded.

'Yes.' Was all he said.

Chapter Five

1965, Greenacre, Sydney

When her daughter and husband got home after Wilfred's funeral, Madge sniffed disdainfully. 'Didn't take you long to clean up your father's place.'

Charles shrugged and murmured something about his father's tools and going out to the shed.

'Hm, his tools would be the only things of value he'd have had.' Madge turned to Liesel and said pointedly, 'The ironing's out in the laundry, Lee.'

'I'll do it now.' Liesel had learned to be meek and compliant with her mother, but she hugged her secret to herself while she carefully ironed and folded the pile of clothes.

She'd a lot to think about. A Jewess! All that stuff written in German! She resolved to start to learn German as soon as she'd finished her teacher training.

***

Liesel couldn't keep the secret of her ancestry to herself. She'd been going out with a boy in her year at college. 'Guess what, Pat?' she said, bubbling with excitement when she met him at lunch time the next day.

'Um, your grandfather left you a fortune.' Patrick Lacey smiled at her and caught her hand as they walked across the campus.

'No, nothing like that.' She wasn't going to tell anyone about the miniature violin. 'I'm a Jew,' she smiled.

'What!' he dropped her hand and stopped walking. 'How can you be a Jew? I thought you were a Catholic, like me.'

'Well, apparently my mother is Jewish, and that makes me a Jew too. My father and grandparents as well. And, anyway, why would you think I was a Catholic?'

Pat frowned. 'Hmm. Well ...'

They continued walking in silence, but he didn't take her hand again, and his sudden coolness put a damper on Liesel's excitement.

Over the next few days, she realised Pat was avoiding her. Having been in love with him, she felt heartbroken and decided not to mention her Jewish heritage to anyone ever again.

***

Sunday 25th April 1965 ANZAC Day

The voice of the commentator at the ANZAC parade in Sydney came over the airwaves. Madge turned off the radio. 'Ridiculous, all this fuss about Gallipoli,' she grumbled. 'Why do they celebrate a defeat? Ridiculous.' She stalked out of the kitchen, muttering to herself.

Liesel sighed and carried on with the washing up, thinking about Gallipoli and the First World War. *Would her grandfather have been involved?*

As soon as she'd finished drying the dishes and putting them away, she hurried out to her father's shed. 'Dad! Would Pop have fought with the ANZACs at Gallipoli?'

Her father turned from the old radio he'd been repairing and stared at her. 'Of course not! Gallipoli was before your grandfather even came to Australia, and the Allies were fighting the Turks there.'

Liesel frowned. 'I don't understand. What did Turkey have to do with it?'

'Didn't they teach you anything at school? Turkey, as part of the Ottoman Empire had an alliance with Germany. Pop would've been fighting for the Kaiser. Go and read your history books.' He turned back to his soldering.

Chapter Six

1914, Frankfurt am Main, Germany.

A lthough Wilfried was still working for his old master, his thoughts were occupied with thinking about how he could save enough to start his own business and marry Liesel, so he wasn't paying attention when his father passed him the *Frankfurter Zeitung* on the night of Monday 29th June.

'Read this,' Manfred said, pointing to the headlines: *ASSASSINATION MAY LEAD TO WAR! On Sunday 28th June, Archduke Franz Ferdinand of Austria was assassinated by a Serb student, Gavrilo Princip.*

Wilfried scanned the article and frowned as he looked up at his father. 'Do you really think this will lead to war?' he asked.

Manfred shrugged. 'There's always problems in the Balkans.'

Wilfried looked at the rest of the news. 'Goodness,' he said, 'Rasputin, the Tsar's advisor, was also nearly assassinated. Oh, and look at this, there's a new Zeppelin route connection, Frankfurt to Berlin. It leaves on Wednesdays and returns on Fridays.' He looked up dreamily. 'Oh, how I'd love to travel in one.'

Manfred smiled and shook his head.

***

Seven days later, Kaiser Wilhelm, the German Emperor and King of Prussia, promised German support for Austria against Serbia.

Wilfried didn't pay much attention to this either—it was just politics—but when on Tuesday, 28th July, Austria declared war on Serbia, the situation changed. That weekend Wilfried went to Mannheim to visit the Goldbergs.

They all sat around the big kitchen table after lunch, discussing the actions of Austria-Hungary. Fritz frowned and looked at Wilfried. 'What will it mean, Wilfried?' He asked, thinking that Wilfried, having just finished his national service, would have all the answers.

Wilfried shrugged. 'It's hard to tell. But it's of great concern because the Russians support Serbia, and France and Russia have a treaty. That means Germany could be crushed between France in the West and Russia and her allies in the East. And the French have never got over our annexation of Alsace-Lorraine in the Franco-Prussian War.' He sighed and looked at Liesel. 'I'm worried that we'll declare war on Russia, and if that happens, we'll be obliged to declare war on France, and then where will it end?'

Wilfried's fears were realised when, on the first of August, Germany declared war, first on Russia and then two days later on France. They followed this by implementing the plan proposed by the German military leader Alfred Von Schlieffen: first sending a small contingent of the military to Germany's border with Russia, believing it would take Russia at least six or seven weeks to mobilise its army; and at the same time, sending the remainder of the German army to invade France by marching through Belgium, the aim being to take France within six weeks. The large network of railways in Belgium would enable the transport of a huge number of troops and supplies into France before the French had time to rally their forces. Then, after six or so weeks, once France had been subdued, a small occupation army could stay there and the remainder of the forces sent to the Eastern front to back up the contingent there and either invade or repel Russia. It was a well-thought-out and logical plan.

Except for one problem.

Germany thought that the neutral Belgians would follow German orders and allow the German army free passage through Belgium to their border with France. However, the Belgians, angry that their neutrality had been violated, blew up railway lines and bridges, and this caused major setbacks for the German army, delaying their invasion of France. Unfortunately, the brave Belgians suffered severe reprisals for their actions, and on the fourth of August, Britain, honouring its treaty with Belgium, declared war on Germany.

Instead of the swift passage of troops through Belgium, German manpower had to try and repair railways and bridges before they could reach the French border, and in the meantime, British and French forces had time to mobilise and thwart the German plans of a quick defeat of France.

***

By the time he left to join his Infantry unit, Wilfried was a crack shot, fit and strong, and an expert in armed combat. He'd just turned twenty-five.

His mother wept inconsolably.

His father turned his head to hide his tears. 'I hope this war will be the war to end all wars,' he said, patting his elder son's shoulder.

Josef regarded his brother with admiration. 'I'll be joining you soon! Once I've finished my national-service training.'

Their mother wept even more at these words.

Wilfried completed his training and joined his battalion on the troop train in late autumn. The smell of soldiers, with their new uniforms, boot polish and sweat, kit and rifles, all squashed in together, all talking and laughing, all eager to fight for their homeland, made it hard for Wilfried to breathe. It was a relief when the train arrived at a Belgian village behind the German line. With the noise and confusion of disembarking, it was a while before he realised that the distant rhythmic rumble that he could hear was the fighting going on at the front—a continual eerie sound. He looked at the devastated landscape—flattened buildings and denuded trees—and saw shrapnel shells exploding in the sky. His stomach turned at the thought that only a few months ago this had been a village, filled with houses and people.

In the beginning, he'd been fired with enthusiasm at the idea of protecting his homeland and family from the neighbouring armies of France, Britain and Russia. They'd been told of British and French aggression and their seizure of parts of Africa. Now, however much doubts assailed him, he had no time to ponder these matters as his platoon was ordered to march. He shouldered his kitbag and, weighed down by his ammunition belt and rifle, trudged through the heavy clay soil, which was wet and sticky from the autumn rains.

His platoon marched to the labyrinth of trenches and dugouts which branched out from the trenches where the men were supposed to sleep. They hadn't been trained for trench warfare. As with previous wars, their Kaiser and generals played mock war games with tin soldiers and horses on a mock battle field, not under mortar fire in trenches.

Wilfried's unit's first task was to dig a new trench around one that had been destroyed by enemy shells. With pickaxes and shovels, he and his platoon laboured all the first day. He was horrified to come across the blackened hand of some poor soul from the collapsed trench sticking out of the mud.

His commander's words sickened him. 'Carry on, men. We'll build a wall around it.'

That night the field kitchen arrived by horse-drawn dray with a cauldron of pea and ham soup. It smelt delicious and Wilfried was ravenous. His fellow soldiers wolfed it down. Wilfried did likewise. He didn't care, pork or not, he felt he could've eaten the whole cauldron.

Two of his unit went on a two-hour sentry duty. It seemed that two hours was the most to be expected before sentries fell asleep on duty. Only two men at a time were allowed to sleep in the cold, hard, and damp dugouts, and only for two hours. The others had to be ready for action. Midnight was his turn on sentry duty. His first. He stood behind a slit in the trench wall, his rifle at the ready and endeavoured to stay alert for two hours in the freezing cold. Tired from marching and digging, he struggled to keep his eyes from closing, stamping his feet while his breath came in white drifts on the cold night air. At last someone relieved him, and he managed to snatch a bare two-hour sleep before the morning roll call. Then it was back to digging, reinforcing the trenches, getting food, water and ammunition from the supply lines and trying to keep themselves clean.

This routine seemed to be never-ending. The monotony only interrupted when mortar shells fell in the trenches or shrapnel hit one of their company. Wilfried didn't think he'd ever get used to the sight of the injured and dead men. Their spiked helmets of painted leather didn't offer much protection against shrapnel, and he wondered if the protruding spike wasn't a target for the French Army.

The dugouts where they slept were just holes hacked into the ground with planks for roofs, and some earth shovelled on top. In heavy rain, the water seeped through and soaked them, making it hard to sleep.

Eventually another platoon relieved them, and they had a spell off duty, relaxing in a nearby village. Well, not exactly relaxing, Wilfried thought; only if you could call being billeted in a rat-infested barn in a flattened village with just a few surly, resentful villagers in evidence as a relaxing atmosphere.

Still, he had time to write letters. First to his parents—a very brief letter, letting them know he was well—then a longer letter to Liesel.

***

A week later a reply came from his father: all was well at home. He waited anxiously for news from Liesel. At last, he received a letter and a parcel from her.

February 1915.

Dear Wilfried,

I hope you are safe; we don't have much news from the front.

Helmut Winkl has asked my father if he can marry me. He has been called up to fight in the war, but he wants us to get married before he goes. My father is keen, because the Winkls have a big farm. He thinks this will guarantee security for me. But my mother isn't in favour of a marriage between us because the Winkls aren't Jewish.

I like Helmut, but I don't want to marry him. I don't want to be a farmer's wife. I want to try and continue my music studies. But it would mean a secure future for my parents. I worry about them.

It's very uncomfortable at home now. I don't know what to do.

Liesel Goldberg.

Wilfried felt distraught at the contents of this letter and wished he'd asked Fritz if he could become engaged to Liesel before he'd left for the war. He'd hesitated, wanting to wait until he had something to offer her. And the war wasn't supposed to last.

He wrote back straight away.

February 1915.

Dearest Liesel,

Please do NOT marry Helmut.

Liesel, I love you. I want to marry you. Please wait for me.

If you say yes, I'll write to your father and ask for you.

I love you, Liesel

Wilfried Schönbaum

He put it with the other letters to be posted and prayed that Liesel would receive it quickly. He was soon back in the trenches, and four long weeks passed before he received her reply.

March 1915.

My dear Wilfried,

I showed your letter to my mother. She was very pleased. I think she likes you, and you are also Jewish. She spoke to my father.

He was very kind. He told me he didn't know that you wanted to marry me. Apparently, he thought that I loved Helmut. I don't know how he could think that! He thought that when Hans and I went to see you in Frankfurt, it was because you were friends with Hans!

YES, Wilfried, I want to marry you!

Helmut has gone to join his unit. He asked me to write to him. I didn't know what to say. He doesn't know that I am now promised to you.

I wish you were here, Wilfried.

Liesel Goldberg.

Wilfried's heart lifted when he read this letter. He also received a letter from his mother with a parcel of food. The German army expected its soldiers to supplement their rations with food from home. Shipping blockades by the British meant that some foods weren't getting through to German ports, and because so many men had been called up to fight, only women or those men too old or unfit to fight remained to work on the farms.

As soon as he could, he wrote to Fritz asking for permission to marry Liesel.

Chapter Seven

Ypres, Belgium

The winter was hard. Frost, snow and ice made the conditions unbearable. Their sleeping dugouts filled with water. Wilfried lay on the hard plank which was his bunk and wrapped his sodden greatcoat around him. He tried to block out the constant dripping of water. His feet felt like soggy blotting paper, but he had no dry socks to change into. Eventually he fell into an exhausted sleep, only to be woken two hours later. His bones ached. Sentry duty was a nightmare. Standing in all weathers in the dark, wet, mud-filled trenches, feet cold and wet, and trying to stay awake and ignore the hunger gnawing at his belly. There seemed to be no letup in this routine.

At last spring arrived, and his company was moved from the front line and posted to Ypres for what would come to be called 'The Second Battle of Ypres.' For two days they suffered bombardment—at least their spiked leather helmets had been replaced with plain metal ones—then Wilfried heard screaming. He peered over the sandbags lining the front of the trench and saw a greenish cloud drifting across no-man's land and into the French trenches.

He frowned at the sight of French soldiers pouring out of their trenches like rats escaping from a burning building and running as fast as they could away from the front. They threw down their rifles and tore off their coats in an effort to run faster. The screams got worse as some of them collapsed on the ground, writhing in agony. One or two in his battalion shot at them, they were easy targets. Then the haze started to drift back to the German line.

With the retreat of the French, Wilfried realised that here was an opportunity for the Germans to advance. He looked around at his commanding officer, but the man hesitated as he saw the effects of the gas on the French. Afraid of what it might do to him and his men as the green cloud drifted back towards them, Wilfried's commanding officer failed to take advantage of the rout. Then French reinforcements came on horseback to defend the line. It was too late.

Germany had started gas warfare. Chlorine gas turned to hydrochloric acid when it touched moisture. The French soldiers' eyes and lungs burned. Many collapsed and died, others were blinded.

***

By 1915 the food situation in Germany had grown so bad that soldiers who were farmers were given leave in the summer to go home and help get the crops in. The thought of Helmut, most probably getting leave and laying siege to Liesel, tormented Wilfried. Though she'd promised herself to him, it didn't stop him thinking the worst.

With autumn came rain, and the trenches filled with water. Some dugouts collapsed, and they had to dig through the heavy clay mud to find comrades who'd been sleeping in the dugouts.

October 1915.

My dear Wilfried,

I hope you are well. I am including some cakes and dried beef. I hope you receive it. Food is getting scarce here. Luckily, we can still get milk and some eggs from Helmut's father.

I'm worried about my mother. She isn't well. She's lost a lot of weight and isn't eating.

Helmut's father has been sending butter and extra eggs when he can spare them for her.

Oh, Wilfried, I am distraught! I wish you were here, I miss you so much.

My mother tries to keep on working, washing and baking, although I help her as much as I can now that I have finished my education. I must stay home and take care of her and my father, and of course my brother.

Please stay safe, Wilfried; I love you so much. I couldn't bear it if anything happened to you!

Your ever-loving Liesel.

Liesel's news upset Wilfried. Poor Hannah. And was Helmut's father trying to ingratiate himself with Liesel on Helmut's behalf? He wondered what to write back. Maybe Hannah's illness wasn't really serious. He sighed and got out his pencil and some paper. It was impossible to find ink to write with a pen.

My darling Liesel,

Thank you for the parcel, the food was very welcome and the socks.

Our clothes get so damp and wet in the trenches.

I am sorry to hear your mother isn't well. Is there any improvement since you last wrote? I hope so.

At the moment we are billeted in a village in Belgium, near Ypres.

We have six days leave before we have to go back.

He stopped and wondered what to say next. That three of his company had been blown to bits? That another had bled to death from a shrapnel wound to an artery in his neck? That any wound could lead to a killing infection of the blood?

I think this must have been a pretty little village once.

We are sleeping in a big barn, and a few of the men have been going out at night trying to shoot rabbits for food.

At least I am a Reform Jew, he thought gloomily. Orthodox can't eat rabbit, and I'm so hungry all the time. He knew the officers had better food than the men in the trenches. Everyone was grumbling about it. They all thought it was wrong.

I am fit and well.

My regards to your family.

What else could he say? Bloated enemy corpses and dead horses lay around on no-man's land with enormous rats feeding on them? That they had been issued with gas masks since the use of chlorine gas?

I can't wait to see you again, my darling.

Your ever loving

Wilfried Schönbaum

***

The war dragged on. During Wilfried's short spells of leave, he had no time to get from the front back to Frankfurt or Mannheim. In the summer of 1916, he was still holed up in the trenches and tormented by the thought of Helmut being at home for the harvest. Did he know that Liesel was spoken for? Was he still coming with milk and butter and eggs? Liesel hadn't mentioned him. Perhaps she was playing a game, and keeping Helmut dangling, in case he, Wilfried, didn't make it through the war. He kept telling himself that she wouldn't do such a thing, but those thoughts kept intruding.

All through the summer and into autumn, Wilfried's company seemed to make advances and then lose their advantage. It was stalemate.

October 1916.

My darling Liesel,

I am sorry to hear that your mother hasn't recovered her health. It must be hard for you all. Christmas will soon be here. I am due some leave, but I don't know when it will happen.

We are all getting weary of this stalemate.

There is another Jewish fellow in my platoon, and we sometimes have discussions about why we are fighting this war.

I think our letters are being censored, so if you see black marks on my letters, it's where the censor has tried to erase anything which I should not have written.

All my love

Wilfried Schönbaum

***

On the few occasions when his platoon managed to take prisoners, Wilfried was astonished at the supplies provided to the British soldiers: good food, tobacco and extra clothes. The British must have better supply units than we have, he thought. He wanted to write and tell Liesel this, but he knew it would be censored. At the end of 1916, he was given seven days leave.

His parents were delighted to see him.

'I'm sorry there isn't much to eat,' his mother said, offering him a dish of swedes. 'According to the newspapers, the British have blockaded the entrance to the English Channel and the North Sea. They're stopping all ships and confiscating any food.' She sounded upset. 'They're trying to starve us into submission.'

'Yes,' his father said, 'and the French and Italians are doing the same in the Mediterranean Sea. So no food is coming from the south, either. And so many farm workers have been called up, there's not a lot of farming being done.'

Wilfried frowned, indignant at this information. 'I learnt at school that Germany didn't need to rely on imported food; we grew enough. We haven't heard any of this at the front, but the British trenches we've captured seem to be well supplied with food. It's probably the stuff bound for us that they're confiscating!'

His father shrugged. 'The harvests have been bad, and it's been said that the nitrates that farmers have been using for fertilisers in recent years have been used for making ammunition instead.'

Wilfried prodded his swedes and potatoes, angry at the British. Perhaps we're right to fight them after all, he thought.

'I heard we have some new underwater boats trying to destroy the British supply ships, *Unterseeboots*,' Josef said, eager to display his knowledge. 'U-boats. They're targeting supply ships in the Atlantic coming from America.'

Wilfried looked at his brother. 'Just don't try and become an officer in one of them.'

The next day, Wilfried got the train to Mannheim to see Liesel. He'd sent a letter telling her on which train he'd be travelling.

He knocked on the door, and she came running, opening the door in a fever of excitement.

He wrapped her in his arms.

'Oh, Wilfried!' She looked up and gasped. 'But you've got so thin!'

He smiled. 'Everyone has, but Liesel, my beautiful darling, let me look at you. Oh! There's nothing of you.'

Fritz's voice interrupted their embrace. 'Bring Wilfried in out of the cold, Liesel.'

Wilfried was shocked when he saw Hannah. She sat by the stove, painfully thin, her yellow-tinged skin stretched over her cheekbones. 'Wilfried, how good to see you,' she said with a smile.

He went over to her. 'Dear, Frau Goldberg, I am so pleased to see you.' *What else could he say?* 'And Herr Goldberg.' They shook hands.

'And who is this young man?' Wilfried smiled at Hans, who grinned back.

'Tell me all about the front, Wilfried, please.' Hans asked, eager to hear all the war news.

'Later, Hans,' Fritz interrupted. 'Let Wilfried have something to eat and drink first.' He paused and looked at Wilfried. 'And how are your parents and brother?'

Wilfried told them that his parents were well and that Josef was completing his military training and would soon be ready to fight.

Hannah looked up. 'Your poor mother, with both sons fighting,' she said. 'We are lucky that Hans is too young.'

Hans puffed out his chest. 'I'm old enough now,' he exclaimed.

Fritz peered over his spectacles at Wilfried. 'How long will this war go on, do you think?'

Wilfried grimaced. 'I don't think anyone knows. It was supposed to be a short war. We had the manpower to implement the Schlieffen Plan, but Belgium wouldn't co-operate and let us through unimpeded. But then we hear all kinds of talk in the trenches, and who knows what is correct?'

He didn't want to discuss his growing disillusionment with the whole process and meaning of this war. To whose advantage was it? It didn't seem that the ordinary people would benefit: people were starving, and thousands of men were being wounded and killed. His face darkened.

Hannah turned to Liesel. 'It must be time to fetch the milk,' she said.

'Yes.' Liesel jumped up.

Wilfried looked up and smiled. 'I'll come too.' He took Liesel's hand and they walked to the farm. 'My darling, Liesel, I've missed you so much.' He turned her to face him and then kissed her.

'Oh, Wilfried, I've missed you too.' A note of anxiety crept into her voice. 'How do you find my mother? Is she much changed since you last saw her?'

He remained silent for a moment and put his arms around her before speaking. 'Yes. Very much, I'm afraid.'

'Oh, Wilfried.' She burst into tears and clung to him.

Gently he held her, rocked her in his arms and murmured useless words of sympathy into her hair.

With a gulp, Liesel took a deep breath and stood tall. 'We'd better get the milk,' she said, taking a handkerchief from her pocket and blowing her nose.

At least Helmut wasn't there.

***

At dinner, they all sat around the kitchen table, except for Hannah, who was too weak, and had no appetite. 'I'll just rest here,' she said, 'by the fire.'

Coal was in short supply, so Hans and Fritz went out into the woods most mornings to collect branches and sticks for the fire to keep Hannah warm.

Liesel put a pot of soup on the table. 'It's not much,' she said with a sigh. 'Turnips and some nettle leaves that I found in the fields, and some soup bones.'

Wilfried said nothing, but he was secretly horrified. This was why Liesel and her family were so thin. And it seemed the whole country was the same. Anger against the British for the blockades and for Serbia and Austria for starting this war boiled in him. 'It's lovely, Liesel,' he managed to say.

She put some soup into a bowl and went to her mother. 'Please, mama, try and swallow some.'

Her mother lay back in her chair and shook her head. 'Maybe later, my dear.'

The meal was soon over, and Liesel started to collect the plates. Wilfried stood. 'Let me help.'

She smiled and shook her head, but then Fritz turned to her. 'We need music!'

'Of course.' She put down the dishes and went to fetch her violin.

***

All too soon his leave was over, and he returned to his platoon, working on the Hindenburg Line—long days of digging and re-inforcing in a line from the North Sea to Verdun with a lot of volunteer labour and prisoners of war. The line was anywhere between ten and fifty kilometres from the front, which puzzled Wilfried since it seemed to be a retreat. He couldn't see from on the ground that the new trench line cut out a piece of French territory where the old line bulged out, making the new line shorter and easier to defend. He worked on the part named the Siegfried Line, which was over a hundred-and-fifty kilometres long. The trenches were about five-metres deep and four-metres wide with reinforced concrete shelters at intervals. Wilfried surveyed the wide barbed-wire entanglements in front of the line with awe.

In that same month, he received a letter from Liesel saying that her mother had passed away. The following week, a letter came from his parents with the news that his brother, Josef, had been killed in action. His enthusiasm for defending the Fatherland evaporated.

What's it all for? He kept thinking. His only brother dead, and he couldn't be with his parents or the woman he loved to support them in their grief. People were starving, and the killing in this war just kept going on and on.

He was to spend most of the rest of the war fighting from that line.

***

In early September 1918, an explosion embedded shrapnel in Wilfried's neck and chest. In the field hospital, the army surgeon took out what he could.

'There's still some in there,' the grey faced and exhausted surgeon told him, 'but it's too near an artery and your throat for me to attempt to take it out. Might work its way out over the years. Get it checked when you're demobilised.' He looked at Wilfried. 'You're lucky it didn't hit your face, unlike some of the other poor fellows. Don't know what their sweethearts will think when they see them ...' He sighed and turned to the man in the next bed.

Wilfried was sent back to a German camp to recover, but before he was able to return to the front, the Allies, with an enormous number of tanks, broke through the line and by the middle of October their victory was in sight.

Wilfried was lucky that he'd been wounded and not captured by the French, who sent most of their German prisoners of war to the North of France to work on repairing and rebuilding the war-ravaged towns and villages.

As soon as he was considered fit enough to leave the hospital, Wilfried started for home. Like a lot of other soldiers who didn't wait for official demobilisation, but just walked away from the front, he walked and hitched rides back to Frankfurt

Chapter Eight

Frankfurt, December 1918.

W ilfried's parents were thrilled to have him back, but his mother couldn't stop crying. A mixture of relief at having Wilfried back and grief at losing Josef.

His father was happy at Wilfried's return, but next morning when he, Hilde and Wilfried were having breakfast, he looked sombre. 'I'd like you to come to the shop with me, son. I need to discuss business with you.'

Wilfried's heart sank; he hoped his father didn't intend asking him to come and work in the shop.

'The economic situation appears bad, my son,' Manfred said to Wilfried, when they entered the furniture shop. 'Food and money are scarce. I'm thinking of closing the store. No-one has any money to buy good quality furniture. I have a bad feeling about the future. If I shut the shop now, I will save on rent, and I'll put the remaining furniture I have in storage until I can sell it. We have enough to live on for the next few years, and then things might improve. I was wondering what you think about my plan. Especially now that Josef isn't here to carry on the business.'

'Oh, Father, you must do what you think best. I really don't know. But if it's all getting too much, and you really think you can manage without the income from the shop, then, yes, it seems a good plan.'

Manfred nodded. 'Thank you. I just wanted to know your views. In case you felt like taking over from me?'

'I want to marry Liesel,' Wilfried said, 'but I think we'll have to stay in Mannheim after we marry. It'll be hard for her father and young brother to cope on their own.'

His father nodded. 'Yes, I can understand that. It's so sad about Liesel's mother. You've both waited so long. The future looks bad, but as a cabinet maker you may be able to pick up some work.'

Wilfried frowned. 'Now that I have my master craftsman insignia from the guild, I was hoping to start my own business in Mannheim,' he said.

Manfred's face darkened. 'Things have changed since you were here last,' he sighed. 'I think it will be difficult to start your own business. You might have to consider emigrating. You learnt Spanish and French at school. Perhaps South America would be a good option. A lot of people are going to Argentina. I'd advise you to look into it while there's still time.'

Wilfried was surprised to hear his father talking like this. 'But you and my mother would be on your own!'

His father's expression drooped. 'We want the best for you.'

'And how could Liesel and I go now and leave Hans and Liesel's father on their own?'

His father nodded. 'I know. But an exit visa is hard to get and can take many months, even years. I suggest you apply now. I have some contacts who may be able to help.'

Wilfried stared at his father.

'If you get established in South America, your mother and I might be able to join you,' his father continued sadly.

'I'll think about it.' Wilfried stood and took his father's arm. 'Come, if there is nothing more to do here, let's go home.'

His father nodded. 'Good to have you back, son.'

His father's words didn't cheer Wilfried. On their way home, he said, 'I've been reading about the Spartacist movement. Some of them have founded the communist party. I'm going to join.'

His father frowned. 'I don't like that idea. They're very reactionary. I've heard they're planning a revolt.'

Wilfried sighed. 'But what's the alternative? The Kaiser has abdicated and gone into exile; who will run the country? People are starving, and the dukes have all the property and money. We need to have equality.'

His father shook his head. 'No, no, we don't want Germany to be like Russia; we don't want a revolution.'

Seeing that his father was getting upset, Wilfried changed the subject.

***

On the train to Mannheim next morning, Wilfried brooded over his father's words. On his way back from the front, he'd been so relieved that the war was over, even though it was a surrender, and he'd been so focused on reaching Frankfurt, that he hadn't noticed the way the towns and villages seemed run down. After the devastation of Belgium and France, the landscape had appeared lush and complete. Now he stared out the window of the Mannheim train with a feeling of gloom. What was the point of it all, he thought. His only brother killed, and it seemed that everyone had suffered.

At last he reached the Goldberg's house, apprehensive at what he might find.

Liesel must have been looking out for him; she opened the shop door as he approached. 'Wilfried. Oh, Wilfried!' She flung herself into his arms.

'My darling, Liesel.' he buried his face in her hair, muffling his voice.

Hans rushed out. 'Wilfried! My father said to come in.'

Wilfried followed Liesel and Hans into the kitchen where Fritz huddled in front of the stove. He stood up as they came in and held out his hand to Wilfried. 'Welcome, dear boy; it's good to see you back, safe and sound.'

'I'm sorry for your loss, sir,' Wilfried said, taking Fritz's out-stretched hand.

Tears sprang to Fritz's eyes. 'My darling suffered,' he managed to say.

Liesel came between them. 'Come, Father, sit down and I'll make some tea.' She gently took her father's arm. 'Tell us, Wilfried, how was the train journey? We've heard there are delays with all the soldiers returning home.'

Conversation turned to general matters. The shortage of food and the rising inflation.

'I'd better start preparing the evening meal,' Liesel said. 'Hans, would you go to the farm and get the milk, please?'

Wilfried wanted to raise the question of his and Liesel's marriage, but didn't quite know how to bring up the subject, then suddenly Fritz turned to him.

'I expect you and Liesel want to get married now,' he said.

Surprised at this sudden turn in the conversation, Wilfried replied eagerly, 'Yes, sir, it's my dearest wish.'

Fritz nodded. 'It will have to be a very quiet wedding.' He paused and suppressed a sob. 'Hannah so wanted to see Liesel and you married. You have my blessing, Wilfried. The eleven-months official mourning has passed; you are free to marry.' He wiped his eyes. 'We'll miss Liesel,' he continued sadly.

'I'm hoping to get work in Mannheim and perhaps stay here with you,' Wilfried said.

Fritz looked up, his face brightening. 'That would be wonderful!' Then he frowned. 'But what of your mother and father? They've lost one son; they'll not want to lose another. They'll miss you.'

Wilfried nodded. 'Yes, that's true,' he said slowly. 'This war has ruined so many lives.'

Both men sat in silence with their thoughts until the kitchen door slammed. Hans came in with the jug of milk, and Liesel announced dinner was ready.

***

Wilfried and Liesel's wedding was subdued. Wilfried's parents came from Frankfurt, and a few other relatives managed to get to Mannheim to help celebrate the occasion. Hans had asked if he could bring a friend and surprised them all by leading a young girl over to introduce to the family. Her fair hair was coiled in plaits around her head. She seemed shy and kept looking at Hans for reassurance.

'This is Marlene,' he said, blushing.

Wilfried smiled. 'Hello, Marlene.' He held her hand in greeting, then turned to Hans. 'Well, done, young Hans, Marlene is lovely,' he whispered. Marlene must have overheard this remark, as a shy smile spread across her face.

Fritz kissed his daughter as he took her to the synagogue. 'My darling, Liesel, you look so much like your mother.'

'It's her wedding dress,' she whispered to him.

'I know; she told me she wanted you to wear it if Wilfried came back from the war.'

Before she'd died, Hannah had asked Liesel to go down to the cellar and find the trunk which held the dress she'd worn to her wedding to Fritz. 'I hope it's still all right,' she'd said, smiling at Liesel. 'I'd like you to wear it; it's hard to get nice material these days.' She'd sighed. When Liesel had returned with the dress, her mother said sadly, 'Try it on, darling; I won't be here for your wedding, but I want to see you in it.'

Tears had risen in Liesel's eyes. The dress had been folded in many layers of tissue paper and she'd unwrapped it carefully. It fitted perfectly.

'Darling, Liesel,' her mother had said, 'I know you'll be happy with Wilfried. He's a good man and will take care of you.'

Now, in the synagogue, Liesel's heart was breaking at not having her mother with her, but when she looked up and saw Wilfried, she felt comforted. *Mother would be happy.*

***

Liesel and Wilfried caught the train to Heidelberg for their honeymoon and stayed in a small *pension* near the centre of the old town. They spent their days walking hand in hand in the forest and their nights making love. A week wasn't long enough. Wilfried thought he was the luckiest man alive. Liesel thought she was the most fortunate woman in Germany.

All too soon they were back in Mannheim. Wilfried found lots of small carpentry work around the area—so many men had been killed in the war that there was a shortage of workers. Money was scarce, and inflation ate into the value of the Mark. Wilfried so wanted to work on making beautiful furniture, not barn doors and window frames. He dreamed of the beautiful furniture he'd make and thought out elaborate designs while working on mundane projects.

About four months later, one hot August morning, he woke early to the dawn chorus of birds. He lay for a while worrying about the future, his arm around Liesel, her head resting on his chest. The weather had been so hot that they hadn't bothered with night clothes and were both naked. He raised himself on his elbow, stroked one of her breasts and traced down the line of her belly, filled with awe at the thought that their baby was growing inside that smooth abdomen.

She stirred at his touch and turned slightly, revealing both breasts and filling him with desire. Gently he stroked her and then stopped. She needed her sleep. She worked hard all day looking after the household. Fritz, her father, seemed to have lost interest in his work since Hannah's death. Wilfried hoped the baby might cheer him up. The worrying thoughts kept going around in his head. The future. The rise of the socialist movement. He should join the German Communist Party. The war had changed everything. Now the German Workers Party was saying that the country had been stabbed in the back and that the Jews were to blame for a lot of what was wrong. Wilfried knew for a fact that, as a percentage, more Jews had fought for their country than any other ethnic group. Perhaps his father was right and he should try and get to Argentina and start a new life. But what about his parents? And Liesel's father and brother? He sighed. He desperately desired Liesel but didn't want to wake her ... maybe in another hour ...

Chapter Nine

11th November 1965, Sydney. Armistice Day

The Armistice Day services and commemoration made Liesel think of her grandfather again and the fact that he'd probably fought with Germany in World War One. But he was the gentlest of men; she couldn't imagine him fighting anyone.

Her chores finished, she went out to her father's shed, took out the box and hugged it to her chest. *Why does being a Jew have to be so hard, Pop?* Slowly she opened the box. *I should really start going through everything.* But she had so much work and exams for college. She took out a piece of paper and peered at it. *Perhaps I could just look at one thing at a time.*

'Kommunistische Partei Deutschlands,' Liesel read. She frowned. 'Communist Party Germany.' She noticed the date, 1919, then pulled out two more pieces of official looking paper: one in German, of which the only words she could make out were *Visa* and *Exit*; and the other in another language, maybe Spanish, with the word *Argentina* all she could understand. An envelope sat underneath. It contained a blurred, old sepia photo of a tall man with a woman wearing a close-fitting hat and holding the hand of a small boy. It looked like it'd been taken at a railway station. She turned it over. On the back in faded black ink was written *Wilfried, Liesel und Carl, 1923.*

Where were Wilfried, his wife and their son, her father, going in 1923? And the visa. Why would he have needed an exit visa? Whatever was an exit visa anyway? She'd have to ask her father, or maybe go to the library. Her father wasn't very forthcoming with information. But hadn't he said they'd come to Australia from Argentina?

She took a deep breath, then heard footsteps. Quickly, she replaced the photo and the box and pushed some tins of paint in front of it.

'What're you doing in Dad's shed, Lee?' her brother asked as he entered.

'Looking for some paint. Pop's kitchen door needs touching up,' she lied.

Not wanting to get involved with any kind of work, Archie kicked an empty paint tin that lay on the floor, then disappeared.

Chapter Ten

1919, Germany

The next time Wilfried went to Frankfurt to see his parents, he asked his father about the exit visa and how to get to Argentina. He'd thought long and hard about it, and there seemed to be no future for him and Liesel in Germany. Already the Jews seemed to be getting blamed for a lot of the social and money problems that confronted the country.

If he and Liesel and the baby could settle in Argentina, they could send for his parents and her father and brother and all start a new life. Fritz might be a problem; he wouldn't want to leave his wife's grave, but perhaps when their baby was born, he might change his mind.

His father was encouraging. 'I'll find out all I can,' he said. 'I think it costs a lot and you have to sell all your assets to the government, but as you don't actually own anything, it won't cost you too much, and Argentina is anxious to attract young workers, especially qualified tradesmen like yourself.'

***

Wilfried tried hard to help Liesel. He saw the tiredness in her eyes as she struggled with the house work—cooking, cleaning and doing the heavy washing for the three men. Wilfried thought back to the dainty, slim woman he'd married. Viciously, he swung his axe into the timber he was splitting for the stove. *I must take her away from this drudgery*. After picking up an armful of firewood, he entered the kitchen and stacked the timber by the stove. Fritz came in with a bundle of kindling, and Wilfried studied him. He'd aged and shrivelled and lost the will to live after Hannah's death.

Wilfried sighed. How would they manage when Liesel went into labour? When he asked her, Liesel had only smiled and said, 'Darling, Wilfried, don't worry. I've made arrangements, and we'll all help each other.' He had to be content with that. If only he could get more work and earn more to pay for extra help.

The birth was hard, and Wilfried was frantic. He paced up and down outside their bedroom, stoked the fire for boiling water and kept asking the midwife what he could do. Eventually, he went outside and split firewood to ease his anxiety.

After a time, he became aware of Fritz standing beside him, smiling. 'You have a son,' he said.

***

Wilfried wasn't surprised when Hans cornered him a few weeks after baby Carl's birth.

'Wilfried! Can I have a word?'

Wilfried smiled. 'Of course.' He was on his way to look at some timber to make a door. 'Come with me; you can help carry the timber back.' After they'd set off, he said, 'All right, what's up?'

Hans hesitated. 'Well, the thing is, I want to marry Marlene, but I don't have any money.' He sighed. 'I wanted to study maths and physics at university, but all the money went on doctors' bills for Mama. Not that I begrudge it!' he added hastily. 'Anything to relieve her pain.' He lapsed into silence.

Wilfried kept walking, staying quiet.

'Well, as you know, instead of studying, I've become apprenticed to my father, as a shoe maker.' Hans sighed again. 'How can I ask Marlene to marry me when I can't provide for her?'

Wilfried slapped Hans's shoulder. 'But there's room at Fritz's!' he said. 'Liesel and I have her old bedroom, and the baby sleeps in our room. You have your room and can bring Marlene there. I'm sure your father will be happy to have us all in the house.'

Hans's face lit up. 'Do you really think so?'

'Absolutely! And I know Liesel is fond of Marlene, too, and she'll be glad to have help in the house.' The thought occurred to Wilfried that with Hans and Marlene in the house, Fritz wouldn't miss Liesel, Carl and himself if they moved to Argentina.

A few months later, Hans married Marlene. They went to Frankfurt and stayed with Wilfried's parents for a few days for their honeymoon. The following year, Hans and Marlene's first baby, a boy they called Samuel, was born, and the small Goldberg house seemed even smaller.

Wilfried became restless. He was finding it difficult to get work, and inflation was beginning to bite. He'd come across a copy of a Frankfurt newspaper at one of the houses where he worked and was dismayed to find that compared to 1921, when it took twelve Marks to buy one US dollar, just a year later, it took over one-thousand marks. That shocked him into realising that he and Liesel must make a move soon, before shipping fares became out of reach.

Marlene became pregnant again and was sick every day. Wilfried saw Liesel having to cope with the extra work in the household. Hans was busy trying to learn his trade with Fritz, as it seemed more people were coming to get their shoes and boots mended, rather than getting new ones made.

The following weekend, Liesel and Carl and he went to Frankfurt to visit his parents. Carl, now three-years old, was enthralled with looking out the train window. Wilfried took Liesel's hand and broached the subject of Argentina.

'My darling,' he said, looking at her solemnly. 'You know how I've often mentioned migrating to Argentina, well, I think the time has come.'

Liesel's free hand flew to her mouth.

'Now that Hans and Marlene are living with your father, there'll soon be two of their children in the house besides Carl. It will be a bit crowded. I think your father won't be lonely if we move out.'

'Oh, Wilfried, do you really think it's wise?'

'Yes, my darling. I've been looking into it, and I think the economy will get worse, and now with the rise of the Nazi party, I don't have a good feeling for the Jewish community.'

'But what of my father and Hans and their children?'

'Well, if we settle down, we'll be able to sponsor them to join us in Argentina—my parents, too.'

Liesel frowned. 'I'm not sure, Wilfried. It's a big step; I'll miss my family.' Her words tailed off and tears came to her eyes. 'I miss my mother.'

'I know, my darling, but Carl and I are your family now, and we must do what's best for Carl's future. I can't see any future for him in Germany. I've been reading the papers, and work is getting even more scare. And there seems to be a rising feeling of animosity against Jews.'

'Why? What have the Jews done to cause that feeling? Oh, Wilfried, I don't understand! But, my darling, if you think it's the right thing to do, then we will do it.' She looked suddenly determined. 'And as you say, we can sponsor our parents and Hans and Marlene once we get settled.'

Wilfried took her hand and kissed it. 'I'm certain it's the right decision.'

***

It took over a year for Wilfried and Liesel's exit visas to come through. It seemed that Manfred Schönbaum had pulled in a few favours to achieve this.

'You won't be able to take anything much with you,' he told his son, as they sat in Manfred's study one evening after dinner.

'We don't have much, except my tools, Liesel's violin and Carl's things.'

'Keep it to a minimum,' his father said. 'I have the money for your passage. Be prepared to leave at any moment, as berths are hard to get. I'll book as soon as possible.' His eyes filled with tears. 'I'm sure this is the right thing for you to do, my son.' He patted Wilfried's shoulder.

Wilfried felt his eyes prickling with tears. He turned away. 'Thank you, Father,' he managed to say and blew his nose loudly to hide his emotions.

Two weeks later, Wilfried and Liesel received a letter from Manfred, telling them they were booked on a ship to Buenos Aires leaving three weeks later and to get ready to travel to Hamburg. They must take only what they could carry.

Wilfried packed his tools and his masterpiece, the miniature violin. He'd need it in Buenos Aires to demonstrate his skill. It didn't take him long. Liesel tried hard to keep everything to a minimum, but as they went out the door, saying their farewells, she turned to Wilfried. 'My violin. I don't have my violin!' Wilfried patted her arm. 'It's all right, darling. I'll buy you a new one when we get to Argentina.'

'No, no, I know I can't take my big violin, I mean the miniature you gave me. I put it to one side, to put it in last, so I was sure it was well protected.' She made to go back into the house to get it.

'Darling, Liesel. There's no time now,' he exclaimed. 'I'll make you another. Come, we'll miss the train and your father will be upset if we have to go through these farewells again.' He took her arm and Carl's hand. 'Come, we must hurry. My parents will be waiting at Frankfurt when we change trains for Hamburg. They'll worry if we don't turn up.'

Reluctantly, Liesel hurried after him.

At Frankfurt station, Wilfried's mother rushed towards them, tears in her eyes. She hugged them and tried to lift Carl up into her arms, but he struggled free, too interested in the engines to pay attention to his grandmother. 'Please take a photograph of them,' she begged Manfred, 'We can send a copy to Fritz. And to you when we get your address,' she said to Wilfried.

Manfred gave Wilfried the paper he'd just bought to hold while he adjusted his camera.

Liesel looked so smart in her cloche hat and slim-fitting short coat, holding Carl's hand and clinging to their tall, handsome son. Hilde and Manfred treasured that photo for many years.

Chapter Eleven

1923, Argentina

O n the train, Wilfried realised he still had the paper his father had given him to hold at the station. *The Frankfurter Zeitung.* He read of the strikes at the dock yard in Hamburg and worried that they'd be delayed boarding their ship. He'd no extra money for accommodation in case of delay. The train seemed to take forever, but at last they arrived. Manfred had bought them second-class passages on the ship. Thankfully the strike had been settled. They had a tiny cabin with just enough room for the three of them. Liesel vomited just after they arrived.

'I think I'm pregnant,' she whispered as they tried to settle down for the voyage.

Wilfried tried to smile. 'That'll be wonderful, darling. A little brother or sister for Carl.' Privately he thought that this wasn't the best time for a new baby.

Liesel gave a wan smile. 'I'll be better soon,' she managed to say.

'What's wrong with mama?' asked Carl.

'She just feels a little sick; she'll soon be better,' Wilfried reassured his son.

He had to care for both Carl and Liesel on the voyage. Carl was no problem, happy to be running around on deck with any other children he could find. The steerage passengers seemed to be all sleeping on the decks, apparently their accommodation below decks was abysmal—cramped and airless. Wilfried felt sorry for them and grateful that his father had somehow found the money to send them second class.

The journey seemed never ending. Liesel hardly left her bunk. Wilfried brought her soup and anything he thought might tempt her appetite.

'Oh, Wilfried, I'm so sorry, but I'll probably feel better when we arrive. The first three months are the hardest. The constant rolling of the ship doesn't help.' She turned over and vomited up the tea and toast that Wilfried had brought.

Helplessly, Wilfried wiped her face and went out to the common toilets with the bowl.

At last the ship docked in Buenos Aires. Pale and weak, Liesel allowed Wilfried to help her dress.

He studied Liesel. 'My darling, we have to be seen by a doctor before we can disembark and then have our papers checked. Are you able to face the doctor?'

'It's all right, Wilfried, if you explain I'm pregnant, I'm sure it'll be all right.' She pinched her cheeks to bring some colour to her face and tried to smile. 'I'll be fine once I'm on dry land.'

The doctor checked them for any signs of contagious diseases or mental instability, then signed their papers. With a sigh of relief, Wilfried led them to the immigration control. The official examined their visas and Wilfried's qualifications, then nodded and waved them through.

'*Gracias*,' Wilfried said.

'Now for our luggage. Are you sure you are all right, Liesel?'

She nodded. Wilfried put his arm around her to support her, and at last they disembarked.

Liesel tried to be cheerful. 'Come, Carl, we have arrived in our new country!'

It was lucky, Wilfried thought, that they didn't have much luggage. His father had given him the name of a Jewish organisation that helped new immigrants. But first they must find the *Hotel de Inmigrantes*, where it seemed all new migrants went initially.

***

Buenos Aires was a shock to Liesel. It seemed so loud. Unlike Wilfried, she couldn't speak Spanish, so everywhere they went a constant unintelligible noise assailed her ears. The boat trip had been bad enough, and the morning sickness hadn't helped. At the Hotel de Inmigrantes, the food wasn't kosher, and some of the other residents weren't very friendly. She had to sleep in the women's dormitory and Wilfried in the men's. Wardens woke them early in the mornings, and they had to queue for food.

'At least I'm over the worst of the morning sickness,' Liesel reassured Wilfried. 'Just a bit, first thing.' She tried to stay positive for him, but the morning sickness hadn't been that bad with Carl. *Perhaps it means it's a baby girl.*

Wilfried hugged her. 'We'll soon settle down in Buenos Aires, my darling. My father has given me the names of some people to contact.' He said this with an air of confidence that she knew he didn't feel. Liesel only smiled; she trusted him completely.

Liesel found it hard waiting in the hostel, the communal facilities and the smells didn't help her sickness. Wilfried took Carl with him to look for the Jewish organisation on his father's list. First, he must find accommodation, then look for work. He didn't have a lot of money. It had been impossible to take money out of Germany. His father had given him some pieces of gold which Fritz had cleverly concealed for him in the heels of his boots. It should last them several weeks.

He found that the Spanish they spoke in Argentina was a bit different from the European Spanish that he'd learnt. He felt sorry for some of the other people who'd disembarked with them; they could speak no Spanish and were completely bewildered. But he couldn't stop to help them, Liesel and Carl were his priority.

At the Jewish organization, he'd been given a list of places that would accept Jews. The first one he went to see was a seedy place that smelt of boiled cabbage. The second one was in the house of a widow, Miriam Martinez, on the outskirts of the city.

He knocked on the door. A small girl opened it and stared at him.

'Hello, my name is Wilfried Schönbaum. I believe there are rooms to let here?'

'Who is it, Ruth?' a voice called.

'I believe you have rooms to let, Señora Martinez,' he called out.

A woman appeared from a back room, drying her hands on her apron. Tall and pleasant featured, her fair hair was cut short in a fashionable bob. Wilfried noticed the faint smell of baking bread.

'I was given your details by the Jewish Organisation, the A.M.I. A.,' he said. 'It's for my wife and me and our son, Carl.' He indicated Carl who was looking wide-eyed into the house.

'Oh, yes, come in. I'll show you the rooms.' She led him up two flights of stairs. 'Two rooms, and share a bathroom and cooking facilities with the family on the next floor. They're very quiet—the Da Souzas, an elderly couple. The toilet is outside.' She was brisk and business like and spoke with a different accent to others in the city. He looked at the room; the bedroom was quite big with a double bed, a wardrobe and a chest of drawers. Pretty curtains hung at the window, and the bed had a matching bedspread.

'I can put a small bed in here for your little boy,' Señora Martinez said.

Wilfried nodded. The other room contained a table and four chairs, some cupboards and an ancient sofa. Although sparsely furnished it was clean and affordable and much better than the Hotel de Inmigrantes. At least they would all be together.

'It seems very suitable. How soon can we move in? By the way, I'm Wilfried Schönbaum, my wife is called Liesel and this is our son, Carl.' He didn't mention the fact that Liesel was pregnant. Señora Martinez mightn't like the idea of a baby in the rooms, and the people upstairs might not like a baby disturbing their peace.

She nodded. 'As soon as you like. Rent in advance, please. One month.'

He handed over the money, and she gave him a key to the front door.

'I'll get my wife straight away. She'll be delighted to come here.'

Señora Martinez smiled at last and held out her hand. 'I hope you will all be happy here.'

Wilfried smiled back and took her hand; he had a good feeling about her. 'Come, Carl, we'll go and fetch Mama, and then we'll be coming back to live here.'

'If you like, he can stay here while you go for your wife,' Señora Martinez suggested.

Wilfried shook his head. 'Thank you, but I think he's had a lot to cope with in the last month, so I'll keep him with me. But it was most kind of you to suggest it.'

Wilfried didn't notice the approving look Señora Martinez gave him.

He and Carl made their way back on the tram to fetch Liesel and their belongings. Very soon he'd have to find a gold exchange to change one of the coins in his shoes.

When they reached their new home, he unlocked the front door and then knocked on Señora Martinez's door.

Ruth opened it.

'This is my wife, Liesel,' he said, introducing her, when Señora Martinez appeared. 'Liesel doesn't speak Spanish.'

Liesel just nodded and smiled. Wilfried had been trying to teach her but she'd been so tired and unable to concentrate. 'Tell Señora Martinez it's lovely, and I'll soon learn the language,' she said to him.

Señora Martinez seemed pleased when he told her what Liesel had said. 'Maybe your wife speaks English?' she asked.

Wilfried shook his head. 'No.'

'It's just that I'm actually American and speak English. I just wondered ...' she seemed wistful.

Wilfried looked at her enquiringly.

'We might have been able to talk in English. I miss not being able to speak English. My late husband was Argentinian; he was working in New York when I met him and we married. Then we came here. When he died, I turned our house into a boarding house to make ends meet ...' she frowned as her voice trailed off.

'I'm sorry for your loss,' was all he could think to reply.

Señora Martinez sighed. "I'm Jewish, but my husband wasn't, so I don't practice anymore.'

Wilfried nodded. 'Thank you, Señora. I'll show Liesel our new home.' Embarrassed, he was anxious to get to their room.

Señora Martinez sighed again, then said, 'Perhaps I should introduce you to the Da Souzas upstairs.'

Wilfried translated for Liesel, and they made their way up the stairs, leaving their cases outside their rooms on their way.

Señora Martinez knocked on the door of the Da Souza's apartment.

'It's Miriam,' Señora Martinez shouted.

A shuffling noise came from the other side of the door, then it slowly opened. A small white-haired woman appeared, followed by a bent old man.

'Señora, Señor, this is Señor and Señora Schönbaum and their son, Carl. They're moving into the rooms on the floor below. Señora Schönbaum doesn't speak Spanish, but she is learning.'

Liesel smiled and shook hands, and Wilfried said a few words.

Señora Da Souza said something and darted back into the room, appearing a few minutes later with a young child's book with pictures and words in Spanish. She smiled and held it out to Liesel.

Wilfried translated. 'She says it belonged to her son when he was very young. You and Carl might like to use it to learn Spanish.'

Liesel beamed. '*Gratias!*'

They said their goodbyes and went back down the stairs.

'Let me know if you need anything,' Señora Martinez said.

***

As soon as they'd unpacked their few possessions and Wilfried had settled Liesel on the settee with the book for Carl, he went out to the market to get food that would be easy to prepare.

Liesel looked around. Privately she was dismayed. Though clean and quiet, it was very basic—not what she'd been expecting—but it was better than the Hotel de Inmigrantes. And it smelt nice.

Wilfried returned with the groceries and they ate a simple meal: bread, cheese and some fruit.

'This is wonderful,' Wilfried smiled at his wife and son, his grey eyes shining. 'Our own little home at last.'

Liesel smiled back. 'You're right; up to now we've been either living in my father's house, or on the ship or at the hotel.' She reached up and kissed him.

Carl was over tired from the excitement and all the new experiences. Liesel settled him into the small bunk that Señora Martinez had set up, and then she sat with Wilfried on their bed and waited for Carl to fall asleep.

Wilfried took Liesel into his arms. She looked so pale. 'I know it's not exactly luxurious, my darling, but it's only until I can find work and then we will move to somewhere nicer,' he reassured her.

Exhausted from the journey and the noise and smells of the Hotel de Inmigrantes, Liesel relaxed into his arms. 'It's fine, my darling,' she said. 'You have done well. And perhaps I will be able to give music lessons once we get settled.'

Señora Martinez's two daughters, Ruth, six and Sarah, eight, were entranced by the four-year-old Carl and loved to play with him and keep him amused when they weren't at school or helping their mother. Señora Martinez spoke English with her daughters at home, so Carl was soon chattering away in English as well as Spanish, which confused Liesel.

***

The enormous influx of migrants into Buenos Aires created a building boom and Wilfried soon found work as a carpenter. Liesel settled into the rooms, doing the shopping with a list that Wilfried wrote out for her.

The first time she went to use the stove in the kitchen, Señora Da Souza was there, cooking something. Liesel smiled and apologised and tried to indicate she'd come back later when Señora

Da Souza had finished her cooking. She went back to their rooms and waited until she heard Señora Da Souza slowly moving up the stairs.

Liesel felt sorry for Señora Da Souza, who she could see had problems getting up and down the stairs to the kitchen and bathroom they shared. She made sure to clean the bathroom and kitchen thoroughly after using them, hoping that Señora Da Souza wouldn't be offended.

About four weeks after they'd moved in, Liesel woke in the night, doubled up in pain, with severe stomach cramps.

Feeling her tossing and turning Wilfried stirred. 'Darling, what is it?' he mumbled.

'Oh, Wilfried, I'm afraid it's the baby!' She pulled back the bedclothes and felt the dampness of her nightdress.

He got up and lit a candle and saw the blood. 'What must I do?' he whispered, not wanting to wake Carl.

'Nothing! Fetch the night pot!' She climbed out of the bed and sat on the pot, doubled over in agony.

'Shall I fetch Señora?' The blood alarmed him.

'No,' she whispered. 'Just strip the sheets and put them in cold water to soak the stains.'

While looking for a bucket in the bathroom, he heard shuffling steps, and Señora Da Souza appeared in a dressing gown. 'I'm sorry, Señora, did I disturb you?'

'No,' she replied. 'I don't sleep very well. I was awake and heard someone moving around down here.' She looked at the blood-stained sheets.

'My wife ...' Wilfried didn't know what to say.

She nodded and took the sheet, put it in the bath and covered it with cold water. 'Go back to your wife; in the morning I will wash it.'

'No, no, I will do it. But thank you.' Wilfried could see that arthritis crippled her hands.

The night seemed endless.

'I'm going to have to tell the Señora,' he said to Liesel later. 'I think she'll be sympathetic. And she might look after Carl while you rest.'

Too exhausted to care, Liesel nodded. 'I'll be all right; you can't miss work when you've only just started.'

Wilfried felt grateful that Liesel understood that he had to work. He saw Señora Martinez as he left. 'My wife isn't well,' he told her—he didn't know the Spanish for miscarriage. 'I think it's a woman's problem ...' He hesitated. 'I left sheets ... I wonder if you'd be kind enough to look after Carl until I come home? I hate leaving Liesel, but I must work.'

'Of course!' she replied. 'I understand you have to work. The poor creature. I'll go and see her and fetch Carl so she can rest.'

Wilfried left, thankful to leave this women's business to the Señora.

Señora Martinez tapped on Liesel's bedroom door and went in. 'My dear, how are you?' she said.

Liesel didn't understand her words, but the sympathy in her voice made her burst into tears. *'Meine bebe!'* she sobbed.

Miriam understood. It sounded like *mi bebé*, my baby. 'Hush, little one; I'll take Carl now and bring you some breakfast.'

'Come, Carl, we'll get you something to eat!' She smiled at Carl, who was looking anxiously at his mother, and held out her hand.

He was happy to go with her, for which Liesel was grateful.

When Wilfried returned that night, he found Liesel sitting up in bed and looking better.

'Señora Martinez has been so kind.' She smiled at him. 'She said to call her Miriam. I think she said she will cook for us tonight. I'm not sure, but I think that's what she said. She looked after Carl all day. I'm feeling better now, darling.'

Wilfried's brow cleared. He knew Liesel was putting a brave face on her loss; she'd been so hoping for a baby sister for Carl.

'I was thinking of getting my hair cut in a bob like Miriam.' Liesel tugged at her long dark hair. 'The change might cheer me up, and it will be so much easier to wash and care for.'

Wilfried's face showed his horror. 'No, no, my darling, I love your hair! Please don't cut it!'

Surprised at his vehemence, Liesel smiled. 'All right! I won't.'

Wilfried leaned over the bed, stroked her hair and kissed her. 'I'd better fetch Carl and get him ready for bed.'

***

Life settled into a routine. Miriam helped Liesel find a school for Carl, and Liesel's Spanish slowly improved.

A few weeks after losing the baby, when she felt better, Liesel wanted to thank Miriam but didn't know how. The Da Souzas had also been kind. Señora da Souza had taken Carl for a few hours when Miriam went out and thought that Liesel should rest. It seemed that Señora Da Souza loved minding Carl, reading to him from a children's book that used to belong to their son when he was small.

Liesel asked Wilfried to write down the Spanish for the ingredients for a German friendship cake. She went with Carl to the local shop, came home and baked three cakes. She and Carl took one cake upstairs to the Da Souza's

Liesel knocked on their door and when the Señora answered it, Liesel smiled and presented her with the cake. She'd prepared a phrase in Spanish saying it was a German friendship cake and hoped they would accept it. Señora Da Souza smiled, took the cake and beckoned Liesel and Carl in.

Liesel nodded and smiled, and the Da Souzas seemed very happy.

Carl chattered in Spanish, trying to explain about the cake. '*Gracias*,' Carl said and gave the Señora a hug.

'Tell your mama, that I notice she has been keeping the kitchen and bathroom clean, and I thank her,' Señora Da Souza said to Carl.

Carl told his mother and she was able to smile and say it was a pleasure.

Then Liesel and Carl took the second cake down to Miriam.

Liesel smiled at her. '*Gracias*, Señora.'

Miriam understood that Liesel was trying to thank her. She smiled at Liesel. '*Gracias*, Liesel.'

***

Wilfried worked long hours to try to save money. He wanted to get settled so he could send for their parents and Hans and Marlene. His work wasn't the fine cabinet making that he enjoyed, mostly just making doors and windows, but he still took pride in his workmanship.

As soon as he managed to save enough for a violin, he told Liesel they were going out shopping. He asked Miriam if she'd mind Carl for a few hours, and then he and Liesel set off.

'Where are we going?' She smiled at him. 'This is exciting; is it a surprise?'

Wilfried put on a serious face. 'No, darling, no surprise.' However, a smile crept over his face as he led her into a music shop.

He pointed to a violin. 'Do you like that one?'

'Oh!' Liesel could hardly breathe. 'But darling, we can't afford to buy a violin!'

'Yes! We can and we will.' He looked up as a shop assistant approached. 'We'd like to look at violins please.' He told her their budget.

Liesel spent the next hour trying the violins, her eyes sparkling with excitement. Soon it seemed the whole shop was standing around listening. She played some old German songs, and the shop erupted into singing.

Startled, Liesel stopped and looked round.'Oh!' she exclaimed, 'I think I got carried away.'

Wilfried smiled. 'Which violin do you like best?' he asked.

'This one.' She held out the one she'd just been playing.

All the way back to the house, Liesel was beside herself with excitement, and as soon as they got in, she rushed straight to Señora Martinez's kitchen. 'Look, Miriam! Look what Wilfried has bought me,' she exclaimed.

They all gathered round and looked expectantly at her as Liesel took the violin from its case and tuned it. Carl looked into the case to see if there was anything in it for him. Then Liesel started to play.

Miriam Martinez gasped. 'Your wife is so accomplished,' she whispered to Wilfried.

Her daughters were delighted and started to clap. Carl joined in, clapping in time to the music.

'Will you teach us, Liesel?' Ruth asked.

Elated, Liesel nodded.

'Me too?' Carl didn't want to be left out.

Then Sarah jumped up. 'We must show the Da Souzas,' she said.

They all trouped up to the top floor, and Liesel played her violin outside the door of the Da Souza's apartment. Slowly the door opened, and the old couple came out, broad smiles on their faces. Wilfried looked at Liesel; he was so proud of his beautiful, talented wife.

Chapter Twelve

1926, Argentina

By 1926 Wilfried had decided that he'd saved enough to bring his parents to Argentina. He thought that by the time they got exit visas he'd have enough to buy a house on the outskirts of Buenos Aires. Known for the quality of his work, and well liked and cheerful, he had no problem getting work. He wrote to his parents to tell them to get their exit visas as soon as possible.

Carl was settled in a school, and Liesel was giving a few violin lessons. They still lived with the Martinez—the rent was reasonable, which made it easier to save, and the two girls loved Carl and were happy to mind him when Liesel was out giving lessons. Liesel and Miriam had become firm friends, and the elderly Da Souzas on the top floor loved getting visits from Liesel and Carl. They also appreciated Liesel cleaning the bathroom and kitchen, and tried to repay her by giving Carl Spanish lessons and helping him learn to read.

Wilfried had also made some nice pieces of furniture so their rooms were more comfortable. Their accommodation suited Wilfried and Liesel very well.

One evening Wilfried came racing up the stairs to Liesel. 'Liesel!' He burst into their room as she was laying the table for their dinner, picked her up and swung her around. 'Guess what?'

'What?'

'I've been asked to make a grand staircase for the major department store in Buenos Aires!' He couldn't contain his elation.

'Oh, that's wonderful, my darling.' Knowing how much he yearned to make beautiful furniture, Liesel was thrilled for him. She'd often seen him sketching furniture in his little note book. This seemed like it might be a start to him having his own business.

This major breakthrough in Wilfried's ambition made him happy. He could visualise the furniture he'd be making in the future.

But soon after, Wilfried noticed a change in Liesel. 'Darling, Liesel, is something wrong? You seem quiet lately; you're not playing the violin as much.'

She looked at him and smiled. 'Oh, Wilfried. That's just your imagination.'

He frowned. 'Are you sure? You look quite pale. Perhaps we should have a holiday. Go away for a few days. I think we can afford it.'

'No, no; our priority is for you to finish the department store staircase and for us to save for a house so our parents and Hans and Marlene can come to join us.'

Wilfried kissed her. He wanted to be reassured.

A few nights later, he turned to her and gently stroked her breasts. He was surprised when he felt her stiffen. 'What is it my darling?' he whispered. 'We'll be very quiet. Carl is sound asleep.' He cupped one of her breasts and then stopped. 'What's this?' he asked abruptly. 'This lump?'

Liesel lay very still, then she went limp in his arms and started to sob quietly. 'I have cancer, like my mother,' she whispered.

Wilfried froze with shock. 'Liesel! Why didn't you tell me? We must see a doctor.'

'I did. Last week I went to see a Jewish doctor. Doctor Isaacs. He said I've left it too late for any treatment. And it wouldn't help anyway. Look at all the money my father spent on treatment for my mother, and she suffered terribly from the surgery, and it didn't help. What would be the point?'

'No, no, that was nearly ten years ago. Things have improved since then, new treatments ...' his voice tailed off. 'Oh, Liesel, my darling, please, please let us get a second opinion.'

'It's too late, Wilfried. I only found the lump a few weeks ago. I thought nothing of it, and then it began to hurt to lift my left arm and I went to the doctor. He told me it was a very invasive cancer and had already spread.'

'So that was why you stopped playing the violin ...' His voice thickened with suppressed tears. 'My darling, Liesel, I couldn't live without you. You are my life.'

'Wilfried. The doctor thinks I maybe have another six months or so. I think it would be good if your parents and my father and Hans and Marlene can come here as soon as possible. You'll need your family around you.' She paused, then continued, 'Wilfried, we've had nearly seven years of happiness together. We have a beautiful son. Treasure that. Not many people have that. Please don't be sad when I'm gone. I've been so happy with you.'

Now Wilfried's tears did come.

They clung to each other for the rest of the night, unable to sleep.

***

With a heavy heart, Wilfried wrote to his parents telling them of Liesel's illness. He asked them to visit Fritz and Hans and tell them that Liesel didn't have long to live. He didn't want to write to Fritz and have him read the awful news. They must all try and get exit visas from Germany and apply to the Argentinian Embassy for entry visas.

Wilfried went to see the Jewish doctor that Liesel had consulted.

Dr Isaacs pursed his lips and shook his head. 'There's no hope,' he said. 'The cancer is a very invasive one and has already spread to other parts of her body.' He sighed. 'I've noticed cancer of the breast in a lot of Ashkenazi Jewish women. It seems to be more prevalent in them than the general population.'

'My wife's mother died of breast cancer,' Wilfried said.

The doctor nodded. 'Come back to me when her pain becomes unbearable. I'll help her then.'

Wilfried had to be content with that.

Liesel gradually got thinner and weaker. Miriam Martinez was a tower of strength. Wilfried began to depend on her. He couldn't afford to take time off work, and by 1928, Liesel was bedridden. Miriam came every morning and washed Liesel and saw to her toileting. Her two daughters were happy to give Carl his breakfast and take him to school.

One morning when the girls had left with Carl, and Miriam was washing her, Liesel put a thin, blue veined hand on Miriam's arm. 'Miriam.'

'Yes, my dear?'

'I've seen the way you look at Wilfried.'

Miriam lowered her eyes and carried on gently drying Liesel's arms.

'When I'm gone, I won't mind if you and Wilfried ...'

'Hush, now, please don't talk like that.'

'And Carl ...'

'I'll make sure Carl is well cared for, Liesel dear.'

Liesel closed her eyes and sank back on the pillow. 'Thank you,' she whispered.

***

One sunny Sunday morning, Liesel smiled at Wilfried and said, 'Darling, it looks like such a beautiful day. Do you think I could sit outside and feel the sun on my face?'

Carefully, Wilfried took her in his arms; she was as light as a feather. He carried her downstairs, calling to Carl as he went. 'Bring a chair for Mama, Carl!'

Carl ran and placed a chair outside the front door. When Wilfried lowered Liesel onto the chair, she put her right foot out to steady herself, but her leg cracked and jutted out at a funny angle—broken. She went white with pain but didn't utter a sound.

Wilfried looked at her with anguish in his eyes. 'I think we'd better get you back to bed,' he said. 'I'm so sorry, Liesel, I was trying to be gentle.'

Liesel's eyes were shut tight, helping her to contain the pain. 'It wasn't your fault,' she managed to whisper.

Gently, Wilfried picked her up and carried her back to their bedroom. 'Fetch Señora,' he said to Carl.

When Miriam came rushing up the stairs and Wilfried told her what had happened, she nodded. 'I'll send Sarah for Dr Isaacs; he'll give her something for the pain and perhaps set the broken bone.'

Two months later, heavily sedated with morphine, Liesel breathed her last.

Wilfried was heartbroken. He could barely rouse himself to get up in the mornings for work and to look after Carl. *I didn't even make her another miniature violin like I promised*, he thought. All the ways in which he thought he'd failed Liesel just kept going around in his head.

Eventually, Miriam Martinez confronted him. 'Wilfried Schön-baum, it's two months since Liesel passed. Carl needs you; he's lost his mother and now it seems his father, too! You must stop this selfish self-pity!'

Wilfried stared at her, anger mounting in his chest. 'She was the light of my life! I can't live without her!'

'Yes, you can, for Carl's sake. He's her son; you have to take care of him. He's grieving, too!'

Her words fell like a shower of cold water on Wilfried. He frowned, his eyes darkening. He forced back the tears, looked at Miriam for a long moment, and then nodded slowly. 'You're right. Thank you,' he said abruptly. He stood up and looked around the room, seeing it as if for the first time; it was a mess. 'Carl,' he called. Carl peered cautiously round the bedroom door. 'Carl my little one. Will you help me tidy up? I don't think Mama would like to see us living in this mess, do you?'

Slowly, Carl came out and nodded.

Wilfried took him in his arms. 'It's just you and me now, son,' he said. 'We'll do our best to do what Mama would have wanted.'

With tears in her eyes, Miriam Martinez quietly left the room.

Chapter Thirteen

Argentina

Wilfried waited anxiously for news from his parents. It seemed that getting permission to leave Germany was getting harder. Not only that, but Argentina had cut back on admitting immigrants. They had all the workers they needed now. And they definitely didn't want any more Jews.

Wilfried found it hard to stay cheerful for Carl. He threw himself into his work to stop his mind dwelling on Liesel. He carefully packed away her violin. There was no money to pay for lessons for Carl. Most of his savings had gone on the doctor's bills and painkilling medication for Liesel and her funeral.

Just when he thought he was making progress, in October 1929 the American Stock Market collapsed. Shockwaves went around the globe and hit Argentina badly. Their main export was beef and now no-one was buying. He was fortunate to be able to get work here and there, but the days of limitless overtime were gone.

The following year was even harder as work began to dry up. He received a letter from Hans.

Dear Wilfried.

I hope all is well with you and young Carl. I have been trying to get exit visas for us all, but to no avail. They are impossible to get. One needs to know the right people, and it's necessary to give up all your money, bank accounts, property and businesses to the state. And then it's impossible to get entry visas for another

country. With the worldwide recession, no one wants immigrants,
and it seems Jews are especially unwelcome.

You were lucky, Wilfried, to have got to Argentina when you did.

I'm worried about my family; there is a lot of bad feeling here
towards Jews. There's no work and people are starving. Inflation
is so bad that the Mark is worthless. We are fortunate to have a
garden to grow some food.

Fritz is well. I heard from your parents about six months ago
and they were well.

I'll try and write again soon.

Your Brother-in-law,

Hans Goldberg

This news didn't cheer Wilfried. Sometimes he wondered if
he'd done the right thing by coming to Argentina. Bringing Liesel
to rented rooms and then for her to die in a strange country, but
perhaps he'd been right, at least for Carl's future.

On the other hand, there was anti-Jewish sentiment in Buenos
Aires, too. Most of the Jewish immigrants were from Russia. Fear
of a revolution like that in Russia stirred up animosity towards
these 'Russos' and hence all Jews.

Just after he received this letter, a spate of anti-Semitism erupted in Buenos Aires. A synagogue was burnt down—expressing an
underlying feeling of resentment towards Jews.

On the sixth of September, 1930, General Uriburu and his
supporters staged a coup and overthrew the elected Argentinian
government of Hipólito Yrigoyen. Large crowds formed in Buenos
Aires in support of the coup.

Wilfried was dismayed when he heard this. Uriburu wanted
to turn Argentina into a fascist state along the lines of Mussoli-
ni's Italy, supported by the branch of the German Nazi Party in
Buenos Aires. He didn't know what to do. He felt trapped. Should

they stay in Buenos Aires, or move to somewhere outside the city? What would be the best thing to do for Carl? He felt powerless, and to make matters worse, there wasn't much left of his savings.

One evening in 1931, Miriam came up to his living room.

Wilfried stood up.

'I need to speak with you,' she said. 'Carl, would you go down with the girls, please?'

Surprised, Carl looked up from his homework. He nodded, collected his books and went out of the room.

Wilfried frowned. He hoped this wasn't going to be more bad news or another lecture. 'Sit down, Miriam.'

She sat at the table and folded her hands in her lap. He sat opposite her. 'Wilfried,' she said. 'I'm going to have to sell the house.'

He started. The thought of having to find new accommodation at this point was daunting.

'I'm going to emigrate to Australia.'

'Australia?' He echoed, his frown deepening.

'Yes. Things are getting serious here. There is a lot of bad feeling towards Jews, and yes, I know what you are going to say ...' She waved a hand at him. 'I know I'm not a practicing Jew, but somehow the authorities know who are Jews. And there's so much corruption and electoral fraud happening; everything is too uncertain. I don't like the idea of fascism. Anyway, there doesn't seem to be any future here for my girls. I have a friend in Australia; I've known her since we both lived in the States. She went to Australia years ago and married there. We've always kept in touch. She's often asked me to visit, and now I think the time has come. She and her husband said I could stay with them for a while until I get sorted out.'

'You're American; you could go back there.'

Miriam grimaced. 'Things are even worse there. And my family never forgave me for marrying a non-Jew and an Argentinian. Australia seems to be the best option. So! I need to sell the house to pay for our passage and get started in Australia.'

Wilfried blinked and continued to stare at her. Then he dropped his gaze and nodded. 'What about the Da Souzas?' he muttered.

'They told me last month that they're moving out to go and live with their son.'

'So you want us to move out.' He looked up at Miriam.

She took a deep breath and swallowed. 'Well, I had another idea.' She paused and looked down at her hands. Then, not meeting his eyes, she continued. 'It's hard for a single woman, a widow, to make it in a strange country. And it will be hard for you and Carl to find somewhere else. My girls think of him like a brother. He's like a son to me, I'd miss him.' She looked at him.

He had no idea where this was leading.

Miriam took another deep breath. 'So,' she paused. 'I thought that if you and I were married we could go to Australia together.'

Wilfried's mouth fell open and his eyes widened.

'Of course, it would be just a marriage of convenience,' Miriam hastened to add. 'After all, I am two or three years older than you.' She stood up. 'Think about it. But you'd have to give up your Judaism. Australia apparently doesn't welcome Jews.'

Wilfried had long turned against any form of religion, so this was a minor detail.

'And change your name. Schönbaum sounds too German, and seemingly in Australia there is a bad feeling about Germans ever since the war.'

Speechless, Wilfried just kept staring at her.

'As I said, think about it. I have the forms ready to fill out.' She turned and left.

Wilfried put his head in his hands. The world was going crazy.

His head spun. Miriam's proposal went around and around in his head. He thought about his and Carl's future. Carl was twelve now. What would be his prospects? He, Wilfried, wouldn't be able to afford to give him a good education, if he could even afford to keep him at school, and then, finding somewhere else to live would be another challenge. Miriam was right about the rise of anti-Semitism. His head started to pound. Perhaps Miriam's offer was the way to go. But that would be disloyal to Liesel. He didn't love Miriam. She was a good person and a good friend. He was fond of her, and she did say it would be a marriage of convenience.

He began to feel it was his only option.

The next night he sat Carl down. 'Carl, my son. Miriam and the girls are going to Australia to live and we will have to move from here.'

Carl looked up, alarm in his eyes. 'But where will we go?' He was silent for a moment and then said eagerly, 'Can we go to Australia too? With them?'

Wilfried sighed. It seemed the decision had been made.

Chapter Fourteen

Argentina

Wilfried and Miriam married three months later. He changed his name to Wilfred Martin and Carl's to Charles Martin. Miriam became Señora Martin. Nothing else changed. Wilfred still slept upstairs in his old bed. However, his and Carl's evenings were spent with Miriam, who now cooked for all of them.

She tried to teach them English. 'You'll need to be able to read and write in English,' she told Wilfried. 'I think you may have to do a written test to get into Australia ... Oh! And by the way, don't ever mention that you fought for the Kaiser and Germany in The Great War. From now on, we speak only English at home.'

Her daughters and Carl thought this was great fun, and Carl learned very quickly. The girls were used to speaking English with Miriam, and Carl had also picked up a lot of English, so it was easy for them, but Wilfried's heart wasn't really in it. However, he'd always been good at languages, and soon was able to read and write basic English. His accent when speaking was another story. Miriam would have to do the talking for them both.

The house was sold, and the visa application for Mr and Mrs Wilfred Martin and their three children was successful—mainly because they were paying their own way and had enough money to keep them for a few months.

It didn't take long for them to pack their trunks. Wilfried carefully wrapped Liesel's violin in tissue paper and then put it back in its case. Perhaps he'd soon be able to afford lessons for Carl. No, he must remember to call him Charles now. Apart from his miniature violin and some clothes for himself and Charles, he didn't have much else to pack. Miriam sold a lot of the furniture he'd made for Liesel to the people who bought the house. She and the two girls seemed to spend ages trying to decide what to take. He left them to it.

***

Miriam booked their passage below decks—a cabin with three bunks for her and the girls, and another small cabin with two bunks for Wilfried and Carl.

Wilfried was pleased he didn't have to face sleeping in the same cabin as Miriam.

'I'll get the girls and we'll go to the bathroom now,' Miriam said, taking her wash bag and towel as she went out of the cabin.

Wilfred nodded. 'Come on, Carl, we'd better go and wash, too,'

Carl laughed. 'I'm Charles now, remember, Dad? Miriam said I mustn't answer to Carl, only to Charles.'

Wilfred smiled. 'Excited, Charles?' he asked as he ruffled his son's hair.

'Yes, this is a big adventure!' Charles grinned back.

Miriam settled her daughters in their cabin, and then came to check on Wilfred. Charles was already fast asleep in his bunk.

'Is everything all right, Wilfred?'

'Yes, and thank you for everything, Miriam.'

'That's all right, Wilfred,' came the calm reply. 'I hope you sleep well. Goodnight.'

***

After the interminable boat journey, they were all relieved to reach Sydney. Miriam had sent her friend details of the ship and the day it was expected to dock. She hadn't seen her friend since she was in her twenties, so she'd no idea what she looked like now, some twenty years later.

'She's called Milly; her husband is Billy.' Miriam laughed. 'Easy to remember! But I don't know how we'll know them,' she continued anxiously.

Wilfred felt apprehensive. He worried about what would happen when they arrived. He kept thinking about when he, Liesel and Carl had landed in Buenos Aires and the Hotel de Inmigrantes. Thankfully they passed through the customs and immigration checks with no problems. Out on the wharf, noise and bustle and people were everywhere.

Then they heard shouting. 'Miriam! Wilfred! Girls! Over here! Where are you? Milly and Billy are here!'

Everyone turned to look at the source of this raucous noise—Milly and Billy.

Wilfried couldn't help smiling.

Miriam waved enthusiastically. 'Here we are,' she shouted.

The crowds parted and let them through, bemused at such an exhibition.

Milly, a big boned woman in her forties, hugged Miriam. 'Welcome. Wow, Miriam, you haven't changed a bit since you were a teenager!'

Miriam laughed. 'A bit greyer!'

Billy, a bulky man with a moustache, shook Wilfried's hand until Wilfred thought it would fall off. 'Welcome to Australia,' he boomed. 'And these are the children? Well, these aren't children; these are young people!' he exclaimed, looking closely at Sarah, Ruth and Charles. 'Welcome, everyone! You'll love it here.' He turned back to Wilfried. 'Your trunks will be a day or too unload-ing and going through customs. I've got a mate with a trailer; we can fetch them later. Now come back with us. You must be tired after the journey.'

Wilfred wasn't so much tired as weary. The journey had been long and boring, and he'd spent every day and every evening trying to improve his English. Now he nodded at Billy. 'Tank you zo much, Billee.' He smiled, indeed very grateful. 'You are zo kind. I tank you zo much!'

Billy clapped him on the shoulder and laughed. 'No worries, mate.'

Wilfred wasn't sure what that meant. The only mates he knew were those ship mates who worked on the boats. He decided not to dwell on it.

Charles looked around in wonder. Wilfred took his hand. 'Come, my son, we must go with Billy.'

'It's pretty basic,' Milly informed them as she led the way to the tram. 'But we were lucky. Billy made a few bob in the gold mines, and we managed to buy a little house in Annandale.'

When they eventually arrived at the front gate, Wilfred paused from puzzling over the bob that Billy made and noticed the cladding on the house. He pointed to it. 'What is the material on the 'ouse?' he asked Billy.

Billy frowned, then laughed. 'Fibro-cement! Cheap and nasty, but does the job.' He led the way into the little one-story house.

'We have the spare room for you and Wilfred,' Milly said, turning to Miriam. 'We thought we could put a mattress on the floor for the girls, and Charles could sleep on the veranda. Billy's made a bit of a sleep-out there.'

Charles' eyes widened at the thought of sleeping on the veranda. He smiled at his father. Meanwhile, Wilfred felt relieved that the girls would be sharing their room.

'It will be all right until you settle down. Hopefully Wilfred will soon find work,' Milly said as she looked doubtfully at Wilfred. 'With the depression, there isn't much work in Sydney. It was a bad time to come, really.' She sighed. 'Anyway, hopefully things will soon improve.'

It seemed she didn't hold out much hope for Wilfried getting work. Not with that thick German accent.

'Put your bags in here. You must be thirsty. I'll make tea.' Milly bustled away. 'Here, in the kitchen,' she called.

'Come, Willy,' Billy said as they sat down at the kitchen table, 'now tell me, what is your trade?'

'I'm a cabinet maker,' Wilfred replied.

'A very fine one,' added Miriam, 'but of course, Wilfred can do all and any kinds of carpentry.'

'Hmm,' Billy appeared doubtful. 'Not much building work going on at the moment. Might be difficult to get a job.'

This made Wilfred subdued; it wasn't what he wanted to hear.

'I think the recession is everywhere, all over the world,' Billy continued. 'But I know there's a vacancy coming up at the slaughter house where I'm working. It hasn't been advertised, yet, but if you come with me tomorrow and offer to work for a few days for no pay, then if you can do the job, they'll probably take you on, if I recommend you. It's not very pleasant ...' He shrugged. 'But it brings in the bacon, so to speak!' He guffawed and turned to Milly. 'Brings in the bacon! Joke, Milly!'

Milly smiled back at him.

Miriam looked quickly at Wilfred, wondering how he'd react. Even though he was a Reform Jew and didn't follow the strictly

Jewish customs, he still couldn't bring himself to eat pork or bacon.

Wilfred just nodded. 'That would be most kind. Thank you, Billy.' He'd seen worse things in the war. Dead bodies and dead horses. *Needs must*, he told himself.

'Great, mate!' Billy boomed. "It's hard to get good workers there. Just until things get better.'

Wilfred smiled and nodded. He found it hard to follow the conversation. What Miriam had been teaching him didn't sound like the Australian accent.

She and Milly soon started reminiscing about their teenage years. Billy and he tried to make conversation, but by nightfall, he felt his head would fall off with nodding and smiling at Milly and Billy, trying hard to follow their accents. On the other hand, he wasn't keen to go to bed. That double bed was confronting. He sighed; he couldn't delay much longer.

Billy got up from the table. 'Well, mate, we'd better knock off for the night. Early start, if you want to come with me tomorrow. I'll give you a shout. G'night then.' He lumbered out of the room.

Wilfred and Miriam rose from the table.

'You and the children go to bed, Wilfred,' Miriam said. 'I'll help Milly clean up, and then I'll come too.' She started clearing the table.

Wilfred gave a little bow to Milly. 'Tank you, Missis Milly,' he said. 'Come, children.' He turned and left the kitchen with the children.

'Girls, you use the bathroom first, and be quick. I'll get Carl's—I mean Charles's—things and then we'll get washed.'

When the girls came into the bedroom, Wilfred indicated their mattress. 'Into bed now while I get Charles settled on the veranda.'

Charles was excited. 'It's such an adventure, Dad.'

'Yes.' Wilfred smiled as he tucked his son into the cocoon of blankets. 'Good night, my son.'

***

In the kitchen, Milly turned to Miriam. 'Oh, he's so gorgeous, Miriam! How did you manage to snare him?'

Miriam shrugged. 'Oh, you know how it is,' she smiled, 'a marriage of convenience.'

Milly winked at her. 'Oh yeah? Very convenient, if you ask me!'

Miriam poured hot water from the kettle into the washing-up bowl and said nothing.

When she finally got to their bedroom, Miriam found Wilfred already in bed. The two girls were asleep on the mattress on the floor, and she was sure that Wilfred was pretending to be asleep. She found her bag and towel and tiptoed outside to the wash room.

When she returned, she put out the lamp and slid into bed beside Wilfred. She sensed he was awake but said nothing, just turned on her side away from him. *All in good time*, she thought as she drifted into sleep.

***

At breakfast the next morning after Wilfred and Billy had set off to the abattoir, Milly said to Miriam, 'Would you like to go into Sydney? We could take the children for a picnic and go to Mrs. Macquarie's Chair.'

Miriam nodded, wondering what was so special about a chair. 'That sounds nice.'

With the breakfast dishes done, Miriam and Milly made sandwiches and put water into empty glass sauce bottles and packed them into a picnic basket, then caught the tram into Sydney with the children.

'They're delighted to be able to run around after being cooped up on board ship,' Miriam said, indicating the children as she and Milly spread a rug on the grass and sat down.

They watched them for a while, then Milly turned to Miriam. 'You're so lucky to have children,' she said softly.

Miriam nodded. 'Yes.'

Milly took out her handkerchief and blew her nose. 'You might think Billy is a bit ...'—she didn't know how to say it—'of a rough diamond, but he's a good man, Miriam. I never mentioned it in my letters, but when I first came to Australia, I was on my own, and it all went to my head. Anyway. I got pregnant. I was desperate. I knew no-one; the father disappeared. I was working in a dismal café and only getting paid in tips, which weren't much. So I had a backstreet abortion. It stuffed me up. A couple of days later, I fainted in the café. The manager was a bitch. She was angry because I'd dropped a plate with this man's breakfast on it. The man was Billy. He threw some money at the woman, picked me up and carried me outside.' She looked at Miriam. 'He's looked after me ever since.'

Miriam took her hand. 'Yes, I can see he adores you.'

'And I love him.' Milly sniffed. 'He'd have loved children. But after the abortion, I got an infection and was unable to have another child. Billy knows about the abortion. Like I said, he's a wonderful man.'

A lump came into Miriam's throat. She put an arm around Milly, just as Charles came bounding over. 'I'm starving, Miriam, did you say we were going to have a picnic?'

Milly gave a wobbly smile, and said, 'You've done a great job with teaching them English, Miriam, even if they do speak it with an American accent!'

***

Wilfred found the smell of the abattoir intolerable, but he kept reminding himself it was no worse than life in the trenches. Several times he felt like vomiting, but he knew he was lucky to have any kind of work.

He must write home to his parents and tell them his new address, at least for the time being. He hadn't heard from them or Fritz since leaving Buenos Aires. He worried about them. It seemed that this Hitler was changing the face of Germany.

He stuck to the job in the slaughter house, though he thought he'd never get rid of the smell of dead carcasses from his clothes. He thought Miriam recoiled when he and Billy got home from work. But perhaps it was his imagination.

She said nothing, but one night as they followed the usual routine with Wilfred getting into bed first and pretending to be asleep, Miriam whispered, 'Wilfred, you seem very down lately. Is your work very depressing ...?' Her voice trailed off. Instead of lying in bed with her back to him, now she turned around.

Wilfred said nothing.

'Are you asleep, Wilfred?' she whispered.

Then he replied, 'No, Miriam. I'm lucky to have work, but I cannot get the smell from my nostrils. Do you smell it? He turned to her to keep his voice low to avoid waking the girls.

'Oh, Wilfred; I smelt it at first, but now I no longer notice it.' Tentatively she put out a hand to his face.

'I'm sorry I can't give you a better life. I think you didn't expect that it would come to living like this, in someone else's home and putting up with these conditions,' he replied, not moving from her touch.

Moving slowly, Miriam put her arms around him. She didn't speak, just held him.

For several minutes he tried to control himself. Then he gave her a kiss on her forehead. 'Thank you for everything, Miriam,' he said.

'It's all right,' she said softly.

Exhausted, he soon fell asleep in her arms.

She smiled to herself. It was a small step.

The next night, Miriam tentatively turned to Wilfred as he pretended to sleep and let her hand rest on his hip. The following week, she was lying with her back to him when he turned and cautiously put his hand on her hip. She smiled to herself as the nights passed, knowing she had to let things develop very slowly. *This must be the slowest ever consummation of a marriage*, she thought. Then, one night when she was sure the girls were deeply asleep, she cautiously turned to him and touched him. He flinched but didn't move. Tentatively she stroked him until he was fully erect. He turned to her urgently and took her quickly, and she had to bite her tongue to avoid moaning with pleasure. He shared no endearments or words of love, but it put their relationship on a new footing. Miriam felt that Wilfred was as relieved as she to get to this stage in their relationship.

***

Milly knew Wilfred and Miriam were worried about imposing on them, so three months later when Milly found out that a couple with whom she was friendly were moving to Adelaide, she mentioned it to Miriam. 'It's only about a ten-minute walk from here,' she said.

'It sounds ideal for us,' Miriam said. 'And you'll get your home to yourselves again.'

'Actually, it's been lovely having you all here.' Milly seemed a bit wistful. 'It's been good, talking about old times in the States.'

Gradually, the economic situation improved. Wilfred was able to get work as a carpenter, and they managed to rent a house in Bankstown, a suburb of Sydney. When Charles was seventeen, Billy pulled a few strings with his mates to get him an apprenticeship as an electrician. Miriam's daughters had found work, Ruth as a shop assistant in Sydney and Sarah as an apprentice dressmaker. Wilfred felt a measure of happiness. Life seemed good. His fondness for Miriam grew. He'd never love her like he'd loved Liesel, he told himself, but their relationship was solid and based on mutual respect. He realised he was content. Theirs was a happy household.

From the news he received from his parents and Hans, it looked like things were improving in Germany. Hitler had got the economy going, building roads and factories, but there was still a lot of resentment towards Jews. Wilfred didn't know what to think. Were they writing this to reassure him, so that he wouldn't worry about them?

Every Saturday he read *The Sydney Morning Herald*, and one Saturday in August of 1936, while reading about the Olympics in Berlin, an article caught his eye

Ominous Reports from Paris: Red Battalions and German Bombers.

He read on:

Foreign intervention in the Spanish civil war is becoming more ominous. Battalions, half Frenchmen and half foreigners, are being formed, and some have already started for Spain to help the Spanish Government. Five-thousand Red volunteers mobilized in Russia have also set out. French Communists will house them in various locations from whence they will be drafted across the frontier.

Herr Hitler has decided to send two more cruisers and some destroyers to the Spanish coast.

It is also reported that the steamer Usuramo *left Hamburg on July 31, with twenty-eight bombing aeroplanes and pilots on board, bound for Lisbon, the capital of Portugal.*

This alarmed Wilfred. Twenty-eight bombing aeroplanes, all ready and waiting? Surely that should send shivers up the spines of the British and French?

The news from Germany didn't improve. It seemed that many Jews were trying to get out of Germany. Wilfried wondered if his parents and Hans and Marlene and their children were safe. He felt helpless.

Chapter Fifteen

1966, Sydney, Australia

A year after her grandfather's funeral, Liesel decided to visit his grave. She knew he'd loved freesias, so she bought a bunch at Lidcombe station and caught a bus to the cemetery. Bewildered by the vastness and the sight of all the gravestones, she knew she'd never find Wilfred's grave without help. She found the office and asked for directions.

As she neared the row number she'd been given, she saw an old man standing in front of the tiny headstone that marked her grandfather's grave. He turned at her approach and frowned. 'Good morning.' He peered at her through thick glasses. 'You Wilfried's granddaughter? I saw you at his funeral.'

Liesel nodded. Tears came to her eyes at the sight of the small headstone that simply bore the inscription: 'Wilfred Martin. 1889 – 1965. Sadly missed.'

She looked around for something to put the freesias in.

Seeing this, the old man turned to her. 'I go and find pot for flowers.' He walked off, and a few minutes later came back with a small vase filled with water. 'It only had dead flowers in it,' he remarked. 'We can borrow it.' He smiled at her, a twinkle in his eyes.

Liesel smiled back; she was sure he'd filched it from another grave. 'Thank you. He loved flowers; he spent a lot of time in his garden. Did you know him well?'

'Yes. I was in Tatura with him.'

'Tatura?' Liesel frowned.

'Yes. We were in Tatura Internment Camp together during the war.'

'Internment camp?' Liesel realised she was echoing his words.

'He kept all our spirits up, teaching anyone who wanted to learn carpentry skills, and making things for our children for presents—wooden trains and little wooden horses.' He sniffed and blew his nose. 'I must go. My wife is buried over there.' He indicated another part of the cemetery. 'I come every week and talk to her. Sometimes I visit Wilfried, too.' He tipped his cap at Liesel. 'Goodbye.' And he walked slowly away.

Liesel stared after him. What had he been on about? The same man had spoken to her at her grandfather's funeral. Where was this Tatura place? She'd have to try and get her dad to herself one day and ask him.

Chapter Sixteen

1938, Australia

R eport in the Australian morning papers:

Statements from representatives at the Evian Conference, France, July 1938.

Australia's representative, Colonel T.W. White, Minister for Trade and Customs:

"Australia has her own particular difficulties ... migration has naturally been predominantly British, and it is not desired that this be largely departed from while British settlers are forthcoming. Under the circumstances, Australia cannot do more, for it will be appreciated that in a young country manpower from the source from which most of its citizens have sprung is preferred, while undue privileges cannot be given to one particular class of non-British subjects without injustices to others. It will no doubt be appreciated also that as we have no real racial problem, we are not desirous of importing one by encouraging any scheme of large-scale foreign migration ... I hope that the conference will find a solution to this tragic world problem."

Wilfred sat in his arm chair one evening watching everyone. Miriam was knitting. Sarah had material spread on the kitchen table and was cutting out a dress. Ruth was in the laundry doing something with her hair. *The Sydney Morning Herald*, which he'd bought on his way home from work as he usually did on a Friday, sat on his lap.

Charles and two of his apprentice friends had come around as Charles had recently found plans in *Radio Monthly* for how to build a short-wave radio. They were keen to make a start.

'Show me your magazine,' Wilfred said, holding out his hand.

Charles handed it to him and then turned to Sarah. 'Come on, Sarah, hurry up and finish that dress or whatever it is you're doing. We want to start building our radio,' he grumbled. 'Dad, tell her please.'

Wilfred looked up from the magazine. 'This looks very interesting, please explain to me how it will work.'

Charles and his friends, Jimmy and Pete, crowded round Wilfred, all talking at once, telling him how a short-wave radio worked. Wilfred looked up and caught Miriam's eye; he winked at her, and she smiled, appreciating his ploy to distract the boys until Sarah finished her cutting out.

'I could make you a nice timber case to hold the radio when it's finished,' he offered.

The boys looked at each other. They liked being able to see all the valves and wires.

'Thank you, Dad, maybe later on,' Charles said.

'You can have the kitchen table now; I've finished,' Sarah said.

Ruth's sudden entrance into the room distracted everyone.

Miriam jumped up, her ball of wool falling from her lap onto the floor. 'What on earth have you done to your hair!'

Ruth's brown hair had changed to a flaming red. Her eyes filled with tears. 'It's supposed to be chestnut!' she wailed.

Wilfred smiled to himself. He loved his family life.

The boys moved to the kitchen table with their radio equipment. Miriam left her knitting and went to the laundry with Ruth. Wilfried heard her saying something about washing out the colour.

Sarah sat on the floor, tacking the seams of her dress.

He was happy. He had a family.

He picked up *The Sydney Morning Herald*, shook out the pages and settled down to read the news. It was Friday the eleventh of November 1938, and he was horrified to read the headlines:

Orgy of Destruction in Germany.

Mobs Wreck Jewish Shops.

Synagogues Burnt: 10,000 Jews Arrested.

His mind blanked. He blinked and read the rest of the article. It had happened all over Germany. The Minister for Propaganda, Dr Goebbels, said it was a spontaneous retaliation after the shooting, by a Polish Jew, of Dr von Rath, Secretary to the German Embassy.

Wilfred's anger built as he read the rest of the article. Then his anger turned to despair. Had his parents been involved? Hans and Marlene? He went cold at the thought. He'd no way of finding out. Heavy hearted he went to the laundry and called to Miriam.

She hurried out, her hands stained pink from trying to wash the dye from Ruth's hair. 'What is it, Wilfried?

He showed her the paper.

'Oh, Wilfred!' She put her arms around him as he tried to hold back his tears.

***

Six weeks later he received a letter from Hans. It bore no address.

Wilfried. We are in hiding. Some good Christian Germans are keeping us. They will post this letter for me.

Last week Marlene and I and the children went to visit Marlene's parents, as you know they live outside Mannheim. When we got back on the Saturday afternoon, one of the neighbours, who knew where we were, walked to meet us. He said it was too dangerous to go home, and he told us that my father's shop had been smashed and looted and Fritz had been arrested. We don't know where he is. None of us are safe here. We are trying to get our children, Samuel and Rebecca to England.

The British Government has agreed to take 10,000 Jewish children.

If Marlene and I don't survive, please, Wilfried, will you find them and look after them. I'm sorry but I have no news of your parents. I don't know if I will be able to write again. I don't want to get this friend into trouble.

Your brother-in-law Hans Goldberg.

Wilfred felt devastated by this news. He wondered if he should show the letter to Miriam. He knew she'd help him any way she could to find Hans and Marlene's children. He decided to wait and see what happened before showing her the letter. In the meantime, he had to keep this to himself. Carefully he folded the letter and put it into the wooden box he'd made to keep his masterpiece miniature violin, along with other documents. He determined that as soon as he had the money, he'd go to England and find Liesel's nephew and niece. He'd find his Mother and Father, too, where ever they were.

***

The news from Germany got worse. It seemed that every time Wilfred picked up a newspaper, he read of more atrocities against the Jews.

And then on Sunday the third September 1939, Miriam turned on the radio, and they heard the voice of the Prime Minister, Robert Menzies: *'Fellow Australians, it is my melancholy duty to inform you officially, that in consequence of persistence by Germany in her invasion of Poland, Great Britain has declared war upon her and that, as a result, Australia is also at war.'*

Wilfred felt sick. Charles was now twenty. Five years younger than he'd been when he'd fought for Germany in the Great War. At least, at that time, Australia had no conscription, so Charles wouldn't be called up to fight. *As long as he didn't volunteer.*

The news from Europe didn't improve as the days passed. Britain paper-bombed Germany with propaganda leaflets. Wilfred didn't understand why the British didn't just bomb the German armament depots with live bombs instead of paper.

He tossed *The Sydney Morning Herald* aside to answer the front door. Someone was making a hell of a noise with their banging. If it was children playing a trick, he'd soon give them a piece of his mind. He flung open the door ready to growl at whoever it was, only to be confronted by two policemen.

'Wilfred ... um Shunbum?' asked one, consulting a piece of paper clipped to a folder.

Wilfred frowned. 'My name is Wilfred Martin; why?'

'Say's here Wilfried Shunbum, also known as Wilfred Martin. See?' He held out the folder.

Wilfred peered at it. 'I was called Wilfried Schönbaum, yes, but my name has been legally changed to Wilfred Martin,' he said.

'Whatever.' The policeman tucked the folder under his arm. 'You're now under arrest.'

'What!' Wilfred blinked, dumbfounded.

Miriam came to the door. 'What's happening?'

'You Mrs Shunbum?' the other policeman asked.

'No, I'm Mrs Miriam Martin, and this is my husband; what's going on?' Wilfred stood back as she confronted the policemen.

'Your husband, here, is under arrest; he's an enemy alien. We have to take him to Long Bay Jail and then he'll be sent to an internment camp.'

'What! Why? I don't understand.' Miriam straightened and stood tall.

'He was born in Germany. And there's a boy, Charles ...' The officer pushed his cap back and scratched his head as he consulted his list.

Miriam was outraged. 'My children were all born in Argentina. I am an American citizen; how dare you come here insulting us.'

'Says here this Charles was born in Germany.'

'I should know where my children were born, officer.' Miriam glared at them and her American accent seemed more pronounced to Wilfred as she raised her voice. 'I shall take this matter to court!'

The police officers wavered. They didn't see Miriam's right hand behind her back with her fingers crossed. Wilfred did and hid a smile. He put an arm around her shoulders.

'Well, anyway. We have to take your husband now. Apparently, he's been sending radio messages to the enemy; we'll have to impound the radio. We'll check on the boy later. If you want to put a few things in a bag for your husband while we put him in the van ...' They led Wilfred away. Five minutes later, they returned. 'We have a search warrant to confiscate the radio'

Miriam was stunned. 'This is ridiculous! My husband was helping our son and his mates build a crystal set; how dare you suggest he's been sending messages.'

The policemen just shrugged. When they reached the kitchen and saw the crystal radio, they grinned triumphantly. The senior officer pursed his lips. 'Circumstantial evidence,' he proclaimed. Quickly they gathered up the radio equipment.

'This is outrageous! How dare you.'

'Missus, I'd take it easy if I were you,' the younger policeman said, trying to be helpful. 'Otherwise we'll have to arrest you too.'

Furious, Miriam found Wilfred's shaving gear and a change of clothes, put them in a bag and took them out to the waiting van. 'This is ridiculous,' she repeated, as she handed the bag to one of the policemen. She tried to look into the back of the van but couldn't see Wilfred. There seemed to be a few other men in there. Distraught, she stood watching as the van drove away.

'Why would they take him, Miriam?' Charles asked when he got home that evening. 'And why would they take our radio away? We spent so much time building it.'

'There are so many rumours going around, and there's a bad feeling here towards Germans.' Miriam sat wringing her hands. 'Somebody with a resentment towards him could have sent in a complaint to the police. It seems someone heard about the radio you and your mates were building in the kitchen and assumed your father was behind it and was sending messages to Germany.'

'What? That's ridiculous! Does that mean one of my mates dobbed him in? Who on earth would have anything against Dad? He's such a quiet person, friendly and helpful towards everyone. It's crazy.'

'I know. But someone round here thinks he's a Nazi spy.'

Charles tried to think who it could be. 'It must have been the parents of one of my mates. Or it could be someone from his work. Someone who resents him for working harder than anyone else and being good at his job.'

Miriam's shoulders sagged. Suddenly she looked older than her fifty-two years. 'I'll try and think what to do.'

She tried everything she could think of to get Wilfred released and lodged an appeal immediately, but heard nothing.

***

Finally, Wilfried managed to sit down and write a letter to Miriam:

My dear Miriam,

We have been moved from Long Bay to this specially built camp inTatura, in Victoria. I'm in No. 1 Camp. It's mostly Germans.

This is our routine:

At half past six every morning there is a bugle call to wake us p.

He didn't mention that he had to queue, naked, with just his towel, with hundreds of other men to shower. Each man allowed under thirty seconds.

At seven thirty, breakfast in the mess hall, then roll call at nine thirty. Another meal at 12 noon and last meal at 5pm. Lights are turned off at 10.30, which is a bit ridiculous as the whole camp is lit by floodlights at night.

He looked up at the ceiling. This letter sounded very like the letters he used to write to Liesel from the trenches in the war.

There is plenty of food here.

Well, not that bit. They'd been starving in the trenches.

They have me on their roll call as Wilfried Schönbaum, not Wilfred Martin. We sleep in dormitories. Twenty men to a hut and there are fifty huts on the compound. Some of the men snore heavily and sometimes it's difficult to sleep. I found a few carpentry jobs that needed doing so I asked if I could work on them.

The superintendent was a bit dubious at first, but he let me do some work under supervision. The tools are brought to me in the morning, and have to be checked out in the evening, and every tool accounted for. The superintendent was pleased, so I am hoping to be able to do more as it's very boring here.

I wonder if you could send me some clothes. For those of us with none of our own, we have to wear old Australian-army uniforms which have been dyed with brown dye. They come out a kind of burgundy colour.

But I am well. I miss you and the children, dear Miriam.

Your loving husband,

Wilfred Martin.

He didn't tell her that it was freezing cold. The only heating was in the tiny mess hall, and that was so crowded that there was no room to sit down. There were no hot showers, and none of the windows over each bed in his dormitory had glass in them.

He was allowed to send two letters a week, each a maximum of twenty-two lines. Miriam wrote to him every Sunday night. She sent him writing paper, envelopes and stamps, and occasionally, chocolate. Charles sometimes included a letter. Often their letters arrived with little windows cut out of them—the censor at work.

Life was hard for Miriam. The only money coming into the household came from Ruth, Sarah and Charles. None of them earned very much, but they kept the family going until Charles finished his apprenticeship a few months later and was able to contribute more.

Milly and Billy often called around and always brought some-thing.

'There was a lot of meat left over this week,' Billy would say. 'Too much for me and Milly. Thought you might be able to help us out.'

Miriam found part time work in a vegetable shop—a godsend as she was able to bring home fruit and vegetables too old or misshapen to sell. Charles worked overtime and they managed.

Christmas came and they were all sad not to have Wilfred with them. It just wasn't the same.

Miriam tried to console them all. 'At least, we know Dad is safe. Not like the poor devils fighting this war.'

The Christmas dinner of a scrawny roast chicken had been picked clean, and just as Miriam, with a sigh, was about to get up to fetch the Christmas pudding, Sarah, unable to control her excitement any longer, stood up and clapped her hands.

Startled, everyone looked at her, except George, her boyfriend, who looked down and studied his hands.

'George and I are engaged,' she announced.

Suddenly everyone was talking and congratulating George, who reddened and smiled bashfully.

'Wilfred will be so pleased, darling.' Miriam got up and kissed her elder daughter. 'I'll write to him tonight.'

The announcement lightened the otherwise sad atmosphere.

Since coming to Australia, there had been no mention of religion in their family, so Sarah's marriage would be a civil one at the Sydney Registry Office.

'Will you give me away, Charles?'

Miriam sighed. 'It's so cruel that Wilfred can't be here to give you away, Sarah,' she said. 'And, Charles, you will have to get a suit to wear.'

She looked at Sarah, who nodded and said, 'I suppose you will, Charles. At least I'll be able to make my wedding outfit.'

'And, Charles,' Miriam continued, 'I have a little money which I've been putting aside, and I've been saving our clothing coupons, so if you don't mind, I'll pay for a suit for you, and use the coupons. It's lucky we have a dressmaker in the family to make most of our clothes.' She smiled at Sarah.

'It's good that we don't need coupons for linen,' Sarah said. 'I'll be able to make you a shirt from a new white cotton sheet, Charles.'

Their generosity touched Charles. 'Thank you, Sarah, and you too, Miriam, but as soon as I can I'll pay you back. After all, I'll be able to wear the suit and shirt for special occasions for years.'

'Yes, for your own wedding!' Sarah laughed and poked him in the ribs. 'As long as you don't put on weight, and once you can pluck up courage to ask a girl out.'

Chapter Seventeen

1938, Sydney

Madge leaned against the counter of the gentlemens outfitters in Sydney, watching a young man hesitating at the glass door of the shop.

She summed him up as a time waster. Probably just checking prices and wanting a cheap suit, not the quality tailoring they stocked.

She was sure she could feel Adam looking at her from the manager's office upstairs.

After disappearing, then reappearing the young man pushed the door and came in.

Madge tossed her head, flicking her hair over her shoulder.

Seeing him standing, looking lost, she approached him, wiping the sour expression from her face.

Her chin high, she smiled at him. 'May I help you, sir?'

'Um, yes; I need a suit for a wedding.'

'Your wedding, sir?' She smiled coquettishly at him.

'Oh, no,' he stammered. 'It's my sister who's getting married.'

'I'm surprised your girlfriend didn't come to help you choose.' She raised her eyebrows enquiringly.

'Oh, I don't have a girlfriend,' he said, his face colouring.

'So "off the shelf" or tailored?'

He looked blank.

'Ready-made or will you have it tailor made?'

This bloke seemed a bit dim, Madge thought, her mind drifting to the previous night when Adam had told her that he loved her wig, it was so natural. Affronted, she'd retorted that she wasn't wearing a wig, that this was her own hair. She'd tossed her head, flicking her hair back over her shoulder. Adam had been speechless. He'd managed to stutter that he'd thought she was an Orthodox Jew and kept her hair covered with a wig. He'd gone quiet and then announced that he could only marry her if she was Orthodox.

'I won't wear a wig and be restricted by those Orthodox views,' she'd told him vehemently. 'It's ridiculous, having to keep your hair covered except in the presence of your husband, and not being able to touch a non-Jew. I'm of the reformed movement and proud of it!' She'd shaken her head again, her long glossy brown hair swinging defiantly.

Adam had just looked at her. 'My father ...' he'd mumbled.

'Your father needs to come out of the dark ages!'

Adam had stiffened, and she'd regretted the words immediately. 'I'll take you home,' was all he'd said.

And Madge had seen her chances of a good marriage to a wealthy man evaporating. Her head held high, she'd allowed Adam to take her home.

'Good night, then,' he'd said awkwardly.

Trying to salvage the situation, Madge had flung her arms around him, but he'd stood rigidly unresponsive, then he'd pushed her arms away, turned abruptly and left.

Back in the present, she became aware of the young man in front of her, who was now staring at her with a perplexed look on his face.

'Oh, I'm sorry, I didn't catch what you said.' She gave him one of her winning smiles.

'What's the difference?' he asked.

'Difference?' Madge had forgotten what she'd said.

'Off the shelf or tailor made.'

'Oh, well, "off the shelf" means a suit that has already been made, which may not exactly fit you, but "tailor made" means you're measured, you choose the material and have it made especially for you. Of course, you'd have to come back and have a fitting. "Off the shelf" is less expensive, though, and if necessary, we can make alterations.'

'I think I'd better have off the shelf,' he said hesitantly.

'Oh! Well, I can help you choose. But first you must be measured.' She glanced up at the office and saw Adam watching her. She wasn't allowed to measure customers. She was supposed to call one of the tailors. *I'll make him jealous! He'll soon come around to my way of thinking.* She took out a tape measure. 'Please take off your jacket, sir.'

The young man took off his jacket. He seemed embarrassed by its threadbare collar.

Deliberately, Madge put the tape measure around his chest. *Hope you're watching, Adam.* 'Forty-two.' She smiled approvingly. 'We have a good range of suits of that size, and if the jacket fits, we can easily adjust the trousers. Come over here; I'll show you suits which might suit you.' She laughed at her joke as she led him to the back of the shop.

She quickly rifled through one of the racks and pulled out a dark-grey jacket. 'Try this on. The material would be suitable for any formal occasion.' She helped him into it, then turned him around to face a mirror. 'Yes, a perfect fit, and you look very handsome in that one. With a nice white shirt and a tie ...' She regarded him appraisingly. *Actually, he'd scrub up rather well.*

He blushed.

'Now for the trousers.' She pulled them off the hanger. 'If you like this suit, you can go to the changing rooms and try on the trousers.' She handed them to him and pointed. 'Over there. Then come out and show me. Oh, and take off your shoes,' she called after him

Five minutes later, he emerged in his stockinged feet.

Madge surveyed him. 'I think the waist needs taking in a bit and perhaps the legs a bit shorter. I'll get one of the tailors to measure you, just wait here.' She hurried off and returned with a small bent man armed with a tape measure and a pin cushion.

'Over here, sir, to the changing room.'

Madge waited expectantly until the young man came out dressed in his own clothes. 'Are you happy with that suit, sir?'

He nodded.

'Right; now if you just put down a deposit, then you can pay the balance when you come to collect it.' She handed him an invoice.

Bemused, he glanced at it, took out his wallet and gave her the money.

She touched his hand as she took the money, which she wrapped in the invoice, put into the container for the cash carrier and pulled the cord. She looked up. *Yes! Adam was still watching her.* When he saw her glance, he quickly turned away.

'It won't take long,' she said, looking up at the young man from under her eyelashes. Then she enquired innocently, 'Have you been to see *Gone with the Wind* yet at the pictures?'

'Um, no.'

'Neither have I, and I'd love to see it, but I've no-one to go with.' She smiled at him, hoping Adam was still watching her.

The young man gulped. 'Um, I wonder ... I wonder if you'd like to come, um, come with me?'

Madge gave him a dazzling smile. 'Oh, that would be ever so nice! What about Sunday night?'

Speechless, he nodded.

'By the way, my name is Madge Steiner.'

'Charles Martin.'

'I'll meet you outside the cinema at seven-thirty, shall I?' Madge said.

He nodded again.

With a clank, the money tube arrived.

Madge gave him the receipt and touched his arm. 'See you on Sunday night, then,' she beamed.

She watched Charles walk out, then glanced up at Adam. He was no longer looking at her. *Well, she'd show him! He'd soon come around to her way of thinking. She'd use this Charles bloke to make Adam jealous, and in the meantime, she'd get to see a good film.* Triumphant, she smiled to herself.

Her mother had been nagging at her for ages to hurry up and get married and produce some grandchildren. Madge's only other sibling, her sister, Naomi, had been married for several years but they'd no children. Naomi's husband, Ron, was some kind of business man—Madge didn't know the details, but they lived in a nice house and had a car.

Madge's mother had been delighted when Madge had started going out with Adam.

'A tailoring business in Sydney!' she'd exclaimed. 'That's the man for you, Madge.'

Madge had glowed.

So when she'd arrived home the day before and told her mother that Adam had assumed she was an Orthodox Jew and had finished with her when he found out she wasn't, her mother was angry.

'But you should have gone along with it.' She glowered at Madge. 'There aren't many suitable men around these days, what with this war! You should've pretended your hair was a wig! Your father would've paid for one for you. I don't know what you were thinking. Adam was such a good catch!'

Madge shrugged. 'Oh well, I can't see me being an Orthodox wife.'

'You could've kept up the pretence until after the wedding.'

'Anyway,' Madge said. 'I'm going to the cinema with a nice man on Sunday. He came into the shop today to buy a suit for his sister's wedding.'

Her mother cheered up at this, no doubt visualising an important, well-off man. 'Invite him for tea one day,' she said. 'We'll get Naomi and Ron to come too. What's his name?'

'Charles Martin.'

'Is he Jewish?'

'I don't know! For goodness sake, Mam, I've only just met him. I didn't give him the first degree just to go to the cinema.' Madge flounced out of the room.

***

Charles walked out of the store feeling a mixture of elation and alarm. He'd bought a suit and asked a pretty girl to go out with him! His temerity amazed him. He'd never been out with a girl before even though he was twenty-three. His stepsisters were always trying to set him up with one of their friends but, somehow, he'd managed not to get involved.

Sunday came and Charles felt nervous. On Sundays they usually had a late lunch. Sarah's fiancé, George, was there too.

Sarah watched him picking at his meal. 'What's the matter, Charles? You're not eating much. Have you heard from Dad?'

'No,' he mumbled. Then he looked at her. 'I'm taking a girl to the cinema.' There. He'd said it.

'Oh, that's nice!' Sarah smiled. 'Tell us all about her!'

Miriam, Ruth and George all looked up.

'Um. I met her when I went to get my suit for your wedding, Sarah.'

'That's great, about time you made a move.'

'What're you going to see?' Ruth asked eagerly.

'*Gone with the Wind.*'

'Oooh, can I come too?'

Charles would love to have Ruth come, but Sarah interrupted. 'No! Of course not. This is Charles's first date.'

Ruth sniffed.

As soon as they'd finished eating, Charles went to his room and changed into clean clothes. He wished he had his new suit, but this would have to do.

He arrived at the cinema half an hour early and paced up and down, trying not to look anxious. Just as the doors were opening, he saw her strolling up to the cinema doors.

'Well, hello Charles.' she said with a smile when she spotted him.

'Hello, Madge,' he said shyly. 'Shall we go in?'

She nodded and followed Charles to the ticket office.

During the film, couples kissed and cuddled all around them. Charles sat stiffly beside Madge, not even daring to hold her hand. He missed bits of the film as he worried about what to do afterwards. He should've asked Sarah.

The film lasted over three-and-a-half hours, but the end came much too soon for Charles. He watched the other men with their girls. Most of them put their hands on their girl's elbow or around their waists and guided them out. Cautiously, he put his hand on Madge's elbow.

Outside the cinema he looked at her and asked if she'd like a coffee or something.

'That'd be lovely,' she simpered. 'Perhaps an ice cream as it's so warm.'

Charles nodded.

They sat on a bench and ate the ice-creams. He was in a panic as to what to do next when Madge suddenly stood up.

'I'd better go now,' she said. 'There's my bus. Thank you so much, Charles. I enjoyed the film and your company.' She held out her hand.

He didn't know what to do with it. Kiss it? Shake it? He ended up patting it and giving it back to her. 'Thank you, Madge,' he managed to say.

He stood and watched as she got on the bus. She gave him a little wave and a smile. A feeling of achievement filled him, but on his way home, he realised he hadn't asked her out again. Damn. Then he remembered that he'd see her again when he went to get his suit.

***

Madge felt happy. She had another string to her bow if Adam didn't come to heel. This Charles seemed all right, a bit slow, but steady men were thin on the ground these days. The war had messed up everything. She felt she'd played it right. Not too forthcoming but not too shy either. He'd be coming to collect his suit the following week. She'd have to think up a good excuse to get him to ask her out again. If only Adam could have seen her with Charles today ...

She arrived home to see her mother peering out the window, looking out for her. 'What kept you?' she demanded. 'You should have been back long before now.'

'The film was nearly four hours,' Madge said with a shrug. 'Then we had an ice-cream.'

'So ... has he asked you out again?'

'Give me a break, Mam.'

'You're not getting any younger, Madge.'

Madge grimaced. *As if she didn't know.*

***

All week Charles wondered what to say to Madge when he went to collect his suit. He listened carefully to Ruth and Sarah talking about their boyfriends. It seemed that a walk in The Domain or the botanical gardens was a possibility. But how to bring himself to ask her?

Madge seemed pleased to see him again. 'Your suit's all ready, if you'd like to try it on,' she said, handing him the hangers.

Remembering to take off his shoes, Charles changed into the jacket and trousers and came out of the changing room with a bashful smile on his face.

Madge nodded approvingly. 'Yes, a lovely fit; you look most handsome.' She smiled at Charles, then took a swift look up at the office. 'You need a nice white shirt and a tie, now.'

'My sister is making me a white shirt,' he mumbled, as Madge said, 'That's nice, now just go and change and we'll look at ties. Bring the suit out with you.'

Charles changed and when he returned, she'd already selected a tie.

'I think this one,' she said, passing him a light-grey tie with a pale-mauve stripe through it. 'Very suitable for a wedding.'

Charles nodded.

'So who's going to the wedding?'

'Oh, my mother, my sister, Sarah, who's the one getting married, and my other sister, Ruth, who's maid of honour. And friends of my mother. And some of Sarah's friends. It's only a small wedding, because of the war.'

Madge nodded. 'So, your father ...' She looked enquiringly at him.

Charles flushed. 'Um, he's away at the moment.' Then, quickly to avoid any more questions, he said, 'Um, would you like to come for a walk on Sunday afternoon? Perhaps the botanic gardens?'

Madge smiled, apparently surprised and pleased. 'That'd be lovely, Charles.'

'I'll meet you at Circular Quay, shall I?' Her smile made him bold. 'Three o'clock?'

'Lovely.' Madge carefully folded and wrapped the suit and tie, and then made out the final invoice.

Charles swallowed hard when he saw the total. Thankfully he just had enough money in his wallet. Lucky they were only going for a walk on Sunday.

Chapter Eighteen

Wilfred felt sad that he wouldn't be at Sarah's wedding to give her away. He'd known Miriam's daughters since they were small girls and he'd grown very fond of them. When he and Miriam had married and Ruth and Sarah heard Charles calling him Dad, it had seemed natural for them to do the same. Their own father had died from the Spanish Influenza when Ruth was just a baby and Sarah only three-years old. They'd always gone straight to Wilfred if they'd done well at school or were worried about anything. Miriam had been delighted that her girls treated Wilfred as if he were their own father. Somehow Charles had never called Miriam mum, though, which seemed strange to Wilfred, now that he thought about it.

He sat down to write back to Miriam. He'd been at the camp over two years and felt he was becoming institutionalised. He shared the compound with a thousand men—fifty huts, each with twenty beds. They all hated the barbed-wire fences and the inability to be alone. They lived in such close proximity. Some of the internees had committed suicide, others had gone mad and had to be removed before inflicting harm on the others or themselves. Some tried to escape, but even if successful, they were soon found and returned to the camp.

When he'd first arrived, the other occupants of his compound had asked him why he was being interned. He'd told them that he'd been accused of sending messages to the Nazis on a short-wave wireless his son had made. That had seemed to impress them.

But he had to tread carefully. They could make his life hell if they knew he was Jewish and anti-Nazi. Soon after he arrived, as he was going into the crowded mess hall for the main meal of the day, he'd been stopped by a small swarthy man, who'd looked all round to check there was no-one listening, then said in a low voice, 'When you go in, take the pork and eat some. They're watching you.' Then he'd walked off.

Wilfred had gone into the mess hall, suddenly aware that the usual chatter and noise had lessened. He made his way to the counter and helped himself to a large portion of pork-and-bean hot pot. Taking his fork, he speared a lump of pork and started to eat it as he walked to a corner of the room where there was space. The noise and talk resumed.

When he'd finished eating, Wilfred went outside and looked for the man who'd warned him. He found him in the vegetable garden that some of the men were cultivating.

'Nice garden you've got here,' he'd said. 'Wilfred Martin's my name. It was Schönbaum.' He held out his hand.

'Werner Schmitt,' replied the other, taking his hand. 'They had you marked as a Jew. I had to warn you.'

'Thanks. I'm glad you did.' He didn't want to think about what indecencies he'd have been subjected to if the bunch of Nazis decided he was a Jew.

'So are you?' Werner asked.

Wilfred shook his head. 'Well, I grew up as a Reform Jew, but I haven't been practicing for years.'

'You look Jewish.' Werner smiled.

Wilfred laughed. 'Is it my nose?'

'Hmm, you just look like a classic Jew. But I think someone noticed that you didn't eat the pork dishes and put two and two together ... you know how it is.'

Wilfred nodded. He'd tried to stay aloof from these Nazis. He wished now that he'd told his captors that he was Jewish. It would've been better to have been in with other Jews.

'How about you, Werner? Are you Jewish?'

Werner shook his head. 'No, I was a member of the German Evangelical Church, but when the leaders were trying to make the church part of Nazi policy, I joined the Confessing Church. I could see what was happening, even people whose Jewish grandparents had converted to Christianity and been baptised were banned from attending the German Evangelical Church. I didn't like the way things were going, so I worked my passage to Australia in 1934. I'd been a welder at the shipyard in Bremen and had no problem getting work in Australia. I was working at Cockatoo Island in Sydney. I married an Australian woman, but I was still arrested and sent here. My wife is finding it hard. I have a new-born baby daughter, who I've never seen.' He paused, his face a picture of sadness. 'Luckily my wife's family are helping.' He frowned. 'Good to meet you, Wilfred.' He turned back to the garden.

Wilfred had walked away, deep in thought. It was lucky that he was a carpenter and able to make things; it kept him from going mad with boredom. The German Club in Sydney had sent thousands of books and musical instruments. Now they were treated to classical music from time to time played by some of the internees. So many talented men, musicians and academics. They held classes, and a lot of the men attended, keen to have something to occupy their minds, and he could get books to read. He'd also made a chess set carved from odd bits of left-over timber, and he'd made a chess board and painted the squares. He managed to sell it, and then someone asked him to make another. A lot of men engaged in similar small enterprises to make extra pocket money.

My Dear Miriam,

Thank you for your letter. Please give George my congratulations on persuading such a wonderful girl as Sarah to be his wife. I am sure they will both be very happy. I'll be sad not to be at the wedding, but I'll be with you all in spirit.

He thought it all ridiculous. He hated what Hitler and his cronies were doing and would've have been happy to fight for the Allies.

I'm sure Sarah will look beautiful and Charles, being such a good-looking young man, will be perfect to give her away. He told me that you'd been saving all the clothing coupons for his suit. You are the best of wives, my dear Miriam. I miss you so much.

It's getting very hot here. There is a small window over each of our beds, but there is no glass or fly screens. We have no mosquito nets either as the authorities think they are a fire hazard. So it gets very dusty here when it's windy, and there are flies and mosquitoes everywhere.

I don't think I told you about Oskar Speck. He paddled his fold-up kayak all the way from Germany to Australia. It took him seven years. The day he arrived on Australian territory he was arrested and interned and sent here to Tatura. Well, he managed to escape! No one knows how. But after three weeks on the run he was captured in Melbourne. Apparently, he was trying to cycle to Sydney!

They put him in solitary confinement for three weeks when he was brought back here. Now he's been sent to another camp in South Australia. We'll miss him. He used to give very entertaining talks about his voyage from Germany. What a man!

I'm fit and well, my dear, and I hope you are too.

Your loving husband,
Wilfred Martin

He often thought about Liesel's brother, Hans, and his wife and the letter he'd had from Hans asking him to find Samuel and Rebecca. Perhaps he'd be able to go and look for them when the war was over. Or maybe Charles would.

Chapter Nineteen

Sarah and George's wedding went off well. Miriam and the girls spent the day before the wedding baking and preparing food. Milly and Billy arrived on the morning of the wedding with a leg of ham and a big pot of potato salad.

Miriam hugged Milly. 'You're the best friend ever!'

After the ceremony, they all returned to the house to celebrate. George and his family, and Milly and Billy, managed to keep the atmosphere light and happy, but most of them were sad that Wilfred wasn't there to see his step-daughter married and share in their joy.

***

Charles and Madge fell into a pattern of meeting most Sunday afternoons. Depending on the weather, they either walked around the harbour or went to the cinema.

'So when are we going to meet this Charles?' her mother kept asking. 'Why don't you bring him next Sunday for tea?'

'I'll wait until he takes me to meet his family.' Madge didn't want to frighten Charles away.

'Maybe he's waiting until you ask him over to meet your family first.' Her mother suggested. 'It's Naomi's birthday next week. Tell him we'll be having a little celebration and invite him. Nothing forward about that.'

The next day after their walk, she said casually to Charles, 'It's my sister's birthday next Sunday. We're having a little celebration. Nothing fancy, perhaps you'd like to come? You don't have to bring a present or anything; it's just tea and a birthday cake.' When she saw Charles hesitate, she continued, 'No problem if you don't feel like coming; it's nothing special.'

Put like that Charles couldn't refuse. 'Thank you. You'd better give me the address and tell me which bus to catch.'

***

Charles told Miriam about the invitation. 'Should I wear my wedding suit?' he asked her.

'Hmm, no, I don't think so. Not if Madge said this is just a casual affair.'

Charles felt nervous getting the bus to the Steiner's house in Willoughby. He'd never been to that part of Sydney before. Madge's family must be well off, he thought to himself as he knocked on the front door.

Madge opened the door. 'Well, Charles, come in.' She smiled and led him along the hall to a kitchen, then out to a covered veranda. 'Everyone! This is Charles.'

Charles nodded and smiled.

Madge's father, Brian Steiner, stood up. 'Hello, Charles.' he said. 'Have a beer?'

Madge's mother looked disapproving.

'Er, yes, thank you.' Charles was happy to have something to keep his hands occupied.

'Charles, this is my sister, Naomi, and her husband, Ron.'

Charles shook hands with them. Naomi seemed quite nice, he thought. She didn't look like Madge. Naomi's hair was short and blond, and she looked plumper. Ron was fleshy with dark, slicked back hair.

'Madge tells us you're an electrical engineer, Charles. Where do you work?' Brian asked.

Charles frowned. 'I'm an electrician,' he said, looking at Madge. *How did she get that idea? Electrical engineer!* 'I'm working for one of the electricity suppliers in Sydney.'

Madge's mother's eyebrows drew together.

'Ah, so what does your father do?' Brian asked.

Charles wriggled on the hard chair in the Steiner's dining room. 'He's a cabinet maker,' he replied, then quickly changed the subject. 'These scones are delicious.' He turned to Madge. 'Did you make them?'

'No, my mother did.'

'Oh.' He turned to Madge's mother. 'Mrs. Steiner, these are quite the nicest scones I've tasted. Perhaps you'd give me the recipe for my mother.'

Mrs. Steiner's bosom swelled with pride. 'Yes, of course.'

After Charles left, Madge's mother reflected on the afternoon and decided that the visit had gone off rather well. She was, of course, disappointed that Charles was only an electrician, not an electrical engineer, but considering Madge's age and all the men killed or away fighting, well, beggars couldn't be choosers. And hopefully she'd soon have a grandson.

***

On Monday the first of June 1942, Charles got home from work and turned on the radio. He was horrified to hear that the previous night, Japanese Submarines had been patrolling around Sydney Harbour at the very time he and Madge had been walking there.

An Australian boat, the Kuttabul had been attacked, killing over twenty service men. *Madge could have been killed.*

In that instant, he realised that Madge had become part of his life. He definitely wanted to take their physical relationship further, but Madge had been coyly resistant. A kiss was as far as she'd go. She'd taken him to meet her family, but he was reluctant to bring her to his home. Her family seemed all right; apparently, they were non-practicing Jews. They didn't keep the Sabbath or any of the other traditions, not that he knew much about the Jewish traditions, even though, according to his father, they were Jewish. Wilfred had taken him aside one day when he was a teenager and told him that they were Jews by birth, but to never mention it. Jews were not welcome in Australia.

He supposed he could ask Madge to marry him, but money was scarce, especially since Sarah had married George and gone to live up the coast. That meant there was only his wage and Ruth's coming in to keep the household going since his father's internment. Miriam's job at the vegetable shop had finished when the owner's daughter became old enough to work there. Miriam had tried to get work cleaning, but no-one could afford cleaners around where they lived. If Ruth married and left home, it would be only him to support Miriam. He didn't know if he could afford a wife. And maybe children. It was a frightening thought.

But Madge seemed to be getting restive.

***

When coming out of the cinema one Sunday afternoon, Madge spotted Adam with a girl on his arm. He didn't notice Madge, though—too intent on the girl beside him. *Don't think much of her wig,* Madge thought bitterly.

Still, it was a blow. And Charles didn't seem in a hurry to make a move. She'd made a few remarks about her friends getting married, but they seemed to go over his head.

Perhaps she should be a bit more forthcoming sexually. Charles had tried to get his hand inside her blouse on one or two occasions in the cinema, but she'd slapped his hand away. He hadn't tried since. And her mother kept nagging her about getting married and providing a grandson.

'Ask Naomi,' Madge had snapped. 'She's been married long enough.'

Her mother's lips had folded. 'I've given up on Naomi. I have suspicions about that Ron.'

'What kind of suspicions?'

'Oh, he seems a nice enough man, but he's a bit too slick for my liking. And there can't be anything wrong with Naomi. It must be his fault they have no children.'

***

Charles worried all week about getting married. He'd noticed Madge's veiled hints about her friends getting married.

Miriam noticed his preoccupation. 'Charles, my dear, you seem a bit quiet lately. What's the matter? Are you worried about your father?' She sighed. 'I miss him so much, and I'm worried about him in the cold. It's winter and they're only in those tin huts, no heating, no windows either. Freezing in winter and boiling in Summer ...'

'No, Miriam,' he said. 'I'm worried because I think I want to marry Madge ...' He reddened as she looked at him sharply.

'You've never brought this Madge home, Charles. Is it because of your father?'

Slowly, Charles nodded. 'I don't know how to explain it to her,' he said miserably. 'There's such bad feeling about Germany and the Germans; I just can't tell her that my father is German and in an internment camp in case he's a spy.'

Miriam nodded. 'Hmm; it's hard. But it's you she'll be marrying, not your father.' She remained silent for a while then stood. 'Ask her to come to tea next Sunday, after your usual Sunday walk. I think Ruth is going out with some friends, so it'll be just you and me.'

Charles smiled, grateful. 'Thank you, Miriam.'

***

Madge was thrilled when they came out of the cinema the following Saturday and Charles asked if she'd like to come the next afternoon and have tea with him and his mother.

Charles and Madge arrived for tea to find the table looking nice, with a pretty tablecloth and a little vase of flowers.

'Welcome, Madge,' Miriam said.

Madge smiled. 'Thank you.' She thought Charles's mother seemed very elegant and welcoming, and she hoped she'd make a good impression on her. 'You said your father is away, Charles, is he still?' She enquired as they sat down at the table.

'Yes,' Miriam replied quickly, then changed the subject. 'Charles tells me you work in a Gentleman's outfitters?'

Talk turned to the tailoring trade and the decline in business since the war. The visit went well and Charles seemed pleased

Eventually it was time for him to take Madge home.

He rose from the table. 'Thank you, Miriam. That was lovely. Can we help to clear the table?'

'No, my dear.' Miriam smiled at him. 'I have all evening to do it. You take Madge home before it gets dark.' She turned to Madge with a smile. 'It's been lovely to meet you, Madge.'

Before Madge could reply, Miriam started collecting the tea cups.

On their way to the bus stop, Madge turned to Charles. 'Why do you call her Miriam and not Mum?' she asked

'She's actually my stepmother,' he replied.

'I guess that explains why you look nothing like her,' Madge continued. 'So tell me about your real mother.'

'She died when I was very young,' Charles replied. 'I don't remember much about her.'

Madge thought he seemed anxious to change the subject away from his family, but then he took a deep breath and said suddenly, 'What do you think about us getting married?'

Taken by surprise, Madge couldn't think straight. 'Is this a proposal, Charles Martin?' she asked.

Charles swallowed. 'I suppose it is,' he said slowly. 'Will you marry me, Madge?'

Madge was overcome with relief. But her practical nature came to the fore. 'Where will we live, Charles?'

'We'll work something out,' he said.

'I'd like an engagement ring.'

'Of course. We'll go and buy one next weekend!'

***

Overjoyed that Madge had agreed to their marriage, Charles felt reckless. Perhaps she'd let him go further than just a kiss now they were engaged ...

That night he sat down to write to his father to tell him about his engagement. He tried to write at least every week or two, knowing his father missed his home and family.

Miriam came and sat at the table while he wrote. She watched him in silence.

Eventually he looked up and smiled. 'I asked Madge to marry me,' he said. 'I'm just writing to tell Dad.'

'Are you sure she's the right one for you?' Miriam asked, looking soberly at Charles.

His elation evaporated. He frowned. 'Didn't you like her?'

Miriam sighed. 'Somehow I don't think she's the right girl for you.'

'Why?' Charles's frown deepened.

She shrugged. 'Just a feeling I had,' she said, getting up from the table. 'By the way, I think you should tell Madge about your father. If she loves you, she'll take it in her stride.'

Charles frowned. 'Perhaps you're right.' He doodled on the writing pad with his pen and made a blob with the ink. He hastily blotted it.

'I'll put your letter to your father in with mine, and post them tomorrow. Good night Charles.'

'Goodnight, Miriam. Thank you for the lovely tea this evening.'

Miriam smiled at him, then walked away, leaving him to his writing. He wasn't her birth son, but she loved him as if he were. She wanted to say that she thought Madge was a hard, calculating sort of girl, but she didn't.

***

A few weeks later, Charles brought Madge back for tea again. Ruth was there, and as soon as Madge and Charles left, she turned to her mother and said, 'I don't like her; she's artificial. False. Somehow I just can't take to her.'

Miriam nodded. 'I feel the same way, but what can we do?' She sighed. 'Charles is totally besotted with her.'

'He's never been out with another woman! How would he know?'

Miriam shrugged. 'I know, darling.'

'And if she comes to live here when they get married, I'm moving out!'

'Oh, Ruth, darling. Don't be like that.'

'Well, as soon as Roy gets back from the war, we'll get married and move out to the country. I'm sick of the city.'

Miriam felt her life was falling apart.

***

Madge didn't take the news about Wilfred very kindly.

She frowned at Charles. 'I don't understand. I know possible spies have been interned, so was your father a spy? Is he a Nazi?'

'No, no,' Charles hastily replied. 'It's a precaution the Government had to take. Everyone born in any of the Axis countries has been interned.'

'Axes?' Her frown deepened.

'No, Axis, that's Germany, Italy and Japan.'

'I don't like the sound of it,' she muttered.

Anxiously Charles looked at her. It seemed she was having second thoughts about marrying him. He bit his lip and lowered his eyes.

'Still, I 'spose we won't be living with him, so it'll be all right.'

Charles sighed with relief.

Chapter Twenty

Some of the men in Wilfred's compound were secretly excavating a room under one of the huts. They made bags with a hole in the bottom and tied the bags inside their trousers near a pocket. They blocked the hole with a piece of cloth and filled the bags with excavated earth. Then they'd go for a walk, removing the cloth blocking the hole. With their hand in their pocket they were able to wriggle the bag to let a trickle of earth out when they could see no one was looking. The guards would've been suspicious of any small heap of fresh earth. Eventually they'd made a small room, lined with bits of wood from timber packing cases and accessed by a trap door, which had been cut in the floor of the dormitory between two beds. It had been cleverly cut so has to leave barely a sign of its presence. Wilfred knew what was happening, as his bed was just opposite the trap door, but he tried to ignore it.

Only a select few were allowed into the room.

They were trying to build a short-wave radio from bits and pieces they'd managed to find. They knew Wilfred had been accused of sending messages using a short-wave radio, so they asked him for his help.

He'd been careful in his reply. 'I didn't actually build the radio. It was my son and his mates. I can't remember exactly how it all went together.'

He could see in their eyes that they didn't believe him. They still regarded him with suspicion.

Eventually, using scraps of tin foil from chocolate wrappers, old valves from the talking picture equipment, and the use of other ingenious components, by early 1943 they managed to get a signal and send and receive information from Berlin. They were all elated to hear from the news broadcast that Germany was winning the war. A newspaper was printed with the news and distributed to a select few in the camp.

'Won't be long before we are freed and the Nazi party takes over Australia,' they said jubilantly.

Wilfred suspected that the information they received was all propaganda, but with no news coming into the camp it was hard to tell. The information they sent was pretty useless, too. Wilfred was impressed with their ingenuity, so it seemed, were the prison officers when they discovered the secret room and confiscated all the equipment.

The years dragged by. Some men who'd settled in Australia had visitors, but the isolation of Tatura and the difficulty with transport and fuel meant that visits were infrequent.

***

Charles and Madge married in 1943. Madge's parents held a reception for them. A lot of Madge's relations attended, but only Miriam, Ruth, Sarah and her husband, and Milly and Billy attended from Charles's side. Charles got the feeling that the Steiners looked down on him and his family, particularly Billy and Milly. Ruth declared them snobs.

Billy and Ron seemed to get on well. Miriam sat amidst the talk and laughter with a glass of wine in her hand and watched them.

She heard Billy ask Ron about his line of business and thought Ron's reply a bit evasive.

'Oh, I have an office in the city, do a bit of business here and there. What about you Billy?'

Billy was still working in the slaughterhouse, but had progressed to being an overseer.

'I'm in management,' he replied, with a wink towards Miriam.

She overheard Billy telling Milly later, 'Bit of a wanker that Ron.'

Charles had asked Miriam if they could move in with her until he could afford to rent somewhere else. Miriam agreed, of course. She didn't know how she'd manage without the money Charles gave her for his board.

True to her word, Ruth went to live with Sarah, to wait until her boyfriend returned from the war.

Miriam did her best to get on with Madge, who she thought was very selfish and expected the world to revolve around her. When Madge became pregnant in 1944, Charles was so excited he wouldn't let her lift a finger. Madge gave up her job as soon as she found out she was pregnant. She seemed to spend all her time sitting down with her feet up, listening to the radio or reading.

The little fibro house sweltered in the hot summer, so Miriam spent a lot of time in the garden, or reading in her bedroom. She couldn't wait for Wilfred to come home, and for Charles and Madge to move out.

'If the baby is a girl, I want to call her Sheila, and if it's a boy, Archie, after my grandfather,' Madge announced one day. 'I really want a boy.'

'If it's a girl, I'd like to call her Liesel, after my mother,' Charles replied.

'But that sounds so German! No. Definitely Sheila.' Madge sounded adamant.

When their baby girl was born, Charles went straight out and registered her as Liesel. Madge was furious. It was the first and only time Charles stood up to her.

Miriam cheered up with the arrival of Liesel, and Madge, despondent not to have a boy, was happy to let Miriam help care for the baby.

Eighteen months later, in 1946, Madge got her wish with the birth of a baby boy. It coincided with Wilfred's arrival home.

***

Miriam saw the change in Wilfred.

'I know the government had to intern enemy aliens,' he said to Miriam in bed the first night. 'But they didn't give me a chance to defend myself. I could have joined the Australian Army! I try not to be bitter, but I've lost six years of my life, and left you to cope with everything.'

He found it difficult to get work; his accent had thickened over the years of being confined with other German speakers and anti-German sentiment was rife. Everything appeared hopeless to him, and Madge didn't help. He detested her, and she couldn't stand him. He retreated into himself and thought back to his *Wanderjahre* days. He'd been so filled with ambition. All the beautiful furniture he'd planned to make.

He took his box from the wardrobe in their bedroom to find his notebook of drawings and sat on the bed, going through the pages. The last page on which he'd drawn was for the department store staircase in Buenos Aires. The last real project he'd built. He gazed into space. It had been such a success, beautiful mahogany timber, the ruby tones glowing in the light of the chandeliers lighting the staircase. And now what had his life come down to? What was the point? He couldn't get work, his and Liesel's only child married to a bitch. And now two noisy grandchildren. He found a pen and started to draw a family tree. Then tore it out, screwed it up and threw it across the room. He heard Miriam calling for him. He quickly picked up the crumpled piece of paper and put it in the box. Miriam would be sad if she saw it. She wasn't on it.

'I'm here, Miriam,' he called, dragging himself through the kitchen and out to the old wicker chair on the front porch.

'Wilfred, dear. Madge is feeding Archie, and I have to go to the shops. Just keep an eye on Liesel for me, please,' she said as she handed the toddler to Wilfred.

Wilfred blinked, unwilling to take the child. But Miriam dumped her in his lap and headed off out the gate.

Wilfred looked at Liesel, who regarded him solemnly with big amber eyes. *Or were they green eyes?* Wilfred peered closer. He thought he could see the likeness of this young child to his first love, Liesel.

He caught hold of her pudgy little hand and she suddenly gave a beaming smile. 'Ganda,' she murmured. *Oh, that smile! It was his Liesel's smile!* For the second time in his life, Wilfred was in love.

When Miriam returned from the shops, she found Wilfred down on his knees playing with Liesel. He looked up and smiled at her. 'She's a sweetie,' was all he said.

Miriam smiled, thrilled to see the change in Wilfred.

He stood up and looked at her. 'I'm fifty-six,' he said. 'I must get work. I can't sit around all day. You have been a wonderful wife, Miriam, putting up with me all these years. I thank you.' He put his arms out and enveloped her in a hug.

Miriam put down her shopping and picked up Liesel. 'I'm so happy to have you back, Wilfred,' she whispered, tears in her eyes. 'Can you bring in the shopping, please?'

***

No love was lost between Wilfred and Madge.

'Charles! We have to move to our own place.' Madge stood at the end of their bed as Charles got undressed. 'I can't stand it anymore in this place. Your father is obnoxious! He detests me! And I can't stand him. He's a miserable old sod of a German Gestapo.'

Charles blinked. He'd tried to explain that like her, they were actually Jewish, and that his father could not possibly have been a spy, let alone a Gestapo. But that didn't stop Madge calling Wilfred those names. The atmosphere had been charged since his father had returned. It hadn't helped that his father's German accent seemed more pronounced. Even Charles found it hard to follow what his father said at times. He realised Madge was right. They must move in order to keep peace in the family. He sighed. She was sullen and bad tempered most of the time and wouldn't let him near her in bed. 'All right. All right. We'll look for a place at the weekend.'

Madge sniffed. 'You'd better.'

Soon after, Madge, Charles and the children moved to a little rented house in the next suburb. They found it hard to make ends meet. Charles did as much overtime as he could to earn extra money, but Madge wasn't happy with that.

'I'm left here all day with the children and all the work to do in the house,' she complained.

Charles felt he couldn't please his wife. If he didn't work the extra hours in order to help her at home, then he didn't earn enough to keep her happy.

She seemed to have turned against Liesel. As far as Charles could see, it was all about Archie. When he tried to make it up to Liesel, Madge nagged him to pay attention to Archie. Archie was turning into a spoiled brat, Charles thought, while Madge was turning Liesel into a drudge, making her do a lot of things in the house. Too much for a five-year-old.

He said nothing. When Madge complained that she was tired from looking after the children and doing all the housework, he said he'd take them over to see Wilfred and Miriam while she had a rest.

'I don't want my son associating with that creepy old German spy,' she said. 'Take them to the park.'

So he did. However, sometimes on the way home, he called in to see his father and Miriam. Wilfred loved to see Liesel, and Miriam tried to keep Archie entertained, but Charles knew she found it hard. Archie was a destructive, obnoxious child, breaking anything he thought Liesel treasured. Charles didn't know what he could do about him.

When Archie told his mother about their visits to Wilfred and Miriam after the park, Madge put a stop to it.

***

Most Sundays Madge went to Willoughby to see her parents. In the beginning she took both children. It seemed no-one except Naomi was interested in Liesel. Everyone else focused on the boy, the coveted Grandson. Her parents indulged him, and Madge resented Naomi, who had a lovely house and plenty of money; and her husband, Ron, was happy to drive her around in his new car. But at least Madge could lord it over her in one respect. She had Archie. Naomi was childless.

Naomi found Liesel enchanting, and she started buying her nice dresses and shoes. At first Madge was pleased, but then, when

Archie wasn't receiving anything, she abruptly curtailed Liesel's visits. The focus should be on Archie. So, after a few weeks, much to her joy, Liesel was left at home with Charles.

***

On her eleventh birthday, Wilfred gave Liesel the violin he'd bought for his beloved first wife. He knew his granddaughter loved music and wanted to learn to play.

Liesel stared at the violin as if enchanted, and cradled it in her arms.

Madge scowled. 'We don't have the money to pay for music lessons, and anyway, if anyone should learn to play it should be Archie. He's the one with talent, Liesel is useless.'

Wilfred and Miriam both cringed at her words. Liesel loved to listen to classical music on the radio whenever Wilfred had it turned on, and one day out of the blue she'd said: 'I love listening to the violin, Granda. When I'm rich, I'm going to buy one and learn to play.'

Wilfred's heart clenched at her words. Archie wasn't the least bit interested in music, but anything Liesel wanted, he wanted.

'Miriam and I will pay for lessons for Liesel,' he said at Liesel's birthday party.

'Yes, and when Archie is eleven, we will pay for him to have lessons too,' Miriam hastily added, knowing that Archie would prefer a toy gun or some kind of destructive toy.

Madge sniffed. She had nothing to say to that.

Liesel loved her lessons and loved practicing.

But Madge complained all the time. 'I can't stand that screeching and caterwauling she makes with her so-called practicing,' she grumbled to Charles. 'It's a waste of time and money.'

Charles made a non-committal reply.

Liesel usually rushed home from school to do her practice, but one day she was a bit early and caught Archie coming out of her room looking a bit shifty. 'Your door was open,' he said. 'So I closed it.'

She ran into her room, closed the door and carefully took her violin case down from her little wardrobe. To her horror, when she opened the case, she found the instrument broken in half.

'Mummy,' she screamed. 'Who broke my violin? It must have been Archie!'

Madge calmly came to the bedroom door and surveyed the wrecked violin. 'I don't think so, Lee. It must have fallen out of the case, or you were careless when you put it away. Archie hasn't been near it.'

Liesel felt heartbroken. When her father came home from work, she wanted to rush to him and sob her heart out.

But her mother forestalled her. 'Poor Liesel, she's broken her violin!' she said to Charles. 'I think she was careless when she put it away last night.'

Charles looked from Liesel's white face to Madge and then to the smirking Archie. He struggled to contain his anger. He knew Liesel would've been careful with the violin, and he could see that Archie was guilty as hell. But what could he say? Or do? His father would be devastated, too. He'd have to go and see Wilfred this evening and tell him; it would be too much for his poor little Liesel to do.

He said nothing but went over and hugged Liesel. 'I'll make it up to you one day,' he whispered before leaving for the washroom.

Liesel started to lay the table for dinner.

***

Rage filled Wilfred when he heard what had happened.

'That boy needs a good thrashing!' He clenched his fists and glowered at Charles. 'He's an evil little monster. Have you no control over him?'

Charles looked down at his hands. 'I can't say anything. You know what Madge is like; she worships him. If I laid a finger on him, she'd probably call the police.'

'I should have kept the violin and let her practice here.' Wilfred paced up and down, fuming.

'But you know Madge always finds some reason for Liesel not to come here.' Charles looked up, his face a picture of misery. 'It's only when I come and bring her, and even that's getting more difficult. Madge treats her like a servant.'

Wilfred looked at Charles. He opened his mouth to say something scathing about Madge, and then changed his mind. 'Bring the violin here. I might be able to mend it.'

When Charles brought the violin the following weekend, Wilfred carefully examined it.

'It looks like it's been held at an angle and had a heavy blow on the back; probably Archie propped it against something and then jumped on it.' He took a deep breath and shook his head. 'I don't think I can do anything with it, but I can try.'

***

One evening in July, Miriam, folded her knitting and stood up. 'I'm a bit tired, my dear; I'm going to have an early night,' she said and kissed Wilfred.

Wilfred looked up from the paper he was reading and smiled at her. 'I won't be long, either.'

The next morning when he woke up, he slipped quietly out of bed and went to make a cup of tea for Miriam. He put the cup and saucer on the bedside table and said softly, 'Good morning, Miriam, my dear; I've brought you your cup of tea.'

Getting no response, he pulled back the curtains, then returned to her side and gently touched her cheek. Her skin was cold. Wilfred's heart seemed to stop. Miriam had died in the night at the age of sixty-eight. Wilfred was beside himself with grief. She'd been a tower of strength to him since the first day he'd met her in Buenos Aires. He missed her dreadfully and felt bereft at losing her.

He had a few friends, some Germans from his internment days, who kept in touch, and as he still worked, he managed to fill the time with work and doing the shopping and housework. He pottered in the garden at the weekends, and looked forward to visits from Charles and Liesel.

'Tell me about Germany,' Liesel said to him one weekend. 'We're learning about Europe at school.'

Wilfred looked at her. 'There is no Germany,' he said.

Liesel frowned. 'I don't understand. It's on the map.'

Wilfred sighed. 'To me, Germany is no more.' He refused to talk about it.

'When I'm big, I'm going to go there and learn to speak German.' Liesel smiled, thinking that would please him.

Wilfred shook his head. 'Life is all about learning to live with loss.'

Liesel frowned, a puzzled expression on her face. 'I don't understand.'

Wilfred looked at her sadly. 'Liesel, I lost my home, my country, my parents, my brother, Josef, my beloved wife, Liesel, my liberty and then Miriam. I never fulfilled my ambition to be a master cabinet maker.' His voice sank to a mutter. 'Eventually, I will lose my health ...'

Liesel stared at him, speechless.

'Leave Granpop alone, Liesel,' Charles said, coming into the room and only hearing part of his father's speech. 'He doesn't like to think about the things that happened during the war.'

***

At seventeen Liesel left school. She wanted to go to university, but didn't mention it to her mother. Like Charles, she knew Madge wouldn't hear of money being 'wasted' on a girl. She'd say that any money available should go towards giving Archie a good education.

But Liesel won a scholarship to a teacher training college. She was thrilled, and since she was already working at weekends serving in a local shop, Madge couldn't find any reason for her not to go. But she still managed to grouse.

'A waste of time,' she said. 'She'll leave college and get married, and that'll be the end of her education.'

Charles and Liesel remained silent. Archie was out with his so-called friends. Thugs, Charles privately called them.

'Perhaps I could come and live with you, Granpop,' she said when she rushed round to tell him the news, knowing he'd be delighted to hear it.

He smiled. 'Yes, that would be wonderful!'

But it would never happen.

The shrapnel, buried in Wilfred's neck since the Great War, had been slowly working its way through his chest. Being Wilfred, he'd never had it checked as the army surgeon had advised. One evening in 1965 while reaching up to a high cupboard, it finally pierced his carotid artery. Wilfried collapsed, lost consciousness, and died.

Chapter Twenty-One

L iesel eventually recovered from her beloved grandfather's death. Pat's rejection, though painful, inspired her to focus on creating a solid future for herself. She concentrated on her studies, put all her energy into completing her teacher training and looked forward to the time when she could get a job and leave home. Nothing else mattered, not even the contents of the mysterious box her grandfather had left her.

The sixties were an exciting time to be young in Australia. There was plenty of work; the contraceptive pill was available, even though the Pope had banned Catholics from using it, and Liesel felt liberated for the first time in her life. After she finished teacher training college, she had no difficulty getting a teaching job in a school in Western Sydney. Most of the pupils were the children of migrants and their language skills left a lot to be desired. However, Liesel loved the challenge of teaching them, and they seemed to love her. They thrived under her enthusiastic but somewhat unorthodox teaching methods.

At last she was able to move out of the family home. Away from the obnoxious Archie, who, not having anyone to torment, turned his attention to drinking and drugs. Madge refused to acknowledge this, blaming his bad behaviour on the company he kept.

But Liesel didn't care about Archie. At last she was free. She shared a house with two other girls. She had her own small bedroom, and they all shared the kitchen, bathroom and a lounge room. She was happy.

One day she noticed another teacher, James Conroy—dark and good looking, with a mysterious air about him—studying her in the staff room on their breaks. Whenever she looked up, he seemed to be watching her, and he'd give a tiny half smile.

One day during her playground duty, he appeared beside her. 'Need any help?'

She shook her head. 'No, I'm fine, thanks, Mr Conroy.' She continued monitoring the little ones and breaking up potential fights between the boys, feeling a little miffed that he thought she needed help.

One afternoon at the end of the day, as Liesel was coming out of the school gates, the heavens suddenly opened. She'd forgotten her umbrella and had no time to run for shelter. *Just have to get drenched.* She put her head down, prepared to make a dash for it, when a car drew up.

James Conroy leaned over and opened the passenger door. 'Quick! Jump in; you'll be soaked.'

Without thinking, Liesel obeyed.

'Where do you live? I'll drop you home.'

'Oh, that's kind of you, Mr Conroy. But just the bus stop will be fine.'

He turned to her with a smile. 'It would be my pleasure. Now, where do you live?'

She told him, then thanked him and sat with her knees together, her big bag of school work on her lap.

He glanced at her and smiled. 'Please call me James. And you are Liesel? A pretty name for a very pretty girl.'

Liesel felt her cheeks getting hot. *Pretty girl indeed! She was all of twenty-three.*

From then on, every few days he just happened to be passing as she was about to cross the road, and he'd stop, lean across and open the door for her.

'I have my bus ticket,' she'd protest, but he'd simply smile and say, 'Quick, I'm holding up the traffic.'

A few weeks later, on a very windy, wet morning, she'd come out of her front door to find him waiting for her outside.

'Thought I'd save you getting drenched or blown away,' he said with a smile.

Liesel felt flattered. 'That's really kind of you; I don't think my umbrella would survive this wind.'

He dropped her at the school gate. 'I'll just park around the corner. See you in the staff room.'

In the staff room, she was sorting through her lessons for the day when he entered. He nodded to everyone, said, 'Morning all,' and gave her a nearly imperceptible wink.

She quickly looked down at her folders.

One Friday afternoon, he stopped to pick her up and drive her home, and as she was about to get out of the car, he took her hand and said, 'Feel like going for a coffee? I'd like to talk to you about a couple of the boys in year five.'

Liesel hesitated, wondering why he couldn't bring it up in the staff meetings.

'Or perhaps you're going out tonight with your boyfriend, and are too busy?'

'No, I'm not going out, and I don't have a boyfriend.'

'Great!' He let go her hand and put the car into gear. 'There's a nice coffee place near here.'

He seemed very interested in her—asked her opinion of the current political situation and really listened to her replies. She felt flattered by his attention, and they fell into a routine of going for a coffee on a Friday afternoon after school.

One Friday they discussed a book Liesel had just finished reading.

'I'd like to borrow it, if I may,' James said.

When he stopped the car outside her house, she invited him in while she got the book.

Neither of her flat mates were at home. 'Annette and Rosemary both work in the city,' she said over her shoulder as they walked inside. 'They don't usually get home until late on a Friday. They go for drinks with their office friends.' She smiled at him and led him to her room. 'This is my little room. Come in, and I'll get the book for you.'

She walked to the bookshelf and reached up to sort through the books on the top shelf.

James came up behind her and put his hands around her waist. 'Liesel,' he said, and his hands moved up under her jumper to her breasts.

She spun round. 'James!'

James jumped back. 'Sorry, Liesel. I've wanted to do that for ages, and to kiss you.'

She just stared at him.

Then he put a hand on each side of her face, drew her to him and kissed her gently.

'Oh,' she gasped, and suddenly, before she could ask him to stop, they were kissing passionately.

James sat her down on the bed and in a husky voice asked, 'Liesel, may I? Can we?'

Mesmerised, Liesel nodded.

He lay her down on the bed, and undressed and caressed her.

She lay transfixed by what was happening to her body.

'Um, Liesel, my beautiful one, are you on the pill?' he whispered into her ear.

She shook her head.

'Then we'd better take precautions.' He searched in his jacket pocket and pulled out a condom.

***

Afterwards, she lay in his arms, her heart singing. *So this is real love!'*

Eventually, he stood and started to dress. He glanced at his watch. 'Too late for coffee. I'd better go.'

Liesel got up and wrapped her dressing gown around her. 'It wouldn't take long to make one,' she said, hoping to keep him longer.

'No, my sweet, I'd best be off.' He gave her a lingering kiss. 'Until Monday! Can't wait to see you again.'

Suffused with happiness she stood at the door and watched him driving away.

A pattern was set. Every Friday he'd take her home, and they made love. Some weekdays he drove her home, kissed her passionately in the car and then drove off.

Liesel was in love.

The other young female teachers seemed to be in love with him, too. They hung off his every word and tried to flirt with him in the staff room during breaks. But Liesel just smiled to herself, knowing James was hers.

One Friday night, a few weeks later, she lay in his arms and said 'Perhaps we can meet over the weekend. We'd have more time ...'

He nuzzled her neck. 'Bit awkward, darling,' he said, his voice muffled by her hair. 'I'm studying for my master's degree.'

'Oh, I didn't know you were studying.' She sat up. 'Of course, I understand. Of course. You must spend your weekends studying.'

The following week she went to the doctor and got a prescription for the contraceptive pill.

One Friday when they arrived at Liesel's place, they found Annette in the kitchen.

She smiled. 'Hi, Liesel; I wasn't feeling well and came home early.' She looked at James.

'Oh, this is James,' Liesel said.

'Hi.' He smiled. 'Well, I'll be off, then. Nice to meet you, Annette.'

'Don't rush off because of me,' she said.

'I was just giving Liesel a lift home from school,' he said, handing Liesel her bag of school work. 'Bye!' And he was gone.

'Hmm, he's rather dishy,' Annette said, looking at Liesel closely. 'Someone you work with?'

'Yes. He teaches at my school.' She turned to go into her room. On the one hand she wanted to say he was her boyfriend, but she wanted to hug that knowledge to herself a bit longer. When he finished his masters, he'd be able to earn more, and they could get engaged. 'Hope you feel better soon. Anything I can do?'

'No. Thanks anyway. Just a really bad headache. Hope I'm not getting the flu.' She disappeared into her bedroom.

Spring turned into summer. School work kept Liesel busy, along with swimming at the weekends and occasionally going home to visit her parents.

Sometimes she wondered when she should tell James about her being Jewish. She felt nervous about telling him, not wanting a reoccurrence of what had happened with Pat. After his masters, she thought, I'll tell him after his masters.

'When will you finish your masters?' She asked James one Friday evening. 'I'm looking forward to seeing more of you.'

'Mmmh, same here,' he replied, taking her into his arms.

***

At the end of the Christmas term, the children put on a Nativity play. Liesel coached her class and felt proud of their performance. Little Johnny Ryan played Joseph. She'd given him the part to try to boost his confidence. He had the habit of picking his nose whenever he felt worried about something, which seemed to be often, but by the night of the performance he seemed confident of his role.

The parents loved the play, too, especially when Mary asked Joseph what they should call their baby. Joseph hesitated, the index finger of his right hand rising towards his nose.

Oh no! Johnny, No! Liesel thought.

His hand wavered, then he suddenly exclaimed, 'Jesus Christ! I dunno!'

After a stunned silence, the tranquil Mary, rocking her baby Jesus doll, said, 'Oh, yes, Jesus is a good name; we'll call him Jesus,' and she tenderly placed the doll in the crib. The stifled giggles from the audience led to an outburst of clapping.

At the end of the performance, which gained an enthusiastic round of applause, Liesel looked for James, hoping to share her elation with him. She caught sight of him going towards the exit, apparently in a hurry to leave. She rushed to catch up with him, but an excited parent waylaid her. Over the parent's shoulder, Liesel saw James turn to a woman at his side as if urging her to leave. The woman turned and caught James's arm. Liesel saw the bulge of her stomach and heard the woman say, 'Wonderful, darling, you have them eating out of your hand!'

Then Liesel saw the wedding ring on his finger.

Appalled, she turned away. She felt sick, but put a smile on her face and accepted the compliments from the parents. Finally, she was able to leave.

You stupid fool, Liesel! She admonished herself. She'd been used! She was stupid. Her mother was right; she was useless. Tears stung her eyes as she blindly made her way back home. He must've been taking his wedding ring off before he got to school! No wonder he wanted to keep their affair quiet. *How many of the staff had guessed?* Her cheeks burnt at the thought.

She flung herself on her bed and sobbed her heart out.

I can't go to school tomorrow! I can't face him!

But when morning came, with her head held high, she returned to school for the last day before the Christmas holidays, prepared to ignore James.

However, in assembly that morning, the headmaster announced that Mr. Conroy had left. He'd been appointed headmaster in a regional school and wouldn't be returning next term. 'I'm sure all the staff and pupils wish him well.'

The heck I do. Liesel thought.

But she missed James, and an ache resided in her chest for a long time. She resolved never to be taken in by a man again.

Reluctantly she went home for Christmas. Her father was pleased to see her. Her mother, too, but mainly so she could help prepare the Christmas meal.

'Naomi and Granny are coming,' she said. 'We have to put on a bit of a show.'

Liesel groaned inwardly. Her mother's father had died a few years before, and her Grandmother was even more cantankerous.

Naomi was still embittered by her divorce from Ron, who'd been having an affair for several years. The affair only came to light when his girlfriend became pregnant. To add insult to injury, the baby was a boy.

Liesel found Christmas lunch an ordeal. Granny Steiner complained all the time about her arthritis and the treacherous Ron.

'Oh, shut up, Mum,' Naomi said eventually. 'I'm better off without him. Good luck to the bitch. She's welcome to him.' She looked at Liesel. 'Keep away from men,' she said giving her a dark look.

Liesel looked up. 'Indeed, I will.'

Liesel was just thinking, *Thank God Archie's not here*, when they heard the sound of a key fumbling in the front door lock.

Charles got up from the table and opened the door.

A dishevelled Archie fell into the hall.

'Archie, darling!' Madge half rose from the table. 'You're just in time to have Christmas dinner! Liesel, go and set another place and serve Archie some turkey.'

Liesel looked at Archie. He was either drunk, or high on something, or both.

Charles guided him to the table, where he lurched and sat down. 'Ev'one,' he slurred.

Liesel put a plate of food in front of him.

'Not hungry,' he muttered, then looked up at her with a leer. 'How you going Cin'rella.' His hands shook as he picked up his knife and fork. He managed to spear some roast turkey on his fork, but missed his mouth.

Naomi looked on in disgust.

Madge remained silent, then after a while said, 'Aren't you feeling well, Archie? It might be that bug you had last week come back again.'

Archie nodded.

Madge looked at Charles. 'Dad, help Archie to bed.'

Charles stood and put his arm round Archie. 'Come on son.'

Archie staggered to his room, cursing and swearing.

Madge said in a loud voice, 'Poor Archie, he keeps getting this horrible flu. Makes him really shaky.'

Liesel could see Naomi about to say something, so quickly she said, 'How's the car going, Aunty Naomi?'

Naomi had managed to get a new Mercedes car, keep the house and a hefty settlement from the divorce. 'Great,' she said, looking happy for the first time since she'd arrived.

The meal dragged on. Finally, Liesel could clear the remains of the lunch and wash up. *Don't think I'll ever get married,* she thought as she stood with her hands in the soapy water. Between her brother, that bastard James and her devious Uncle Ron, she hadn't seen much to recommend being tied to a man. Her grand-mother had never seemed very happy either. She suddenly felt sorry for James Conroy's wife. *Imagine being married to a maggot like him.* No. Marriage was out as far as she was concerned.

'Liesel, make some tea, and we'll all watch the Queen's speech,' her mother called from the dining room.

'We won't stay,' Naomi said. 'Come on, Mum. We can watch it at home, and I'll be able to have a drink.'

Madge was affronted. 'We have wine here, you know.'

'Can't drink and drive,' her sister replied.

At last they were gone. Madge settled in front of the TV with a cup of tea and a box of chocolates that Naomi had brought.

Liesel wondered what to do for the rest of the day. She went out to the shed where her father had retreated as soon as his in-laws had left. 'How're things, Dad?' she asked.

He sat on a stool, carefully cleaning his secateurs. 'So-so, Liesel. What's been happening with you?'

'Not a lot, just work.'

He nodded.

'Dad, Archie's on the downward slope.'

He sighed. 'I know, but what can I do? I think he's been stealing money from your mother, too. You know how careful she is to put money away each week for the bills. Well, it's disappearing.'

'Oh, Dad! What can we do?'

Charles put down the secateurs.

'Don't know. I've already lent him most of our savings to buy a car. He said he needed one to get a job. Then he crashed it into someone and had no insurance, so I had to lend him the money to pay for that.' He put his head in his hands, then looked up. 'Sorry, Liesel; it isn't your problem. But your mum won't accept that anything's wrong; she believes him when he tells her it's always someone else's fault.'

Liesel nodded.

He studied her. 'You don't look that well, Liesel. You're very pale.'

'Last school term of the year is always hard, Dad.' She tried to think how to change the subject. Then she remembered her grandfather's box. Somehow with college, her new job and moving out, not to mention James Conroy, she'd never had time to learn German and sort through the papers in the box. 'I was thinking of taking Grandad's box back with me,' she said.

Her father nodded and pulled a tool box from a shelf. 'Do you remember? I hid it behind these old paint tins. Your mother would never think of looking here.'

Liesel smiled. 'Thanks, Dad. I'm going back to my share house tomorrow. I'll get it before I leave. I'll get an old carrier bag to put it in. That won't arouse any suspicions.'

Charles made a sound halfway between a snort and a laugh.

Liesel managed to get through the rest of the Christmas period unscathed by her brother or mother. Once back in her bedroom in the share house, she put the box on her bed, carefully took out all the papers and spread them on the bed. Several years had passed since she'd last looked at the contents, but, now, she resolved to get a German dictionary, hopefully the next day. Then she carefully packed everything back in the box.

Next day, armed with her new dictionary, she opened the box again and took out the notebook she remembered looking at after her grandfather's funeral. Each page contained beautiful drawings and designs of stunning furniture. She sat back and looked up at the ceiling. *This must be what Pop meant about wanting to make beautiful furniture.* She closed the notebook and picked up the next piece of paper. She'd seen it before but hadn't been able to translate what it said. It took her half an hour to figure out that it proclaimed Wilfried a member of the German Communist Party. That was a bit of a shock. She shuffled through the rest of the papers until she came to a letter from a Hans Goldberg.

With the help of the dictionary, she struggled to translate it and was appalled by what she could make out. It seemed that her grandmother's brother, Hans, had sent his two children to England at the start of World War Two and had asked Wilfried to try and find them if anything happened to him.

Surely Hans would have perished in the Holocaust.

She scanned through the other papers, but this was the only one from Hans.

She sat for a while, then came to a decision. She'd go and find these long-lost cousins. She was certain that was what her grandfather had wanted her to do, what he'd meant when he'd told her father she was the only one who could fulfil a request.

Bugger that James Conroy, she thought, calling him all kinds of names in her mind. *I'll do what my darling Grandpop would have done if he'd been able.* First, she must learn German and translate all the documents properly. Then she would find out what had happened to Samuel and Rebecca.

***

In January, at the start of the next academic year, Liesel enrolled in a night class to learn German.

An elderly woman replaced James at her school, and Liesel thought this new English teacher's classes must be pretty boring compared to James's. *Care factor low*, Liesel told herself. She applied herself to her German lessons, and though she thought some of the other students were rather nice—one in particular—she made a resolution not to let herself get involved. *Never again.* She was obviously a poor judge of character.

Eventually the day came when Liesel had saved enough money for her fare to England. She applied for a visa which allowed her to work for five years in the UK. From what she'd heard, they were crying out for teachers in London.

Her father seemed pleased when she told him her plans. 'That will be a great opportunity for you,' he said. 'Well done, love.'

But her mother was displeased. 'Waste of money,' she sniffed on the way to the airport. 'You could put the money down as a deposit on a house instead of frittering it away travelling.'

Liesel just smiled and winked at her father. 'Yes, that would've been a better option, Mother, but it's too late now.' She gave them both a quick kiss on the cheek, put her small travel bag over her shoulder and lugged her suitcase to the check-in counter at Sydney Airport. 'Give Archie my regards!' she said gaily.

The journey seemed to take forever. After five stops, she eventually arrived at Heathrow Airport on a damp, drizzly morning at the end of August. *So this is an English summer's day!*

She'd arranged employment from Australia and was due to start work at a council school in London the first week in September. One of her friends from college had moved to England two years before and told Liesel that she could stay with her until she got settled.

'It's only a bedsit, but you can sleep on the floor until you get your bearings,' Jane had written.

Chapter Twenty-Two

England, 1968

It always seemed to drizzle in England—fine, soft rain, not like the tumultuous downpours in Sydney, which were often followed by sunny skies. Liesel thought it made the sky seem low. She found everything strange. But London buzzed, and Liesel soon became caught up in the excitement. Her teaching job was much the same as in Australia, except that the children mostly had Cockney accents—it took her a while to get used to them. The others were Jamaicans, Indians and a mixture of other nationalities.

Her friend Jane immediately included Liesel in her social life, and Liesel had a wonderful time, but one evening two months after she'd arrived, Jane drawled, 'Love having you here, Liesel, darling, but it's getting a bit awkward. I'd like to invite Pete over for the night, but ...' She paused from painting her nails to look at Liesel.

'Hmm. Okay, I guess I'd better start looking for my own place.' Liesel felt a bit guilty about imposing on Jane for so long.

'You know my friend Jennifer?' Jane concentrated on her left little finger. 'Well, she's in a share house with two others and one of them is moving out ...'

'Sounds good!' Liesel said briskly. 'Do you think she'd be happy to have me?'

Jane smiled. 'Absolutely!'

Liesel moved the following weekend.

***

At the end of the Christmas term—her first term working in England—Liesel thought back twelve months to the James Conroy episode. She'd come a long way since then.

She found the build up to Christmas exciting with the dark evenings, Christmas lights and carol music everywhere. So different from Christmas in Australia.

Christmas Day found her in the share house on her own. The others all had family to go to. They'd each asked her to come to their family homes for the day, but Liesel didn't want to be the stranger at the feast.

'Thank you, but I have other plans,' she'd told each of them.

She slept late, then took her breakfast back to bed, enjoying being able to just loll around in bed. Eventually, she stretched, got up and dressed, and wondered what she'd do for the rest of the day, which seemed to stretch out in front of her. She turned on the radio. A church service was being broadcast, and the ponderous tones of the service soon made her turn it off. She turned on the tiny black-and-white television in the shared living room, but the same church service was being screened. She turned it off.

I'll go for a brisk walk.

After an hour walking through the quiet streets, she came back to the flat. *I'll write home.*

Half way through her letter, while wondering what on earth to write, a thought suddenly struck her. She'd done nothing to trace Hans Goldberg's children! But where to start?

She fetched a note book and sat down to make a plan. At the top of the page she wrote, *Procedure for finding Samuel and Rebecca Goldberg*, then she underlined it and sat sucking the end of her pen while she thought. Next, she wrote: *Children's Rescue Transport; Find a synagogue and ask if there is an organisation for refugees.* Then under that, *Look in the telephone books for people called Goldberg.*

She couldn't think of any other items, but a tattered phone book sat on a shelf behind the TV, so she took it down, then got out the box containing the papers and her miniature violin, which she kept carefully tucked away under her bed.

Hans, who was her grandmother's brother, had married Marlene, and it seemed they'd had two children. These children, Samuel and Rebecca would be her father's cousins. So that would make them about her father's age. Probably Rebecca would have married and have a different last name. She should focus on Samuel Goldberg.

Feeling a mounting excitement, she opened the phone book, quickly found the G's and then lots of Goldbergs. And a lot with the initial S. She looked at the cover of the phone book and discovered it was only for a small area of London! Her shoulders sagged. He could be anywhere in England. Or Scotland. Or Wales. There could be hundreds of S. Goldbergs.

She turned on the television again. It broadcast the Queen delivering her Christmas message. Liesel left it on and went into the kitchen, made herself a sandwich, then found a bottle of wine and spent the rest of the day in front of the television, feeling homesick.

***

Liesel woke early on Boxing Day, wondering why she always wanted to sleep in on a school day, but woke early at weekends and holidays. Her head pounded from too much wine the night before, so she got up, made a cup of coffee and then went back to bed with two painkillers.

The house was quiet without the others and the bustle of getting ready for work. She lay and thought about her next step in her search for her what? Great uncle? Second cousin? Maybe learn some more German? She'd go to Germany as soon as she had money for the fare. Perhaps in the Easter holidays.

The sound of the front door opening roused her from her doze. One of her flat mates had returned. Liesel pulled on her dressing gown and walked out to the kitchen.

'Hi there!' Jennifer smiled. 'Did you have a nice Christmas?'

Liesel returned the smile. 'Lovely, thanks, and you?'

'Yes, but it's good to be back. Christmas is so exhausting, trying to keep the peace with all the family.' She sat down at the table. 'Mmm coffee smells good.'

Liesel jumped up and put the kettle on. Then had a thought. 'Jennifer, if you were trying to find a long-lost relation, how would you go about it?'

Jennifer sat back in her chair and frowned. 'Dunno.' Then after a moment, she added, 'Well, I suppose the phone book, or maybe an ad in the paper.'

'An ad in the paper! What do you mean?'

'Oh, you see them all the time, in the personal columns. "Looking for Fred Bloggs, relation of Joe Bloggs, used to live in Birmingham. Contact Box no xxx" that kind of thing.'

The kettle boiled. Excited, Liesel got up to make the coffee. 'What do you mean, 'Box no xxx?'

'Well you put the ad in the paper and they give you a box number. People write to the paper stating that box number and then the paper will forward their letters to you. I think you have to pay for them to be posted on to you. Not sure, something like that, anyway.'

A thrill went through Liesel.

Jennifer cradled her cup of coffee in her hands and studied Liesel. 'Why? Who are you searching for?'

'Oh, a cousin of my father who came here during the war ...' Liesel said casually. 'What paper would be good?'

Jennifer tilted her head thoughtfully. 'Not sure. Go and buy one or two of the most popular ones and see what kind of notices are in their personal columns.' She got up and yawned. 'Might lie down for a bit, late night last night and too much to eat and drink. Happy Christmas; glad it's over, Liesel!' She gave Liesel a grin as she went off to her room, leaving the mug of half-drunk coffee on the table.

'Happy Christmas!' Liesel echoed. She put the cups in the kitchen sink, then found her notebook. She'd go to the newsagents in the morning. Filled with enthusiasm, she got out her German books and started to learn a few new words.

Chapter Twenty-Three

England, 1969

*E*lderly gent requires housekeeper ... No. *Nanny to care for two delightful toddlers ...* Definitely no. Liesel scanned the rest of the personal ads. Ah, this one was more like it:

Betty Baker, last heard of in Plymouth, went to Plymouth Grammar School in 1954. Her friend Bridget wants to get in touch. Contact Box No 8612.

Liesel looked for the advertising section and found the details of how to put an ad in the personal columns. She'd try the main London papers first, then perhaps the regional ones. *I'll go to the library when they reopen after the Christmas holidays and check out the regional papers.*

She spent a while forming her advertisement, finally coming up with:

Seeking Samuel Goldberg, son of Hans Goldberg, who came to England with sister Rebecca with the Children's Refugee Transport in 1938. Please contact Box ....

Pleased with her ad, she went to the post office to get postal orders and stamped self-addressed envelopes for the replies, then she posted her advertisement. While she waited for a response, she decided to visit a synagogue to see if she could find out about the refugee children.

***

The first synagogue she visited couldn't help. When she asked about the Children's Refugee Transport, the young rabbi shook his head.

'Don't really know much about it,' he said, 'but I have heard of it. It's called the *Kindertransport* now. Apparently, there was a group who organised the evacuation of Jewish children, but I don't think they'd give out any information without the consent of the evacuees.' He looked at her, a smile on his face. 'So you're a Jew, yourself?'

Liesel nodded. 'Apparently, yes.'

'Orthodox?'

Liesel noticed him studying her hair. 'No.'

'Ah. Well, but you're welcome to our synagogue,' he said.

'Thank you, Rabbi.' Liesel held out her hand.

The Rabbi looked at it, then nodded his head. 'Any time I can be of service.'

Disappointed, Liesel went back to her bedsit. Every evening after school, she checked the mail that had plopped onto the doormat. Apart from the odd letter from her father, nothing of any interest arrived.

After a month, she decided to try the regional papers. She'd gone to the local library and found a list, but there were hundreds of them. She was beginning to think this whole quest was a waste of time, but decided to put ads in five regional papers before giving up. It was beginning to get expensive.

She sent off her stamped, self-addressed envelopes and postal orders for the ad, and the days went by. The only replies seemed to be from lonely people who wanted to keep writing to her or losers thinking there must be money in it for them.

The cold winter turned to spring. Liesel's first in England. She was delighted when the bare trees started to show a hint of green and the leaves appeared as the weather warmed.

Her flat-mates and Jane included her in their activities, and Liesel felt happy and secure in herself. Then one day she picked up the mail from the bristly doormat and found one for her. She left the others on the hall table and went to the kitchen. *Cup of tea first*, she thought.

Cup in hand, she went to her room, kicked off her shoes and sat on the bed, her legs stretched out, toes wriggling in bliss. She tore open the envelope and took out the letter, expecting the usual begging letter or offer of employment.

Dear Box Number,

I saw your advertisement in the Western Gazette. My father is called Samuel. His sister, Rebecca, died some time ago. They came to England on what has come to be called the Kindertransport, in 1938. I spoke to my father, and he said his father, called Hans, had a sister called Liesel. He thinks that sister went to Argentina.

I've never replied to a box number advertisement before so I'm uncertain as to whether your advertisement is genuine. I'd be pleased if you could supply more information as to the purpose of your query.

Please reply to

Benjamin Goldberg, c/o The Post Office, Street, Somerset.

Liesel sat up on the bed, her heart thumping, finding it hard to breathe. 'Yes!' she shouted. 'Yes! I've found them! Grandpop, you'd be so happy!'

She suddenly realised she was crying. Taking a deep breath, she got her writing paper and pen and wrote back.

Dear Mr Goldberg,

Thank you for your letter. I'm so thrilled. It seems we might be related.

My grandfather, Wilfried Schönbaum married Liesel Goldberg, and they emigrated to Argentina sometime in the 1920s. Liesel died young, of cancer, and Wilfried subsequently remarried a few years later and changed his name to Martin when he migrated to Australia.

My grandfather received a letter from his brother-in-law, Hans, in 1938 telling him that he was trying to get his children, Samuel and Rebecca to England on a children's evacuation plan, and if he didn't survive, for my grandfather to find them and look after them. Unfortunately, the war intervened and my grandfather didn't get the opportunity to carry out his brother-in-law's wishes.

Before he died, my grandfather told my father that he thought I might be able to find his nephew and niece. After he died, I found the letter from your grandfather and resolved to see if I could find out what happened.

Liesel stopped. Should she tell him anymore? No. See what he had to say. Although it seemed genuine.

Can you tell me the name of your grandfather's wife?

If he wrote back and said Marlene, then she'd know he was authentic. Should she continue using the box number or put her actual address on the letter?

I look forward to hearing from you.

Yours sincerely,

Liesel Martin.

Taking a chance, she put her address on the top of the letter. Excitement filled her as she hurried out to the letterbox to post it.

***

Every evening after work, she rushed back to her bed sit to check the post. It took a week for a reply to arrive.

Dear Miss Martin,

Thank you for your letter. Yes, it certainly seems we may be related. Your family history matches what my father remembers his father telling him about his Aunt Liesel. My grandmother's name was Marlene. I wonder if you could make a copy of the letter from my grandfather to your grandfather? My father would be interested to see it.

Yours sincerely,

Benjamin Goldberg

Next morning Liesel went to school with the letter from Hans to her grandfather in her bag. At break she asked the school secretary if she'd mind copying it for her.

The secretary frowned. 'We're not really supposed to do this for private correspondence, Miss Martin.'

Liesel's shoulders sagged. 'Oh, I see. Thank you, anyway.'

'But as it's just one sheet, I can make an exception.' The secretary smiled. 'Beautiful writing,' she added when she came back with the letter and the copy.

'Thank you so much!' Delighted, Liesel hurried back to her class.

***

Dear Mr. Goldberg

I enclose a copy of the letter as requested.

Yours sincerely,

Liesel Martin.

***

Dear Miss Martin,

I'm sorry to take so long to reply, I had to wait until I got some time off work to visit my parents and show my father the letter. He was quite speechless when he read it. Thank you for sending it.

He was sixteen when he came to England on the Kindertransport, so he was still able to read the German easily and translated it for me. He has asked if it would be possible to meet you. It would seem that he and your father are first cousins.

I see by your address that you live in London. My father and mother could come up to London on the train and meet you and your family if you could let us know a convenient date and time.

Yours sincerely,
Benjamin Goldberg

***

Dear Benjamin (I hope you don't mind me calling you that as I think we must be second cousins!)

My family all live in Australia, so I'm the only one living in England. I'm here on a visa, teaching at a school in London. I'd be delighted to meet your parents.

Any weekend is fine for me. Sunday is best because I often have school activities on Saturday mornings.

Regards,
Liesel

***

Dear Liesel,

How strange that you're a teacher. So am I! As you're here on your own, my parents suggested that you might like to come to

Somerset one weekend, possibly in the Easter school holidays and stay with them for a few days. They live in Bath. There's a good train service to Bath. You have to change trains at Reading.

I teach in a private boarding school in a small town called Street, and I have to work most weekends. I'd like to meet you, too, so the school holidays would be more convenient. At the school where I teach, as we have to work on Saturdays, our school holidays start a few days before the government schools.

Regards,

Ben.

***

Liesel was thrilled to get this letter. *Relations in England!* She'd be able to tell her flat-mates that she would be visiting relatives in Somerset at Easter when they'd be going to see their families.

After school she went to a stationer, bought a map of England and found Bath in the South West. Then she bought a map of the southwest of England and hurried back home to look up Street.

She was poring over the map when Carol, her other flat mate, came in. Flopping down at the table, she kicked off her shoes. 'Is the kettle boiled?'

'Just made a pot of tea,' replied Liesel. 'Shall I pour you a cup?'

'You're a darling! Yes, please.' She glanced at the map. 'So where are you off to with your map?'

'I have cousins living in Bath, and they've invited me to stay for a few days over Easter. I was just looking at where Bath is. Their son works in a school in a town called Street. At least that's what he said. How can a town be called Street?' Liesel put the cup of tea in front of Carol.

'Thanks. You'll love Bath,' Carol said as she took a sip of tea. Then she looked at Liesel and added, 'Teaches in Street? There's a very expensive private school there; I forget the name. I wonder if that's where he teaches.'

'Mmmh. Don't know.'

Carol got up with her cup of tea. 'Going to put my feet up for a bit.' She went into her room.

***

Liesel was bursting to write to her father and tell him all about Ben and what she'd found out, and that she'd be going to visit them at Easter. But, how could she? Her mother would get the letter, read it and want to know what it was all about. Liesel could just picture her mother with a sour expression on her face, saying, 'How come I wasn't told about letters to that old German Nazi!' which would put her father on the back foot.

Dear Mum and Dad,

I hope you're both well. It's Spring here now, but still quite cold. My job is going well; the kids are mostly very nice.

How could she let her father know that she was making progress on the family search?

I've found out some interesting things about violins, and I'm thinking of starting to learn to play again. I've found someone by the name of Goldberg, who might be willing to give me lessons.

Yes! Surely her father would realise what she meant! She didn't think her mother knew her grandfather's first wife's maiden name, but her father would get the connection.

My flat-mates, Carol and Jennifer, are very nice.

Love from Liesel.

Chapter Twenty-Four

England, Easter 1969

T he approach of the Easter holidays filled Liesel with excitement.

'What do people wear in the country here?' she asked Carol, who laughed.

'The same as they wear in town, unless they're huntin'-shootin'-an-fishin' types with their wellies and Barbour jackets,' she said. 'But it's probably unlikely your relatives are like that. Just wear your normal clothes. Maybe a pair of good walking brogues in case they're country walking types.'

'Brogues! What on earth are brogues?' Liesel's eyebrows arched.

'Just strong leather shoes. Don't worry, whatever you wear for walking will be fine.'

Liesel packed her bag and her grandfather's box and set off on Good Friday. The train was crowded, but she managed to get a window seat. The countryside fascinated her—so different from Australia. It was early April and the bare trees just showing hints of pale green. She loved the train journey to Somerset: the green countryside; the little fields; the sheep and lambs, and the old farmhouses with paddocks and horse jumps that dotted the landscape. And she loved the names of the stations where the train stopped.

Ben had told her that his parents would meet her at Bath Spa station. She didn't know what to expect. How would they know her? She needn't have worried. As the train pulled into the station, she saw a man and woman about her father's age anxiously scanning each carriage. She pulled her bag down from the overhead rack, got off the train and walked towards them.

The man she'd seen approached her. 'Excuse me, are you Liesel Martin?'

'Yes, are you the Goldbergs?'

'We are. How lovely to meet you.' Samuel Goldberg greeted her. 'This is my wife, Evelyn.'

They all shook hands. 'Come, our car is outside,' said Samuel, taking her bag. 'Ben will be here soon; he had a few things to sort out for his work.'

Liesel felt shy, unsure what to say to these new relations, but they soon put her at ease. She'd been expecting the Goldbergs to live in the kind of house she'd seen in the pictures of Bath—elegant sandstone terraces—but Samuel finally stopped the car in a cul-de-sac outside a small brick house in a row of terraces.

Liesel thought that all the houses she'd seen in England had the same layout. You went through the front door and into a hall, where a passage led to a small kitchen, then two other rooms, a dining room and a lounge. And to the side of the passage way stairs led to the bedrooms and a bathroom at the top of the stairs. No laundry, and usually only one toilet, upstairs in the bathroom. The Goldberg's house was the same.

Evelyn opened the front door, and with a flurry of scrabbling, an enthusiastic spaniel came rushing to greet them.

'Down, Bessie.' Evelyn turned to Liesel. 'Do you like dogs? Bessie is getting on now, but she still likes to welcome visitors.'

'I love dogs,' Liesel bent to pat Bessie, whose stubby tail seemed to propel her whole rear end in a crazy dance.

'I'll show you your bedroom.' Evelyn Goldberg smiled. 'I expect you'd like to freshen up after your journey. Have you had lunch? You must be hungry.'

'I had a sandwich on the train, thank you.'

'Oh, British Rail sandwiches! Come down when you're ready. I'll put the kettle on.'

Liesel smiled to herself. She'd noticed that English people always had a kettle ready to boil to make a cup of tea. 'Thank you; that would be lovely.'

'Our spare bedroom is only small,' Evelyn said apologetically, leading the way upstairs. 'This is the bathroom, and your room is here.'

'It's charming.' Liesel beamed. A pretty little room, it had matching curtains and bedspread, and a little bedside table—no wardrobe but a coat rack with coat hangers on it.

'It's still a bit chilly at night, so I put an extra blanket at the end of the bed if you need it,' Evelyn said.

'You're very kind.'

'My husband is so thrilled you've come. You mightn't realise it, but to have contact with his family after all these years is amazing ...' Evelyn shook her head in wonderment. 'My family are all from around here, but he's never had anyone. Right. I'll make the tea.' Then she had a thought. 'Oh, would you prefer coffee? I know young people seem to prefer coffee these days ...'

'Tea would be lovely.' Liesel smiled.

Evelyn left and Liesel went to the bedroom window and looked out onto the front garden—just a pocket handkerchief of grass with a few spring bulbs showing. After using the bathroom, she combed her hair and washed her hands, drying them on the towel Evelyn had left at the end of her bed. She peered out the bathroom window and saw Samuel getting out of his car and opening the doors of what looked like a shed, but must be a garage, at the end of the garden. He parked the car and then came out and started to walk down the garden path. There seemed to be a road giving access to the back of the houses.

Back in her room, she opened her bag, carefully took out her grandfather's box, and took it downstairs.

'In here,' Evelyn called, as she carried a tray with tea things on it into the dining room.

'Can I help?' Liesel asked.

'No, no, it's all done.' Evelyn turned to her husband. 'Put a match to the fire, Sam, please; it seems a bit chilly in here.'

Liesel looked around the room. Plum coloured velvet curtains framed a big window which looked out onto the back garden, bare except for a few daffodils and snowdrops. Two comfortable-looking armchairs sat on either side of the fire place, and a sideboard, dining-room table and chairs and a large bookcase filled with books made the room feel warm and inviting.

Evelyn followed her gaze. 'The garden will be pretty again, as soon as the weather warms up.'

Bessie jumped up and raced out of the room at the sound of a door opening.

'It's Ben.' Evelyn went out to meet him. 'Ben, your cousin is here!'

Liesel was surprised to see a tall, well-built young man with fair, curly hair and grey eyes enter the room. She'd expected someone with dark hair who looked like a younger edition of her father.

Smiling, he held out his hand. 'Welcome, Cousin Liesel.'

She put the box on the table and took his hand. 'Hello, Cousin Ben. This is the box my grandfather, your Uncle Wilfried, left to me,' she said nodding at Samuel, who didn't seem able to stop staring at her.

'Just give me a few minutes to take my stuff upstairs,' Ben said. 'Don't start without me.'

Evelyn smiled at her son. 'Come, Liesel, sit down.' Evelyn indicated a chair at the dining room table, then she sat down and took the embroidered tea cosy off the tea pot. 'I'll pour the tea, and please help yourself to cake.' She looked at Liesel and raised her eyebrows. 'Do you like your milk in first?'

'Yes, please, no sugar.' Liesel took a piece of the cake. 'Um, this is delicious.'

Ben came in and sat down. 'Thanks, Mum,' he said, taking his cup and saucer.

The Goldbergs all looked at Liesel's box.

Liesel took a sip of tea and then looked up at their expectant faces. 'Except for the violin, it's really only papers.' She said as she opened the box. She took out the papers, put them to one side, and then carefully lifted out the velvet-wrapped miniature violin. As she unwrapped it from the velvet, Samuel gave a gasp.

'*Gott in Himmel*,' he exclaimed.

His wife looked at him in surprise. She'd rarely heard him speaking German.

He held out his hand for it. 'Where did you get it? It was my Aunt Liesel's. She left it behind when she went to Argentina.' He could hardly get the words out. 'I thought it was lost after *Kristallnacht* when my father's shop was looted. Your grandfather's name is written inside. He made it for her.'

'No,' Liesel replied slowly. 'This has my grandmother's name inside. Liesel Goldberg. Look inside. You may need a magnifying glass to see it.'

'I'll get one.' Ben stood up.

Samuel's face went white. His hands shook as he took a handkerchief from his pocket and wiped his eyes.

When Ben handed him the magnifying glass, Samuel peered inside the violin. 'You're right. The one my aunt left behind had Wilfried Schönbaum written inside. I'm sure of it. My father had it put away, but I distinctly remember one year, when I was about ten years old, he took it out to show us what a fine craftsman Wilfried was. He said Wilfried put his name inside so Liesel wouldn't forget him when he went to do his national service and then fight in the war.'

Liesel frowned. 'My father told me that my grandfather would have been on the German side in the First World War.'

Samuel nodded. 'All young German men had to.' He sat back in his chair, a faraway look on his face. Then he shook his head. 'I cannot believe this.' He suddenly pushed back his chair and stood up. 'Excuse me for one moment.' They heard him going upstairs. Ben got up to go after him, but his mother put out her hand.

'Leave him, my dear.'

He sat back down at the table, studying Liesel.

Evelyn turned to Liesel. 'Ben said you're a teacher. What do you teach?'

'At the moment, I'm teaching in a London primary school. It's quite a challenge. Some of the children have very poor language skills, and my Australian accent doesn't help. Sometimes I don't understand them, either. It makes for interesting classes!'

'Yes, I can imagine.' Evelyn continued to make conversation. 'And where is home for you in Australia?'

'A suburb in Sydney called Greenacre.' Liesel laughed. 'Well, it probably had very green acres at one time, but now it's all houses.'

'Yes, that's happening here, too,' Ben said.

Hearing Samuel coming back downstairs, Evelyn got up. 'I'll put more hot water in the teapot.' She left the room and checked on

Samuel. A few minutes later, they both came back into the dining room. Samuel looked more composed.

He smiled at Liesel. 'I'm sorry; this has all been a bit of a shock to me. It's brought back a lot of memories.'

'Perhaps you'd like to look at all these papers, Mr. Goldberg,' Liesel suggested. 'I've tried to translate them, but my knowledge of German isn't very good. I'd appreciate it if you had time to translate them.'

Suddenly Ben, who'd been silent until now, interrupted: 'Perhaps he made two violins.'

They all looked at him.

'Wilfried, I mean.'

Liesel nodded. 'Yes, that's a possibility.'

Samuel stared at his son. 'I wish I could remember all that my father told me about his brother-in-law. I got the impression that he rather idolised Wilfried. I cannot believe I have a family in Australia that I never knew existed until now.' He got out his handkerchief and blew his nose. 'I wonder if your parents could come to England? I'd love to meet them, especially your father. My cousin.'

Liesel couldn't imagine what these kindly people would make of Madge. 'I don't think that's very likely,' she replied after a pause. 'My family aren't well off.' She didn't mention the fact that most of her father's savings went on bailing Archie out of trouble. She couldn't invite the Goldbergs to her shared flat. There was no room for one thing.

Samuel nodded. 'I understand. We, also, are not well off.'

Evelyn said, 'Sam, you're a bit pale. Why don't you take these papers Liesel has brought and sit by the fire and read them? Then after supper you might be able to tell us what they say.'

Ben also looked at his father, concern in his eyes, then he turned to Liesel. 'Perhaps Liesel might like to see something of the town,' he suggested, looking at his watch. 'It's only three o'clock. We could visit the Roman Baths.'

'That would be lovely.' Liesel's eyes brightened.

'A good idea.' Evelyn stood. 'Get some fresh air before supper.'

'It isn't far,' Ben said as he and Liesel left the house.

They walked briskly into the centre of the town. Although it was April, and spring, the air was quite chilly. The houses surrounded by snowdrops and daffodils entranced Liesel. 'It's so beautiful,' she said, looking up at Ben.

He smiled at her. 'I guess it's quite different from Australia.'

'Everything is so old! I love it.'

They walked along in companionable silence, until Ben said, 'Thank you for coming, Liesel. I think it's good for my father to talk about what happened in the past. He's never mentioned it to me, and I don't think to my mother either.'

'I'm only sorry I didn't ask my grandfather more about his past.' Liesel sighed. 'But every time I tried to talk about it, he just clammed up. He was interned during the last war, and I didn't know until after his funeral.'

'Goodness. That must have been hard for him. For how long was he interned?'

'I think about six years.'

Ben shook his head, and they continued in silence until they reached the Roman Baths.

'You mean these baths have been here since the Romans were here?' Liesel asked. 'When was that?'

'Oh, I think maybe eighty AD.'

'What! One-thousand, nine-hundred years ago!' she exclaimed, overawed.

Ben looked at her with a smile, then took her inside the baths and they strolled around the museum. 'I think they close at sunset, and it's starting to get dark; we'd better go,' he said eventually. 'We can come back another day, if you like.'

Liesel smiled at him. 'This has been just the greatest day; thank you, Ben.'

As they walked back to the Goldberg's Liesel turned to him and asked, 'Tell me about your work; what do you teach, Ben?'

'Maths and Music. The violin and piano. I know that might seem a strange combination, but the Maths was in case I wasn't good enough to make a career in music.'

Liesel stopped walking. 'No wonder you looked at the miniature violin so closely! My father told me that his mother, Liesel, was a violinist, but he can't remember much about her. My grandfather gave me her violin on my eleventh birthday. I was learning to play it, but then ...' She stopped.

'Then?' Ben prompted.

'Something happened to it.' She didn't want to launch into how her obnoxious brother had broken it.

'That's a pity. Perhaps you could start learning again. I could ...' He paused. 'We'd better hurry; it'll be dark soon, and my mother will worry.'

Liesel looked at him with a frown. 'Worry?'

'Well, you know mothers!' He smiled. 'They worry about everything and nothing.'

Liesel didn't think her mother had ever worried about her.

***

After supper that night, which to Liesel seemed to be more like a dinner, Evelyn Goldberg said, 'Sam has lit the fire in the sitting room, so we can go there and be nice and cosy. We usually have a cup of tea about now, would you like one, Liesel?'

'Yes, that'd be lovely. Can I help you?'

Evelyn shook her head. 'All prepared,' and she led the way to the front room, which was simply furnished but overflowing with books, and with a piano against one wall. Liesel looked around. Bessie spread out in front of the fire, and books lay every-where—on the coffee table, the settee and stacked up against the wall by the fireplace. Evelyn pushed aside the books on the coffee table to make room for the tea tray.

'What a lovely room,' Liesel exclaimed. 'It's so welcoming. I love reading, and it looks like you do, too!'

Evelyn smiled. 'Yes, we all do.' She poured the tea and set the cups and saucers on the coffee table.

Samuel Goldberg shifted uneasily in his armchair. His wife sat down in the chair opposite him. Ben moved some books to make room for Liesel and indicated that she sit on the settee.

Samuel Goldberg suddenly coughed and then said, 'I was think-ing that perhaps I should tell you a bit about your family, Liesel, from what I can remember.'

'Oh, that would be wonderful!' Liesel sat forward on the settee. Ben too. He'd told Liesel that his father had never spoken about his past.

Samuel seemed nervous. 'I don't know anything about your other great grandparents, Liesel, that would be Wilfried's parents, but I can tell you about your great grandfather, Fritz. He was such a kind and well-liked man. His wife, my grandmother, died before I was born.

'My mother, Marlene, had received a message that her mother wasn't well. They lived in a village called Ladenburg, about three hours walk from Mannheim where we lived. So that particular week, my mother begged my father to take us there. It was a Wednesday, not really a good day, but Rebecca and myself were having difficulty getting to the Jewish school. You see, Jewish children were banned from going to the public schools, so Jews had to form their own schools. We all had to wear armbands with the Star of David on them. Even Jewish people who had converted to Christianity were still classed as Jews. I heard recently that the Mormon Church supplied the Nazis with lists of Jews. I don't know how true that is.' Samuel paused to drink some of his tea. 'The shop wasn't busy, and my mother was worried and restless. She was adamant that we all had to go. My grandfather, Fritz, said he'd be all right in the shop, and he wasn't up to the long walk anyway. We left early in the morning. It was midday when we reached my other grandparent's little house. They were happy to see us ...

'My father did a lot of jobs around the place, brought in firewood and my mother did some things around the house—cooking and washing as my grandmother had been too ill to do much, and my grandfather was quite old and infirm. By the time they'd done all these things, it was dark and too late to walk back to Mannheim. So we stayed the night. I forget where my parents slept, but Rebecca and I slept on thin mattresses in the kitchen in front of the stove.' Samuel appeared distressed.

Evelyn took his cup and saucer. 'I'll get you another cup of tea, my dear.'

He nodded and then continued, 'The next morning, after breakfast, we started to walk back to Mannheim. We were not far from home when we were met by one of my grandfather Fritz's friends, who was a Christian, I think. He knew where we'd gone and walked to meet us. He told us the terrible news. The synagogue had been torched, shops and houses belonging to Jews had been burnt and ransacked, including ours, and my grandfather had been arrested. Then he told us there was no point in going home that night. The place had been looted then gutted. He had friends who would shelter us. My father and I went to see the shop next day ... there was nothing left ... just a burnt-out empty shell.

'It came to be known as *Kristallnacht*, the night of broken glass. I'm sure you've heard of it, Liesel?'

Liesel felt her face go red. 'No. I'm afraid my knowledge of German and Jewish history is very poor.'

Samuel nodded. 'Yes. Best forgotten.' He went quiet.

'What happened then?' his wife prompted.

Samuel's eyes focused on her. 'Well, my mother wanted to go back to her parents; she thought we might be safer there. We'd heard terrible things about the concentration camps. My father was worried about us. He was afraid I'd be put to work for the Nazis and was even more afraid for Rebecca. Well, these kind people took us in. My father knew that my grandfather had hidden some gold in the back garden. He told this friend where to find it, and he went and got it and brought it back. My father had already found out about the Children's Refugee Transport. It was difficult to get on that. You had to be sponsored by someone. The Quakers, good people, brought a lot of Jewish children over to England. The British Government said they would take ten thousand children, but no parents. And they had to be either sponsored or have fifty pounds to keep them. Fifty pounds was a lot of money in those days.'

Samuel stopped again. He seemed to be reliving the past. 'Anyway.' He gave his head a little shake. 'This friend managed somehow to get the money from changing the gold. I don't know how on earth he did it. I was lucky. I was sixteen at the time, and there was an age limit of seventeen.' He took a deep breath.

'Rebecca and I left for England. Our parents were devastated. It must have been so hard for them to let us go.' He looked at Ben, as if wondering if he would've been able to send Ben away. 'That must have been when my father wrote to your grandfather.'

Liesel inclined her head in a gesture of acknowledgement. The atmosphere felt so tense. She could feel Ben beside her on the settee; he seemed to be holding his breath.

'Somehow, Rebecca and I were taken to Mannheim station and got the train to Frankfurt with other Jewish children. That was the last time we saw our parents. I'll never forget their stricken faces.' He paused and blew his nose. 'Then from Frankfurt we went to Bentheim and then Holland. The journey seemed endless. I tried to stay close to Rebecca, and when she went to the toilet and didn't return, I was frantic. When I saw her again, I was weak with relief. Then we got a ferry to Harwich, in England. We were sent to a disused holiday camp. It was winter, and the camps weren't designed for the cold.' Samuel drifted off again.

Evelyn stood and put a hand on Samuel's shoulder. 'I'm going to make a fresh pot of tea, my dear.' She turned to Ben. 'Ben, dear the fire needs more coal.'

'Of course, Mum.' He jumped up. 'Out of the way, Bessie.' He pushed the snoring dog away from the hearth and, using the coal tongs, carefully positioned lumps of coal on the embers.

Liesel watched him, fascinated. Then she suddenly remembered her visitor's duties and got up and followed Evelyn to the kitchen. 'Please let me help,' she said.

Evelyn turned to her and smiled. 'No need, my dear, but I'm worried about my husband, he has never ever mentioned any of this before. I'm not sure if it's a good thing. He seems so drained and exhausted by it.'

'Oh, it's all my fault!' Liesel clapped a hand to her mouth. 'I'm so sorry, perhaps I shouldn't have come and opened up these old wounds.'

'No,' Evelyn said slowly. 'I think it may be better for him to talk about it. Perhaps it's a form of release.' She lit the gas flame under the kettle.

'Shall I wash these cups and saucers?' Liesel asked.

Evelyn smiled and put her hand on Liesel's shoulder. 'It's wonderful that Sam has found a relation he never knew he had.'

The fresh pot of tea made, they went back to the sitting room.

Samuel appeared more composed. Ben looked at his mother and raised his eyebrows. She nodded in understanding, and Liesel marvelled at how this family all seemed to understand each other.

The English seem to live on cups of tea, she thought, taking her cup and saucer from Evelyn.

Samuel took a deep breath and smiled. 'So! Rebecca and I were in England. She was put in a girls' dormitory, and I was put in a boys'. I asked that we wouldn't be separated. It was a bit chaotic. When they saw that I was a fairly big and strong boy, the organisers decided I should be sent to a farm to work. I couldn't speak any English, but there was a kind woman who translated for me. I told her that I absolutely had to have my sister with me. I think they understood and did their best. The next thing we knew, we had labels pinned on our coats, and we were put on a train with some other children and a supervisor. Rebecca and I were lucky. We were sent to a little village in Somerset. A farm. I was put to work, milking cows and feeding cattle with *manglewurtzels*.'

'*Manglewurtzels!*' Liesel exclaimed; she couldn't stop herself from interrupting.

Samuel grinned. 'It sounds strange now, but it was a very nutritious winter cattle food that was easy to grow and stored well. Sometimes they're just called *Mangolds*.'

'I'm sorry, I didn't mean to interrupt, but that sounded so like something scary out of a children's book! Please, do continue.'

'You're thinking of Worzel Gummidge, the scarecrow,' Ben said.

Now Liesel was completely confused.

Samuel took a breath. 'Anyway, it was freezing. Rebecca was also at the farm, but was sent to school. They found an old bike for her, and she cycled the six miles to school every day with Mary, the farmer's daughter. Didn't matter what the weather was like. Then she helped after school with making butter, looking after the hens and the housework. The school she went to had classes from eight in the morning until twelve noon and then another school that had been evacuated from London used the school from midday until four o'clock. So she had all afternoon to help on the farm. In the evenings she and Mary taught me what they'd learnt at school. And so I became fairly proficient in English.'

He looked at Liesel, his eyes twinkling. 'Do you detect a German accent in my speech?'

Liesel thought for a moment, then shook her head. To be honest she'd heard so many different accents since coming to England that she couldn't hear any difference in Samuel's.

'Luckily,' Samuel continued, 'because I was already fairly proficient in Italian and French, I was able to learn to speak English quite quickly. And it's a Germanic language so that helped. Rebecca showed me her textbooks, but I have to say that I found Shakespeare and Chaucer very difficult.'

Hmm, Liesel thought, *actually, so do I!*

'As soon as I turned eighteen, I wanted to join the forces and fight the Nazis. The authorities were in two minds. Not sure if I should actually be interned as an enemy alien, or whether to use my German-speaking abilities as a British spy.'

Evelyn drew in a sharp breath. 'Samuel! Why haven't you told me any of this before?'

He shrugged. 'My darling, it's all in the past. Not relevant—no good going back. I'm only telling this now as I think Liesel deserves to know her family background.' He looked at Ben, who had sat up straight and was frowning at his father. 'Yes, you probably should know this too, my son.'

Ben sat back, took a deep breath, but said nothing.

Liesel wanted to take Ben's hand, but didn't like to; she'd heard that the English were very reserved.

Tears came to Samuel's eyes. He paused and took his handkerchief from his pocket. As he blew his nose, Evelyn stood.

'Goodness,' she exclaimed. 'It's half past nine! I think Liesel must be tired after such a long day. I think we might get ready for bed.' She smiled at Liesel. 'Come, my dear, I'll make a hot water bottle for you. I know it's Spring, but it's still chilly at night.'

'Of course, Mrs. Goldberg, I'm sorry to have taken so much of your time.'

'Oh, Liesel, please call me Evelyn.'

Samuel stood and gave Liesel a watery smile. 'My dear, it's been a delight to meet you and have you to stay. Forgive me for getting a bit emotional, and, please, call me Sam.'

Liesel took his hand. 'I'm so grateful to you for sharing my family history with me. I know it must be painful.' She didn't know if she should give him a hug, but he patted her shoulder with his other hand.

'Goodnight, my dear.'

Ben stood up and took the tea tray. 'Good night, Dad.' He nodded at his father.

***

Liesel lay awake going over in her mind all that she'd heard. It had been an eventful day. *Imagine if my grandfather hadn't gone to Argentina.* He'd have been arrested, and my father would have been sent to work until he starved to death. And I wouldn't have been born! Eventually she fell into a deep sleep.

A loud gurgling noise which seemed to come from the room next door woke her with a start. Then the gurgling stopped, and she heard what sounded like an alarm clock. She needed to go to the toilet—*all that tea!*—so she pulled a cardigan over her pyjamas and tiptoed to the bathroom. Voices came from the bedroom next to hers. The gurgling couldn't have been anything very serious, like drains or anything.

On her way back to her room, the door next to hers opened, and Evelyn Goldberg appeared, a dressing gown wrapped around her.

'Oh, my dear,' she whispered. 'I hope our Teasmaid didn't wake you?'

'No, no,' Liesel replied with no idea what a Teasmaid was.

'Would you like a cup of tea? There's only enough in the pot for two cups, but I can go downstairs and make you a cup. Or would you prefer coffee?'

'That's lovely of you, but can I make a cup of coffee for myself? That's if you don't mind. I'm sure I can find everything.'

Before Evelyn could answer, the other bedroom door opened, and a tousled looking Ben came out, tying his dressing gown and suppressing a yawn.

His mother turned to him. 'Oh, Ben, Liesel would love a cup of coffee; would you make her one?'

'Love one myself,' Ben said with a smile. 'Go back to bed, Mum. Your tea will be getting cold.'

They wandered down to the kitchen. Bessie, who had her basket in the kitchen, stretched and began wagging her tail.

Ben yawned, filled the kettle and put it on the gas ring, then, bending down and patting Bessie, said, 'Come on, old girl, outside for a wee.' He opened the back door and let her out. 'Only instant coffee, I'm afraid,' he said to Liesel as he got the cups and saucers from the dresser.

'That'll be fine,' Liesel said, pulling her skimpy cardigan around her shoulders. *At least I'm wearing pyjamas, not a nightie. Mental note: buy some kind of elegant dressing gown.*

Ben looked at her. 'I was thinking,' he said, 'that perhaps it would be a good idea to leave my parents alone today; if you like I could take you for a drive. Would you like to see Glastonbury Tor? It's near where I teach. It's Easter Saturday, so it'll be pretty busy everywhere, but the Tor should be fairly peaceful.'

'Oh, that'd be lovely.' Liesel really was pleased to be able to visit the area.

'Then there's Wells Cathedral, which is pretty special,' Ben continued.

'Are you sure? I don't want to put you out if you have other plans. I'm happy to wander around Bath.'

Ben handed her a cup of coffee. 'It'd be a pleasure.'

'Thank you, and oh, I wanted to ask you; what's a Teasmaid?'

Ben burst out laughing. 'It's a machine to make tea. I bought it for my parents as a Christmas present. It's an electric kettle with a metal tube coming out of the top. At night you fill the kettle with water, put tea in the tea pot and adjust the metal tube so that it goes into the tea pot. Then set the alarm. Five minutes before the alarm is due to go off, the kettle boils, the water evaporates up into the tube and is syphoned out into the tea pot. After a few minutes, the alarm goes off and a light comes on, and voila! Tea is ready to pour out!'

Liesel grinned. 'I heard this strange gurgling noise ...'

'Yes, I don't know why they bother with an alarm; the noise of the tea pot being filled is enough to wake the neighbourhood. But my parents love it. My father used to go down every morning and make my mother a cup of tea, now the jolly old Teasmaid does it!'

'Sounds like a lovely idea.'

When Ben mentioned at breakfast that he and Liesel were going to visit Glastonbury, Liesel felt that Evelyn was somewhat relieved.

***

Liesel settled back in Ben's old Austin A30, and they set off to Glastonbury.

The names of the villages they passed fascinated her. 'Farrington Gurney! How cute,' she said, then, 'Wow, Chewton Mendip. How did those towns get their names?'

'No idea,' Ben replied. A little later, he said, 'Liesel, it's been so good meeting you,' then, tentatively, 'so ... do you have a boyfriend waiting for you back in Australia?'

Liesel paused before replying, 'No, Ben. No boyfriend. There was, but it didn't work out.'

He glanced at her and saw her set expression. 'I'm sorry.'

'Don't be. He was married and I didn't know.'

'Oh. That must have been tough.'

'Yes.' Liesel looked resolutely ahead. They drove on in silence until she said, 'How about you? Girlfriend?'

Ben sighed. 'No. There was, but at that time I was playing in a youth orchestra. She didn't like the fact that I was working at night and weekends, and then travelling. Orchestras have to play at night and travel! She found someone with a nine to five job that was more secure.' He shrugged. 'And then the government funding for the orchestra was cut, and I was out of work. I managed to get this job teaching maths and music.' They both fell silent after that.

Several minutes later, Ben took a sideways glance at her and said, 'We're coming to Wells. Would you like to see the cathedral or Glastonbury first?'

'Glastonbury please.'

***

They walked up to the top of Glastonbury Tor. Liesel looked around at the countryside. 'It quite flat,' she said

'This area is called the Somerset Levels. Jesus came here with his uncle, Joseph of Arimathea. In those days, the Levels were flooded and the Tor was like an island.'

Liesel frowned.

'Jesus and Joseph walked to the top of the Tor,' Ben continued. 'Joseph stuck his staff in the ground before they left, and it grew into a bush, and flowers twice a year.'

Liesel looked at him sceptically. 'Really? So what were Jesus and his uncle doing in Somerset?'

'They came to get tin from the mines all along the south west, mainly Cornwall, but they must have got swept up the Bristol Channel,' Ben said matter-of-factly.

'Why would they want tin?'

'They smelted it with copper to make bronze.'

'You really believe that?'

'Of course!' he said, with a twinkle in his eyes. 'All good Somerset people believe that!' He laughed. 'Come on, race you to the bottom!'

Liesel felt over-awed by the antiquity of Glastonbury and Wells. It seemed that everywhere she looked, Ben had a story about ancient times.

Eventually, after they'd had lunch at an old pub in Glastonbury, looked at a few shops and seen Wells Cathedral, Ben said, 'I guess we'd better head for home. I think my father might have more to say about his experiences in the war.' He smiled at her. 'Thank you, Liesel, it's been amazing to hear Dad talk about all these things; I had no idea.'

Liesel nodded. 'Yes, it must have been awful for the Jews in Germany at that time. Do you keep the Jewish faith, Ben?'

He hesitated. 'Um, no. I think my maternal grandmother is Jewish, but she doesn't practice. Her husband, my maternal grandfather isn't Jewish, and we've never observed any Jewish traditions. I really don't know what my father thinks about religion. It's funny, but it's never been a subject we've talked about. Strange now I think about it, since we've had animated discussions about just about everything else!' He gave a small laugh. 'How about you?'

'About the same as you. My parents never spoke about religion. In fact, they didn't talk much about anything. Not like your family, Ben.'

They lapsed into a comfortable silence until they reached Bath. 'Thank you, Ben. It's been a lovely day,'

Ben turned to her. 'It's been lovely for me too, Liesel. It's interesting to see familiar places through the eyes of a foreigner. I never realised what an amazing heritage I have.'

***

After their evening meal, they sat in the sitting room. Samuel turned to Liesel with a smile.

'Perhaps we should hear more about your side of the family before I continue with my story.'

'Oh!' Liesel blinked. She hadn't expected this. 'Well, I don't really know that much. My father, Charles, was born in Germany, then, apparently, when he was about four or five, his father, Wilfried and his mother, Liesel, emigrated to Argentina. I think Wilfried had joined the German Communist Party and that was banned in Germany at some stage. Anyway, after they'd been in Argentina for two or three years, Liesel died of cancer.'

Evelyn drew a sharp breath at this. 'Was it ...' She indicated her breast.

Liesel gave a slight shrug. 'I don't really know. But after a couple of years, Wilfried married his landlady who was an American with two daughters, and he changed his name to Wilfred Martin. His new wife, Miriam, had friends in Australia, and because things were getting hard for Jews in Argentina and the rise in fascism they migrated to Australia.' She paused. 'I've only recently got this information from my father. He never spoke of it until my grandfather died.'

Samuel nodded. It seemed he could relate to that.

'Well, that's about it really,' Liesel continued. 'When war broke out my grandfather was interned for about six years. During that time my father married and my brother and I were born.'

'So what does your brother do?' Evelyn asked with a smile.

Liesel studied her hands. Should she tell them the truth? She looked up at them. They were good people; she couldn't lie to them. She dropped her gaze. 'Um, I'm afraid he's a bit of a waster; doesn't do much at all.'

Ben reached over and took her hands, and Evelyn stood and walked over to her. She touched Liesel's head. 'I understand, my dear. That happens in families. Now, how about I make a fresh pot of tea?'

Liesel smiled through the tears that started to form. 'Thank you,' she said, her voice husky. 'I'll come and help you.'

***

Back in the sitting room, everyone looked at Samuel expectantly. It seemed they all thought it was his turn to continue with the family saga.

Samuel appeared vague. 'I think I might be repeating myself ... my sister and I arrived on the ferry and were taken to this holiday camp. Except it was winter and freezing cold. But we were given hot food. When it came to night, my sister didn't want to be separated from me or I from her. It was very awkward. We ended up sitting in the entrance vestibule together. Some people came and gave us blankets. I was terrified of being separated from Rebecca.

'Anyway, next morning they gave us breakfast and told us we'd be getting the train to a family who would take us in ...'

Chapter Twenty-Five

1938, Samuel and Rebecca

A friendly woman pinned labels on Samuel and Rebecca's coats. The labels bore their names and the name and address of the family who'd agreed to take them in. She then beckoned them to follow her.

Mutely they did as they were told. She took them to a railway station where the woman spoke at length to the guard and then indicated that they should get on the train.

Bewildered, they got into a carriage where noise and bustle, and a language they didn't understand, surrounded them. When they arrived at a station with a big sign saying, 'Paddington', the guard came and got them and indicated that they should get off the train.

They stood on the platform, confused, until another woman came forward, examined the labels pinned to their coats and said, 'Come with me.'

It sounded a bit like, *'Kommen sie mit!'* They followed her to another platform.

The woman found the guard and spoke to him, then she put them in a carriage, gave them a packet of sandwiches each and said, 'You get off in Somerton. SOMERTON.' Then she gave them a piece of paper with *Somerton, Mr Marshall* written on it. 'The guard knows,' she said, then walked away.

Samuel looked at his sister. She was close to tears. He opened his packet of sandwiches and handed her one. It had some kind of pink stuff in it, but he was hungry and quickly ate his. He wondered if Rebecca would eat hers. She was sniffling. *Better wait and see.*

The train trundled on through the English countryside. Eventually they both fell asleep, until the train came to a juddering halt, and the guard called 'Somerton'. Luckily, he was a kind man and came and looked for Samuel and Rebecca.

'Come on, kids! You must get out here!' He shook them awake, and they hastily grabbed their small bags and followed him.

They stumbled onto the platform, shivering with the cold. There weren't many people there.

'Be you Samuel and Rebecca?' A kindly looking man, cloth cap pulled down on one side of his head, approached them and peered at the labels on their coats. 'Yes, you are. Come with me.'

Bewildered, Samuel and Rebecca stood, looking around.

'Come on! Can't keep the hoss waitin'' It sounded like *Kommen.* They followed him outside to a waiting horse and cart. 'Up you get!' He helped them up into the cart. 'My name is Mr Marshall. You'll be staying with me and my wife at the farm.'

Samuel thought it sounded like the man said *'Meine namen ist Mr Marshall.'* He replied, *'Meine namen ist Samuel.'*

'Aye,' said the man. 'And your sister is Rebecca.'

Samuel nodded; he thought he understood. *'Ja.'*

They continued their journey in silence. With the bare trees, the countryside looked much like winter in Germany. He pulled his thin coat around him, put an arm around Rebecca and drew her to him.

Mr. Marshall, seeing this, leaned back and pulled an old blanket from behind him. 'Wrap this around you,' he said.

After what seemed like an hour, they reached a small village.

'Yer we be,' said Mr. Marshall briskly, stopping in front of a rambling two-storey stone building with a thatched roof. A low stone wall fronted it, and bare bushes stood behind. 'Open t'gate, young 'un.' He nodded towards the gate.

Samuel interpreted the nod, jumped down, opened the gate and shut it after the horse and cart had gone through.

Mr. Marshal smiled at him. 'Told me you didn't speak English! You'm smarter than they thought!'

A woman and a young girl came out from the house as Rebecca got down from the cart and looked about her. The girl, who had mousy-coloured straight hair and wore thick spectacles, came forward.

'I'm Mary.' She looked at the label on Rebecca's coat. 'You are Rebecca. Welcome.' And she smiled.

Rebecca nodded and gave a sigh of relief. *Wilcommen* was what she heard.

'My mother, Mrs Marshall.' Mary spoke slowly.

Rebecca understood. Mother, *Mutter*.

Mr Marshall beckoned to Samuel to follow him to the stable and showed him how to take the harness off the horse and put the cart away. He seemed to be of the opinion that you start the way you mean to continue.

Mary seemed enthusiastic. An only child, she now she had a companion close to her own age. She took Rebecca up to her room. 'Look, Dad has put a bed in here for you, next to mine. Do you want to unpack?' Mary put out her hand to take Rebecca's bag.

Rebecca clutched her bag to her chest, then put it down on the bed behind her. It only contained her toothbrush, a pair of dirty knickers and pyjamas. She felt reluctant to take these out of the bag in front of this girl.

Mary frowned slightly, at a loss for what to do. Rebecca hadn't spoken since she came. 'Come, we'll go down to the kitchen. It's warmer there.'

Rebecca followed her. Samuel and Mr Marshall were already there, and Mrs Marshall was asking if they'd like a cup of tea. Mr Marshall was saying he had to get the cows in to milk and did Samuel want to come and help. The two German children, however, understood nothing. They looked around helplessly.

Mary suddenly said, 'What about the vicar's wife? She might be able to speak German. Didn't she go to Switzerland last year?'

Her parents looked at her with relief. 'Yes! Quick, run around to the vicarage and ask vicar's wife if she can come around. Explain the problem.'

Happy to be of use, Mary pulled on her coat and skipped off.

'I'd better get to the milking,' said Mr Marshall, leaving his wife and the two children alone.

Mrs Marshall, indicated chairs at the table, took a jug of milk, put a mug each in front of Samuel and Rebecca and raised her eyebrows. 'Milk?' she said.

'*Milch?*' they heard. '*Ja, danke.*' They both replied.

'*Yes, Thank you.*' Mrs Marshall poured out the milk and looked at them.

'*Ja*, Tank you.'

The children sat in silence, and Mrs Marshall wondered if this had been such a good idea. The vicar had asked if anyone could take in Jewish children who were being evacuated from Germany due to persecution, and of course, her husband, softie that he was, had immediately said yes!

It seemed like ages before Mary returned with the Reverend Davey's wife.

Mrs. Marshall brewed a pot of tea and got out a cake she'd made that afternoon.

'Oh, the little darlings,' cooed the vicar's wife. 'Look, I found a German phrase book that I had last year when I went to Switzerland.' She produced a slim blue book. 'This should help.' She opened the book. 'See it's got the numbers, one, two, three and so on *eins, zwei* ...' she opened another page. 'Ah, here we are: *My car has broken down.*' She paused. 'Hmm maybe not that phrase. Ah, this is more like it: *Waiter, another fork*; *Kellner, noch eine Gabel.*' She looked up triumphantly.

Samuel and Rebecca looked at her, puzzled. What had waiters and forks to do with anything?

When she saw their faces, Mrs. Davey frowned, then smiled. 'Anyway, I'm sure this little book will help! I must be on my way now; there's choir practice tonight. Are you coming Mrs Marshall?'

Mrs Marshall shook her head. 'No, but Mary will. And perhaps she can bring Rebecca?'

'Of course!' Mrs Davey took off with an airy wave of her hand.

Mrs Marshall took Samuel up to the attic. 'I'm sorry but this is the only spare room we have,' she said. 'Rebecca is in with Mary. Leave your bag here and come down for supper. Oh, and the toilet and bathroom are here.' She took him downstairs to the next floor. 'That's Mary's room and that's mine and my husband's.'

Samuel didn't understand what she was saying, but he guessed he'd be sleeping in the attic room, and toilet sounded like *toiletten*. He nodded. 'Tank you.'

They ate their evening meal mostly in silence. Samuel and Rebecca didn't know what to say, and the Marshalls were puzzled as to how to address their guests.

After the meal, as Mary helped her mother clear the table and wash the dishes, Rebecca got up to help. Mary put a tea cloth into her hands and showed her the clean dishes to dry. 'Plate,' she said, handing Rebecca a plate.

Rebecca repeated, 'Plate.'

Mary smiled, enjoying the new situation. It had been great taking Rebecca to choir practice. They'd been the centre of attention. Of course, Rebecca hadn't been able to sing from the hymn sheet, as she couldn't read the words, but Mary had demonstrated that she could hum instead.

That night in bed, Mary heard muffled sobs coming from Rebecca's bed. She lay for a while wondering what to do, then she had an idea. She turned on the little torch she'd been given for her birthday, crept out of her bed and rummaged in a cupboard, coming out with a big knitted rabbit. Gently she pushed it in with Rebecca.

'*Danke*,' came a muffled sound.

'Thank you,' Mary automatically replied.

***

The next day, being Sunday, the Marshall's got ready for church.

'What'll we do with Samuel and Rebecca?' Mr. Marshall said to his wife.

She shrugged. 'Well, we can't leave them here on their own, and there's no Jewish place around here, so I suppose they'd better come with us. Learn about a proper Christian God.' She pursed her lips. 'And their clothes! It looks like those are the only ones they've got. I'd better find something of Mary's for Rebecca; she can't go to church dressed like that.'

William Marshall looked at the children and scratched his head. 'Look out something of mine for the boy. It'll be too big for him, but at least it'll be clean.'

The two children obediently followed the Marshalls to the church. They really did look like orphans: Samuel in baggy pants and a much too big jacket, and Rebecca in a dress and coat that hung on her emaciated frame. They'd never been inside a church before. They looked up at the stained-glass windows in awe. It was just a village church, with a small congregation, most of whom studied these newcomers with interest.

When the vicar started his sermon, he indicated the children. 'We welcome these poor, unfortunate, persecuted children to our village,' he announced, his plummy accent giving weight to his words. 'They have had to leave their own home and family, and the Marshalls have been so generous as to welcome them into their home. We must all do what we can to help them.'

Everyone turned to look at the Marshall's pew. Mary's heart swelled with pride. She thought she'd like to be a missionary when she left school.

'Now, our sermon for today is based on the parable of the Good Samaritan,' continued the vicar.

'Don't look German, do 'em?' one woman whispered to her husband.

Her husband wondered what German children were supposed to look like.

When the Marshalls got up to take communion Rebecca and Samuel hesitated, then stood up to follow them. Mary shook her head and indicated that they should sit back down. Slowly and enunciating every word, she said in a loud whisper, 'You have to be confirmed first.'

After church and a heavy meal of roast beef and Yorkshire pudding, Mary went up to her room and came down with a blackboard and chalk. She took off her glasses and polished them.

'We will have an English lesson,' she said, speaking very slowly to the Goldbergs. Then she wrote on the board, *My name is Mary*, pointed to herself and repeated the words.

Samuel and Rebecca understood quickly.

Thirteen-year-old Mary decided that perhaps teaching would suit her better rather than being a missionary. Missionaries sometimes got boiled alive and eaten. She'd seen scary pictures in one of her books. That didn't happen to teachers.

***

After doing all their chores, Mrs Marshall said to Mary, 'Don't forget your music practice, Mary.'

'Of course, Mum,' she said, then turned to Rebecca. 'Come, Rebecca.'

Silently Rebecca followed her to the parlour. Her eyes widened when she saw the piano. She went over and stroked the keys.

Mary opened her music book and put it on the stand. 'I can teach you how to play,' she said.

Rebecca stared at her.

'Sit down. I'll show you Middle C and explain.' Mary patted the music stool.

Obediently Rebecca sat down then looked at the music. '*Für Elise*,' she said.

Mary clapped her hands. 'Well done, Rebecca. You're really learning English quickly.'

Rebecca gave her a bewildered look, then put her hands on the keys and started to play.

Dumbfounded, Mary stood watching her.

The door suddenly opened and her mother burst in. 'Well done, Mary, you're really coming on with that piece ...' she started to say, then when she saw who was sat at the piano her expression changed. 'YOU are supposed to be doing your music practice, Mary. Not the refugee.'

Rebecca stopped playing at the tone of Mrs Marshall's voice and stood up, hanging her head. '*Entschuldigung*,' she said softly.

'I think she means sorry,' Mary said to her mother, then, 'Mum, Rebecca is so good. Can she come to music lessons with me?'

Her mother frowned. 'There's no money for extra lessons.' She turned and left the room.

***

Eager to do their bit, the villagers searched their wardrobes for clothes that might fit the refugees. Very few of the clothes seemed suitable, or were even appropriate for teenagers. But Samuel and Rebecca expressed their gratitude and tried to appear in Church wearing an item at least once. Gradually they settled down in their new home.

They learned to speak English, albeit with a West Country accent. Mr. Marshall found an old bike for Rebecca, and he and Samuel cleaned and oiled it and put on new tyres. Rebecca was thrilled, she'd never had a bike before and would now be able to ride to school with Mary. Although she was a year older than Mary, the headmaster put her in the same class as her at the grammar school, hoping that she'd soon catch up.

Rebecca excelled at French and Maths. The French teacher lent her a German/English dictionary, and with its help she managed to do well in Chemistry and Physics, which didn't need pages of

English, like History and Literature. She found History difficult. She'd never learned about the English Kings and Queens before, only the German Emperors and their battles.

Samuel worked hard on the farm, and in the evenings, he diligently taught himself to read with the help of Rebecca's dictionary.

Chapter Twenty-Six

Bath, England. 1969

S amuel took a deep breath. His wife, Ben and Liesel just looked at him. Each engrossed in their own thoughts.

How awful, Liesel thought. She tried to imagine what it would be like at fourteen-years old being sent to a country where you didn't know the language or know anyone, and with only your brother for company. And you might never see your parents again! Well, with her brother, she'd gladly leave him in a foreign country on his own. And Samuel had been sixteen. She looked at him now. He looked exhausted.

'Shall I put the kettle on?' Liesel stood, making the others jump.

'Oh, yes please, my dear! I think a nice cup of tea is just what we all need!' Evelyn rose from her fireside chair. She put a hand on Samuel's shoulder. 'I think that's probably enough for tonight, my dear.'

Ben got up too. 'Yes, that's a lot to think about.'

His father sat, deep in his memories.

***

The next day, Easter Sunday, Liesel woke to the usual gurgling of the Teasmaid. With a smile, she pulled her long woollen cardigan over her pyjamas and went downstairs to put the kettle on. Bessie got out of her basket, wagged her tail and stretched.

'Come on, Bessie,' Liesel whispered, unlocking and opening the back door.

Just as the kettle started to boil Ben appeared. 'Happy Easter, Liesel.' He presented her with an enormous chocolate Easter egg.

Liesel's eyes widened, taken aback. 'Oh, my goodness! How lovely. Thank you, Ben. But I didn't think to get you one.' She reached up and gave him a kiss on his cheek.

A deep blush suffused his face. To hide this, he got mugs from the dresser and started spooning instant coffee into them.

Liesel laughed. 'One spoon is enough, Ben.'

'Yes, of course.' He tried to spoon some granules back into the jar, then he turned to her, serious now. 'Thank you, Liesel, for coming here. I know it's been an ordeal for my father to go over all these experiences, but I think it may have been cathartic for him to get it all out; stuff he's been keeping bottled up for years. Let's go into the sitting room. I think it's still warm from the fire last night.'

They sat with their hands around their mugs, each thinking their own thoughts.

'Would you like to go somewhere today?' Ben asked out of the blue.

'Yes, but I really don't want to take up too much of your time. I didn't expect to have a tour guide for my visit here, you know.'

'I'm really enjoying our outings.' Ben smiled at her. 'I thought you might like to see Clifton Suspension Bridge, and perhaps Bristol Zoo?'

***

'Ben makes everything sound so interesting,' Liesel said when they got back that afternoon. 'I'd never heard of Isambard Kingdom Brunel before. Ben's a good teacher.'

Ben smiled. 'Not really; I'm sure if you took me around Sydney, you'd be equally good at telling me about its history. I wouldn't know the names of Australian bridge builders.'

'Somerset is beautiful. I think I could live here very happily.' Liesel quickly changed the subject.

'Wouldn't you miss the Australian climate and your family?' Evelyn asked with a smile.

Liesel smiled back, then, anxious to change the subject, she turned to Samuel. 'Will you tell us more about your experiences when you came here?'

Evelyn looked at him, a frown creasing her forehead. 'It won't be too much for you, Sam?'

He shook his head. 'Well ... in 1940 there was a lot of ill feeling about enemy aliens. Winston Churchill was under intense pressure when he said, 'Collar the lot!' meaning intern all people born in Germany or Italy over the age of eighteen. Well, the next thing I knew, a policeman turned up at the Marshall's farm to say I was under arrest. He was very apologetic. I think he was probably embarrassed as he knew the Marshalls well and knew they wouldn't have been harbouring a spy.

'It was awkward as by this time Mr Marshall depended a lot on me. Two of his farm hands had gone off to join up. I think they thought being in the army was better than getting up at half-past four every morning to get the cows in and milk them, and again in the evening.

'I was taken to a prison for a few days, and then to the Isle of Man to an internment camp. It was really rather nice. They'd put barbed wire around a section of guest houses. You see, The Isle of Man was a popular holiday resort for the English, so there were lots of boarding houses. It was full of Austrians and Germans and most of them were professionals, teachers, doctors, musicians and so on. I suppose some of them may have been Nazi spies, but they didn't show it. They soon organised schools and activities. I loved it!' Samuel gave a sheepish smile. 'I know it sounds strange, but instead of having to get up at dawn every day and work hard, I was able to relax and go to classes and learn things. Also, to speak German again. Rebecca and I had agreed that we'd only speak German if we were on our own together, which didn't happen very often. The worst thing was having to leave Rebecca. But I knew she was reasonably happy and well cared for ...'

He paused, lost in thought, as the memories came back. 'I asked some of the other inmates if they knew what had happened to the men arrested during *Kristallnacht*. The consensus was that they'd have been sent to Dachau or another concentration camp.' He sighed, then continued. 'Well, then the authorities interviewed each of us and we were divided into categories: Category A was for the hard-core Nazi sympathisers; B was for people who could be released, but with restrictions; and category C, for those who could be released unconditionally. I came within the Category C, and they told me to join the Pioneer Corps. I think because I was young and strong. We were basically set to doing labouring work. Building Nissen huts and clearing the bombed towns and cities.

'Then, after about eighteen months of this, I was asked to go to London for an interview. I was asked lots of questions and then told I'd been selected to join a special unit, because I could speak fluent German.'

Evelyn interrupted. 'I must start the dinner, can we continue later, Sam?'

'Of course, my dear.'

Chapter Twenty-Seven

1942, Rebecca

A t least, living on a farm, they didn't get bombed. But they often heard the Luftwaffe going overhead to bomb Bristol. And once a German plane came down in a field close by. That caused a lot of excitement.

The farm meant they had enough to eat. Rationing wasn't as hard for them and everyone did their bit. Mary and Rebecca kept rabbits, gathering dandelions every evening after school to feed them. They mixed bran with used tea leaves, which the rabbits seemed to like. While Mary and Rebecca were at school, one of the farm hands dispatched the young rabbits and sent them to the local butcher.

With Samuel gone, there was even more work to be done around the farm. Mary and Rebecca did their best, helping with feeding the cattle as well as their usual duties. Rebecca missed her brother; in some ways it was good that she was so busy or she'd have felt even lonelier. She was brilliant at maths and physics, and soon got through her homework.

Mrs Marshall wasn't happy that Mary would ask Rebecca for help with her maths, not liking to think that a foreigner could do something that her daughter couldn't. She pursed her lips with disapproval, and said, 'I'm sure you can do it without Rebecca's help.'

'But, Mum! I don't understand it, and Rebecca is so good at maths! Thank goodness I'm not taking physics.'

Rebecca wanted to go to university to study maths and music, but she'd need to pass the Matriculation in English and Latin. She spent long hours studying these subjects, much to Mrs Marshall's annoyance.

'There's butter to be churned and the hen house to be cleaned out,' she grumbled.

Rebecca always jumped up and readily did these chores.

It seemed that every week in assembly, the Headmaster would read out the name of an old pupil who'd been killed in action. Some of whom had been at school only a year or so before and known to the girls.

The most exciting diversion was the arrival of the Americans, with their currency of cigarettes, chocolate and nylons, who were stationed near their school, much to the delight of the senior girls. As all the road signs had been removed to confuse the enemy in case there was an invasion, the girls were sometimes stopped by tanks and asked directions by the tank drivers.

Mary left school to take a secretarial course in Bridgwater, a market town a few miles away, where she stayed with relatives, only coming back to the farm on weekends. With Samuel interned, Rebecca was the only one left at the Marshall's during the week, so she'd a lot more work to do when she got home from school.

One morning at school assembly, the headmaster announced yet another casualty of the war who'd been a past pupil, and then said, 'I'd like to see Rebecca Goldberg in my study after assembly.'

Rebecca's heart stopped, and then started to pound. *Had Samuel been killed?* Slowly she made her way to Mr. Rose's study. She'd never had occasion to be summoned to the headmaster's study. She knocked on the door.

'Come!'

She opened the door and stood nervously staring into the book-lined room.

Mr Rose looked up from behind his large desk. He took his pipe out of his mouth, tapped it on his desk and smiled at her. 'No tobacco; it's only a habit,' he said. 'Sit down.' He indicated a chair facing him.

Rebecca trembled, steeling herself for bad news.

'Rebecca. One of my Cambridge associates has contacted me and asked about possible students who are fluent in German and good at maths for a secret mission. I put your name forward.'

Rebecca let out her breath.

The headmaster pushed his glasses down his nose and studied her. 'Is that a problem?'

'I really wanted to try for a scholarship to university,' Rebecca said in a timid voice.

'Yes, well, there is a war on, as you know.' He frowned at her. 'This is a chance for you.'

'But what is it exactly?'

'I haven't been told. Apparently, it's top secret.' He stood up, so Rebecca did too. Then he leaned over his desk and handed her a piece of paper. 'Ring this telephone number and you'll be told what to do.'

She looked at the piece of paper. 'I don't understand.'

'Well, I'm sure it will all be made clear in due course. Now, run along, child! Oh, and you can use the phone in my secretary's office.'

Rebecca nodded. 'Thank you, sir.' She studied the piece of paper as she made her way to the school secretary's office and knocked on the door.

'Come in!' The school secretary looked up from her typewriter. Her desk had been pushed to one side of the room to make space for a second desk for the secretary of the school which had been evacuated from London. It was very cramped. 'Yes?' She frowned at Rebecca.

'Excuse me, but Mr Rose said I can make a telephone call from here.' She handed the piece of paper to the secretary, who stood up and studied it.

'One moment.' She went to the telephone, dialled the operator and asked for the number Rebecca had been given. Once connected, she handed the receiver to Rebecca.

'Hello, who is it?' said a voice on the other end.

'My name is Rebecca Goldberg. My headmaster, Mr Rose, gave me this number and told me to ring.'

'Did he say why?'

'No, he just said it was because I speak fluent German and I'm good at maths and physics.'

'Yes.' There was a pause, and then, 'Have you paper and pencil?'

The secretary, overhearing the conversation pushed some paper and a pencil towards her.

'Yes.'

'Write down this address, then come here at one o'clock next Wednesday afternoon.'

Bemused, Rebecca wrote down the address. 'Um, how do I get there?' But the line had gone dead.

The Secretary shrugged and smiled. 'London! How exciting!'

Rebecca didn't think so. She'd no money of her own; how was she supposed to get to London?

She didn't know what to do. After the classes had ended for the day, she cycled back to the farm. Should she tell Mrs Marshall? What a pity neither Mary nor Samuel were there to ask. She didn't like to ask Mrs Marshall, who, she felt, resented having a German refugee living with them.

She did all her chores and then waited until Mr. Marshall had brought in the cows ready to milk, then she went to the milking shed. 'Mr Marshall?'

'Yes, m'dear?'

She was fond of him. He was a lovely, gentle man, who treated her and Samuel with kindness and respect. 'My Headmaster called me in today. Oh, nothing wrong ...' She smiled, seeing his startled look. 'He's put me forward to do some kind of secret work for the war. I have to go to London next Wednesday for an interview.'

'Well, I hope it's not dangerous work.' He frowned. 'I can't let you do anything dangerous.'

'No, I don't think so. But I don't know how to get to London.'

He nodded, apparently understanding why she'd come to him. Mrs Marshall would be unlikely to give Rebecca money for the train. 'Don't you worry, m'dear. I'll make sure the morning milking's finished early, and I'll take you to the station myself.'

'Thank you, so much, Mr Marshall. I'll get up extra early to do all my chores.'

'I'll make it right with Mrs Marshall.' He winked at her.

With a sigh of relief, Rebecca went to hen house to collect the eggs.

***

Mary was very excited when she got home at the weekend and Rebecca told her the news.

Mrs Marshall folded her lips. 'Top Secret indeed,' she muttered. 'Plenty to do here instead of gallivanting off to London.

Wednesday came and Rebecca was filled with anxiety. She'd never been to London before and had no idea what to do when she got there.

Mr Marshall came into the station with her. 'Return ticket to London, Paddington,' he said at the ticket counter, then he paid for her ticket and asked the ticket clerk about return trains. 'Now, my dear ...' He took a ten-shilling note and some small change from his wallet. 'This is for you. When you get to London, find a policeman and ask him how to get to the address.'

Rebecca gulped. Policemen were bad news. The ones in Germany had been brutal, and an English one had taken her brother to be interned.

Seeing the alarm on Rebecca's face, Mr Marshall smiled. 'Policemen here aren't like in Germany; they'll help you. Now, all being well you should be back on the four-o'clock train, which gets here at six o'clock, and I'll meet you.' He patted her shoulder. 'It'll all go well, don't worry.' Then he opened the door of the train which had just arrived at the station. 'Jump in!'

***

Rebecca sat twisting her scarf in her hands and looked out the window of the train. She'd dressed in her school uniform, having nothing else smart enough for an interview. The last time she'd been on a train was when she and Samuel had come on the Children's Refugee Transport four years ago.

Paddington station was crowded with service men and women, but at last she found a policeman standing near the exit, discreetly observing everyone going out.

'Excuse me ...' Rebecca looked up at him. 'Can you tell me how to get to this address?' She showed him the piece of paper.

He looked at it and then looked at her. She looked very young in her school uniform. Taking a pencil from his top pocket, he took her piece of paper and wrote down directions. 'Just outside the station here, there's a bus stop. Get the number twenty-three bus and ask the driver to set you down at Piccadilly Circus. This place is just around the corner.

'Thank you, sir.'

She got the bus and eventually found the address she'd been given. She didn't have a watch and wasn't sure of the time, so just rang the bell. A man in service uniform answered and asked her name. He checked his list and showed her to the waiting room. 'Wait here, miss.'

Rebecca sat, her stomach rumbling with hunger. She hadn't eaten since six o'clock that morning, and she'd been too nervous to have more than a piece of toast with a scrape of butter. She was afraid the other two girls waiting with her would hear her stomach.

Eventually her name was called and she was taken into a room where five men sat behind a long table.

'Sit down,' one of the men said, indicating a chair opposite them.

They asked questions. One spoke to her in German and she answered.

Another showed her a piece of paper with a puzzle on it. 'Can you do that, please?'

Rebecca finished it in less than a minute.

The men looked at each other and nodded.

'I understand you have a brother?' one said.

'Yes.'

'He's in the Pioneer Corps?'

'Yes, I think so.'

'Very well. You may go now. We will be in touch. Thank you for coming.'

Rebecca wanted to ask about the money she owed Mr Marshall for her fare, but she didn't have time. One of the men took her arm, led her outside and called the next person waiting.

Rebecca just managed to get the four-o'clock train from Paddington. She still hadn't eaten anything since her breakfast but didn't like to spend any of Mr Marshall's money on a sandwich.

At last she got to Somerton and was relieved when she looked out the window of the train and saw Mr Marshall sitting on a bench cleaning his nails with his penknife.

'Hello, m'dear.' He smiled at her as he got up, took her arm and they walked out of the station to the waiting horse and cart. 'Look, I thought you might be hungry. I brought you a bit of bread and cheese.' He pushed two slices of bread and butter and a small piece of cheese into her hands.

'Thank you, Mr Marshall.' *He's the kindest man,* she thought.

'How did it all go?'

'I don't know,' she mumbled through a mouthful of bread and the farm butter. 'They'll let me know.' Then she took out the money from her blazer pocket. 'I didn't need all the money,' she said, slipping it into his jacket pocket.

He smiled at her and urged the old horse on. 'Soon be home,' he said.

Chapter Twenty-Eight

Bath, 1969

After the washing up and the regulation pot of tea brewed, they all sat around the fire, looking at Samuel expectantly.

Then Liesel said, 'What I don't understand is how the Nazis knew who were Jews. I don't think anyone in my home suburb would know the religion of any of our neighbours. Apart from the devout people who go to Mass or Church every Sunday.'

'Yes,' Samuel said. 'That's an interesting question, and I sometimes wondered that, because we were Reform Jews, and apart from our immediate neighbours, no-one would really know. But then, in the internment camp, there was a professor of Applied Mathematics who had managed to escape to England in 1937. He told us that there was a machine developed by a German called Hollerith and built by International Business Machines in America. Hundreds of them were leased and maintained in Germany. All the data from all the previous census years had been encoded onto these special cards. If I remember correctly, they were called punched cards. Each person had a card with their names on it and holes punched in it denoting their religion and where they were from, and anything special, like being handicapped or a Roma Gypsy. So that enabled the Nazis to print lists of people that should be arrested and taken to camps. The punched cards showed if the person was fit enough to be worked to death, or just starved to death.'

'Oh!' Liesel's mouth fell open.

Ben frowned. 'Are you sure, Dad? I haven't heard any of this.'

'Well, that's what this professor said, and he believed it, because it was a money spinner for IBM. They didn't care that it was being used to exterminate people; they leased their machines to the Nazis and sent engineers every few months to service them. Apparently, they had them in every concentration camp and most towns. IBM had to have known what was going on.'

Silence descended while they all digested this.

Then Samuel said, 'Well, anyway, Rebecca went to Bletchley Park, one of Churchill's Geese.'

Liesel frowned. 'One of Churchill's Geese? I don't understand.'

'Oh, Churchill said the people trying to crack the Enigma code were the geese that must lay the golden egg and win the war.' Samuel smiled. 'You've heard of the Enigma machine? Or the Ultra?'

Embarrassed, Liesel shook her head.

'Not surprising; no-one outside of Bletchley did until last year when one of their intelligence officers published a book called, *The Ultra Secret*. I have it if you'd like to read it.'

Ben nodded. 'Yes, please.'

'The Nazi's had a machine which they used to send messages to their submarines and war ships and bombers. The messages were encoded and the codes kept changing. Britain could intercept the messages, but couldn't decode them. The people at Bletchley Park were working on trying to decode the messages. But they were all sworn to secrecy. They weren't even allowed to tell their families exactly where they were working or anything about their work. Not even a hint. The authorities thought that if word got out, then the Germans might target Bletchley with bombs. But in the end, instead of Bletchely Park, Rebecca ended up in a place called Withernsea, near Hull. I think she may have had something to do with receiving messages from German ships. I don't really know. She only ever said she was doing clerical work.

Ben and Liesel both looked at Samuel in amazement.

'I think they'd discovered she had a brother who also spoke German and, although not as bright as Rebecca, might be able to help them, because a few weeks after Rebecca left, I received a letter telling me to report to The Combined Services Detailed Interrogation Unit. Some of the more important German Prisoners of War had their rooms bugged, and their conversations were secretly recorded from the time they woke in the mornings. My job was to translate their conversations to see if we could glean any vital information.

'Those Nazi POW's didn't appear to realise they were being bugged, and we translated a lot of important stuff. However, after a few months I wanted to do something more challenging.' Samuel sighed. 'I was young and very bitter. I wanted to avenge my grandfather's death and most likely my parents. I heard of a new unit Churchill had set up, called the Special Operations Executive, or the SOE, and I asked to be transferred to it. The authorities were doubtful at first. Anyway, I had to go for special training, and when I passed that I was sent to the Western Highlands of Scotland for assault training. We had to be one-hundred percent fit.'

Ben sat up straight, and frowned. 'So you were a Commando?'

'No, not quite. We had slightly different training. We had to be issued with a false name and papers. I took the name of Marshall.' He smiled. 'It was easy for me to remember! I took on the persona of the son of a farmer, who had joined the Royal Fusiliers. Then if I was captured that would be my cover story. The story was that I spoke German because my mother was German and had met my father when she was working as governess in the big house where my father leased a farm. We spent days practicing our cover story.

We had to really believe our stories and become that person. Often after training all day, running with heavy kit for hours, followed by an assault course, we'd be in a deeply exhausted sleep and then roughly woken by someone shaking us and shouting *'Wie heisβen Sie?'* We had to be able to give our English cover names without even thinking about it.' He paused.

Ben shook his head. 'Why haven't you mentioned anything about this before?'

Samuel sighed. 'We were all sworn to secrecy. I can't tell you about the missions I was on. It's all still classified information.'

'That's ridiculous!' Ben sounded angry.

'Well, that's the just the way it was. Rebecca also had to take an oath of secrecy. For the rest of her life.' He was silent, then added softly, 'For what was left of it.'

Chapter Twenty-Nine

Rebecca continued ...

F our weeks later, a letter came addressed to Rebecca. It contained a rail pass and instructions to go to an address in Albany Road, Bedford the following Monday. She would be staying there for two weeks.

Mrs Marshall wasn't impressed. 'What on earth do they want with a slip of a girl like you, and how am I expected to manage with no-one to help me?' she muttered.

Rebecca didn't know it at the time, but she'd been enrolled in a cryptography course.

After the two weeks was up, she was allowed to go back to the farm, given a rail pass and told to report to Bletchley Park the following Monday.

'So, what will you be doing?' Mary asked that weekend.

Rebecca shrugged. 'I think it's some kind of clerical work for the Foreign Office.' She shook her head and frowned. 'I don't know, and I really don't want to go,' she replied. 'I'd prefer to go to university.'

'And who would pay for that?' Mrs Marshall glowered at her husband.

'There's a war on; you'll have to do your bit,' Mr Marshall said. 'But we'll miss you.' He'd become fond of the Goldberg children.

Mrs Marshall merely sniffed. For her it just meant one less to do the work around the farm and the house. 'And anyway,' she said, glaring at Rebecca, 'if it's clerical work, our Mary'd be much better suited than you.'

'I don't think I'd like to move so far away.' Mary tried to be diplomatic.

Her father looked at Rebecca. 'You know you must treat our house as your home and come back here whenever you have time off.'

His wife just folded her lips.

Rebecca smiled at him. 'Thank you both.'

'Yes.' Mary jumped up. 'I shall miss you. Come and show me what you're going to pack.'

The two girls went up to their room. Rebecca knew what she had to pack: a few dowdy clothes that the local village women had given her.

Mary had saved her clothing coupons, and with her first few weeks wages had bought a pretty blouse. 'I think it suits you better than me,' she said, holding it up against Rebecca. 'Try it on.'

Rebecca hugged Mary. 'No, Mary, you look very pretty in it.' She knew how much Mary loved the blouse.

Mary pushed her glasses up her nose and gave a half smile.

The following Monday, Rebecca got the train to London, managed to get the tube to Euston station and then changed for Bletchley Park.

The admitting officer looked at her sternly. 'You are never to talk about your work, or your location to anyone. Either at home, or between your work mates or boyfriend. *Anyone, ever,*' he emphasised. 'To do so would make you a traitor. The punishment for treason is ...' He made a cut-throat gesture across his neck.

Rebecca stared at him, horrified.

'That means either a firing squad or hanging. Understand?'

Rebecca nodded, took the pen and signed her name to the Official Secrets Act.

'And best not to ask questions,' he continued as he rang a bell and another man came in.

The officer nodded to her. She stood up and followed him in through the big guarded gates.

After several hours sitting in a cold waiting room a woman came to get her. 'Ah, Miss Goldberg, there is a little problem; you should have been assigned to Y-Service, because of your fluency in German.'

Rebecca had no idea what Y-Service was. *Best not to ask questions*.

They sent her on another two-week training course in Wimbledon, where she learnt how to receive and log live German Naval messages. From there she was posted to Withernsea as a linguist. Her job, along with several others, was to intercept radio transmissions from German ships. Their radios were located in a little hotel on the seafront, and there they ate, slept and worked day and night on shift work. Rebecca found the work mind numbing at times, constantly twiddling knobs to try and pick up a signal. It could be hours before she heard voices through the static, and then she had to write down exactly what she heard. If she missed a word, she had to leave it blank. No guessing allowed.

Withernsea, a small, dismal town near the mouth of the River Humber was freezing cold in winter and somewhat fresh in summer. It was miles from Somerset and the Marshalls. Rebecca felt very alone. The other girls were kind and friendly, but most of them were in the Women's Royal Naval Service, and although they tried to include her in their group, Rebecca still felt like an outsider. And she worried about Samuel. She hadn't heard from him for several weeks. Eventually she received a letter from him.

Dear Rebecca,

I'll be coming near Hull next week on my way back from an intensive training course. Do you think you will be able to have a few of days off so we can meet? A couple of the other chaps will be with me. We'll be staying in the Red Lion Inn. We'll be there on Wednesday. I'll book a room for you in case you can get time off.

Love

Samuel

Rebecca was thrilled. She asked her supervisor if she could have time off and was told that, yes, as Rebecca hadn't actually had any time off in over a month, she was due a break.

On the Wednesday morning, Rebecca got the train from Withernsea to Hull and found the Red Lion Inn.

As she walked into the reception area, a great shout went up. 'Rebecca!' Sam came rushing over to her.

'Oh, Sam.' Tears came to her eyes. 'It's so good to see you.'

Samuel stepped back and looked at her. 'What's happened to my little sister?' he said. 'You've grown up!'

Rebecca blushed. 'Well, what's happened to my big brother, who is now even bigger?'

'Come and meet my friends.' Sam took her hand and led her over to three other men. 'John, Will and Mike.'

Rebecca shook hands with John and Will, murmured, 'Hello,' and then came to Mike.

He took her hand.

She looked at him, and he looked at her.

'Hello, Mike,' she said, almost whispering.

'Hello, Rebecca,' he said, staring at her.

'Okay, what are you having, lads?' Samuel asked. 'Lemonade for you, Rebecca?'

She nodded, still looking at Mike.

'Well, and what do you do up here, Rebecca?' asked Will, looking at her admiringly.

She smiled. 'Just office work,' she replied, giving the standard reply she'd learnt. The threat of treason still weighed heavily on her.

***

After they'd eaten and laughed and joked, Samuel said, 'Okay, I think I'll hit the sack, and you look pretty tired too, Rebecca.'

Mike stood. 'Perhaps you'd like to get some fresh air first, Rebecca? We could have a little stroll outside.'

Sam glanced at him and then at Rebecca, who was nodding, her face reddening. He shrugged. 'Don't be long.'

Mike and Rebecca went out into the cold night air. Mike held up her coat for her. Outside, he looked around, checked that no-one was in earshot, then said softly in German, 'Do you believe in love at first sight?'

Stunned, Rebecca turned to him. 'Are you German?' she whispered.

'Yes. My name is actually Mikkel Wendt. Mike Webber is my special operations name that I've assumed. We all speak English when together with your brother and our friends. Especially in public.'

Rebecca hugged her coat around her. 'Should you be telling me this?'

Mike shrugged. 'No. But you're Sam's sister. You know the score.' He took her hand. 'So ... my question? I'm twenty-six,' he said, 'but as soon as I saw you, I knew you were the woman for me. I've never felt this way before.' He turned her round to face him then gently kissed her.

Rebecca's heart thumped, but she remained silent.

'I'm sorry. Perhaps I shouldn't have declared myself so soon. But life is short, Rebecca. Now I've shocked you.'

'No,' she said. 'I just don't know what to think or say. Perhaps we should go back inside.'

Mike nodded. 'I'm sorry. You're right. Forgive me.'

They went back into the inn and to their separate rooms.

It took Rebecca a long time to go to sleep, even though she was exhausted from a few days on night shift.

The next morning, Mike came down early for breakfast. He sat at a table with a cup of tea, watching the door of the dimly lit pub dining room. It wasn't long before Rebecca appeared. When Mike saw her, a smile spread across his face. He stood and walked over to her.'Good morning, Rebecca. Can I help you get breakfast?'

She smiled as she shook her head. 'Good morning, Mike. I think I can manage, thank you.' She helped herself to toast and marmalade and a cup of tea, then went and sat opposite him. She took a bite of toast, but it seemed to stick in her throat.

'Rebecca, I'm sorry for being so impetuous last night, but I have to see more of you. I don't know where we'll all be going, or when my next leave is due. It's secret.'

Rebecca looked at him and nodded. 'It's the same for me,' she said.

Mike's eyes lit up and he leaned forward. 'You mean you feel the same way about me?'

Rebecca looked down at her toast. 'I mean, the same for my work. It's all secret.'

'Oh.' Disappointed, Mike sat back.

Then Rebecca said in a low voice. 'But I couldn't stop thinking about you last night. I would like to see more of you.'

Mike told her later that he wanted to make a joke and say *I'll strip off now and you can check me out*, instead he said, 'Perhaps we can arrange to meet? Will you write to me?'

She nodded.

Just then Sam came into the dining room with John and Will. Sam looked at his sister and Mike, who were so engrossed with each other that they didn't seem to notice him.

'Good morning!' Sam smiled as Mike and Rebecca both looked up with startled expressions. 'You two seem to be plotting something.'

Rebecca blushed and Mike laughed. 'Just wondering what was the plan for today.'

'Maybe go for a wander round and look at the bombing damage, then go to the pictures if there is still a cinema open. How does that suit you, Rebecca?'

'Lovely, thank you.'

'All right, so shall we all meet up about nine? How about you two?' Sam turned to John and Will.

John decided he had letters to write, but Will said he'd come with them.

***

On their walk, Mike managed to stay with Rebecca while Will and Sam strolled ahead.

'Looks like Mike is smitten with your sister,' Will remarked. 'Don't blame him, if I didn't have a girlfriend already, I'd be fighting him for her!'

Sam glanced back at Mike and Rebecca who seemed to be deep in conversation and walking more and more slowly behind them.

'Hmm.' Sam frowned. 'She's too young. I'd better break them up.' He made to turn back to them, but Will put a hand on his arm.

'No, Sam. Please don't. Mike's a good man. He'd never do anything to hurt her. And Rebecca's what? Eighteen? I don't think she'd appreciate you interfering. She seems pretty happy at the moment.'

'I suppose you're right,' Sam muttered. 'But she's my little sister, and all I've got.'

'I understand. Probably like you, I don't know what's happened to my family back in Germany. That's why all of us German speaking men have volunteered for the Special Operations Troop.' The two men walked on, each thinking their own thoughts.

'I don't know Mike's story,' Sam said eventually. 'I'd like to know a bit more if he's going to be hanging around Rebecca.'

'You don't need to ask him. He told me,' Will said. 'However, I don't feel at liberty to tell you. It's his story. But I can tell you this much. He lost all his family, either in the gas chambers, or worked to death. He's one of the best. Believe me. I've known him for a long time. Have no fear of him hurting Rebecca.'

Sam nodded. 'Thanks, Will.' He sighed. 'It's hard to believe she's grown up. This is the first time I've seen her for over a year.'

'Look, here's the cinema,' Will said. 'Let's see what's on while we wait for the lovebirds to catch up. We can have lunch somewhere then come back.'

Sam thought about what Will had said. If Rebecca had to fall in love, it was much better for it to be someone he knew and approved of, rather than some casual soldier or sailor that happened to be around.

***

In the dark of the cinema, Rebecca couldn't concentrate on the film. She sat between Mike and her brother, and as soon as the lights went down, Mike took her hand. Her heart fluttered. Was she in love? Was there such a thing as love at first sight? She'd never felt this way before. It wasn't as if she'd never had any contact with the opposite sex. There were service men everywhere in the area and many had asked her out. She'd never felt inclined to go out with any of them. But now ... she wanted Mike to kiss her again. She looked sideways at her brother; he seemed engrossed in the film. But she daren't move closer to Mike. She looked to her other side and could just make out Mike looking at her. She saw the white of his teeth as he smiled at her, then squeezed her hand.

'Good film,' Sam said as they came out of the cinema. 'What did you think, Rebecca?'

'Yes, very good,' she agreed, hoping Sam wouldn't start questioning her on any of it. Her head had been too full of how she could meet Mike again.

Later that afternoon, Sam looked at Mike and Rebecca. 'How about you show Rebecca around the gardens,' he said to Mike.

Rebecca's face lit up, and she smiled. 'That'd be nice, if Mike doesn't mind.'

Mike definitely didn't mind. He'd been wondering all afternoon how he could get Rebecca to himself and away from her brother.

At the bottom of the pub grounds, Mike and Rebecca came across a small bench surrounded by bushes. Mike took out his handkerchief and wiped the wooden seat, then turned to her. 'Rebecca. I know this might be sudden, but I want to marry you. I don't want to rush you but ... Well, actually, yes, I do want to rush you.' He took her hand. 'I knew as soon as I looked at you. Please say yes.'

Rebecca hesitated. 'I don't know what my brother would say.'

'If he's happy, would you say yes?'

She nodded and smiled.

Gently he took her into his arms and kissed her.

After a few minutes, Rebecca said breathlessly, 'I think I'd better sit down. My legs have gone all weak.'

It was some time later that they went back to the pub.

***

Mike found Sam alone in their room.

'Hello, Sam,' he said. 'I'm glad you're here by yourself. I have something to ask you.'

Sam looked up from the book he was reading. 'I don't have a good feeling about this conversation.'

Mike grinned. 'I want to marry Rebecca.'

Sam blinked. 'I was right. Not a good feeling.'

'I love her, and she loves me. You know what it's like with the war. We can't wait until it ends. We don't know when or if it will end, or whether Hitler will invade England. We have to take our happiness now.'

Sam nodded. 'But she's so young.' He sighed. 'I'll go and talk to her now.'

Mike nodded. 'All right, but please don't try to dissuade her!'

Sam went to Rebecca's room and knocked on the door. 'Rebecca, it's Sam. May I come in?'

'Of course. It's not locked.' Rebecca sat on her bed, a big smile on her face.

'Rebecca, I've just been talking to Mike. He said you want to get married.'

Rebecca stood. 'Yes, Sam. I've never felt this way before. I'm quite determined.'

Sam's eyebrows rose in surprise. Rebecca had always been so very quiet and biddable.

'Sam, please be happy for me. This is not a sudden thing. Well, yes, it is sudden. But I know it's the right thing.'

Sam put his arms around her and gave her a hug. 'If you're sure, then I won't stand in your way.'

Her eyes glittered with tears of joy. 'Thank you, dear Sam. I hope one day you'll find the right woman and then you'll know how I feel.'

He smiled. 'Come down to the lounge and we'll celebrate. I'll just fetch Mike. See you down there.'

Mike wasn't in their room. Sam walked down the stairs to the lounge and met Will and John coming in. 'Come and have a drink with us,' Sam said. 'Rebecca is on her way down. Mike is around somewhere.'

'No; we met him as we came in. He was in a rush. Said he was going to the Registry Office before they closed. Didn't stop to tell us why.'

'Erm ... I think I know why, but perhaps we should wait for him to come back. Here's Rebecca. I'll get drinks; sit down all of you.'

Talk remained general until half an hour later when Mike came in. 'Here you all are!' He smiled at Rebecca.

'Now, what was your haste, Mike?' Will asked.

Mike looked around at them all, a broad smile on his face. 'Rebecca here has agreed to marry me, so I went out to find the registry office to enquire how to get a special license to get married.'

The three men looked at him. Rebecca blushed.

'But in my haste, I didn't know Rebecca's date of birth or her full name, just Rebecca—though I guessed Marshall like Sam here—or where she lives or anything. They must have thought me quite stupid in the registry office.'

'Sit down. You need a drink,' Sam said. 'We were just about to celebrate your engagement.'

Mike sat down next to Rebecca. 'Thank you, Sam.'

Will and John looked at each other.

'This is all rather sudden,' Will said. 'But congratulations, I hope you will both be very happy.' He raised his glass. 'To Mike and Rebecca.'

***

All too soon Rebecca had to return to Withernsea and the men back to their training. Mike got the special marriage license and Rebecca's details, and four weeks later she got permission to leave Withernsea for a few days to travel to London where she and Mike were married.

'It's not in a synagogue, but we can do that later if you want,' Mike said to Rebecca on their way to the registry office.

'That's all right,' she said. 'I haven't been to a synagogue since I left Germany.'

Sam gave her away, and Will and John were witnesses.

Rebecca thought of asking Mary to be her bridesmaid or maid of honour, but there was no time to contact her and anyway, Rebecca doubted if Mrs Marshall would have let her come.

Chapter Thirty

Bath 1969

S am shook his head. 'All these memories,' he said. 'Then we'd finished part of our training and were on our way to London via Hull. I knew Rebecca was working near there, so I managed to contact her and she got the train from Withernsea. I don't think that line exists anymore. Anyway, I was there with three other men who were training with me. The amazing thing is that Rebecca and Mike instantly hit it off. They were married a month later.'

Liesel gasped. 'So soon?'

'Well,' Sam said, 'things were different in the war. There was a sense of urgency; who knew if you would be killed in an air raid or on active service.' He sighed. 'And it was obvious they were made for each other. Mike was a great person, and Rebecca just seemed to glow when she was near him.'

'Was a great person?' Ben said. 'What happened?'

'He never returned from a mission we were on. I survived somehow, but we never found out what happened to Mike. I was always afraid that he was captured and tortured to death.'

There was a stunned silence.

'Poor Rebecca,' Liesel murmured.

'Yes. It was like that inner light in her just went out.'

Evelyn stood and went over to Sam. 'I think we've talked enough for tonight,' she said.

'I'll put the kettle on.' Liesel walked to the door, followed by Ben.

***

After their visit to the Clifton Suspension Bridge and the zoo, Ben and Liesel were both feeling hungry. Evelyn had prepared lamb and mint sauce for their evening meal.

'This is lovely,' Liesel said as they sat around the table. 'But I feel bad that you're going to so much effort, and I just waltz in and eat your lovely cooking.'

'Nonsense, Liesel; it's a real pleasure to have you here. Please tell us more about your life in Sydney.'

'Not much to tell, really.' Liesel suddenly realised that was true; unlike Samuel, and even Ben, she thought, looking at him as he carefully carved the leg of lamb.

'Well, what do you do on the weekends and after work?' Evelyn seemed interested.

'Most evenings I'd be marking and preparing the next day's class.' She heard Ben give a snort at this and turned to look at him. 'Then sometimes there's school sport on a Saturday morning. As often as I can, I get the train to Bondi and go swimming with my friends. Sometimes go to a concert, but the tickets are very expensive.' *That sounds pretty boring and pathetic.*

'I've heard of Bondi Beach,' Ben said. 'Is it very beautiful?'

'It's nice, but there are lots of other lovely beaches. Manly is nice too.'

'And the weather?' Evelyn prompted.

'Well, it can get quite hot in the summer, but most of the time it's very pleasant. Winter can be cold, but we don't get snow in Sydney. In the Blue Mountains it can snow, but that's quite a distance from Sydney.'

Ben served the lamb, and Liesel remained quiet as conversation turned to general subjects. Later Liesel looked at Evelyn and said, 'So, Evelyn, if it's not classified information can you tell me what you did in the war?'

Evelyn smiled. 'Oh, I did nothing very exciting. I was just a nurse.'

'Just a nurse!' Samuel exclaimed. He smiled at his wife, his expression softening. 'Evelyn only saved my life.'

They smiled at each other, and Evelyn shook her head. 'Your father is exaggerating,' she said to Ben.

'I'd been badly wounded—half my back blown away—and was lucky to get back to England. Don't remember much. Apparently, they gave me up for dead, but this young nurse sat beside me holding my hand as I drifted in and out of consciousness. It was as though she was telling me I had to stay alive. When I came to, I thought I'd died and gone to heaven because this beautiful angel was holding my hand.'

Evelyn smiled. 'Your vision was impaired by the pain killers!'

They seemed to still be in love even after all these years.

Samuel smiled. 'The funny thing was that after I was well enough to go to a convalescent home and knew I'd recover, I wanted to see this lovely young nurse again. So I wrote to her, care of the hospital, but got no reply.'

Evelyn laughed. 'I received this letter, thanking me for looking after him in hospital and asking if we could meet, signed Sam Goldberg. Well, I had no idea who this Sam Goldberg was, had no recollection of nursing anyone of that name.'

Samuel grinned. 'I forgot that I'd been admitted under my assumed name of Samuel Marshall, and when I didn't get a reply, I didn't know what to do. I knew I had to find her.'

Evelyn took up the tale. 'Well, I wasn't going to go out with someone I didn't know!'

'As soon as I was able to walk,' Samuel continued, 'I went back to the hospital every evening when I knew her shift would be finishing and lurked outside. I thought perhaps she already had a boyfriend, but if that was the case then I was going to steal her from him. I wasn't going to give up! Then five evenings later, I saw her. I went over to her and said, "Hello, Nurse Brown, do you remember me? Sam Goldberg." She looked all surprised and said, 'You're Samuel Marshall, how nice to see you walking.'

'Then I realised that, of course, she didn't know my real name. I think she was so embarrassed that she said yes when I invited her out.'

Evelyn blushed and smiled at Sam. 'I'm so glad I did,' she murmured.

Liesel sighed. *How lovely to still feel like that after so many years of marriage.* She suddenly stood up, breaking the tense atmosphere. 'Shall I put the kettle on?'

Ben stood, too. 'Liesel and I will make tea. You two lovebirds sit here and make sheep's eyes at each other,' he said with a laugh.

In the kitchen, Liesel turned to Ben. 'I hope I haven't stirred up a hornet's nest, or opened Pandora's Box or whatever the expression is,' she said. 'It seems like the last few days have been pretty traumatic for your father.'

'Mm, yes, but perhaps it's a good thing. He must've had this stuff all bottled up for years.'

'Well, if it's classified information, I guess it would seem better not to mention any part of it.'

Ben nodded and went to the pantry. 'I think mum had some chocolate biscuits somewhere.'

'What about the giant Easter Egg you gave me? We'd better make a start on that!'

***

The next day, Easter Monday, Evelyn said at breakfast, 'Samuel and I have to go back to work tomorrow, but you're most welcome to stay on here, Liesel. I'm sure Ben would enjoy your company.'

'Yes, indeed.' Ben smiled.

Liesel looked at them all. 'That's so kind of you, but I couldn't possibly impose on your goodwill any longer. I'd love to be able to invite you to London, but I share a flat with two other girls ...'

Samuel laughed. 'That's all right, my dear. We quite understand. But please. Consider this as your family home away from home. After all, you are indeed family, and I think I can speak for all of us when I say that we love having you here.'

Ben and Evelyn both nodded.

'There's a train at half-past twelve, if perhaps Ben would take me to the station?' Liesel turned to Ben.

'My pleasure.'

She said her goodbyes to Samuel and Evelyn. 'It's been so wonderful to find such amazing relations,' she told them, giving them both hugs. Reserved or not, they didn't seem to mind.

At the station, Ben lifted out her bag and walked with her to the ticket office.

She turned to him and took her bag. 'Thank you so much, Ben.'

'I was wondering about the summer holidays,' he said. 'We get six or seven weeks from mid- July. I was thinking about going to Germany and looking up the places my father mentioned.'

'Oh, what a good idea!'

He kept looking at her.

Liesel frowned. He seemed to be waiting for her to say something. 'Well, I'd better find my platform.'

'Liesel, would you like to come?'

'Come? To Germany? Oh!'

'I'd really like it if you did.' His face grew red.

'Well. I don't know if I'd be able to afford it,' she said doubtfully. 'But I can try and save up.' She turned and went to the gate, showing the ticket inspector her ticket.

'I'll write when I find out more details, shall I?' He raised a hand in farewell.

'Thank you again, Ben.' She turned and waved to him, then hurried to the waiting train.

She found a window seat and settled down. *So much to think about.* Amazing that she'd found a new family of relations! And such a history. She wondered about going to Germany in the school summer holidays. Would she be able to afford it? It was all too much to think about. Meanwhile she'd try to learn some more German.

***

Ben walked back to his car, deep in thought. Why had he suddenly asked Liesel if she'd like to come to Germany with him? And he hadn't even been thinking about it at all. It had unexpectedly occurred to him as he was saying goodbye to her. The more he thought about it, the more attractive it seemed. He'd do some investigation. Surely his father would remember the address where he'd lived in Mannheim. And where Liesel's Grandfather had lived. When the Public Library opened on Wednesday, he'd go and get some books on Germany. He'd keep Liesel informed.

***

Back in London, Liesel's flat mates asked her if she'd had a good time in Bath.

'Oh, yes!' She wanted to tell someone, anyone, about her new relations, but it seemed they had only asked out of politeness. They weren't really interested. She tried another tack.

'Have either of you been to Germany?' she asked as she made a pot of tea the next evening.

'Jennifer looked up. 'Germany? Why do you ask?'

'Oh, I was thinking about going in the Summer holidays,' Liesel tried to sound casual.

'No, I haven't. And if I was going abroad, I'd go to Majorca or somewhere like that, nice beaches and sun!' Jennifer looked at Liesel and smiled. 'Oh, of course, you come from a land of beaches and sun. Suppose you'd want to go somewhere different.'

Liesel shrugged and smiled back. 'True.' She resolved to go to the local library when they re-opened and do some research. She could write and tell Ben what she'd discovered. Perhaps she could go to a travel agent and find out how much fares cost and whether if she saved hard, she'd have enough money for a trip to Germany.

***

Liesel discovered that a train went from London to Dover, and from there she could take a ferry to Calais and then a train to Mannheim or Frankfurt. After finding out the rough cost of the fares, she wondered how much it would cost for accommodation for around two weeks. She consulted her flat mates, and they told her she could stay in youth hostels, which were cheap.

She wrote and told Ben that she'd probably be able to save enough to go for two weeks if they stayed in youth hostels, but she'd have to find a part time job for the rest of the school holidays. She posted her letter, got back to the bedsit and found a letter from Ben on the door mat.

Dear Liesel

I was thinking that perhaps I could get a very early train to London one Sunday, and we could meet, have lunch and talk about travel plans. Then I could get a train back in the evening.

It seems as if you like the idea of going to Germany.

My parents are well and send their regards.

Best wishes

Ben Goldberg.

Liesel smiled to herself. It looked like the German trip was on! She wrote straight back to Ben suggesting the following Sunday week. The next day she joined a German night class.

***

Liesel met Ben on a crowded and noisy platform at Paddington station. She elbowed her way through the crush of people and was just thinking that he must have missed the train, when a voice behind her said, 'Hello, Liesel. You're looking for me in the first-class carriages. I was down the other end.'

She turned to see him smiling at her, then they stood awkwardly. Ben seemed to be wondering if he should shake her hand, and Liesel considered whether or not to give him a hug. She nodded at him instead, then looked at her watch. 'It's a bit too early for lunch. Why don't we go back to my bedsit? We can spread out maps and stuff and talk about it there.'

'Great idea! Lead on McDuff!' He smiled.

Liesel led the way to the tube. 'Not far.' After several times getting on in the wrong direction and having to get out at the next stop and go back, she now felt proud of how much she'd learnt about the London Underground.

As they walked up the stairs to the flat, she heard Jennifer's voice ask, 'Can I borrow your blue top?' A muffled reply followed.

Liesel turned to Ben as she unlocked the door. 'It's only small; Jennifer and Carole have the two bigger bedrooms, and I have the smallest—I was the last to join them.'

Ben nodded. 'I get the picture.'

She introduced him to Jennifer and Carole.

'This is my cousin, Ben.'

'How do you do.' Ben smiled, and Jennifer and Carole suddenly weren't in such a hurry to go out.

'Ben and I are going to put maps on the kitchen table, if that's all right,' Liesel said, looking at the table which had the weekend papers, empty paper bags and a dirty coffee mug on it.

'Yes, of course, I'll move my stuff.' Jennifer cleared the table. 'Liesel told us you're a teacher, Ben, what subjects do you teach? Liesel hasn't told us much.'

The two girls seemed to hang on his words. Liesel thought they'd never go. Eventually she had to look at her watch and say, 'Well, Ben and I have a lot to plan, if you don't mind.'

'Oh! Of course.' They disappeared into their rooms and emerged a few minutes later ready to leave.

'So nice to have met you, Ben,' they chorused as they left.

Liesel closed the door behind them and turned to Ben with a smile. 'Do you usually have that effect on girls?'

A bit embarrassed, he shrugged, then smiled. 'Come on; I thought you said you had maps.'

Liesel got out a notebook. 'I've listed trains and stations and rough costs. We can get a train from London to Dover, then the ferry to Calais, then a train to Lille, then change and get another train to Brussels, then to Cologne, then on to Mannheim.' She looked up with an expression of triumph.

'You've done very well. That's excellent research,' Ben smiled at her. 'However, I was thinking we could take my car and drive there.'

'Drive!' Liesel blinked. 'But they drive on the wrong side of the road!'

Ben sucked on his teeth and nodded. 'That's true.'

'It would be dangerous.'

'I've driven to France a couple of times.' A grin spread across his face. 'I think you'd be safe with me.'

They spent an hour planning routes and stops and deciding which of them would find out about youth hostels until Ben looked at his watch and said, 'I'm starving! What about we stop now and have lunch before I head back to Bath? Perhaps I can come again in a couple of weeks, and we can carry on, and in the meantime we can each do more research.'

'Sounds good! Did I tell you I'm doing a night class in German? *Sprechen Sie Deutsch?*' Liesel gave a wry smile. 'Or something like that.'

***

Later that afternoon she waved goodbye to Ben at Paddington Station and went back to her bedsit feeling strangely light hearted. It had been a great day.

When she let herself into the flat, Jennifer looked up from the kitchen table. 'Hi, Liesel, have you any more cousins like Ben? He's a dish!'

Liesel blinked. 'Is he?'

'Come on, Liesel. Surely, you've noticed. He's the most gorgeous hunk I've met in ages!'

Carol came out of her room. 'Yes, Liesel; come on, tell us all. Is he spoken for?'

Liesel shrugged. 'I think he's recently split up with his girlfriend.' She smiled. Ben *was* very nice looking. She was starting to get excited about this trip. But first she had her German homework to do before the class on Monday night.

Dear Ben,

I enjoyed Sunday. Thank you so much for coming up to London.

I'm wondering about other places we could visit besides Mannheim. I went to a travel agent and got some brochures. We could look at them the next time you come to London. Or I could come to Bath for the day if you prefer that.

Regards

Liesel.

***

Dear Liesel

The Whitsunday long weekend is coming up soon. My parents suggested you might like to come to Bath for a few days and we can do more planning there.

I admit, I haven't been able to do a lot. My feeble excuse is school work!

Regards

Ben

***

Dear Ben,

I'd love to come for the long weekend. Please thank your parents.

I'd really like to get something for them; they've been so kind to me. Have you any suggestions? I can't think of anything suitable.

I'll bring all my notes on places to visit. I think two weeks might not be long enough!

Do you think your father would mind if I practiced my German on him?

How is school? Probably the same as me. Flat out.

Regards

Liesel.

***

The May bank holiday seemed to come around very quickly. When Liesel looked out the window of the train and saw Ben on the platform, her heart gave a little leap. *He's your cousin,* she reminded herself.

'Hello, Liesel!' He smiled and took her bag.

'Thanks, Ben; so nice to see you.'

'Yes, and the weather forecast is good, a change from the recent rain and cold winds.'

Liesel nodded and followed him out of the station to his little car.

As he was about to start the engine, Liesel put a hand on his arm. 'Ben. Before we go any further, please will you tell me what happened to Rebecca? I don't want to put my foot in it by saying something inappropriate.'

Ben turned off the ignition and sat looking straight ahead. 'I only vaguely remember her. She died of cancer. I think she must have been in her early thirties. I don't know what she did after the war. It's so sad that her husband died so soon after they were married.'

'Yes, did she ever remarry?'

'I don't think so. Dad never talks about her. I think it must have been so hard to lose his only living relative like that.'

***

Liesel and Ben sat at the dining room table making their arrangements. Evelyn watched in amusement, thinking they looked so at ease with each other. She saw Sam studying them as well. He caught her eye and smiled. She knew he was thinking the same; Liesel seemed to fit right in to their family.

'So! We have our plan.' Ben looked up. 'Liesel, I'll pick you up in London on the Saturday morning, and we'll drive to Dover and get the afternoon ferry.'

'Oh, that would be too much out of your way!' Liesel protested. 'I could get the train to Dover and meet you there.'

Evelyn stood. 'I'm going to make a pot of tea,' she said, 'and Liesel, why don't you get the train down to Bath on the Friday and stay the night here; then you can get the car packed up together and leave early on Saturday morning.'

Ben and Liesel looked at each other.

'Good idea, Mum.' Ben smiled. 'It would be about the same for Liesel to get the train to Bath as to Dover, and then there's no fear that I'll get lost in London or lose her in Dover.'

'*Wunderbar!*' Liesel looked at Sam, who smiled.

He smiled. *Ja, gute idee.*

***

'Have you got a sleeping bag?' Jennifer demanded as Liesel tried to organise her luggage.

'No. Do I need one?

Jennifer rolled her eyes. 'If you're going to stay in youth hostels, then of course you'll need one.' She looked at Liesel's suitcase. 'And that case is far too big and unwieldy. I'll lend you my back pack and sleeping bag. I won't be going anywhere this summer.'

Liesel looked helplessly at her suitcase.

'And you won't need all that stuff. How many pairs of knickers have you got there? You only need two pairs plus the pair you wear; you'll be able to wash them every night at the hostel.' Jennifer smiled at Liesel. 'Like me to help you? Anyone would think you'd never been on a holiday before.'

Liesel didn't want to tell her that no, actually, she had never been on a holiday before.

The last day of school arrived and Liesel was ready.

Ben met her at Bath Spa station and eyed her backpack with approval. 'I was a bit worried you might turn up with a big suitcase, but I see you have a sleeping bag rolled up there with a waterproof cover. You've done well!'

'Actually, it was Jennifer who got me sorted,' Liesel confessed.

'Good for Jennifer!'

Chapter Thirty-One

Europe

The next morning Sam and Evelyn waved goodbye as Liesel and Ben headed off on their holiday armed with sandwiches and flasks of tea.

Sam turned to Liesel with a smile. 'I think my mum has packed enough food to last us the whole two weeks.'

Liesel nodded. 'She's wonderful.' She was about to say he was lucky to have such a mother, but then stopped. Ben didn't need to know everything about her.

'I managed to get the address of my grandfather's shop in Mannheim—9 Pfeffer Strasse. Apparently, it was in an old part of Mannheim on the outskirts, all cobblestone roads. It might have been built over since the war. He didn't know where your great grandparents lived, except that it was in Frankfurt and that they had a furniture store.'

'Perhaps we can have a look around Frankfurt anyway.'

Liesel looked at Ben, who nodded and said, 'I asked him if he'd thought of going back to Germany, and he said, no. He didn't think he could bear it. He can't believe that so many people said after the war that they hadn't known what the Nazis were doing to the Jews and gypsies and handicapped people. They had to have known.'

Liesel nodded. 'I can understand that. It's how my grandfather thought too. He said that there was no Germany any longer. I think that's what he must have meant.'

When they reached the Port of Dover, Ben said, 'Have you been on a ferry before?'

'Um, only the Manly ferry,' Liesel replied.

'The weather forecast looks good, and it's only a short trip, so I think you'll be all right.' He gave her a smile. 'Thank you, Liesel for coming with me.'

Surprised, she smiled back. 'But I want to find out more about my roots, too. I'm so pleased I've been able to find you and your father; my Grandfather would've been so pleased. I feel I've done what he asked.'

When the boat docked, they drove out to the check point, and showed their passports.

Ben said, 'Now, Liesel, I'll need to you to be my offsider if I want to overtake.'

'What do you mean?' Liesel asked with a frown.

'Well, my steering wheel is on the right, and I'll be driving on the right, so I won't be able to see what's coming the other way if there's another car in front.'

Liesel took a deep breath. 'Okay ...'

'And you'll be navigator. I assume you can read maps?'

Liesel wasn't sure about this. Perhaps it would've been better to go by train. She could read timetables, but she'd never had reason to use a map before. 'Um, perhaps you could show me?' she suggested in a quiet voice.

Ben grinned. 'I like someone who can admit when they don't know something.'

Liesel remained silent.

Ben frowned. 'I didn't mean that in a nasty way. I really meant that I don't like it when someone implies they know something and they don't and then stuffs up.' He put his hand on her arm and turned to her. 'Have I upset you?'

Liesel smiled. 'Of course not. I hate it when people aren't honest about what they think and feel.'

'Thank you, Liesel. It's so nice being with you.'

Liesel's heart gave a little leap. 'I feel the same way.'

They stopped when they got off the ferry and Ben looked at the map. 'Here's the youth hostel, and this is where we are.' He pointed to both places. 'So, we must drive along this road and then turn here.' He traced the route with his finger. 'Think you'll be able to direct me?'

'I'll try.'

'Don't worry if we make a few wrong turns; we have plenty of time.'

Liesel nodded. 'I'll do my best.'

She managed to navigate with only one wrong turn, and they arrived at the youth hostel late in the afternoon.

'We'll register and then go and find some shops and buy some food to cook for our dinner. The food in France is so nice.' Ben had stayed in hostels before and knew the procedure.

***

Liesel found everyone very friendly at the hostel, and she enjoyed listening to the chatter of conversation in different languages in the communal kitchen. She was happy to sit and watch as Ben found a frying pan and cooked the bacon, eggs and garlic sausage they'd bought.

'Plates and cutlery are over there,' he said, indicating a cupboard.

Liesel jumped up. 'Sorry, I was day dreaming. I'll make the salad, shall I?'

'Sure'

It's so nice to be able to work together preparing our meal, Liesel thought.

After they'd eaten and washed up, Ben said, 'I suggest we get our backpacks from the car and have an early night. Be careful of your money belt and passport.'

Liesel nodded. He'd already shown her the women's dormitory where she'd sleep.

'We'll be able to make an early start in the morning after breakfast,' he continued. 'What about if we meet in the kitchen at seven o'clock?'

'Sounds good, Ben. Okay, see you in the morning. Good night, sleep tight.'

'And don't let the bedbugs bite,' he replied with a smile.

Liesel's eyes widened with horror. 'Bed bugs?'

'Only joking!'

***

Liesel arrived in the kitchen just before seven the next morning, after she'd showered and packed away her sleeping bag.

Ben was already there, making toast from the left-over baguette they'd bought the day before. 'Good morning.' He looked up and smiled. 'This okay for you?'

'Perfect, thank you.' Liesel smiled as she fetched mugs from the shelf and spooned instant coffee into them.

When they'd finished and cleaned up, Ben got out his map. 'This is our next proposed stop.' He showed Liesel the route on the map.

'Okay; I'll do my best.'

They fell into a comfortable routine of an early breakfast, driving and having a picnic lunch, then driving to the next hostel on their route to Mannheim. After registering and doing some shopping for food they had time to wander around each town. Liesel realised on the fourth day as they drove along that she felt happy. Happier than she'd ever been.

Mannheim was a big city. When they arrived, they went straight to the town hall to look for a street map, but they had no success finding Samuel's grandfather's and father's shop. Either Samuel had got the name of the street wrong or it had been bulldozed and rebuilt after the war.

They strolled around Mannheim, trying to picture what it would've been like for Samuel and Rebecca growing up there. 'Imagine it, my grandfather, Wilfried, and your grandfather, Hans, were both living here after the First World War,' Liesel said.

Ben nodded.

Liesel suddenly felt overcome with emotion. She sniffed and took out her handkerchief.

Ben turned to her, and seeing the tears coming to her eyes, put one of his arms around her and drew her to him. 'It's awful to think what they went though,' he said.

Liesel blew her nose. 'Yes,' she said in a muffled voice.

With his free hand, Ben raised her chin, bent his head and kissed her forehead. Then as if he'd suddenly realised what he'd done, he coughed and released her. 'We'd better find the hostel for tonight,' he said briskly.

'Good idea,' Liesel's voice came out shaky. Ben's arms around her had felt so nice.

After shopping for their evening meal, they walked to the river and sat on the bank. After sitting in silence for a while, Liesel said, 'We should write all this down for our grandchildren.'

'*Our grandchildren?*' Startled, Ben turned to look at her.

She stared straight ahead. 'Well, I suppose you'll eventually marry and have children and grandchildren; and perhaps I might decide to get married. You never know.' Liesel's brow furrowed. 'I don't intend to marry, but it would be nice for everything we've learnt to be written down.' She sighed. 'I wish I'd asked my grandfather more, but he never wanted to talk about his past.'

Ben grunted. 'You're right.' He looked at her again, but she was still looking resolutely ahead. 'Liesel,' he began.

She suddenly jumped up and said, 'I'm hungry, time to go back and prepare dinner.' She looked down at him, smiled and held out her hand. 'Come on lazy-bones.'

He caught her hand as she pretended to pull him up. 'Liesel,' he began again, but she'd turned and started towards the car. With a sigh he followed her.

***

The next morning when they met for breakfast, Liesel suddenly said, 'Ben, I've been thinking.'

He looked up from buttering some bread. 'Mmmh?'

'I don't think we've made much progress trying to find out about our grandparents and their parents. We could go to the authorities and try and find birth and death records, but I don't think my German is up to asking the relevant questions or searching through records; that's if any records even exist.' She sighed. 'I feel your grandparents must have been taken to concentration camps and either been killed or worked to death. The same for my grandfather's parents. Surely if they'd lived, they would've tried to find your father and Rebecca and my grandfather. Perhaps I'll have to improve my German, do more research and come back in a year or two ...'

Ben looked at her and nodded. 'You're probably right.'

'So, I think we should perhaps give up our search and just enjoy the holiday.'

Ben frowned and said nothing.

Liesel looked at him, willing him to say something.

Finally, he sighed. 'I think my father will be disappointed, but as you say we seem to be getting nowhere and need to do more research as to what facilities there are to trace our families.' He suddenly smiled. 'Yes. You're right. Let's be tourists for the rest of the time, and we only have another few days anyway. Well then where do we go next? What would you like to do?'

Liesel looked at him and then quickly looked away. What she'd *like* to do would be to put her arms around him and kiss him. Instead she shrugged, and replied, 'What about Heidelberg and the Black Forest?'

Ben smiled. 'Good idea. Now we know more about Germany, we can carry on our research at home and come back next summer. Perhaps stay longer than two weeks?'

***

The rest of their trip passed quickly. Having decided to stop their research and just enjoy their holiday, they both relaxed. On the last day, while they sat in the queue of cars waiting to board the Ferry at Calais, Ben turned to Liesel and said suddenly, 'I wish you weren't my cousin.'

'Oh!' Liesel frowned. 'What do you mean? Haven't you enjoyed our trip together?'

'Yes, of course. I just wish we weren't related. I've, um, I don't know how to say this Liesel, but I just love being with you. In fact, I'd like to always be with you.'

Liesel was speechless. She just looked at him.

'Sorry! I shouldn't have said that.' He turned away from her and started to get out of the car, muttering something about going to the toilet.

'Ben! Stop.' Liesel put her hand on his arm. 'I feel the same way.'

He turned back, his expression changing from embarrassment to relief and then joy. He got back into the car, then leaned over the steering wheel and tried to kiss her.

Liesel laughed and put her hand on his face. 'I've wanted this for a long time,' she whispered as she kissed him.

The honking of the car behind brought them back to earth.

'We're only second cousins. That doesn't mean anything,' Liesel said as Ben drove up the ramp onto the ferry.

***

Once out of the car and up the stairs on the deck, Ben took her hand. 'How long have you known?'

'Known what?' Liesel gave him a sly grin.

'Oh, you know, that you felt like this?

'Like what?'

'Oh, Liesel! You know what I mean!'

'No, I don't; tell me.'

'That you wanted to do this.' He kissed her.

'Stop! Everyone is looking at us.'

'Seriously. How long have you known?'

'Since we decided that we'd stop searching for Hans's shop, and you asked me what I'd like to do. And I said how about Heidelberg and the Black Forest. But actually, I was thinking that what I'd really like was for you to take me in your arms and kiss me. What about you?'

Ben regarded her as if she were a messenger from Heaven. 'When you said we should write all this down for our grandchildren. Suddenly the thought of us having children and grandchildren together was like a light shining into my life.'

Liesel watched him with awe. 'I love you Ben,' she said. 'I never thought I'd say that to anyone ever again. But I do.'

Slowly, Ben cupped her face in his hands. 'I love you, Liesel. Promise me you'll never leave me.' And he kissed her.

***

The drive back to Somerset passed in a dream: talking of how they each had first realised that they loved the other; their first impressions of each other; and particular things they loved about each other.

'You know the weirdest thing?' Ben asked.

'What?'

'We owe all this to fish and chips!'

'What!' Liesel frowned. 'Whatever do you mean?'

'Normally I rarely buy the local paper, and never read the Personal Ads section, but one night I was out and bought fish and chips and it was wrapped in a few pages from the Western Gazette. The name Samuel Goldberg caught my eye and I could just read the ad through the grease and vinegar!'

'Wow! So, this was all meant to be?'

Ben smiled. 'Yes!'

They drove on in silence until Liesel broke the spell. 'What does it all mean, Ben?'

He gave her a sideways look. 'I hope we'll get married and you'll come and live with me in Street. Or Glastonbury, if you prefer.'

A warmth spread through Liesel. 'I'd love that,' she said. 'When do we tell your parents?'

Ben was silent. 'Don't know. They may not approve, since we're cousins.'

Liesel felt like a cold shower had hit her. Of course, it was too good to be true. 'Whatever you think,' she said in a low voice, turning her head to look out the side window.

Ben drove until he found a place where he could stop the car, then he turned to her. 'Liesel,' he said, taking her face and turning it towards him. He saw the tears glittering in her eyes. 'I love you, Liesel. We will be together. I promise. I just feel I must introduce the idea to my parents slowly. I owe them that.'

Liesel nodded. 'Whatever you think is best.'

'Liesel! It's not WHATEVER! It's FOREVER!' He kissed her fiercely and she couldn't help responding.

'Oh, Ben!' Then she took a deep breath. 'Whatever's best. Come on, we'd better go. I have to get back to London tomorrow, ready to go to Kent and start hop picking!' She tried to smile.

Samuel and Evelyn were waiting for them, eager to hear all the news about their findings.

'Not a lot of progress, I'm afraid,' Ben told them.

They nodded. 'We didn't really expect much,' his father said.

'I've got the dinner ready, let's eat,' Evelyn said. 'You'll probably looking forward to good old English cooking!'

Ben and Liesel exchanged looks. They'd had wonderful French and German meals, but they nodded and said that yes that would be lovely.

***

The next day Ben took Liesel to the station. 'When will you be back from Kent?' he asked her, taking her backpack from the car.

'I'm working until the week before term starts,' she replied.

'Can I come up to London then, and we can meet?' he asked, carrying her backpack to the ticket office.

'That'd be lovely!' She smiled at him. 'Ben, I'm so happy. I hate leaving you, but I have to work. I spent all my savings on this trip.'

Ben nodded, contrite. 'I know. I'm sorry. My fault.'

'Ben!' Liesel admonished him. 'It was wonderful! I loved every minute.'

He walked to the train with her and handed her the backpack as she got into the carriage. She leaned out the window, waving to him as the train left.

He stood for a long time watching the train disappearing along the tracks.

Back home, he found his mother in the kitchen.

'I'm making a cup of tea, Ben,' she said.

'Lovely.' He smiled at her.

Not looking at him, she said carefully, 'Do you have anything to tell me, Ben?'

Startled, he looked up. 'What do you mean?'

'Oh, nothing. Just thought there might be something you've forgotten to mention.'

Ben felt himself colouring as he took the tea tray from her and went to the dining room.

***

The three weeks hop picking in Kent was exhausting. Liesel thought she'd never felt so tired. She collapsed into her bunk bed every night after dinner in the communal dining room and had no time to think of Ben. But she was delighted to earn some extra money and replenish her bank account. She only got paid on her teaching job for the hours she worked, so she hadn't been paid since the middle of July.

At last she was on the train back to London and her flat.

She let herself in. A bath and then bed were all she could think of, but a pile of letters for her sat on the hall table. Quickly she looked through them—one from home and several in Ben's handwriting. Hugging them to her, she thought she'd wait until she'd had her bath and sorted out her stuff and then lie back and read Ben's letters. She'd save the one from home until last.

With her dirty clothes in the washing machine, bathed and feeling clean, Liesel stretched out on her bed and opened Ben's letters. Her heart lifted as she read each one. The message was clear. He loved her. He wanted her, and he couldn't wait for them to be together. He'd come up the Saturday before school started back ...

With a sigh, Liesel closed her eyes, imagining living her life with Ben.

She picked up the letter from home. It was in her father's writing.

Dear Liesel

Can you come home? Your mother has had a breakdown. Archie is in prison. He was caught selling drugs. I can't cope with your mother.

I'm sorry to ask this of you, but I don't know where to turn.

I thought of asking your grandmother but she isn't well herself.

I'm sorry Liesel.

Dad

Liesel's heart sank. *I knew it was all too good to be true*, she thought bitterly. *I was never meant to find love and be happy.*

Slowly she got out pen and paper.

Dear Ben,

I'm so sorry. There's an emergency at home. I'll have to go back to Sydney as soon as possible. I'll go to the travel agents tomorrow and try and get a ticket.

It was a lovely dream. Just not meant to be.

Forget me, Ben.

Liesel.

She folded the letter, put it in an envelope and addressed it, found a stamp and wondered if she had the energy to go and post it. Tomorrow, she thought, on her way to the travel agents. *And I'd better write to Sam and Evelyn.* Then she gave into the tears.

***

Ben felt heartsick when he got Liesel's letter. He told his mother something urgent had come up and he had to go to London.

Evelyn watched, bewildered, as her son slammed around and eventually went out to his car.

'Bye, Mum,' he called as he got into his car and drove off. With the help of a street directory and stopping to make enquiries, he managed to find Liesel's flat in London. He jumped out of the car, ran up the steps and rang the bell.

Jennifer answered it and smiled when she saw who it was. 'Oh! Ben, how lovely to see you. Are you looking for Liesel?'

'Yes.'

'Oh, what a pity; she left for Heathrow about an hour ago. Why don't you come in, tell us all about your trip?' She held the door open.

'No, thanks anyway. I'll try and catch her.' Leaving Jennifer open mouthed, he ran down the steps and into his car. He had a vague idea of the way to Heathrow.

'It'd be quicker to get the tube!' Jennifer shouted after him.

After passing the same row of shops twice he stopped the car. *This is ridiculous. What kind of emergency couldn't she tell him about?* He'd never find her at Heathrow. His mind went around in circles. Her parents had had an accident? But that would be no reason to break off their relationship. She owed him an explanation. He'd have to write to her, but he didn't know her address in Australia. Her flat-mates would. He turned the car and went back to the flat.

Jennifer opened the door. 'Ben! Did you find her?'

He shook his head and grimaced. 'No, and I realised I didn't know which airline she'd be on, or which Terminal.'

'Come in. You look exhausted. I'll make a cup of coffee.'

'Thanks, that'd be good. I came back to see if you had Liesel's address in Australia.'

'Oh. Afraid not. But she stayed with an Australian friend, Jane, when she first came to England. She might be able to help.'

'Can you give me this Jane's address?'

'I'll look for it while you drink your coffee.'

Ben closed his eyes and sighed. Something didn't add up. Why couldn't she tell him what the emergency was? Perhaps her last boyfriend, the married one, had got divorced and sent for her. Anger built inside him. He drummed his fingers on the table.

Jennifer came out of her room with a piece of paper. 'Here you go. But she may have moved since Liesel was there. You might be lucky. It's not too far from here. I'll draw you a map.'

'Thanks. Have you any idea what the emergency is that made Liesel take off so quickly?'

Jennifer paused from her sketch and shrugged. 'Dunno. She just said she had bad news from home and had to go back as soon as possible.'

Ben stood and took the piece of paper. 'Thanks for the coffee, Jennifer. I'll call at Jane's now.'

Jennifer had said Liesel had received *bad* news from home. If it'd been her old boyfriend, surely, she wouldn't have said *bad*? For a few seconds he brightened. Then his mind went around in circles again.

He rang Jane's doorbell, but received no reply, so he wrote a note asking her if she could let him have Liesel's address in Australia. Then he put it through the letterbox and drove back to Bath.

His mother and Bessie greeted him at the front door. 'Hello Ben. Is everything all right?'

'I don't know, Mum,' he answered. 'Liesel's gone back to Australia unexpectedly.'

'Yes, I know.'

'What!'

'Yes, we got a letter in the post today.' She led the way to the dining room, and held the letter out to him.

He sat down at the table as he took the small piece of paper.

Dear Sam and Evelyn,

Unfortunately, I've had to go back to Australia at short notice. I'd have liked to have had time to visit you and personally thank you both for everything. It was wonderful to be able to fulfil my grandfather's wishes.

Thank you again,

Regards

Liesel.

Ben frowned. 'She doesn't say what made her take off like that.'

'I do hope she's all right.' Evelyn sighed. 'It's strange; it seems so out of character for her to just go without telling us why. And she hasn't put her Sydney address on the letter either. Do you think it's something very bad?'

'Like what?' Ben looked up at his mother, his frown deepening.

'I don't know; I just thought maybe something so horrible that she couldn't bring herself to tell us.'

Ben stood up. 'I'll take Bessie for a walk. Stretch my legs. Driving all day.'

His mother nodded.

Ben had never felt like this before. When his last relationship had ended, he'd been sad but relieved at the same time. He knew in his heart that he and Liesel were meant for each other; he'd never loved anyone like he loved Liesel. He walked until Bessie got slower and slower and then suddenly sat down.

'Sorry, old girl. We'll go home now.' He turned around and Bessie stood up and plodded beside him. 'You liked her, didn't you, Bess?' he asked.

She looked up at him and wagged her tail.

'I won't give up. I'll find her,' he said to the spaniel.

Chapter Thirty-Two

Sydney

L iesel reached Sydney at six o'clock in the morning; exhausted, she went through customs in a daze. She'd written to her father as soon as she'd booked her flight, but doubted if he'd received her letter. She wished they had a telephone. Surely most people had them these days.

She saw no sign of her father at the arrival terminal, so she dragged her case and bag out to the bus stop. The few Australian dollars remaining from when she'd left for England would cover her fare.

It was nearly midday when she eventually arrived at the house in Greenacre. She knocked on the door—not having lived at home for several years, she felt she couldn't just walk in.

Her father opened the door. Surprise, followed by relief showed on his face when he saw her.

'Dad, it's Wednesday. Shouldn't you be at work?'

He shook his head. 'Haven't been able to leave your mother,' he said. 'Come in.' He took her suitcase. 'Whatever have you got in it? It weighs a ton.'

'Yes. I wrote to you, but I think the letter hasn't arrived yet.'

Charles shook his head. 'No.'

'Dad, you must get a telephone installed.'

'I know, I know. I will.'

Liesel heard a crash, and a voice screamed out. 'I can hear Lee! It's all her fault! She had it in for Archie from the moment he was born. Her fault, and that bad company he fell in with.'

Charles sighed. 'Your mother. The doctor said the change of life and the shock of Archie being arrested sent her off the rails. She just shouts and screams, then collapses in a heap and stares into space. I don't know what to do, Liesel. I can't leave her alone.'

Suddenly Liesel's parent's bedroom door opened and her mother lurched out, her unkempt hair standing on end. She saw Liesel and pointed at her. 'I knew it was her! It's all your fault! You always hated him and made him do bad things. Get out; get out!' she screamed.

'Now, now, Madge, Liesel's just come home from England. She's tired. Why don't I make us a cup of tea, and you take some of that nice medicine the doctor left for you.'

'That's not medicine; that's poison! You're trying to poison me, Charles Martin, trying to get rid of me. You always took Lee's side against Archie. You're to blame too.'

Liesel looked on, appalled.

Then suddenly, Madge crumpled onto the sofa and started to sob.

Charles went to the kitchen and returned with a small glass beaker with pink liquid in it. 'Sip this lemonade, my dear,' he said, holding it to her lips.

She drank it in one gulp. 'I'm so tired, Charles. I think I'll lie down for a while.'

'Good idea; come, I'll help you.' He led her to the bedroom.

Liesel sat at the kitchen table and closed her eyes. *I hope I'm dreaming this.*

Her father returned and put the kettle on. 'Well, you've got the picture now,' he said. 'That's how she is most of the time. I don't know what to do. She won't let me wash her or comb her hair. I have to do as best I can after she's taken the medication the doctor gave her and is dopey and sleepy. She hardly eats anything—just picks at the food I give her.'

'I don't know what to say, Dad. What does the doctor suggest?'

'Not much. Just give her the medication when she gets hysterical, and hopefully it'll pass once she's over the change. But it was Archie who triggered it. When the police came, she wouldn't accept that he'd done anything wrong. She was trying to beat them off. I had a job to restrain her. Then Archie kept saying he was innocent and it was wrongful arrest.'

He made the tea, then sat down. 'It was awful, Liesel.' He put his head in his hands. 'Thank you for coming home. I just don't know what to do.'

'What about Aunt Naomi?'

'She's no help; she just said, "What do you expect, Charles Martin, Madge has spoilt that boy rotten since he was a baby." Then she gave me a look and said, "There's bad blood there somewhere," as if it was all my fault.'

'But, Dad, if you have to stay home with her, what about your work?'

'Haven't been able to go to work for the past few weeks. Luckily, I had some long service leave due. I'll be able to go back now you're home.'

'What!' Liesel stood up. 'What about my work?'

Charles looked down at the table and picked at the frayed tablecloth. 'You're her daughter; it's your duty,' he muttered.

'Dad, that's not fair! What will I do for money? And my career?'

'We'll work something out.' His words were barely audible. After a pause, he stood. 'Are you hungry?'

Liesel shook her head. 'No, just jetlagged, tired and in need of a shower. I'll take my case to my old room and make up the bed.'

'Thanks for coming home, Liesel.'

She put her hand on his cheek. He looked so old and worn out. 'Yes, we'll work something out, Dad.'

He nodded. 'I'll see if I can get some night-shift work in a factory, and then I can stay with your mother while you work.

'I should be able to get relief work, but I'll need the telephone, Dad. The schools just ring you when one of their teachers is sick and they need a substitute, often just the night before or very early in the morning.'

'Would you organise that, Liesel?'

'Okay; I'll just lie down for an hour, then go to the post office.'

'And then perhaps you can tell me about how you got on in England.'

Liesel gave a rueful smile. 'I found your cousin, Samuel,' she said.

Charles blinked. 'Really?'

'Yes. I thought you'd twig it from my letter.'

Charles shook his head.

'Never mind. I'll tell you another time. I'm too tired now.'

Chapter Thirty-Three

Bath 1969

September arrived and with it the start of a new school year for Ben. His mind see-sawed from anxiety to anger, but at least work kept him busy. The first weekend he returned to Bath his mother looked shocked at his appearance.

'Ben,' she exclaimed, 'are you all right? You've lost weight!'

He shrugged and tried to smile. 'Miss your home cooking, Mum.'

His father walked out of the dining room, where he'd been reading the weekend newspaper. 'Hello, son.'

'Dad.'

'Any news from Liesel?'

Ben gave his father a stony look. 'No.'

'Have you tried to telephone her?'

Ben frowned. 'No, I don't have a phone number for her.'

'What about her parents? Can you contact them? Get their phone number from directory enquiries?'

'I don't have their address, Dad.' He tried to stay patient.

Evelyn suddenly said, 'Didn't she say they lived in a suburb called Greenacre? I remember because she said it may have once been green acres but was now all houses.'

Ben looked up, feeling hopeful. 'Yes, and she said her father had been called Carl, and it was changed to Charles when they went to Australia.'

His mother took him to the hall where the phone sat on a little table. His father followed and handed him paper and a pencil.

Half an hour later, he came into the dining room, his shoulders slumped. 'They couldn't find any Charles Martin with a phone in Greenacre.'

At dinner that evening, Evelyn and Samuel exchanged a look, then Sam said, 'Ben, we were thinking. Um, you're obviously very fond of Liesel, and we are too. In fact, we were rather hoping maybe um ...'

Evelyn broke in: 'We were hoping there might be a romance happening between you two.'

Ben looked up with a frown. 'I thought perhaps you'd be against it because of us being cousins ...'

'Ben,' his father said, 'Liesel is your second cousin. Unless there was some kind of known genetic problem, then there's nothing to worry about. And I know of nothing like that in our family.'

Ben thought back to what he'd said to Liesel about waiting to tell his parents. Maybe that was the problem. But she'd said a family emergency. He closed his eyes and sighed. 'Maybe I gave her the wrong impression. But how can I tell her? She's just disappeared.'

'We were thinking,' said Sam, 'that it might be a good idea to go to Australia and look for her. Surely this Greenacre place must have a post office; you could enquire there. We thought you could go during the Christmas school holidays, perhaps your school would give you an extra week off ...'

Ben smiled, feeling lighter all of a sudden.

'And we'd like to pay for your fare as a Christmas present,' he continued.

Ben blinked and blew his nose to hide the tears coming to his eyes. 'You're the best parents,' he mumbled.

'You're the best son,' Ben and Evelyn said together.

'Now,' his father said, 'next week call in to the travel agent and find out about flights.'

His mother smiled at him. 'Yes, dear, this is really eating you up. We think you must find her and sort things out.'

Ben sat in a daze, trying to convince himself that this cousin business was behind Liesel's sudden flight. He stood. 'Thank you for the dinner, Mum. It was lovely. I think I'll take Bessie for a walk and think it through.'

Chapter Thirty-Four

Sydney

The school term leading up to the Christmas holidays was always hectic for relief teachers. As the academic year progressed, the numbers of sick teachers seemed to increase, so Liesel had no lack of jobs. And the phone had finally been installed.

On the last day of term, she got home early at three o'clock and slumped onto a chair at the kitchen table.

Her father came out of his bedroom. 'I'll be off, then,' he said. 'I gave Mum her medication just after lunch; she should be all right for a while. I had a bit of a nap too. I made dinner for you and Mum for tonight. Just heat it up.'

Liesel nodded. 'Thanks, Dad. Have you got your sandwiches?'

'Yes, love.' He gave her a quick peck on her cheek. 'I hope you'll be able to relax a bit over the Christmas holidays; you look wrecked.'

Thanks for the compliment, Dad. She didn't need reminding.

'I'll have to go and see Archie this weekend.' He picked up his lunch box. 'My shift finishes at two. Bye, love.'

Liesel got up from the table and took her school bag to her bedroom. Her bed looked so inviting; she was just thinking of lying down for a quick nap when the doorbell rang. *Damn, I hope that hasn't woken Mum.* She hurried to the door before the bell rang again and opened it ready to scowl if the caller was a salesman or a religious sect.

It was Ben.

Her mouth fell open. 'Ben!'

He dropped his backpack, held out his arms and drew her to him. 'I thought I'd never find you,' he mumbled into her hair.

'Oh, Ben, what are you doing here? Oh, come in, do.'

'Wait!' He kissed her until they both had to stop for air.

Liesel led Ben into the kitchen, suddenly feeling conscious of her appearance. 'I've just come from work. I look awful,' she said.

'Liesel, you look beautiful to me. I got to Sydney at eight o'clock this morning, and I'm wrecked too. I had a hell of a job trying to get here. I found a tourist place at the airport, and they gave me a map of Sydney. I had to get a bus, but I was on the wrong side of the road. I was all confused, the sun is in the wrong place!'

Liesel laughed. 'I know; I was confused when I went to London.'

'Anyway, I managed to get to Greenacre and found the post office. I thought I'd have a quick check of the phone book and found C Martin and this address. I didn't ring in case I scared you off. I just hoped you'd be here, or at least your parents would know where you were. I had to find you, Liesel.'

'We only got the phone in a few months ago.'

'Who is it? Is it Archie? I can hear a man's voice.' Liesel's heart sank as Madge came tottering out in her nightie. She jumped up. 'Mum, please; it's not Archie, this is Ben, a friend of mine.'

Ben stood up and held out his hand. 'How do you do, Mrs Martin?'

'Mum! Put your dressing gown on!'

'Ooh,' Madge simpered, 'how nice to meet you, Ben. Are you a friend of Archie's? He's innocent you know. It's all Lee's fault.' She scowled at Liesel, who'd fetched her mother's dressing gown.

'Mum, put it on.' Liesel held it out for Madge, but she batted it away with her hand.

'Please, let me help you, Mrs Martin.' Ben took the dressing gown and held it out.

Madge meekly put her arms in it.

'There, that's a very pretty dressing gown,' Ben said, pulling out a chair for Madge.

Liesel stared at him in amazement.

'So how is Archie?' Madge asked him. 'When did you see him last?'

Ben looked at Liesel, but she just looked at him helplessly, so he turned to Madge with a smile. 'Archie's doing really well,' he said.

'It's all Lee's fault,' her mother repeated, frowning at Liesel. 'She never liked him, sibling rivalry, you know.' She nodded at Ben knowledgeably. 'Then he got in with a bad crowd.' She sighed. 'He's such a good boy, such a caring son. Not like Lee here, who just leaves everyone in the lurch and skips off to England.' She gave Liesel another black look.

'I'll make a pot of tea,' Liesel said.

Ben stood. 'Can I help?'

'No, no.' Madge put her hand on his knee. 'Stay here and talk to me. Since Archie left, I have no-one with any intelligence to talk to.'

'Of course, Mrs Martin.' He sat down again.

'Oh, call me Madge! Now tell me, where do you work, Bill? Have you seen Archie recently? The naughty boy hasn't been to see us lately, but he has some kind of high-pressure job, so he's very busy. I expect you work with him, and he's sent you to tell us all his news.' She rambled on until Liesel came in with the tea tray.

'It's time for your medicine, Mother,' she said, indicating the small beaker of pink liquid.

Madge frowned. 'I'm not taking it! Your father is trying to poison me. I know very well what he's up to! He has a big life insurance policy on me. He just wants to get rid of me and get his hands on the money.' She clenched her lips and folded her arms defiantly.

Ben reached over and took the beaker. 'How about we share it?' he said, holding it to his mouth and pretending to drink.

Madge giggled coyly as he held the beaker to her lips. Keeping her eyes on him, she drank the liquid all in one go.

Liesel stared at Ben, who was still looking at her mother.

'See, we're both all right! Not poison at all.' He smiled.

Madge's eyes started to close. 'I'm feeling a bit sleepy, Lee. Bill can you help me to bed please?'

Ben stood and put his arm around her as Liesel came to her other side and guided them towards the bedroom. They sat Madge on the bed, then Liesel lifted her legs onto the mattress. Madge sank back onto the pillows, and Liesel drew the covers around her.

'She'll sleep now for a few hours,' she said with a sigh.

Ben followed her out and closed the door gently behind them. He took Liesel's hand, sat her down at the table and then sat down beside her. 'All right. Give.' He commanded. 'Was this the emergency?'

Liesel nodded, feeling the picture of misery. 'Yes. She had a breakdown when the police came and arrested my brother for drug trafficking. He's in prison. Dad couldn't cope. He's at work now. He's working nights, and I've been doing teaching relief work during the day. Between us we've been looking after her.'

'Liesel, my sweet, why couldn't you tell me this? Did you think it would make any difference to me? To how I think of you?' He put a finger under her chin and tilted her face towards him. 'I love you, Liesel. How could you think me so shallow?'

Tears filled her eyes. 'That's the problem, Ben. I know you. But the thing is, how can I marry, and perhaps have children, when

I have a mad mother and a drug addict brother? I must have bad genes, bad blood. I might end up like my mother! I can't inflict that on you, Ben. That's why I didn't tell you. I knew you'd say it wouldn't make any difference. But it does, Ben. It does!'

She stood and paced around the kitchen, rubbing her hands together in a futile gesture.

'I think that's my decision, Liesel. The fact is that even if you did end up like your mother, I would still love you and want to be with you. And we would have many happy years together. How old is your mother?'

Liesel shrugged. 'I think maybe late fifties. She's never said.'

'And you're what? Twenty-four?'

'Nearly twenty-five.'

'Well then, we'd have at least thirty wonderful years together even if it did happen. I'm sure this hasn't affected your father's love for your mother.'

Liesel nodded slowly. 'My aunt always said my father adored my mother from the day he first met her.'

Ben took her hand and kissed it.

'And what about my brother? Not only is he an addict but he's also a mean, cruel person.'

'Oh, Liesel! That doesn't mean a child of ours would turn out like that!'

Liesel raised her eyes and looked at him. 'I love you, Ben Goldberg,' she whispered, her eyes full of tears.

'When does your father get home?'

'He's working until two, so perhaps three o'clock in the morning.'

'And your mother will sleep for another two hours?

Liesel nodded.

Ben stood, still holding her hand. 'Which way to your bedroom?'

She looked at him, open mouthed.

He smiled. 'Liesel, my darling, if you intend to lose the plot when you're fifty something, then we only have, oh, what? Thirty years left? We have to make the most of them, starting right now.'

She hesitated.

'What's the matter?'

'I don't have my nice underwear on.'

Ben laughed, bent over and picked her up in his arms. 'Oh, Liesel! I'm not actually interested in your underwear just now. Show me the way!'

***

A feeble voice calling, 'Charles, Charles,' roused them a few hours later.

'Oh, damn, my mother's awake.' Liesel sprang out of bed and started to pull on her clothes.

Ben lay watching her. 'Come here.' He held out his arms.

'No; she'll be wandering around tripping over and moving stuff around.'

As if on cue, they heard a crash and a murmured expletive.

'What are you doing, Mum?'

'I have to get the dinner; your father will be home soon. What's this in the oven?'

'Mum, you're in the laundry, and that's the washing machine, not the oven.'

'Of course, I knew that. I'm not stupid. I wish you wouldn't keep putting things away in the wrong places, Lee. Can't you do anything right? You're useless!'

'Come, Mum, how about you sit down, and I'll make a cup of tea and get the dinner on.'

'Where's that nice friend of Archie's? Bob?'

'I'm here, Mrs Martin.' Ben appeared in the doorway.

'Oh, Bob.' She smiled and batted her eyelashes at him, then slipped out of her dressing gown and took his arm.

Liesel was horrified to realise her mother was flirting with Ben.

He gave Liesel a wink and said to Madge, 'Why don't we get your dressing gown on and sit down.'

Liesel picked up the discarded dressing gown, and Ben helped her mother put it on.

'Come and sit down,' he said. She followed him meekly, then he said, 'Mrs Martin, I'm afraid I have to leave now. I have to find somewhere to stay.'

Madge's face dropped. 'No, you can't leave; you have to tell me all about Archie. Lee! Bill can stay here, can't he? He can sleep in your room, and you can sleep on the couch. We have to keep Archie's room free; he could be back any minute.'

Ben looked at Liesel with a grin. 'Thank you, Madge, but I couldn't possibly turn Liesel out of her room. Perhaps I could sleep on the couch just for tonight, and then in the morning I can find somewhere to stay around here.'

Madge pouted, then looked gratified when Liesel turned to her and said, 'Mum, I think that's a good idea of yours because if *Ben*,' she emphasised his name, 'were to sleep on the couch, Dad would get a shock when he comes home in the dark and finds a strange man sleeping on the couch.' She looked at Ben, a smile hovering around her eyes. 'Now, let's have dinner. Dad said he'd prepared something, so we just have to heat it up. And *Ben* must be starving.'

'Oh, yes, indeed I am.' Ben looked at Liesel, a wealth of meaning in his grin.

Liesel blushed, hurried to the kitchen and opened the fridge. A big pot sat on the top shelf. She put it on the kitchen counter and took off the lid. 'Dad's a star; he's made a big pot of stew, heaps for all of us.' She put it on the gas stove and started to lay the table.

'Um, Liesel, do you think I might freshen up? I've not had a shower since I left England.'

'Oh, Ben! I'm so sorry; I didn't think. Let me find you a towel. Bring your bag into my room.'

***

Ben returned from the shower, glowing and freshly shaved. Liesel looked at him with mounting desire. She couldn't believe how good he was with her mother. Usually Madge would say she wasn't hungry and have to be coaxed to eat. She'd lost a lot of weight.

'Now, Madge, will I serve you some stew? It looks delicious,' he said.

'Madge simpered at him. 'Thank you, Bill, I mean Ben.' She giggled.

Liesel cringed. *Oh, Mum, stop it.*

'It's quite delicious; your husband is a good cook,' Ben told Madge.

'Thank you,' she replied with a gracious air, then ate everything on her plate, glancing at Ben with each spoonful and receiving approving smiles.

At last the meal was over. Liesel got up to clear the table and wash up.

'Please, let me.' Ben stood, but Madge took his arm.

'No, no, you sit and talk to me, Bob,' she said. 'Lee can manage.'

Liesel smiled. 'Thanks, Ben, but there isn't much.' Then she whispered, 'It's nearly time for her medication, so just keep her quiet.'

'Oh, look, Liesel's brought that lovely lemonade for us, Madge,' Ben said when Liesel brought the medication. 'Shall we share it again?'

'Ooh, you naughty boy; yes, but don't drink all of it, save some for me.'

Liesel put her hand to her forehead. *What on earth must Ben think?* She finally managed to get her mother to the bathroom and then to bed. She came back into the living room and flopped down beside Ben.

He took her hand. 'What do the doctors say about your mother?'

'They don't really know. Her doctor thinks it might pass and she'll eventually recover. But without the medication she's quite unhinged.' She lapsed into silence. Then looked at Ben. 'When I think about it, I'm sure my dad loves my mother, and feels the same way about her as your dad feels about your mum.' Slowly, she continued, 'and the way I feel about you. It wouldn't matter what happened, I'd always love you.'

Ben leaned over and kissed her. 'I'd really like to make love to you, my darling Liesel, but I'm totally jet lagged and stuffed. In fact, I can hardly see straight. But I've found you, and that's all that matters. Liesel,' he turned her to face him, 'I thought I'd lost you, that you didn't want anything to do with me. I have my parents to thank for getting me here.'

'Really? I thought they'd be against us being together on account of us being second cousins.'

'No, quite the opposite.' Ben gave an enormous yawn. 'Liesel, I've been under so much stress trying to find you, and now I have, and I am so happy, but so tired.'

'Come on, into my bed. But I'll sleep on the couch!' She looked at him mischievously. 'Else I wouldn't let you sleep!'

Ben nodded, his eyes half closed, and followed her into the bedroom. He took off his shoes and fell onto her bed.

Liesel covered him up and kissed him, but he was already asleep. She checked that her mother remained asleep, then got the doona from Archie's bed and settled down on the couch, thinking that she'd never been so happy. She lay awake for some time, going over the day's events in her mind. It seemed she'd only been asleep for a few minutes when she felt her father urgently shaking her.

'What's wrong, Liesel? Why are you on the couch? Is Mum all right?'

She sat up, instantly alert. 'Oh, Dad,' she sighed. 'Everything's fine. Remember I told you I'd found your cousin? Well his son came today and is sleeping in my bed. Go to bed, Mum's all right.' She fell back into a deep sleep.

***

Ben woke at five in the morning and opened his eyes, feeling totally confused. Then reality hit. He'd found Liesel! They'd made love in this very bed! For the first time. And she loved him.

He got up and looked at his watch, then crept out into the living room. Liesel was sound asleep on the couch. He stood and looked at her for a few minutes before going to the bathroom.

When he came back, he found Liesel stirring.

She opened her eyes, saw him and sat bolt upright. 'I thought it was all a dream,' she whispered.

He held out one hand, putting a finger to his lips with the other, and led her back to her bedroom.

Two hours later Liesel whispered, 'I'd better get dressed and see to Mum and let Dad sleep for a bit. Would you like a cup of coffee?'

Ben nodded.

They heard Madge coming out of her bedroom, mumbling, 'Where's that nice Bill?'

He quickly pulled on his pants and came into the living room. 'Here I am, Madge. Did you sleep well?'

'Oh yes, indeed.' She looked at Ben from under her lashes.

'Now, how can I help?' Ben raised his eyebrows at Liesel.

She went to the fridge and looked inside. 'I usually go shopping on a Saturday morning so there isn't much to eat except toast and there're some eggs here, how about scrambled eggs?'

'Lovely,' said Ben.

Liesel looked at her mother. 'You too, Mum?'

Madge was watching Ben. He nodded at her. 'Yes, lovely,' she replied.

'After breakfast I'll go shopping with you, Liesel,' Ben said, 'and then I must find somewhere to stay.

Liesel's father came into the living room. 'I thought I heard voices,' he said.

Ben stood up and held out his hand. 'I'm Ben Goldberg,' he said. 'Your Uncle Hans' grandson.'

Charles mouth fell open. He stared at Ben as if at an apparition as Liesel came out of the kitchen carrying a tray with crockery and cutlery.

'Dad, this is Ben.'

Charles nodded. 'G'day,' he said, taking Ben's hand.

'Liesel tracked down my father, Samuel, in England. I'm so pleased to meet you. I think you must be my second cousin, once removed. Something like that, anyway.' He turned to Liesel, 'Didn't you tell your father all about us?'

Liesel reddened. 'Somehow I couldn't. I couldn't bear talking about you, knowing it was all lost.'

'Bob knows Archie,' Madge suddenly said, taking Ben's hand.

Charles flinched and frowned.

'I'll explain later, Dad,' Liesel said. 'Would you like breakfast? I've made scrambled eggs.'

Still staring at Ben, Charles shook his head. 'No thanks, love.'

Liesel walked back into the kitchen and returned with plates of scrambled eggs and a rack of toast. 'Ben, help yourself. Mum, here's your plate. Do you need help?'

Madge glared at her daughter. 'I'm perfectly capable of feeding myself, Lee,' she said, taking a piece of toast and daintily buttering it.

Charles stared at his wife. It seemed she'd changed overnight. At last Charles found his voice. 'So you live in Australia, Ben?'

'No, no. I live in England.'

Charles brow furrowed. 'I don't understand. What are you doing in Australia?'

Ben looked at Liesel, who blushed. 'Long story, Mr Martin. Perhaps I could have a word with you later. But first I must find accommodation, a youth hostel, if there's one near here.'

Charles sat down suddenly at the table, then gave a strange laugh. 'You're joking, of course. It's Christmas in four days and peak holiday season. You won't find a place anywhere. You'd better stay here in Archie's room.'

At this, Madge blinked and frowned at her husband. 'Archie might come home at any minute,' she said.

Ben took her hand. 'Madge, Archie's very busy; I don't think he'll have time to come home for a while. But I'm sure he'll be thinking of you all.'

Madge's face broke out into a huge smile. 'Of course, how silly of me! He's very busy, and of course you can stay in Archie's room, Bill, I mean Bob.' She continued placidly eating her breakfast.

Charles looked at Liesel in bewilderment.

Liesel shrugged and shook her head. Her mother had totally changed since Ben's appearance on the scene.

Ben turned to Charles. 'That's very kind of you, Mr Martin.'

'Charles, call me Charles, please.' He looked at each of them and then stood. 'I'll go and shower—if you'll be all right with your mum, Liesel.'

'Of course, Dad.' Liesel turned to her mother. 'Mum, are Aunt Naomi and Granny coming for Christmas Day?

Her mother looked at her vacantly.

'Christmas Day. It's in a few days. I need to get shopping; will they be coming?'

Her mother nodded. Then shook her head.

Liesel sighed. 'I'll ask Dad when he gets out of the shower. I'll just clear up here. Ben, I'll show you Archie's room; I'd better check that it's all okay in there.' She led Ben down the hall and opened the other bedroom door. 'I'll put fresh sheets on the bed.'

Ben caught her wrist and drew her into his arms. 'Darling Liesel, I have my sleeping bag and a mat. I can just put that down. No need to go to any trouble. In fact, I'd prefer it.'

Liesel nodded. 'Yes, I can understand that. All right. Thank you, Ben.

He closed the bedroom door and kissed her.

***

Liesel was dreading Christmas Day. Her Grandmother and Aunt Naomi were coming for Christmas dinner as usual.

Ben watched her as she made out the shopping list on Christmas Eve. 'Darling, I can help.'

Liesel looked up. 'No one has ever called me darling before.'

Ben smiled. 'Good. Keep it that way.'

'As soon as Dad gets home, we can go shopping.'

'Why don't I go and you stay with your mother?' Ben stood up and held out his hand. 'Give me the list. And the shopping bags—no arguments.'

Liesel just stared at him. 'How will you know where to go?'

Ben scanned the list. 'Butcher, baker, candle-stick maker.' He looked up, smiling. 'Oh, sorry, grocer, vegetable shop. Right?'

Liesel nodded. 'I guess.'

'I'm not just a pretty face, you know.' Ben grinned and drew her to him. 'Anyway, I have to go to the chemist.' He gave her a wink.

She blushed. Somehow neither of them had been prepared for love making. Best not to take any chances!

After he'd left, Liesel sat at the kitchen table, finishing her cup of coffee. It felt so strange to have someone who loved her and wanted to help her.

***

Christmas Day found them all seated around the table, Christmas crackers pulled and silly paper hats on their heads. Liesel's grand-mother, Aunt Naomi and her mother each tried to impress Ben. Her father focused on carving the turkey.

Liesel looked at Ben and smiled. He was so amazing. It felt as if he'd cast a magic tranquilising spell over the table. Instead of the usual bickering and arguing, everyone was being civil and well behaved. And with no prospect of a drunken Archie falling around the place, perhaps it would be a good Christmas for once.

She thought back to the last Christmas. She'd been on her own in London, now she had Ben. And the Christmas before that! That awful time after finding out about James! How could she ever have imagined that she loved him? Now she knew what real love was!

He father looked at her and smiled. 'Wake up, Liesel, and serve the turkey.'

***

Liesel and Ben spent hours discussing what they'd do in the future.

'I'd really like you to come to England and live,' Ben said.

Liesel sighed. 'Yes, I'd like that, too. But what about my mother? I can't really leave Dad on his own with her.'

Ben wanted to say, 'She's not your responsibility, Liesel. You have your own life to live.' But he knew it was no good to say that. If the situation was reversed and it was his mother who was sick, could he leave his father to cope on his own? 'It seems I must try and get a job teaching in Australia and a visa to come here and live,' he said.

Liesel frowned. 'It's very difficult. If I have to be here to mind my mother while my father is at work, it would mean we'd have to live here. And then when Archie comes out of prison ...' Her shoulders slumped. 'It would be unbearable and impossible.'

'How about if we rented somewhere near here and you just come over when your Dad is working?'

Liesel brightened. 'That's a possibility. Oh, darling Ben, why is life so difficult?'

He took her in his arms. 'We'll work something out.'

***

All too soon, it was time for Ben to return to England. At the departure gate, he gave Liesel one last kiss. 'Promise me you won't run away again, or change your mind,' he said. 'We'll sort it all out. As soon as I get back, I'll apply for a permanent residency visa. Hopefully I'll be able to get work.' He took out his handkerchief and carefully wiped the tears from her eyes.

'Oh, Ben, I don't want you to go!'

'I know, darling. It won't be for long, then we'll be together for ever.' He smiled. 'Perhaps I should have done like Rebecca's Mike and got a special license and married you here and now. Just to make sure you wouldn't change your mind!'

Liesel gave a watery smile as he let her go and picked up his backpack.

"Bye, darling. I love you.' They each said.

Chapter Thirty-Five

1970

*M*y darling Liesel,
    I got back to England safely. I told my parents that I'd found you. They were delighted, and when I explained about you wanting to end our relationship due to your mother's illness and your brother's problems, they understood.

They'd been hoping that you would come to England to live, but when I told them the situation with your mother, they could see that the best solution in the meantime was for me to migrate to Australia.

I've been doing some research, and there's something called a £10 Assisted Passage. Apparently, Australia will pay my fare, it just costs me £10. I'd have to give up my passport when I arrive, and if I want to return to England within two years, I'd have to repay the Australian Government what my full fare would have c ost.

I've sent off for all the paper work. I have to have medical exams and police checks etc. but I think that will all be fine.

I cannot wait to be with you again, my dearest Liesel.

Please write soon.

With all my love

Ben

***

Liesel didn't get many calls for substitute teaching for the first few weeks of the new school term. Which was good, because she'd started feeling sick in the mornings. When she realised she'd missed her period, she knew she must be pregnant. It must've happened during those first two days of Ben's visit, when they hadn't used any protection.

At first, she was thrilled to think she was carrying Ben's baby. Then the reality hit her. What would Ben think? Should she tell him yet? It might not be a baby; it might be a false alarm, and anyway would he want a baby? How could she look after her mother and a baby? Her thoughts went all over the place. Definitely not an abortion. Were they even legal in New South Wales? She rushed to the toilet with another session of vomiting. She had Ben's parents' phone number and the number of his school in Street in case of emergencies, but she decided to wait before letting him know.

Luckily her father was asleep in the mornings when she had the worst bouts of morning sickness, but only a few weeks later, he heard her vomiting in the bathroom and came to see what was wrong.

'Are you all right, love?' he asked.

Liesel wiped her mouth with a tissue and flushed the toilet. It was a shameful thing to have to admit to being un-married and pregnant, but she thought she'd have to tell him at some stage. It was now the end of February. She stood up. 'Dad, I'm pregnant. I'm expecting a baby.'

Her father just stared at her. Then frowned. 'Is that good?' he asked.

Liesel gave a weak laugh. How like her father to respond like that.

'I don't know, Dad.'

'Is it Ben's?'

'Of, course, Dad! Who else's would it be?'

'Does he know?'

'Not yet; I don't know what to do.'

'You'd better tell him. If he won't marry you, then he'll have to pay maintenance.'

Liesel stared at her father. She felt suddenly weak. 'I must lie down for a bit, Dad. Please don't mention it to anyone, especially not Mum.'

He nodded. 'Go and lie down; I'll bring you a cup of tea.' He patted her shoulder. 'Don't worry, love. I'll look after you.'

Liesel's eyes filled with tears. How lucky she was to have such a kind father.

***

Dearest Ben,

That is great news about the £10 passage. I've heard of it, over here they call those English migrants £10 Pommies ...

I have some news. I hope it won't shock you too much. And if you change your mind about coming to Australia and marrying me, I'll understand.

I'm pregnant. The baby is due sometime in August. It must have happened the day you arrived.

Oh, Ben. I hope it's not too much of a shock for you. I've told my father. He was all right about it, which is unusual. No-one else knows. Ben, what should I do?

I love you Ben,

Liesel

Liesel posted the letter with a heavy heart. How would he react to the news?

***

Ten days later, at nine o'clock at night, the phone rang. Thinking it was a school wanting a replacement teacher, Liesel answered it.

'Hello. Liesel?'

'Yes!' Liesel's heart thudded. It was Ben.

'Liesel, how are you? Are you all right? Liesel, your news about the baby is wonderful! I just wish I was with you!'

She swallowed, suddenly unable to speak.

'Liesel! Are you there? I can't hear you.'

She managed to find her voice. 'Yes, Ben. I'm here. I was worried that you'd want me to get rid of the baby.'

'Liesel! How could you think such a thing? I love you, and a baby will be wonderful.'

Tears of relief filled Liesel's eyes. She sniffed. 'Oh Ben, I miss you so much.'

'My darling, I need to be with you as soon as possible. I don't know how long this ten-pound thing takes. I must ring off now; I'm calling from a phone box in Street, and my coins have run out. Love you ...'

The line went dead.

Liesel flopped onto the floor and wiped her eyes. She seemed to have become so emotional since getting pregnant.

Her mother drifted into the hall. 'What is it, Lee? Why are you on the floor crying?'

'It's all right Mum. Is it time for your medication?'

***

Dearest Liesel

I told my parents your news. They were overjoyed! And they wanted to give me the money for the fare to Australia, so I could come as soon as possible instead of waiting for the £10 scheme. But I have enough savings.

I've given in my notice at work, but I have to stay until the end of term. I'm organising visas and stuff and am hoping to be with you after Easter.

Darling Liesel. Everything will be fine.

Our baby will be beautiful.

All my love

Ben xxx

PS Perhaps you could look at places to rent near your parents. Nothing too expensive.

Liesel burst into tears when she read this letter. Suddenly everything looked bright. Ben would be here after Easter! She was sure he'd soon get work teaching.

She checked her bank statement. Somehow there wasn't a lot in her account. She only got paid for the hours she worked, and of course there'd been no work over the Christmas school holidays. She sighed.

Dearest Ben

I'm so thrilled you will be coming soon. I can't wait to see you. xxx

I don't have enough money to get a place for us yet. I only get paid for the hours I work, and you have to have a month's rent in advance and the same amount as a bond.

I'll see what I can do. Dad might know someone with rooms to let.

As you know, there is only a single bed in my room ... and really no room for a baby.

Mum is about the same and Dad is okay. He said that Archie might be coming out on parole at Easter. I can't bear the thought of being in the same house as him.

All my love,

Liesel.

***

Ben worried when he got this letter. He had some savings and hoped it would be enough to rent somewhere and keep them until he found work.

The following weekend when he went to see his parents in Bath, they seemed a bit edgy. 'Are you all right, Mum? Dad?'

His mother beamed, looked at his father and said, 'We've been thinking. We wanted to give you a nice wedding present, but we think it would be best if we gave you money instead. When you get to Australia, you and Liesel will want to get married and have your own place. And we hope to be able to come and visit you when the baby is born, so it'll be nice to be able to stay with you.'

Ben just stared at them.

'So we want to give you some money towards settling down, renting somewhere and so on.'

Ben stared at the cheque for . 'No, that's far too much for a wedding present.'

'It's what we both want to do.' They smiled at him, both seemed so happy to be able to do something for their only child.

Ben blew his nose. 'Thank you.' He hugged them both.

***

By Easter, Ben had managed to transfer some money to Liesel's bank account, and she'd found a place to rent. Fortunately, she managed to buy some furniture from the outgoing tenant, and then only needed the minimum to make the place comfortable. Her father helped her take some of her things there, but she waited for Ben to come before she moved in.

The day of Ben's arrival finally came. His flight got to Sydney in the afternoon, and Liesel went to the Airport to meet him. She cried when she saw him. *Pregnancy makes you so emotional!*

'Darling Liesel! Let me look at you!' He wrapped his arms around her. 'Mmmh, there's a bit more of you than when I saw you last!' he said with a smile. 'I've brought a lot of stuff. Do you think we can manage on the bus?'

Liesel frowned. 'Probably, but we must get straight back to my Dad. He has to work tonight, and he'll be waiting for me. You can sleep in my bed, and I'll sleep on the couch. Tomorrow we can go and look at our new home and sort things out. Let me help with your stuff.'

'No, darling! No heavy lifting!'

Liesel laughed; she thought she would burst with joy.

By an unhappy co-incidence on that very day, Archie was let out on parole.

Back at her parent's house, Liesel opened the front door, walked in, and the first person she saw was Archie. Her mother hovered in the background, mumbling about darling Archie being 'home from his important work'.

'Well, look who's here!' Archie exclaimed, then he looked Liesel up and down. 'Well, well, looks like my big, smart sister's either put on weight or some bloke's got her up the duff!' He gave a mocking laugh.

Ben entered in time to overhear this exchange. He walked over to Archie and caught him by the throat. 'Don't ever talk to my future wife like that again,' he growled.

'Oh, a ten-pound Pommy!' Archie managed to say.

Charles came out from the bedroom. 'I'm off to work,' he started to say, then saw the situation.

Ben let go of Archie, who shook himself, turned to his father and sneered. 'I suppose the only way Lee could get a husband would be to get pregnant.'

Charles stepped forward and clenched his fist. 'Enough of that talk or you're out of this house!'

There was a stunned silence.

Liesel had never seen her father stand up to Archie before. She didn't know what to do. She didn't want to stay in the house with Archie there, but she had to stay for her mother.

Charles looked around at them all. 'Welcome, Ben. Nice to see you again. You and Liesel must want to go to your new home. Archie, do you think you could give mum her medication in another hour and get her into bed and stay with her? She should sleep through the night. I'll be back about three o'clock.'

Liesel opened her mouth to say, no, you couldn't trust Archie to stay in or to give his mother the right medication, but Ben gave her hand a warning squeeze.

'Oh, of course I can. I can take care of my dear mama, can't I, Mum?'

Madge nodded vigorously. 'So lovely to have Archie home again.'

Charles looked at Archie. 'Come into the kitchen. I'll show you what she has to have. Tablets at seven o'clock and then the medicine at eight, and she'll go to the bathroom and then to bed.

Maybe make her a hot drink, and there's dinner all prepared, just heat it up. Think you can do that?'

Archie shrugged. 'No problem. I'm not an idiot.'

Charles turned to Ben and Liesel. 'You two go now. We'll be all right.'

Liesel went to her bedroom and gathered a few things. She found Ben outside waiting on the path.

He looked ruefully at his bags. 'Is it far?'

Liesel laughed. 'About five minutes' walk. We can go slowly, and I can carry something. Really, I'm not an invalid.' They walked slowly along. 'I hope Mum will be okay with Archie,' she said.

Ben nodded. 'Yes, well, we can only hope.'

'Looks like you might be staying awhile,' Liesel said, indicating the baggage.

'I'm planning to.' Ben smiled. 'Oh, Liesel, it's wonderful to be with you at last. I've been so worried about you on your own. How soon can we get married?'

'I think it takes about a month. I'm not sure. I was waiting for you to come.' Liesel gave him a sideways look. 'I wasn't sure if you'd actually come.'

Ben stopped walking and frowned at her. 'Really? You really didn't trust me?'

'I do, now that you're here. But when you're so far away, doubts creep in.'

'Well, I'm here now, so no more doubts. At least, that's if you still want to marry me ...'

Liesel laughed. 'Oh, I might as well, now you've come half way round the world!'

'How much further is this place? I'll show you "Might as well"!'

***

Banging on their door at four o'clock in the morning woke them.

'What the ...' Ben pulled on his pants and went to the door.

Liesel's father stood there, distraught.

'Ben, where's Liesel?'

'Come in, Charles!'

Liesel came running out of the bedroom, pulling a dressing gown over her shoulders. 'What is it, Dad?'

'Your mum. She's lying on the sofa; I think she's gone! Oh, Liesel! I got home from work, and your mum's out cold with an empty bottle of sleeping tablets in her hand, and Archie's on the floor snoring, and I can't wake them. I think your mum is gone! Oh, Liesel, what shall I do?'

Ben took charge. 'We'd better call an ambulance; we don't have a phone here yet. I'll run back to your place and make the call. I think I can remember the way. Just let me put on a shirt. Liesel, get dressed and walk your dad back.'

The house lights were on and the front door wide open when Ben reached the Martin's house. He looked at Liesel's mother and took her pulse. Nothing, and she wasn't breathing. Archie lay on the floor snoring. This wouldn't look good, he thought. *Too late for Madge, but poor Charles doesn't need any more stress with Archie.*

He dialled 999 on the phone, then remembered it was triple zero in Australia. He asked for an ambulance and explained that a lady seemed to have taken too many sleeping tablets by mistake. Then he dragged Archie into his bedroom and hoisted him onto his bed.

Charles and Liesel arrived just before the ambulance, both in tears.

Charles knelt beside his wife and held her hand. 'Madge, oh Madge,' he said. 'I'm so sorry.'

Ben put his arms around Liesel. 'I shouldn't have left her with Archie,' she sobbed.

'Sorry, mate; I think she's gone,' one of the ambulance men said as they lifted Madge onto a stretcher. 'What happened?'

Ben stepped in. 'Her husband here was working night shift and just got home to find his wife like this. Their son, Archie was minding her, but she must have woken up and found the bottle while Archie was still sleeping.'

The ambulance man looked at Ben. 'Who are you?'

Ben sighed. 'This is her daughter, Liesel, and I'm her boyfriend. We live just down the road. Charles came running to us in a panic. He didn't know what to do.'

'We'll have to call the police; don't touch anything.'

They all stared at the ambulance men as one of them radioed to the police station. 'We'll have to wait for the police,' one of them explained.

'I'll make a cup of tea. Is that all right?' Ben said, looking at the ambulance men. 'I think Liesel and her father are in shock.'

The ambulance men nodded. 'Good idea. Her husband looks pretty shaken.'

Charles sat on the lounge, white faced and shaking.

'Where's the son, then?' said one of the ambulance men.

'I think he's still asleep,' Ben said. 'He's not well.'

'Better wake him up.' The ambulance men stood when they heard the police siren in the distance.

Ben looked at Liesel and her father. Neither of them seemed able to move. He walked into the kitchen and put the kettle on, then went to Archie's room.

'Archie!' he said softly, shaking him. 'Wake up. The police are here. They want to know what happened to your mother.'

'Wah? Wassup?' Archie lolled over in the bed.

Ben went to the bathroom, dunked a hand towel in cold water, came back and sloshed it over Archie's face.

Archie sat up. 'What you do that for? Fuck off!' he snarled.

'Get up, Archie. The police are here.'

What!' Archie leapt up. 'I've been okay—no drugs. wadda they wan?'

'Your mother is dead.' Ben's anger made him brutal.

Archie blinked. 'Pommy bastard; get out, leave me alone.' He tried to aim a punch at Ben, who just looked at him with distaste.

'You'd better calm down. They'll want to question you about your mother,' Ben said, then left to make tea.

Archie stumbled out of his bedroom and went quiet when he saw the police. 'I gave her the medicine and her tablets and settled her in bed, just like Dad told me to,' he whined. 'Then I went to bed and next thing I knew, everyone was here.'

The policemen took their statements.

'Looks like accidental death,' one said. 'There'll have to be an autopsy and an inquest of course.'

Charles and Liesel looked bewildered.

'Thank you,' Ben said to the ambulance men as they took Madge's body out.

'And thank you, officers.' He nodded to the policemen. 'Do you know when the autopsy is likely to be? When will we be able to arrange the funeral?'

When he saw them staring at him, Ben rubbed his eyes. 'Sorry if I seem a bit abrupt, but I only got off the plane from England today; I'm a bit jet lagged, and my girlfriend is expecting our baby, and I'm worried what this shock will do to her.'

'Okay, mate. We understand. It all looks straightforward. Shouldn't be a problem.' He tipped his cap at Ben. 'Good night.'

Ben closed the front door.

Archie looked at them. 'I'm going back to bed,' he slurred. 'I took two of mum's sleepin' tablets, feel a bit drowsy.'

Ben said nothing. He turned to Charles. 'Come, Charles; drink this tea, then I think you should go to bed, too.'

Charles shook his head. 'No. I'll just sit here. You take Liesel back to your place. She needs her rest.'

Liesel still looked very pale.

'No. Come, Liesel, into your old bed. I'll sleep on the couch here.' She let him lead her to her old bedroom, where he gently tucked her up in the bed. 'Try and rest, my darling,' he whispered.

Back out in the lounge, Ben lay on the couch.

Charles sat opposite him in the old arm chair. 'I loved her, you know. She was my life,' he muttered.

'I understand,' Ben said and closed his eyes. He hadn't had any sleep for two days what with the long flight and all that had happened. Charles rambled on, but Ben didn't hear; he slept.

***

The autopsy confirmed barbiturate poisoning and probable accidental death. The funeral was a week later and a very small affair. Madge had few friends, but her mother and sister, Naomi, were there, and several of Charles's friends came to support him.

Archie was absent. He'd disappeared the morning of the funeral and hadn't returned.

Ben thought privately that it was a blessing. When he was still missing several days later, however, Charles started to panic.

'He's probably breached his parole,' he said the following Sunday when Ben and Liesel went over to have breakfast with him. He twisted his fork in his hands as they sat eating. 'But I'll be all right here on my own, Liesel; don't worry about me.'

'Oh, Dad! Are you sure?'

Charles nodded. But Ben was concerned that Archie would come back and start abusing his father. Nevertheless, he and Liesel had to get on with their own lives. At least Madge's death had relieved Liesel from the responsibility of being available all the time when her father was working.

'Maybe you can work days again, Dad. The night shift has been ...' Liesel paused, about to say, 'killing you,' but then continued, 'affecting your health.'

Charles nodded. 'I'll try.'

**

At last Ben and Liesel settled into their rented home. They had the phone installed, and Ben found temporary work as a relief teacher.

'Would it seem callous if we were to get married so soon after your mum's funeral?' he said to Liesel as they washed up a few nights later.

Liesel shook her head. 'We'll just make it a very small affair. We have to go to the registry office in Sydney and fill out forms and stuff, and then a month later we can tie the knot.' She smiled at Ben.

'Can we go tomorrow? I don't have a class. Do you?' Ben asked.

'No classes tomorrow, so yes, we'll take the phone off the hook, just in case a school rings up between now and tomorrow morning!'

**

They were married a month later. Liesel's father gave her away, and her Aunt Naomi and a few of Liesel's friends also came to the registry office. The wedding reception was a small affair at a local hotel.

'I'm sorry I can't afford a big wedding for you, Liesel,' her father whispered to her as they went into the registry office.

'It's all right, Dad! We both understand, and anyway, neither of us want a big wedding.'

After the ceremony, Liesel looked at the gold band on her finger. 'I can't believe I'm now Liesel Goldberg! It's like everything we've learned has come full circle.' She looked up at Ben.

He smiled at her. 'Yes, indeed, Mrs Goldberg. Full Circle.'

They spent a week in a small seaside town on the south coast, chosen because they could get there by train.

Liesel worried about her father, though. 'I think Dad must be very lonely,' she said to Ben. 'There's always been someone in the house, and now suddenly, there's no one.'

'Hmm,' Ben murmured, wondering where this was leading. He kept his thoughts to himself.

Back from their honeymoon, they called round to see Charles and were surprised to find him just coming out the front door with a dog on a lead.

He smiled at them. 'Welcome back. This is Goldie.' He indicated the dog. 'One of my mates had to go into a nursing home, and he couldn't take his dog. He asked me to look after her.' He bent down to pat the rather overweight Labrador, who wagged her tail and licked his hand.

'I always wanted a dog,' Charles continued, looking at Liesel, 'but your mother wasn't keen. She said they made too much work, dropping hair everywhere and muddy paws. I was just taking Goldie for a walk ...'

'That's great, Dad,' Liesel said. 'Perhaps you can call round later on.'

'Can I bring Goldie?'

'Of course!' Ben stooped to pat her. 'I love dogs. I miss my old spaniel. Perhaps we can get a dog?' He looked up at Liesel.

She nodded. 'Yes, that'd be lovely!'

They watched Charles walk briskly along the road.

Liesel turned to Ben. 'I've never seen Dad so bright and cheerful; it looks like Goldie's given him a new lease of life!'

***

Their baby, a son, was born at the end of August. They called him Samuel Charles. Ben's parents came to stay a few weeks later.

Charles felt a bit nervous about meeting his long-lost cousin. 'Are they posh?' he asked Liesel before they arrived.

'No, they're both lovely.'

Evelyn was enchanted with baby Sam. 'Oh, he's so like Ben when he was a baby!' she exclaimed.

Samuel looked at his grandson and nodded. He turned to Charles. 'Does he remind you of anyone?'

Charles shook his head. 'Not really.' He frowned and looked at Liesel. 'But maybe his nose?'

Liesel tried to change the subject. 'Dad, you and Samuel do have a likeness to each other, you know.'

The two men soon relaxed, and Charles was fascinated to hear all that Samuel could remember about his childhood in Mannheim and their grandfather, Fritz.

Samuel sighed. 'After Ben and Liesel went to Germany to try and find out what happened to Fritz and my parents, Evelyn and I thought we should make more enquiries. Well, we didn't have a lot of success. Apparently, the Nazis destroyed a lot of the records from the concentration camps. We can only assume that my parents and your other grandparents perished in the camps.'

Both men fell silent.

***

Several months later, Archie's body was found under a disused railway bridge. It appeared he'd died from an overdose of heroin. Liesel was relieved that Archie hadn't turned up while Ben's parents had visited. Now that worry would no longer bother her.

Chapter Thirty-Six

Sydney, 2019

I was thirteen when my Grandmother Goldberg gave me the box. It was just after Pop Goldberg's funeral. Nan Goldie, as we called her, to distinguish her from our other granny, Nan Peterson, seemed to deflate after Pop's funeral. I know that sounds weird, but they always did everything together and finished each other's sentences and stuff. I think she really missed him. But then she said she had something special for me. Naturally my interest was piqued. So I was disappointed when she sat me down at the kitchen table and brought out this old box.

She placed it reverently on the table and looked at me. 'Open it,' she commanded, still fixing me with that gaze.

I did, and was disappointed to find a load of old papers.

'Take those papers out,' she said. She seemed excited, as if she couldn't wait for me to be blown away by what was there.

At the very bottom, I found something wrapped in velvet. I reached in.

'Careful!' she shouted. She was going a bit deaf, so she tended to shout a fair bit.

When I took it out and unwrapped it, I discovered a miniature violin. I saw her watching me all excited looking, kind of. I didn't want to disappoint her. 'Awesome!' I said, trying to make my voice sound enthusiastic. That wasn't difficult because it was around that time that my voice started changing. So, it started with a deep, 'Awe,' and then ended with a squeaky, 'some.'

'My grandfather made it for my grandmother,' she said, touching it with one of her arthritic knobbly fingers. 'Look inside. Can you see my name?'

I peered in and could just make out the words Liesel Goldberg.

'But I thought you said he made it for *your* Grandmother.'

'Yes, but I was named for her. My maiden name was Martin. But then I married your grandfather who was called Benjamin Goldberg!' She smiled triumphantly.

I thought I got the picture.

'So,' she said. 'Your grandad and I wrote all that part of the family history down. We were going to write a book about it, how his father and his sister escaped from the Nazis, and my grandfather was interned during the war, and so was Ben's father. Now, isn't that a coincidence, and how my grandfather met my grandmother, that would be your great-great grandmother, Shannon ...'

She rambled on, but I was completely lost at this stage, and have to admit, I drifted off, thinking about the soccer match on Saturday. And then I drifted back as she went on about a Wander something and a *Waltz Sein* and how it meant going on the road on your own and that's where we got the song *Waltzing Matilda*.

I nodded a few times, and mumbled, 'That's great, Nan.'

She stopped and looked at me with a beaming smile. 'Then you will?'

'Will what?'

She sighed and made a kind of *hmpf* sound, like old people do when you haven't been listening.

'Will you take all these papers and turn them into a book?'

I just stared at her. *Hello!* I thought, *you're talking to the grandson that only likes to read comics and play computer games. I can't write a book!*

'It's all here; you don't need to do much, just put it into the computer and print out a book.'

'I don't think it works quite like that, Nan.'

'And then turn it into a block-buster movie. You could be the star. You're good at acting.'

I love my Nan; she always told me I was special, and she really seemed to believe it. She looked at me with that kind of eager expression, as if she was offering me a box of chocolates and couldn't wait for me to eat them. What could I say? 'Okay, Nan. But I won't have time to do it for a while. I'm busy with school work and soccer and stuff.'

Her face lit up. 'I knew I could count on you!'

Then I had a thought. 'What about Isabel? She'd be better at it. She's a girl—they like writing stuff and romance and stuff.'

She frowned. 'Your sister's too young. I want to see this book published before I die.'

'Nan!' I exclaimed. 'You're not going to die for yonks.'

She just smiled.

I had another thought. 'Or Dad; he'd be better at it than me.'

But she gave me a look that meant, 'Yeah, right, as if,' only she wouldn't say that because Dad's her son, Samuel Charles. Anyway, Dad's not the literary type. He teaches maths and physics, and he's away with the pixies most of the time.

'I want *you* to do it.'

'Okay,' I nodded and started putting everything back in the box.

'Careful!' she shouted as I picked up the violin and started to wrap it in the velvet. I looked at it again. It was pretty amazing with all this white stuff making a pattern.

She seemed so pleased with everything. 'Put the kettle on, Shannon. We'll have a nice cup of tea, and I made some of those ginger biscuits you like.'

Actually, I didn't like the ginger biscuits she made anymore. Her eyesight isn't the best, and I think she must have got mixed up and keeps putting curry powder in instead of ground ginger.

'That'll be lovely, Nan.'

I had a knack of pretending to eat them, but secretly putting them in my trouser pockets. At first, Mum got annoyed as I forgot to take them out, and they all melted and got stuck in one of her good pants in the washing machine. Well, after that I pretended to tie my runners and put an extra knot in the laces to remind me. Then when I got home, I gave them to the dog. The biscuits, not the laces.

***

So, now, here I am, and I'm seventeen. I've left school. I didn't do very well in my exams. Mum and Dad kept asking me what I wanted to do when I left school, and I said I'd like to be an actor or else develop computer games.

Dad rolled his eyes at Mum, and she rolled hers back. Now see? How could I write a book when I write things like that? As if Mum and Dad were playing marbles with their eye balls.

Anyway, I got a job stacking shelves in the local supermarket.

Nan Goldie was the only one who believed in me.

One Sunday morning Nan invited us round for breakfast at her place, but Dad insisted we go out instead. I think he'd suffered the ginger-biscuit heartburn syndrome.

'Have you finished the P. R. O. J. E. C. T yet?' Nan shouted. She tried to wink at me, but it just looked like she had an itchy nose and was too polite to scratch it in front of everyone. She thought that if she spelt it no-one else would understand. Like spelling W. A. L. K in front of the dog.

The others just looked at me, then shrugged and went on eating their eggs benedict.

I gave Nan the thumbs up sign and a wink.

Well, I figured that as I was working nights with the shelf stacking, I might as well look into this book thing. And then I was hooked, and Nan was right. It really was already written, just had to be typed up.

I kept thinking about the other violin, the one that my great gran nan had left behind and that got looted. Wouldn't it be a hoot if I found it? I went onto eBay and did a search. I found heaps of miniature violins, but none with Wilfried Schönbaum inscribed inside. So, I created an alert in case one showed up. Then I forgot about it.

Nan was right. It'd make an amazing movie.

I dreamed of being the star, and sometimes dreams come true. I would be the lead actor. *Ha ha.* No, that's just a dream. But guess what? I'd just finished putting the book together and had published it on Amazon when I got a message to say that someone in Germany had the other violin.

I got a paperback of the book printed for Nan and took it round to her. She was stoked, so then I told her about the violin on eBay. She just looked at me—I don't think she understands eBay, so I got out my iPad and showed her the picture.

'How much is it?'

I told her they wanted six-hundred Euros. She didn't know how much that was, so I converted it into Aussie dollars and she nearly fainted.

'Shannon,' she said eventually. 'Go down to my bedroom and open the top drawer of my dressing table.'

I was loath to go poking in an old lady's drawers.

'There's a pair of black socks in there under some hankies. Bring them here.'

Well, would you believe it, but she had hundreds of dollars rolled up in the socks.

'Take that money and buy it.' Tears came to her eyes as she picked up the book. 'I knew you could do it,' she said, clasping the book to her chest.

I was pleased I'd finally written the book as two weeks after that she had a heart attack and died.

Well, as you probably know, the book was turned into a movie, and I'd like to say that I played the part of my grandfather, Ben, but the producer cast me as Archie, Nan's cretin brother. Still, it was pretty amazing, even if it wasn't a block buster, more an art-house movie. And I did buy the other violin. Nan would've been so proud of me if she'd lived to see the movie.

Afterword

All characters in this book are fictitious and any resemblance to real people, living or dead is purely coincidental.

Acknowledgements

I'd like to thank

My amazing Beta Readers: Barbara Spence, Trish Behan and François Beugels.

Dr. Dimuthu Gamage for his medical insights.

My awesome and most patient editor, Tahlia Newland.

Reference material used for research
Storm of Steel: Ernst Junger;
Nazis in our Midst: David Henderson;
Walls of Wire: Joyce Hammond;
Churchill's German Army: Helen Fry;
The Bletchley Girls: Tessa Dunlop;
IBM and the Holocaust; Edwin Black;
The Tatura Secret Radio: Haakon Nilsen

About the Author

Lyn Behan grew up in the English West Country. She spent her working life as a systems analyst and computer programmer in Europe and Australia.

She now lives on the south coast of NSW with a variety of chooks and a dog.

Also By Lyn Behan

The Men and the Medium – Based on a true story. When radio inventor and spiritualist, Leslie Carter meets the beautiful psychic healer, Lily Bancroft, he is immediately entranced and knows she's his soulmate and that he could love only her. But Lily has her own path to follow, determined to become a healer and spiritualist medium. Through two world wars and three marriages, she struggles to fulfil her dreams. Leslie stands by her as each of her marriages fail. Will his love ever be returned?

***

Stolen Love, Fractured Lives – An incurable, hereditary disease haunts the lives of three generations of women and the men who love them. When Jessica discovers the terrible truth she is devastated. When her marriage ends and she loses her job, husband and home, she doesn't know which way to turn. Adding a baby to her problems results in a tangled web of lies and deceptions.

***

The Unpredictable Past – When a mysterious man, Will, moves into the house opposite hers, Elizabeth's quiet village life is turned upside down. Their friendship develops when Will helps with researching the involvement of one of her ancestors, Edward, in the last revolution in England. This friendship sets the neighbours gossiping and infuriates Elisabeth's daughter, who is convinced Will is a con man preying on her mother, thus raising doubts in Elizabeth's mind. Elizabeth and Will delve more into the past and attempt to solve the mystery surrounding the death of Edward's son, Edmund. How can Elizabeth find out the truth about Will? Is he who he seems?

***

Did you enjoy this book? If so please write a review, even a brief one, as this would help other readers decide if they would like to read it. Goodreads.com or the point of sale from which you purchased this book

Discussion points for book clubs

1. Discuss the impact of transportation on the Jewish children, many of whom were never reunited with their parents.

2. In a similar situation to the parents of these children, would you have made the same decision?

3. Were you surprised by the involvement of IBM in the holocaust?

4. If your country was at war with a foreign power how would you envisage the internment of people allied with that power?

5. Discuss Oskar Specks incredible journey paddling from Germany to Australia.

6. The practice of "wanderjahre" has been revived in Germany. Would this be a good thing for today's apprentices?